Teardrop SHOT

TIJAN

Edited by Jessica Royer Ocken
Photograph by Rafa G. Catala
Models: Andrea Swreda, Oliver Buendia
Proofread by Kara Hildebrand, Paige Smith, Heather Brown, and Chris O'Neil Parece
Beta readers: Crystal Solis, Amy English, Eileen Robinson, and Rochelle Paige
Formatted by Elaine York, Allusion Graphics, LLC
www.allusiongraphics.com

Teardrop
SHOT

TO THE READERS!

To the ones who are going through something
or have gone through something that is unexplainable to others.
Hopefully, here are some of the words.

CHAPTER ONE

"Lucas is busy forking his new girlfriend, but if you're feeling vengeful, I can pop in my dentures."

Those were the words I heard as three things were happening at once.

One, I was just dumped.

The message was being delivered from Newt, my boyfriend's—no, my very, very recent *ex*-boyfriend's—grandfather, while I was standing on his doorstep.

Two, my phone started ringing.

I glanced at it, half hoping it was Luc-*ass*, but it wasn't.

I gulped because the person calling was a blast from my past, like my way early past before Lucas, before the guy I was using Lucas to get over, before even him. *That* far back, and while the person calling me was a guy, he wasn't a romantic guy. At all. It was more the group of people he represented, a group that I left in my dust years ago.

So, hence the gulp, because none of them had called for at least six years. Give or take.

While both those events were hitting me at once, the third was what shirt Newt was wearing—my Reese Forster shirt.

I pointed at him. "You stole my shirt!" And because I was getting flooded with everything happening, the question blurted out of me. "If an owl could talk, what accent would it have?"

My neck was getting hot, furiously hot.

Newt was the one in front of me, so I was dealing with him first.

Who did he think he was?

A thief, that's what.

I loved that shirt. I lived in it. Slept in it. Drooled even. I did so many things in that shirt. And there was no way he could claim it wasn't because the collar was ripped. I put it there, one time in frustration when I watched Forster get the ball stolen from him during the West Conference Finals.

Reese Forster was the Seattle Thunder's star point guard. They had other star players too. In fact, their team was stacked this year, but it was Reese.

It was *my* shirt of him.

I got it the first year he was drafted, when he was nineteen, and while my obsession with basketball had waned over the years, my obsession with him had not.

I kept up on his stats. He was lined up to have one of his greatest years this next season.

Goddamn. I'd have to get a new shirt. Maybe a jersey even?

"Is that a no on the revenge sex?" Newt countered.

"I hope your dentures get glued to the bottom of someone's saggy ass and you have to go to the emergency room to get them removed. You old fuck!"

I stormed off after that, but my phone kept ringing.

Shit.

Looking down, seeing a name I never thought I'd talk to again, I faltered in my storming away. I couldn't lie, even to myself because I wasn't sure how to proceed.

Too many things were all converging at once.

But Luc-ass.

Was I devastated? No.

Was I annoyed? Yes.

Lucas and I bonded over our love of Reese Forster and he'd been the first guy I could tolerate in over a year so I was using him. The whole mantra of getting under someone else to get over someone—well, I'd been trying to test that theory out with him.

It hadn't worked.

So no, I wasn't crushed about Luc-asshole's cheating. I mean, it made sense. In a way. I could never bring myself to practice human corkscrewing, as he'd put it. He'd tried selling me on role-playing opening a bottle of wine.

I'd be the wine bottle, and...

Ring!

Okay. It kept ringing.

In the past, the *very* distant past, if they tried calling, it was only once.

They'd call. I wouldn't answer. They'd leave a voicemail, which I usually deleted. There'd been a few I had kept saved in my mailbox and depending on how much I wanted to suffer, I might listen to them over a box of wine and Cheetos.

This was different.

He called. He called again.

He kept calling.

Oh boy.

Taking a breath for courage, my thumb lingered over the accept button. I mean, why not? The day had already gone to shit. Might as well add another to the pile.

But if I was going to answer it, I was going to do it my way.

"If you had to pick an alcoholic drink to be the title of your autobiography, what would it be and why?" Pause. A breath. Then, "Heya, Trent."

CHAPTER TWO

Eight hours later, we were drinking.

Yeah. I was surprised myself.

At noon I was being dumped via a saggy pervy grandpa, then I answered my phone, and bam. We were here. I mean, that's not exactly how it worked. There was an awkward call.

Trent just landed in the city, and his usual person he called to stay with wasn't in. He explained it was me or a hotel. His gut had a word with him, and he chanced it, figuring he had nothing to lose.

Why I answered, I don't know. I didn't know then. I didn't know now. Maybe I'd look back later and know the answer, but when he asked if he could stay at my place for a night, I heard myself giving him my address.

Then there was a whole disjointed meeting.

I blurted out that I was dumped, cursed Newt to him, and then told him about the real travesty of the day: my Reese Forster shirt had been stolen.

Trent was quiet at first, standing there as I told him all of that, but both of us knowing the big elephant in the room was my disappearing act from our group of friends, or really: the why I faded from the group.

He knew the reason. I knew the reason. Even Lucas knew the reason. None of us were talking about it.

4

"Charlie, uh," he coughed. "The grandpa. The boyfriend." He frowned, shaking his head. "This is a new boyfriend, right? I don't recognize that name."

"Oh, yeah." My throat burned.

Somewhere an elephant was doing whatever sound they do, raising their trunk up, spraying water everywhere.

A bad taste rose up in my throat, and I clamped a hand on my stomach. "Oh no."

I knew more were coming. They were never pretty.

"Do camels' backs actually break?"

The words rushed out of me. I couldn't stop them. I was biting my tongue, suppressing the rest.

I wanted to ask if he ever wondered if mimes enjoyed making sexual gestures more than the others?

What was the name of his imaginary pet chicken?

Did he actually have an imaginary pet chicken because everyone should have an imaginary pet chicken. Pros and cons, please.

Trent was eyeing me sideways. "You still do those, huh?"

I nodded. When things got too much for me, weird and random things came out of my mouth.

"So." Another big sigh from him. He folded his head down, his hands in his pockets and he asked, "Wanna go get drunk?"

"If Jesus were alive, you think he'd be good at Jerkin dance?"

He just shook his head.

. . .

He yelled in my ear as we were dancing, "You should come with me."

We were at the bar two blocks from my apartment.

For whatever reason, Trent decided to give me a break and not push for explanations and apologies that he deserved. Instead, he'd been on this new persuasion of getting me to go with him when he'd go back to our stomping grounds in the morning.

The music was now blaring, and I'd already sweated out two of the tequila shots, so I'd moved on to a Long Island Iced Tea.

Which wasn't much better alcohol-wise because dammmn they were tasty. And when I say dancing, I really mean we were bobbing up and down like apples floating in a barrel for a bad Halloween game—with random arm flailing.

I liked to pretend it was the surprise grouse attack. You're walking, walking, things are great, calm, the world is beautiful, and whoosh—a grouse shoots up from the ground and you just peed your pants. It was that kind of arm flailing. Trent had it down perfectly. He was convinced he should be in a dance crew.

"What?" I stuck a finger in my ear, yelling back, but I was lying. Again.

I was a bad friend because I knew what he was asking me to do.

Echo Island Camp.

The name is deceptive. It wasn't a total island, smack in the middle of the largest lake in Minnesota—well, the largest inland lake. Not Lake Superior. But it was scary big.

Despite all this, I *did* have a soft spot for Echo Island Camp.

It was a sanctuary place, kinda, for me. I went there as a kid, graduated to junior counselor in training during high school, then joined their summer staff full time after that. My family didn't live far, so it'd been a second home to me. Kitchen. A brief stint on the maintenance crew. A counselor. I did it all.

That group of friends I ran from, they continued to get together every year—without me.

And Trent was asking me to go back. He was hired for a speaking event there tomorrow night.

The tequila had made all my thoughts and feelings fuzzy.

Is there such a thing as a tequila meltdown? Because I was nearing it.

I tapped his shoulder, and as he leaned down, I yelled into his ear, "Pee."

He nodded, flashing me a smile. I started moving toward the bathroom, and when I glanced back, Trent was already angling toward a hot blonde back on the dance floor. Judging by the smile on her face, I knew he wouldn't miss me any time soon.

Knowing that, I slipped out to the sitting area. A few tables were full, but I grabbed one toward the edge. Though we were outdoors, there were plenty of televisions and games like foosball and air hockey. There were a couple pool tables too, but they were at the other end. They tended to be surrounded by *serious* players, i.e., douchebags trying to look all tough and manly. Newt had probably been one of them in his younger days.

At the thought of him, I started growling. To myself. Because I was demented now. But he'd stolen my Reese Forster shirt. That pretty face didn't belong over Newt's saggy chest and balls. He deserved to be resting over me, keeping me warm—I had to stop myself. I noticed I'd started to caress my drink like it was Reese Forster.

And sitting alone at a table, that wasn't a good look.

"......*Forster's brother is going to damage his season? What do you think, Kat?*"

I snapped around, hearing the sportscaster's voice.

A few other guys were standing in front of the TV, one pointing a remote control and upping the volume level.

I went over, standing behind them to hear Kat's response. "*We all have to remember that this scandal isn't Reese Forster's scandal. It's his brother's. It's getting coverage because of his relation to Reese, and I hope it doesn't affect his season this year, but who knows? It very well could.*"

On the screen, one of the other men at the desk leaned forward, his suit wrinkling. "*You have to feel for the guy. Reese Forster is known to be private. He's intense on the court. He's a leader for that team, and now his name is being connected to what his brother—*"

"*—what his* estranged *brother—*" Kat interrupted.

He motioned toward her, nodding. "*Yeah. What his estranged brother has done.*"

The first guy that spoke leaned back in his chair, frowning. "*I do believe it's Forster that's estranged from his family. Not the other way around. That's the one thing we know about his personal life—an ex let that slip.*"

7

Kat barked out a laugh. *"Oops. What an ex-girlfriend, huh?"*

The first guy smirked. *"Probably why she's the ex now."*

Kat nodded. *"And getting back to the estranged part, it should be the other way around, shouldn't it? I mean, when you have a brother sexually assaulting women—"*

"Allegedly." The first guy pointed his pen at her, grinning out of the side of his mouth. *"We have to use that term, remember?"*

The second guy snorted, picking up his papers and organizing them. *"Yes. We must use 'allegedly' or our own lawyers will be hitting the red light for us."*

All three of them looked up, past the camera, and laughed.

"And there you have it." Kat leaned forward, the camera zooming in on her. *"Our lawyer just spoke. We'll be right back to talk about where the Seattle Thunder are allegedly going for their preseason training camp."*

The second guy laughed. *"We'll allegedly hear from our sponsors right now."*

They started laughing again as the screen switched to a sports drink commercial. If I drank the purple drink, and if I was wearing an almost see-through bathing suit, climbing out of a pool, then I'd be so sexy that I'd have to bat the boys away.

More like I'd scare the boys away.

I snorted to myself, and the guy with the remote control looked back, along with a couple of his friends.

I'd forgotten I was at a bar, and that I'd had four shots of tequila before coming here. Interest sparked in a couple of them. As their gazes roamed over me, I also remembered I hadn't cared what I wore. I wasn't dressed skimpy, but I hadn't changed since I left Newt's house, and I'd been dressed for Lucas. He always gave me crap about not being sexy for him, so I'd put on a black, high-collar halter tank top. It was cashmere, and I'd paired it with a silver skirt that had a slit up the side.

"Uh. Hey guys." I waved, still backing away. "How about Forster's brother, huh? What do you think his favorite strain of weed is?"

The closest to me leaned forward, leering. "You like basketball?" His breath reeked of cigarettes, chew, and alcohol. I was a fan of only one of those things.

"Charlie!"

I sagged in relief, hearing Trent shout my name.

I pointed over my shoulder. "Gotta go. Catch you on the rebound."

I'd taken three steps before I realized how that sounded. My cheesy basketball humor only made me seem desperate. Damage done. I headed toward the tables in time to see Trent going back inside. I waved, and he saw me, his eyebrows rising.

He held his arms out, weaving around to me. "Where'd you disappear to?"

I gave him a knowing look. "Like you weren't having fun in there with Miss Boobs-a-Lot."

He lowered his arms, but I caught the stupid grin on his face. And the way his cheeks got the slightest bit of pink in them.

He took the seat across from me at the table and raked his hands through his hair. "Her name is Claudia, and she was actually really nice."

"Nice, like you want to head home with her tonight nice?"

"Har. Har." He shot me a look, but I saw the interest in his eyes. He was Boobs-a-Lot smitten. I started to wave my finger in the air, the Trent and Boobs-a-Lot Sitting in a Tree song on the tip of my tongue, when he snatched my finger and shoved it back down on the table.

He glowered. "Don't start. You're about to break out in a full rendition with clapping and hand motions, and before we know it, I'll be taking you to the hospital because you broke your nose trying to breakdance on the floor."

My nose began smarting just at the mention, and I cringed. "Okay. One, I *was* a breakdancer at one point in my life."

"Never. Never. You had two breakdancers in your cabin that summer, but *you* weren't a breakdancer. Knowing two lock-and-pop moves doesn't make you one of them, and those were with your wrists."

I ignored him. "And two, that softball came out of nowhere. Literally. We didn't know there was a game being played on the other side of that building. I thought I was in the clear to show you all my skills." I smoothed out my shoulders, pretending to brush off some dirt.

He rolled his eyes. "Same Charlie. Funny and deluded."

Okay. *Ouch.* "Rule number one of hanging out with Charlie: you can't tell me I'm deluded until I say it first." I smacked my hand on the table. "Take that, Motivational Marathoner."

He shook his head. "You did—three times on the walk here. And don't think I don't know what you were doing. You were trying to distract me from talking about camp." He was trying to keep a straight face. Trying...and he was failing. He laughed, shaking his head. "Man, I've missed you."

There went that moment.

Eight years. It was a long fucking time to stay away, and I was sore from all the cringing on the inside. Including right at this moment.

He hadn't pushed me to talk about *him* or why I faded from everyone. While I knew I was being a coward, I'd been grateful.

It was time. Long past time, because I was glad that I answered his call and I was glad he'd gone dancing with me tonight. But I was *really* glad that I just saw him again.

I'd forgotten how much I missed everyone.

I looked down at the table, the words burning in my throat, but I had to say them. Or say something, at least. I wasn't a total jerk.

"I know I went MIA—"

"Hey." His voice was gentle, and he laid a hand on mine. "I know enough to realize you were going through something bad. You don't have to apologize to me or explain anything."

That made the burning worse.

"Trent..."

I tried again. I had to. He was a good friend to try after eight years of me ghosting, and since he'd showed up, it'd been drama overload. I never used to be a shitty friend.

I didn't think so, anyway. But that might've been something else I was deluded about.

"You gotta know it wasn't *just* the camp group," I said. "It was everyone. I ghosted on everyone in my life. My family too."

"I know."

The music blared as someone opened the door. *BOOM, BOOM, BOOM!*

He waited until the door closed again, until it was just *Boom, boom, boom*, and then he leaned forward, his forehead almost touching mine across the table.

"I knew you were going through it. We all did, and some of that's on us too. You know, when you and..."

Damian.

It was time his name was said.

He hesitated to say his name. Hell, even I did at this point.

He cocked his head to the side. "When you began dating Damian, I'll admit that some of us didn't handle it the right way. I know I got pissed—not because you were with someone, but because I couldn't call you at three in the morning to talk about whatever girl I had in my bathroom and figure out how to get her out of my apartment. At some point, you were no longer our Charlie, but *his* Charlie."

I picked at the table. Some dickhead had scratched *penis* into the wood, and damned if I wasn't going to turn that i into an upside-down actual penis. Just needed to add some girth and another ball. Or I was stalling. Again.

I glanced up, meeting Trent's knowing gaze. Why'd he always look at me that way? Like he was an all-knowing wise owl.

I raised a shoulder, feeling guilt bloom in my chest. "You should've been able to do that, except Damian should've joined the conversation."

God.

One year ago. That's how long ago I'd left that relationship, and I'd been such a mess that it took eleven months to realize I needed something drastic to get me back in the land of the living— and social media.

Hence my Lucas mistake. We met at my gym, gushed over Reese Forster, and I'd given a reckless *yes* to his suggestion we grab a beer, which had ended with Newt. Good old Newt.

I sighed. I was starting to miss the old grandpa.

But not his thieving ways.

Trent nodded. "Yeah. Maybe. Maybe I can't talk, but I know all our other friends, and I never had the relationship with any of them where I could call at three in the morning to plot Operation Remove Forgotten-Name-Nice-Lady." He bumped my arm with his fist and ducked his head to meet my gaze. "I'm kinda scared this is an aberration, so I mean it. You should come with me to camp. Keith—"

Boo. Hiss. Thunderbolts.

I hated Keith.

Keith, the boss.

"—said that whoever booked the island, they have it for almost three weeks. He asked me to come back a couple times for their stay. He's only using old staff. He wants the ones he can trust, so whoever it is, they're a big deal. You should come."

"And work there? Be your assistant? Get you coffee? A fan on command?"

He rolled his eyes. "No. I mean, didn't you say you were trying to write a book?"

Oh, fuck. Either my social skills were seriously lacking or my tolerance to tequila was in the trenches.

"I said that?" I felt my face getting hot. What else had I said?

Trying to write a book hadn't been my idea. It'd been my therapist's, and yes, after eleven months, Lucas and the therapist had both been my attempts at getting a life again. And that was an exaggeration about writing a book. She might've said journal, but here's me. I either overly commit or I don't commit at all, and I walked out of that session hearing I needed to write a book.

Yeah. I'd written nothing.

"What?" Trent asked.

"Huh?"

He shook his head. "You zoned out on me."

"I told you I was going to write a book?"

He nodded. "Were you not supposed to?"

"No, but it's embarrassing."

"Why's that embarrassing? I think it's a good idea. You can write about your life, about what you went through with Damian. It's like an intensive therapeutic technique."

Holy shit. He'd been talking to my therapist. Or Newt.

"My life sucks. It'd be the most depressing book ever."

He laughed. "You'd be surprised. But hey, getting back to my question—are you still working at that data place?"

I used to work with data sets, but it was something I quit on behalf of my dignity. The owner had asked if I stole her laptop. I said no, and I quit. Okay. I might not have quit per se, but I still left without pointing out that it was her cheating husband who stole it. For his mistress. And I knew that because the mistress had come in the day before with the same laptop. He hadn't even taken off the sticker that said *Boss Bitch*. Instead, the mistress had crossed it out and written *Mine Now*.

I felt she'd fired me because I kept quiet. But the mistress herself was revenge enough. I went in the other day to grab my last paycheck—she wouldn't even mail it to me. And I saw she'd hired the mistress for the desk clerk position.

The two of us had a shared smirk moment.

I felt like I was telling her, "Give Meredith hell." And the mistress was telling me, "I already have been, with him. In bed."

She might not have been thinking that, but I had high hopes. She was probably more thinking, *That's the loser who got fired for what he stole for me.* And she probably thought I was thinking, *I'm scared of you, but please come clean so I can have my job back.*

See? Joke was on her. Ha.

Either way, I'd decided to accept the assignment my therapist gave me: write about my life. I was embracing the idea. I did have a small nest egg in my savings account, and if there was any time to try something new, it was now.

Right?

Who was I kidding? I was scared shitless. I needed to get a new job and stat.

"Who do you think would win: a cockatoo or an otter?" I asked. Followed shortly by, "hashtagImight'vebeenfired."

He didn't respond, not right away. He just stared at me, and after I snuck a look at him, he rolled his eyes. Again.

"I'm not even going to ask, but hello?" He nudged my shoulder over the table. "This is perfect timing. You're coming. Decision is made."

It was like being in the last cell in a block, and one by one, I heard the doors shutting. I knew mine was coming, and I wanted to bolt, but I also knew I couldn't. Long-term, it was better if I sat tight.

Lucas had dumped me.

I lost my job.

I had a book to write.

Get the feeling the universe is trying to tell you something?

Trent was looking at me, so smug and somehow I knew I'd just committed to this too.

Whether I was ready or not, Echo Island Camp, here I come.

Again.

CHAPTER THREE

I felt like a thirteen-year-old, all awkward and scared, not like my twenty-seven years. Oh, who was I kidding? My life had been more together back then than it was now. Maybe Trent was right. It *was* fate that I was coming here.

Trent had called ahead, making sure Keith had a position for me to fill. Trent had to leave after his speaking event tomorrow, but I'd be staying so we were going in separate cars the next day. My old boss had hired me for the whole three weeks whoever-it-was had booked the entire island.

He said I'd have to sign a non-disclosure agreement, and I tried to keep from gagging. Keith always made a big deal about any campers. They mostly catered to wealthy campers, but even the 4-H campers got the celebrity treatment. At this point, the island could've been rented out for a makeup consultants convention and Keith only needed us to staff concessions or the gym courts.

In my case, it was the gym courts.

That's what I learned when we arrived, four hours later and severely needing coffee. We'd taken off the morning after what I now called Tequila and Regrets Night. Trent had gotten up, the ambitious overachiever he was, and went for a run.

"Just the gym courts?" I signed the NDA with a little flourish under my name.

Keith started to take the paper away, and I couldn't help myself.

I added two dots over the i in Charlie.

He paused.

I was done.

He started to take it again.

Wait. I had to add a line under my name.

He raised an eyebrow. "Are you done?"

"Is your name Keith?" That was tame, even for me. I nodded. I didn't like Keith. I never had.

He'd been my boss every summer I came here, and each year, his belly got bigger and bigger, and so did his arrogance. He always had on a golf shirt with a mug that spelled out BOSS with the B being the handle (Maybe I was attracted to always being an employer for those types of bosses? The asshole kinds?), and he wore khaki shorts with white socks and white sneakers underneath. It was the same uniform every single day—with a bounce in his step as he strutted around the campgrounds that made me grit my teeth.

And then there was his hair. There was a small amount of curl on top, a blondish brown color. Or maybe it was his laugh. He would always echo out a "HAR HAR HAR" laugh at the end of his jokes. Not anyone else's. His.

When Trent and I had arrived and walked into the office, I'd braced myself for some suggestive, snide comment. There was usually something sexual from him, at least with me. It was what he did, what he leered about, what he suggested with an appraising look, or a slightly dirty joke, but I'd been surprised.

He hadn't said a word, just shoved over the NDA, announced I would get paid a little less than the normal rate and I wasn't special because I was older. Then he'd picked up the B-oss mug and taken a sip.

When I finally let him take the NDA, he left his mug on the counter as he took the papers over to his desk. I eyed it. I was tempted to knock it on the floor, but this was my first day back. Probably not a good idea.

"Is that okay, Charlie?"

I'd been lost in Boss-mugland. "Huh?"

He came over, a key in hand. "You're in charge of the basketball courts, the outside and inside ones. I don't know what they'll need, but make sure they don't take our equipment or damage anything. You're there to watch everything, and help with whatever they need—towels or snacks or whatever. You're in charge of that too."

I stared at him. *Huh?*

Basketball courts...

"It's a basketball camp?"

Trent smothered a laugh beside me.

What had I just signed?

But it was gone. Dickhead Boss had already taken it.

"Yeah. It's a basketball camp."

Both guys were watching me, silent, waiting for something. No doubt waiting for me to clue the hell in on what was going on.

"Who's coming?"

I started going over my list of ideas as I asked. It could be anyone. The Coyotes? Fuck. That'd be a dream job. Sit back and watch them play all day? Reyson got traded a few years ago. Marley before that... I ran down the list of who I thought was still on the team. But what if it wasn't them? It could be a private school. Or a special league. Or... The possibilities were endless.

"Who is it?" I asked again.

Keith smirked. "I'm not telling you. That's what you get for not reading the form."

A surge of anger rushed through me. "How did you ever escape the #MeToo movement?"

Okay. Maybe not so random right there.

Keith ignored my question, his gaze on the front of my shirt. He smirked.

Oh, you—I started to raise a fist in the air, but Trent checked me.

He shoved my hand down, slamming his side to mine and hiding my fist behind us. His laugh was forced, as was his smile. "That sounds great, Keith. Thank you." He cleared his throat, stretching his neck a little. "So, uh, where are we all staying?"

Keith was glowering at where our hands would've been, but rather than comment, he just flicked his eyes back up. "You're in the main lodge," he told Trent. "You got room 222." He turned to me, his eyes hardening. "You, missy, got the fish cabin."

The fish cabin?

"Huh?"

"Oh." Another forced laugh from Trent as he shifted to face me, letting go of my fist. His hand came down on my shoulder, as if he was holding me back. "I told him you were writing a book, so he thought the fish cabin would be a good idea."

Keith's lips were mashed together, his dimple showing (I hated his dimple). His shoulders shook with repressed laughter.

The prick.

The fish cabin had been given that name for a reason. That's what it had been used for. Cleaning fish. They'd stopped using it for that purpose after a local game warden threatened to report the camp. He'd been half-joking, but the next week a camper threw up from the fumes, so Keith declared it abandoned.

Until now, apparently.

I've mentioned he's a dickhead, right?

Fine. Whatever. I gave him a closed-mouth smile, though it was painful as hell to my cheeks. "I'm sure I'll love it."

He held up his hands. "I was just thinking about your writing. It's the most private place on the island."

For a reason.

He laughed. "Besides, it's not that bad anymore. We've had it cleared out over the last few summers, so just spray some of that nice-smelling stuff you girls wear and it should be as good as new."

"I'll make do."

The fish cabin was at the tip of the island, closest to where the bridge and road came on to the island. My cabin would be north of the main lodge in the center of the island, and to the west of the village that had the nicest cabins. That was Morningside. There was a patch of trees between the main lodge and the basketball courts to the south, so my walk would be a nice long one each morning.

"What about the staff headquarters?" I asked.

That was a building in Morningside that the staff used mostly during weekends. It was a bit more relaxed than the rest of the camp facilities, but I knew they had jazzed it up recently. I saw pictures of it on social media.

"It's not available. All the rooms are booked up."

The definition of asshole: exhibit A. Keith, such a bitch boss. He'd put me in the smelliest cabin, farthest from everyone I knew, and the closest cabins to me would be booked with campers—campers I still hadn't identified. Lovely.

"Where's Helen?"

At least she'd be a welcome change. In her early sixties, she was the main receptionist at camp. She didn't live too far away from the island, so it was an easy drive back and forth. Plus, she hated Keith as much as I did. We'd bonded over it, and I missed her.

A flash of guilt settled in my gut.

She'd been another one I stopped coming back to visit, stopped checking in with. Crap. The last I knew, Helen's husband had medical problems. He could be dead by now.

Way to go, Charlie. Way to drop the ball on everyone.

Keith's nose wrinkled and he rested his hands on his stomach. "Helen won't be here for the three weeks."

"What? Why?"

Trent nudged my elbow, nodding toward the pile of NDAs on Keith's desk. I got his implication. Helen sucked at keeping secrets—hence a very old friendship with her. My uncle had visited me from Missouri one time. He was going through the area and wanted to say hello. Keith made him sign an NDA.

My uncle still talks about how we must have had the country's president at our camp.

He would've been sorely disappointed.

It'd been a group of sixth grade boys for fishing week. In fact, I was certain that's when the camper had retched from being in the fish cabin.

"Because she had a family emergency."

I narrowed my eyes.

Keith looked away, starting a drum solo on his stomach.

He was lying, but I got it. And damn, I was really wondering who these people were that were coming.

I sighed. "Just tell me if these people are going to be assholes."

I realized who I was asking and rotated to face Trent. "Am I going to want to kill these people?"

He cocked his head to the side. His eyebrows went up, and he raised a hand to scratch behind his head. "Well..."

Fuck. I was.

"I mean, you don't have the best record at liking people, so..." He faltered, his eyes locking on Keith's. "Help me out here."

Keith deadpanned, "You hate people. You'll hate them."

I hated *him.*

And I wanted to ask if a hot air balloon could ever use cold air instead.

I raked a hand through my hair. "Okay, then." I punched Trent's shoulder. "Help me move in?"

"Uh." I didn't miss the way his eyes returned to Keith. "I need to go over my talk."

Right. Because he'd been *asked* to come here. I had been foisted on the camp. Got it. I swung around to Keith.

"So where's the rest?"

I knew Owen and Hadley from our group had moved back from when I was still on the email chain. Even though I never replied, I'd been happy for them. Owen's dream was to run this place. Though evidently he hadn't gotten there yet.

Trent flashed me a grin, ducking out into the hallway.

It was just Keith and me. This was a scene in one of my nightmares, but Keith didn't seem disturbed. He had sat down behind his desk and started going through some papers.

"They're around," he said, distracted.

I saluted him. "Way to be helpful."

I picked up one of my bags and started for the door. Apparently, I needed to de-fish a fishing cabin.

I took two steps to the door and heard, "And Charlie?"

My heart sank. I didn't look back.

"You're looking real good. You've not let yourself go."

I looked now, glaring, and he smirked. He never gave a shit. Well, neither would I now, and I extended my hand, my middle finger very prominent as I waved it at him.

"Fuck off, Keith. Fuck off."

I left, his smug laughter trailing behind me.

"Always the joker, Charlie."

Owen was always the most responsible, kindest, and organized of our entire group. He probably would've earned a promotion a long time ago. Maybe I'd be proactive in helping him get that promotion.

A lot proactive. Keith had to go.

CHAPTER FOUR

The trail to the fishing cabin wasn't very big, just wide enough for my car to fit. Barely. Tree branches scraped the side, but I had to prioritize: save my already-piece-of-crap car from maybe one or two scratches or save myself a broken back from carrying all of my stuff on foot.

After further thought, I *reprioritized* and grabbed one of the golf carts the camp used. I was fairly certain I needed to sign a whole other form to be allowed to drive one of them, but that was Keith's fault. That was my rationale. If he hadn't been such a dick, I might've gone through the appropriate channels, which would've meant getting one of the maintenance guys to drive me. But I knew who that would've been, and that was another history hill I didn't want to climb. Not yet, anyway.

When I arrived, a station wagon was already there, the back end opened up, matching the windows and the two doors to the cabin, which were also propped open.

And as I walked in through the side door, a voice blared from the bathroom, "Did someone let the dogs out?"

Another voice chimed in, "Woof! Woof!"

I found Owen dancing in the living room, a purple bandana on his head, tied at the base of his neck. He wore an old camp staff shirt. It was faded in patches and ripped at the sleeves. He threw his head back, his mouth forming to howl at the next words, and he jumped backward on one foot. Eyes closed, he stopped and did a full-body twirl, a purple feather duster in his hand.

He wasn't alone.

Hadley came dancing in to join him from the bathroom.

She'd been a petite thing back then, and she still was, but she didn't dance like it.

Baggy jeans rode low on her hips with the legs rolled at her ankles, '80s-style. She had a shirt hanging off her, with the sleeves cut off and the ends rolled and stuffed under her sports bra straps. Both had gone with the purple theme today—even Hadley's hair ties were purple at the end of her two French braids.

Her eyes were closed, her hand in the air, her head down, and she was doing a running-man-inspired dance. Her feet were pumping as she inched toward her man, one bounce at a time. When she stopped feeling the hand in the air, she put both in front of her and started doing a jig, kicking her feet out to the side.

This.

These two people. This dancing. Knowing that when I made myself known to them, they wouldn't be embarrassed. They might turn the music up and dance around me in circles.

I had missed *this* too.

The song changed, and a slow bass began—Eminem's "Ass Like That." As one person, they jumped toward each other. Hadley leapt high enough to turn all the way around, her ass doing its own dance.

Owen crouched around her, pretending to frame her booty like he was a photographer giving his model instructions.

Then he looked up, and his mouth dropped.

Hadley continued popping it with the rhythm, then leaned back and pretended to slap someone's ass in front of her. When she backed into Owen and realized he had stopped, she looked up.

Her mouth dropped too.

I waved. "If you're having a dance-off, is there a way to cheat?"

They paused. One second.

"Charlie!" Hadley screeched.

Owen offered his own awkward wave. "Hey, Charlie."

She launched herself at me. I hadn't seen this woman in eight years, but that didn't matter. She leap-frogged and stuck to me like a window suction animal—legs around my waist, arms around my shoulders, and she climbed up, settling into a better position.

I reacted on instinct, grabbing her so she didn't pull us both down.

That's how my hand landed on her ass, and she wiggled it, mewing into my neck. "Aw, she's missed us too, D. And there's no cheating in a dance-off."

"Whoa." I hugged her tight. "Okay. Extrapolate."

She laughed, letting go and standing on her feet again.

Owen moved up behind her, a protective hand coming to her shoulder as they perused me.

These people.

We were all in our late twenties. I knew these two had a kid, maybe two by now, but they looked like they were still in their teens. It was the camp air. Had to be the camp air, all fresh and no toxins. What kind of animals enjoyed breathing that stuff?

"I'm hoping the D stands for Owen." I wasn't sure if I wanted to pose that as a question.

Owen's tanned cheeks flushed, so yep. Got my answer.

"Okay. Hug time." I pointed at D. "If you leap-frog at me, you're going to hit air."

He laughed, came forward to hug me briefly before Hadley squeezed me tight again. She rocked me left and right. "I've missed you so much."

Owen motioned around the cabin, taking his bandana off his head. "We were trying to help clear it out for you." Hadley stepped to his side, and his arm slid around her waist. They were two pieces of a puzzle coming together.

"We heard what Keith did to you," he added.

Hadley grimaced. "What a jerk."

I grunted. "You're telling me." I studied Owen. "How do you do it? Work with him all these years?"

He shifted, rolling his shoulder. I'd forgotten he did that. An old car accident had messed up his back. He shook his head. "It is what it is. It's only been two years, though."

"Oh." *Crap.* I'd forgotten that part too. They'd come here because her parents died. The Managing Director position opened at camp, and they wanted to leave her hometown.

I wasn't sure what to do now: 'fess up, apologize, or change the subject like an asshole.

"Why isn't it Dragons and Dungeons?"

They frowned at me.

I smiled and pretended to swing a bat. "Look at that." I was committed here. I pretended to hit a ball, and I pointed, showing the high arch it would've taken, whistling in appreciation. "Home run with that subject change, huh? Am I right?"

Owen laughed, but it was weak. He was humoring me.

Hadley's face tightened, and I saw hurt flare for a moment.

Asshole: me.

Genuine friend: her.

"I'm sorry. I... Yeah. Eight years, huh?" A nervous laugh escaped me, and for whatever reason, they both seemed to soften.

A sad smile lingered on Hadley's face and her hands caught mine, squeezing. "It's been too long, if you ask me."

Owen's smile loosened up, and just like that, these two saints forgave me.

"Trent said you're writing a book while you're here?"

It was ten minutes later when Owen asked from the couch, *after* they'd both helped bring all my stuff inside.

A quick recap: they'd offered. I said no. They ignored me and walked ahead of me to my car.

Saints, I tell you.

Despicable.

"Uh, yeah. Sorta." Holy crap, did I not want to talk about that project. "It's more of an excuse to come back here for a bit. I'm manning the gym courts?"

Hadley leaned back, pulling her feet up on the edge of the couch and hugging her knees to her chest. As she checked out, Owen checked in.

Leaning forward, he grew serious. "Yeah. You've done it before, but it'll be longer hours. That's why Keith wanted one person just to handle the gym. You need to have it open every morning at five—"

Cue my choking on an invisible ball.

Five? In the morning? When I was at camp?

Nuts. They were all nuts.

I was back to hissing at Keith in my head.

"—get whatever they need, but they'll have their own trainers here too. Keith wants you to keep a daily list of all our equipment so nothing gets taken back to the cabins—"

I nodded.

When things left with the campers, even if they went to their cabin, the chances of getting them back were small. There was usually a Thursday night cabin raid every week. It was disguised as a camp-wide activity, but it was really to help us snoop and grab whatever had been taken from the facilities.

"—Mary and Grant will help keep everything clean, but you know, help them out with that, and then you'll close the courts at midnight too."

Midnight. Five am to midnight. I'd have no life. Or bathroom breaks.

I groaned. "This isn't legal. Keith's not paying me enough for those hours."

Owen grinned, leaning back next to Hadley. He stuck his foot up, resting it on the coffee table. "You can close it during meals, and I'm sure the campers won't always be there."

Speaking of, I still didn't know who was coming. I opened my mouth to ask, but we heard a shout from outside.

"Yo! Charlie." The screen door pushed open and Trent came inside. "It doesn't smell that ba—"

He saw Owen and Hadley, and I braced myself for Hadley to leap-frog over me. She didn't. She stayed put, just smiling at Trent as both she and Owen said their hellos.

"Hey, guys." Trent chuckled, crossing to sit in the last open chair in the small room. An old fishing net hung above him with three light bulbs in the middle like a chandelier. He looked up, saw it, and cursed. "I forgot how kooky this place was."

Hadley laughed. "There's an old reel by the toilet. It holds the toilet paper now."

I smiled. Yeah, the place was odd and quirky, but there were good parts—the view outside the front door with the lake right there, the entire side wall covered in old hooks to hang things from. I saw a line of crystal lights strung through them, and I would bet money Keith had never done that before.

Trent and Owen and Hadley caught up for the next thirty minutes, but after a while, everyone fell silent. It was as if they'd rehearsed it, because all three turned to me, waiting, silent.

It was my turn.

I felt the back of my neck heating up. I felt bad for not sharing, but I couldn't do what they wanted. There were no words to describe what I'd gone through, so instead, I threw Newt under the bus.

"Before this, I was informed I'd been dumped by my recent ex's grandpa, then propositioned in the same sentence."

I waited.

Owen frowned.

Hadley blinked a few times.

Trent merely smiled.

"Uh—what?"

I nodded at Owen, who spoke for Hadley. "He offered to pop in his teeth if I wanted some revenge sex. I turned him down."

Hadley's mouth was now hanging open. For the booty shaker she was, I had blown her mind.

Oh yeah. "And I was fired, so ta-da. You're all caught up with me. When's dinner? Is Betty working back there still?"

"Wait." Hadley's eyebrows bunched together. She lowered her feet and leaned forward, resting her elbows on her knees. Scooting to the edge of the couch, she asked, "A recent ex? As in Dam—"

"Oh." I waved that off. "That's old news. This was a new guy, but again, I think the grandpa part was the most traumatizing point of that story. And we're here, so everything's good now."

I wanted to run.

It wasn't the best way to end a conversation. It wasn't even a polite way. In fact, it was probably rude and awkward, but in my state, it was the best I could do. So there I was, pretending I wasn't there, and they were all staring at me, because...I was there.

This wasn't working.

I cleared my throat. "About Betty..."

"Oh. Uh." Owen took the bait, always the respectful one. "No, actually she isn't here either. She and Helen are off-island. Keith and Trent are handling the welcome reception tonight, but we're in the kitchen for the weekend."

"Just you guys? How many people are coming for this three-week thing?"

"Maybe around thirty?" Owen seemed to be asking Hadley.

She shrugged.

"I think that's right," Trent said. "Yeah. Plus their extra staff."

I did the math, which surprised even me. "So, what? That's, like, forty people you have to feed? Forty-two, adding Mary and—"

"Well, only half the staff is here, but yeah. We're twelve total."

"You guys are taking care of all of them?"

Hadley shrugged, getting comfortable on the couch again. "We'll be fine. You fed two hundred people alone one time, remember?"

Shit. I had. "We're lucky I didn't burn down the main lounge."

That had all of them laughing, remembering when the grill caught fire. Keith had moved me out of the kitchen after that. I'd gone back to the camping staff personnel team. I think everyone was relieved, particularly the firemen from town. The fire captain came out once after that for an event, and when he saw me in the kitchen, I swear he paled.

I'd thought he was getting the flu and told everyone we were going to get sick. They'd stocked up on antibacterial soap and hand sanitizer and thought that's what had stopped it from happening. Nope. It'd probably been that the fire captain was not contagious, just terrified of me.

I shouldn't have felt some pride about that, but I did.

My power to instill fear was legendary. Except with Keith.

Boo, hiss.

"Wait!" I shot my hands out, remembering to ask. "Who are the campers for this thing?"

CHAPTER FIVE

They wouldn't tell me.

They laughed at me, so I kicked them out.

Full disclosure: the real reason was because I wanted to take a nap. The day had already gotten long with the *waking* up after dancing and boozing, then the *driving* after dancing/boozing, and *then* the whole dealing with Keith. But seeing Owen and Hadley, sitting and talking a bit, had been nice. It was good.

It felt normal.

And I needed normal, especially after waking up from my nap.

I'd been dreaming that Newt was chasing me, threatening to smack my ass with his dentures. Behind him, Trent was dancing with Owen and Hadley, and Keith was the DJ. I didn't know if we were in a nightclub, but whatever it was, it was horrifying. I kept running from Newt, and Keith was always there. I couldn't get away from either of them.

I had chills when I crawled out of bed, until I saw the time.

I had five minutes.

There was a strict late rule when it came to meals at camp. If you weren't there on time, you didn't eat. That was it. This was for staff, not campers. Those guys could stroll in forty-five minutes late, and it'd be fine, but if staff was a minute late, no food for you.

After cleaning up a little—traveling had a smell—I grabbed my sneakers and tore down the walking path with the most direct line to the main lodge. It connected to another path, so I had to veer to the right halfway there. As I did, I was already thinking of ways to make a straight path just for me. I doubted the board would allow it, so I was going rogue.

Call me Camp Badass.

My stomach growled, and I kicked up my speed.

I burst through the front doors, expecting the cafeteria to be busy with activity.

There was nothing. No one. Not a peep.

I skidded to a halt.

The good news: I could still eat and not have to sneak a plate somehow.

The bad news: we were still eating, right?

"Hello?"

The office door was closed so I passed it, going into the cafeteria. On one side of the large room was the kitchen. Campers would line up, grab a tray, and go through the line. They'd grab their drinks, stop so the kitchen staff would hand out food, then move farther down the line for the rest of the meal.

This three-week thing didn't seem full, with only forty people to feed, so I wasn't surprised to see only a few tables set up. The back half of the room had been left open for an indoor gym, the carpeting rolled back to reveal a hardwood basketball court. Sometimes a volleyball net was strung up, or a stage could be pulled out from the wall if there was a show going on during the meals.

The gym area had its lights on, but the table area was dark.

I saw lights on the other side of the kitchen, though the sliding wall was still pulled down. It was locked at night so no one could sneak into the kitchen, but it was lifted during the serving times. The fact it was still down said that they weren't expecting anyone immediately; otherwise everything would be out and uncovered.

It was like the camp gods had decided to answer me, because as I was about to call out again, the front doors opened behind me.

I turned, almost expecting to hear church choirs singing.

A lone guy wearing a business suit was there.

That was it.

He moved forward, a tired look on his face, a bag thrown over his shoulder, and two more guys in business suits came behind him.

I was used to having wealthy campers. Echo catered to them, and the random celebrity had been known to rent out the whole place before, so I was used to seeing nice things. Nice clothes. Nice shoes. Nice bags.

These three guys? They were the definition of nice.

Their faces were manscaped. Clean. Their teeth were white. They had an air of authority and confidence—not arrogant, but strong. They were sure of themselves, so sure that I moved back a step.

These guys were known, whoever they were.

Custom-tailored suits. Italian shoes. Their bags, I didn't recognize the brand, but wealthy people used them. There was a look to them. The first guy was normal height, but trim. The two behind him were giants.

And then all the air was sucked out of the room. It started spinning.

The first guy looked at the office door and at me. He pointed. "That's where I go?"

"Argu*cham*," came out of my mouth.

I didn't recognize the language myself. Maybe it was something foreign, or maybe it was a future alien language, because that's how I played it off. I smiled, blinked, and nodded as I felt like I was about make a crash landing on the floor.

He frowned briefly, but went to the office. A soft tap and he opened it, stepping inside.

The two other giants went with him. Neither spared me another look.

Why would they? Because the reason I started speaking Alien was because I'd recognized one of those giants. He was a former NBA All-star, had been on the All-NBA team, on the All-Defensive Team, and had won six NBA championships.

He. Was. A. Legend.

And I couldn't breathe.

Do platypuses walk backward?

I was hyperventilating.

When you're eighty, will you look back and wish you'd been a psychic?

Winston Duty retired six years ago, but he was now the head coach for the Seattle Thunder.

Oh.

My.

God.

The Seattle Thunder.

I was wheezing.

How many records is too many to break for the Guinness Book of World Records?

I bent over, my hands on my knees, but I couldn't get any air out. I was panicking and pissing myself from excitement all at the same time. And I was about to pass out.

"Charlie!" Hadley hissed my name from behind, and I tried to turn around. I really did.

She was probably motioning for me to get to safety. Hide and die. But I couldn't. My knees were melting. My feet were already in a puddle. I was sure that really was pee dripping down my legs.

This was my dream come true, if I lived to relish it.

A hand wrapped around my arm and jerked me backward. I clutched it and raised my head. I was pretty sure that was Owen's hair just in front of me. He pulled me into the kitchen's office and shoved me in the chair. They pushed my head between my knees, and Hadley kneeled in front of me.

"Breathe, Charlie. Breathe." She patted me on the back.

I couldn't. I kept shaking my head, pointing past them and out the door. Did they not know who was out there? No. The joke was on me. They did.

The Seattle Thunder. Reese Forster. My favorite all-time team and player.

Those were his coaches. If they were here, it meant one thing.

I was so unbelievably stupid.

The Seattle Thunder was having their training program here. HERE! AND I WAS HERE TOO!

All the fangirling, fanatical fan/obsessive stalker inside of me was freaking the fuck out.

Aliens. I'd talked like an alien, and it seemed I wasn't done.

"Whobegodan *ham—*"

They were snickering at me. They were laughing.

I darted forward, knocking my hand against the back of Owen's knee as he turned for a moment. He went down, but caught himself, shaking his head.

That was the old Charlie. I did annoying stuff like that, but it was payback this time.

I glared as I tried to keep breathing. *Nostrils, open on my command.*

"You fuckers," I finally managed.

They bent over in laughter. Hadley was leaning on Owen's arm.

"The look on your face." She pointed at me.

I whipped out a hand, knocking it aside. "What's your favorite sexual position—" I caught myself. "Please don't answer that."

She just pointed again and smiled. "We never do. We ignore your questions."

Years of friendship here. We were past what was polite. It was like the eight-year absence never existed, and then I was laughing too. I mean, I was trying not to think about who was out there— and maybe now standing in the front office's hallway—because if I did, it's straight to the language of the Arguchamites.

"What's going on?" came another voice from the kitchen. There was an attached doorway between the two.

I didn't even look at Trent. He'd been in on it too.

"She found out who the campers are," Owen reported.

"Oh." Trent laughed. "That's fucking awesome." He leaned forward, resting his hands on his knees and raised his voice. "Can you hear me, Charlie?"

I glared at him. "If everyone was deaf, would anyone speak?"

"She started hyperventilating."

I shot Hadley a dark look. I was still hyperventilating. There were birds in the room. Goddamn birds.

One of them flew through Trent's head. He didn't notice. It came out the other side.

A cocky smirk tugged at his mouth. "Live, Charlie. Live. Are you going to live? Do I need to give you a motivational talk on how to soothe your inner fan?"

I punched him in the stomach.

He dropped. "Oomph."

Owen and Hadley started laughing all over again.

"Can animals besides parrots and elephants dance?" spilled out of me.

I couldn't think about who was in the hallway. If I did, the walls in my brain started bending and everything flipped upside down. So therefore, we had normal, wealthy-prick campers out there. I was just here to waste some time, write a little for a novel I'd probably never finish, and deal. I was here to deal. That was it.

As I repeated that, I felt myself calm down.

I could breathe normally. My chest wasn't threatening to cave in.

I started feeling my feet and legs again, enough where I could stand up.

My three A-hole friends all stopped laughing and moved forward, their hands out to catch me. I was tempted to flip them off. That's the least they deserved for laughing at me in my moment of stupidity.

"You better now?"

Aw, Hadley. She was nice, and tenderhearted.

Trent snorted. "You mean is she more sane now?" He gently rapped his knuckles against my head. "Did you scramble these tonight?"

Hadley started laughing.

I take back the tenderhearted part.

Owen lifted his shoulder, knocking it back in place. I swear, that wasn't even about his injury anymore. It was his "we need to get going" signal. That or his "I'm uncomfortable; let's change the subject" signal.

I waited.

We all did—the two other A-holes quieted too.

"If they're all here, we should start checking that the food's still heated."

On cue, we all moved.

Hadley and Owen went to the kitchen to do their thing.

Trent went out the regular office door. I didn't know what he was doing, but I figured it had to do with the job he'd been hired to do here. And me? My job didn't start—well, shit. I didn't know. Tonight? Tomorrow morning?

I went to the kitchen.

Owen was checking the thermometers.

"Do I open the courts tonight?"

"Yeah. I think so." He was distracted, going through all of the steam drawers. "Keith didn't say?"

Hadley came from the dishwashing area carrying two serving spoons that were still wet from being cleaned. She waved them in the air, helping them air dry. "He mentioned that after dinner they'd do the opening reception with Trent," she said. "Then maybe they'd all want to congregate on the courts after."

No way I was going to ask Keith about this directly. "You're thinking I should open it after the welcome ceremony and close it at midnight?"

Owen pop-locked his shoulder back. "Yeah. I think that's a good idea. You can close them if no one shows up."

I clipped my head in a nod. I almost saluted him—I was that grateful he hadn't told me to go to Keith.

I glanced around.

I was still pretending I didn't know who was filling up the cafeteria, but we were all hearing their voices.

"What can I do to help?" I asked.

Owen was already moving around me toward the door.

Hadley eyed me. "Are you going to be okay? Got your question habit in check?"

I nodded. "I'm working on it. I used to have it in check."

She nodded. "You always did like the dishes?"

It was said as a question, but also a suggestion. And she was right.

There was a whole mess of dishes already there, asking me to clean them. I could hear their voices. *"Charlie. Wash us. Make us shine again. Pleeease."*

Okay, that was creepy, but there's something about holding a power washer in your hand and aiming at any surface you want to punish.

The window to the cafeteria was open, where the dishes would be stacked, but I wasn't paying attention. I wouldn't pay attention. Walls. I needed them up and erect in my brain. I reached for that powerful nozzle.

The handle felt like it'd been waiting for me all these years. I almost heard it saying, *"Welcome back, my little Charlie."*

And I smiled.

CHAPTER SIX

There was Garth Carzoni.

I almost fell into the dishwasher.

I should've stopped gawking, but I couldn't.

The randoms were bouncing in my head, though I'd put a block on them. Every time I felt one coming, I bit down on my lip. I'm pretty sure I was bleeding, but what else could a slightly stalkerish-girl do to keep sane?

Apparently, bleed.

And ignore the one player I'd probably pee myself if I saw. I couldn't handle knowing whether he was here, so he was locked in that special place in my mind.

They had all eaten, and Keith and Trent were at the front giving everyone the run-down on the campgrounds and rules. I knew this routine. When they stepped away, the coaches would step up and continue with whatever needed to be said.

After that, I didn't know.

But until they took off, my inner basketball fan was melting down inside.

Terry Bartlonguesen.

I made a weird-sounding gurgle. It started as a sigh, but I caught myself and barked out an alien something again. I wasn't sure what it was.

I couldn't breathe. My heart nearly stopped working as he leaned over and whispered something to Matthew Crusky.

Matthew Crusky, everyone! The Cruskinator. The Cruskimachine.

Double-down on the weird alien sigh.

I sagged again, but grabbed for the sink and caught myself.

Right.

Look away. Brain walls. Brain walls. They needed to be erect.

Firm.

Standing upright and ready.

I felt my knees going.

I couldn't stop myself.

I went back to my stalker/gawking mode.

Beau Michems.

The crowd surges to their feet and gives a standing ovation. *Ahhhh. Ahhhhh.*

And he was sitting next to Juan Cartion.

Juan Cartion. Juan the Speedster Cartion! His other nickname was the Chia Pet because his hair would frizz up during every game. The announcers loved teasing him about it. He wasn't the Chia Pet here, though. His hair had been slicked down and combed to the side. He was the shooting guard, and—I was about to embark into Pure Insanity Mode, so I had to guard myself, ram up the shields—he was Reese Forster's best friend.

My mouth dried up, just thinking of him, thinking his *best friend* was in the room. His best friend was *twenty* feet from me.

Me. *From me!*

"Settle down, Cherry Popper."

"Cherry Popper?" I turned around and raised an eyebrow. "Are you using reverse psychology on me? Hoping I'll want to pop *your* cherry."

Trent laughed. "I was hoping for projection. I'm projecting my fantasies onto you."

I snorted. "Hate to break it to you, but my cherry was popped long agooo...oo...oh shit."

Keith stood on the other side of the dish window, a scowl on his face.

The dirty bastard was going to take it and run. I knew how he worked.

But he just grunted, waving that B-oss mug in the air. "Trent, we're going to start."

Damn. He was all business. I was slightly disappointed... Slightly. I didn't want to get ahead of myself.

But I couldn't help it. "Hey, Keith?"

He paused and looked back.

"If you needed to confess one sin to save your life, what would it be?"

"Keep it up, Charlie. We have other alumni staff we can call." He turned away.

"Oh yeah? How many of them can ask you—" A hand clapped over my mouth.

"Keep walking, Boss," Trent called. "I got her handled."

No one handled me.

Well, except Trent just now, and I needed it.

I gulped down some oxygen once he lifted his hand. "Thank you. I almost lost a second job there."

He moved back, but his chuckle was strained. "I gotta go, but you need to get yourself in check. I mean it. I have to leave tomorrow for another speaking event, and I won't be back till the end of their stay. You going to be okay till then?"

I nodded.

Once the camp weeks started, it wouldn't be hard to avoid Keith. He tended to only show up for meals. He'd stay in the office other than that, so as long as he wasn't poking his nose in at the gym courts, I would be fine. I could do the dishes and squirrel away a plate of food.

"You'll help rein her in if she needs it?" Trent called to Hadley, walking by.

She threw him a smile over her shoulder, not stopping. She went out, picked up a steamer, and brought it back. "No problem," she said as she passed us again. "Though I've always enjoyed Charlie's feisty side."

"For some reason, I'm not reassured."

I slapped Trent on the arm. "Get on. I'll be fine. And if nothing else, I'll whisper my random questions."

He gave me a dry look. "Right. Because that's not creepy."

I shrugged, going back to the dishes.

The players had started to migrate out the doors, leaving all their dishes on the table.

Normal camps had a process where campers were told how to collect plates on one tray, silverware on another, throw away their trash, etc. Adult camps were just told to take their dishes to the dish window, but these guys were none of those. I wasn't surprised to see that not one of them brought their stuff to the window. That would add thirty minutes to the cleanup.

But just then Owen whipped through with a cart.

Owen was bringing the window to their dishes. It was decked out, even with a soaker tub for the silverware.

"Okay. I'm going to go." Trent still lingered. "You haven't asked about your baller crush."

Hyperventilating.

Do you regret anything you did five days ago? Five weeks? Five months? Five years?

I was biting down hard on my lip. None of those questions spilled out, and I was damn proud of myself.

Then I heard Trent say, "He's not here. He's coming tomorrow."

Oh good God.

If you can see a fart on a thermal camera, could you see a climax too?

CHAPTER SEVEN

I t didn't take as long to clean as I thought.

I was walking out of there thirty minutes later. Hadley had set a plate of food aside for me before they put everything away. I could've kissed her when she gave it to me because my stomach was doing some serious growling and rolling. I could've intimidated bears if I needed to, but because I was scarfing down my food, I was also cutting through the back of the lodge, heading for the gyms.

I wasn't sure how long they'd keep everyone at the opening/welcome ceremony, but I hadn't checked out the gyms yet.

Big mistake.

That was always one of the number one rules. Actually, we didn't really have a list of rules. They were all considered the most important, and we had to figure it out from there. My personal number one rule had always been eating, so there you go. Smart girl priorities.

Anyway, I was in a bit more of a rush than I normally would've been, and I slammed through the screen door leading into the inside gyms, only seeing the silhouette at the last second.

"Oh shit!" I tried swerving around him, but I failed.

I hit the guy smack in the center of the chest, and down we went. My food rained on top of us.

Fuuuuck.

Is rain only called rain if it's the liquid form of water? Could my food have snowed down on top of us too?

I bit my lip so hard as I rolled to my feet. "Sorry."

I wasn't sure if I should look, but I did. I sighed in relief. "Oh, Grant. It's only you." And then I immediately seized up in a mouth-twisting-biting-hands-wringing moment because I hadn't meant to imply he didn't matter—like I hadn't purposely *not* asked about him, because I knew he was here or he would be here, and yeah. I was sucking at this whole thing.

I still couldn't bring myself to look him in the eye, but I was very aware of our surroundings. Even in the dark, I was already taking inventory. There were two indoor gyms and in the corner was the cage where I'd be sitting and trying to write out a lame and overly committed-to therapeutic exercise. I'd come in through one screen door, but straight across from us, another screen door led to three brand-new outdoor gyms. Leaning to the side, I could see that the last court had a volleyball net up and shit. That's probably why Grant was here.

"Are you here for the net?" I asked.

I was aware of how he hadn't moved since I jumped to my feet. He was still on the floor, and I got a glance in before I panicked, just quick enough to see my roll sitting on his jean's zipper, right where a whole other type of bread was.

Ahem.

I made every effort to change my thoughts, because I could feel all the sexual-themed questions coming, and with my history with this guy, I did not want to take that on.

He grunted, finally standing up. "That's all you're going to say to me?'"

Well...what else was there?

I mean, besides the fact that for all the crap I took from Keith about "dating" my guy friends, I hadn't dated any of them. Yet, this was the one guy who actually came close to entering that zone. The dating zone.

That'd been Grant.

And no one knew. *No* one.

They just knew he'd been my best friend for six summers in a row. They didn't know we'd kissed on the hanging bench my last summer here, and we'd held hands on the walk to my car—right to where I had it packed with all my belongings. We drove our separate ways, and that was the end of our summer.

Grant went north four hours to finish his last year at college, and I went south to meet Damian. Life took a turn after that—a big, fast, and dramatic turn, and sometimes I felt like I'd taken that turn so fast, my car had rolled in the ditch and I'd never woken up.

My throat suddenly had an STD. There was burning, more burning.

"How's Damian?" Grant asked.

We were going serious right off the bat.

"If everyone started using *shiitake* as a curse word, would we switch things and call them shit mushrooms?"

He snorted, rubbing a hand over his jaw. "You're exactly the same."

No, Grant. No, I wasn't actually. I was very, very different inside, but it was all covered up in lame questions and stupid jokes because I couldn't admit the truth or I would collapse. That was the real Charlie, and I clamped her down because I couldn't even handle her myself.

"Well..." His voice lilted with sarcasm. "I'm engaged. Do you give a shit?"

I looked up at him now, finally. His eyes bore into me, and I swallowed.

"Yes," I whispered.

I rolled my eyes at myself. I wasn't a meek and timid mouse, but that's what was coming out. Coughing, I hit my chest with a fist and exclaimed, "I mean, yes, I do."

Oh, Lord.

It came out booming now. All I had to do was throw my arm out to the side and it would be as if I was announcing the Seattle Thunder's starting lineup.

His lip twitched.

That relaxed me. My lungs weren't so shriveled up.

"Congratulations."

His looked at me and lowered his head, seeming to study me. After a moment, he shook his head. "Yeah. Okay, kid. You and I can do our dance later." He gestured around us. "Boss wanted this cleaned up and the net taken down. I'll handle it." He nodded to the cage. "You need to count everything in there."

The cage was just what it sounded like: a small room set in the corner with two large doors, but only one was used to enter and exit. The other one had been cut in half. The bottom had the door handle. It could swing open and closed, but the other section of the door had been taken off, cut in half again and glued over the top so it looked like half a concession stand.

Years ago, it had looked rough, but they had made it look better. It looked like an equipment room any top-notch facility would use now. The budget had been good to this place.

Heading in, I switched on the light. The cage had been organized. All the balls were in place, the equipment in its spots. I scuffed my foot over the floor. Even that had been cleaned.

"Grant, you did this?"

He'd just cleared the screen door, but hollered back through it, "Nah."

Grant wasn't a liar, so that meant Mary had done it.

I yelled back, "Thank your mom for me, please."

He raised a hand in response, crossing the first of the two courts.

I got myself to work, and I was kneeled down behind a partition, going through the second rack of hockey equipment, when I heard the first voices. They came closer and closer, and I couldn't move.

Grant had left twenty minutes ago, so no one knew I was back here. I squeezed my eyes shut and took a breath. Meditation, bitches. I'd need to become a namaste maestro by the end of these three weeks, but Reese Forster wasn't here.

I whispered that to myself, over and over again. I hoped fervently it would give me some form of bearing so I wouldn't get swept up in the craziness.

"—gotta call the woman and check in."

Yes. I recognized that voice. I'd heard it from locker-room interviews, but I wasn't going to name the Cruskinator. If I did, I'd be nutso.

I wasn't going to be nutso.

Someone else responded, "You have a four year old, right?"

"Yeah. He's such a little punk—"

He sounded so fond of his kid.

The Cruskinator kept talking, but the word *rascal* did it for me.

I could rattle off his stats for four years in a row—not the last four years, but a few years before that—yet hearing him call his kid a rascal grounded me.

He was a father, and a good father from what I'd read.

A different voice: "You guys seen Aiden?"

The door to the cage rattled, but it held firm. I forgot I'd locked it. It'd been an automatic motion for me, a policy Keith hammered into our heads so no campers could get in and steal the equipment.

That same voice: "Door's locked. We don't have any balls to shoot with."

"Half the guys are heading to the cabins to call their families."

That guy grunted. "True. We could come back later?"

Cruskinator asked, "When's Forster showing up?"

The squeak of their shoes on the floor. They were moving away.

The screen door protested as someone hit it open.

"I thought tomorrow..."

They faded away after that, and I let out a deep breath.

Okay. I'd been acting like a twenty-something, which I was, but I needed to rein it in. I was twenty-seven. I was almost an adult. Kind of. God help everyone, but I was annoying even myself.

Yes, these guys were some of my idols. Yes, I had watched them when I was with Damian—and my throat was burning again.

Damian.

Being back here shouldn't have brought him to my mind, but he was everywhere. Everyone grew up. Everyone had formed a family—got married, had kids, got divorced. One guy went to prison. Working here, we'd all had dreams, together, and my dream had been shattered.

And no one knew why.

46

I felt a tear slide down my face.

The gym's lights were on a timer, which chose this moment to turn off. It seemed fitting, so I didn't move. I remained in place—no questions bouncing in my head, no jokes on my tongue—and for the first time in a long while, I let myself feel. A monsoon of grief pushed through me, tearing everything in me and commanding I deal with it.

Well. Fuck that.

Feeling sucked. Who liked to cry? I couldn't do it.

I thought I could. I changed my mind.

I was pushing myself up from the floor when the lights switched back on. The screen door shoved open. I heard angry stomping coming across the room as the door slammed shut, and before I could prepare myself, Reese Forster was standing smack in front of the cage, his stormy eyes locked on me.

"I need a ball."

Shit. I was going there. I tried to stop myself, but, "What's your criteria for determining who you choose to be a fuck buddy?"

CHAPTER EIGHT

H e scowled. "The fuck you say?"
Oh shitty crap.

My idol was scowling at me, and I swallowed over a piece of bark in my throat. I had to go for broke here. If I didn't, I'd forever be a freak in his eyes. I could *not* go to my grave knowing Reese Forster—who was overwhelmingly live and livid and lovely— would think of me as that *freak* fan.

(Though, I kinda was.)

(Slightly.)

(Okay. Completely.)

So, taking a breath, I rushed out, "I didn't mean that the way it came out." *I might've.* "I have a problem."

The scowling lessened, but his eyes were still narrowed at me.

"It's just something weird I do. It'll go away. I hope," I explained. "I just—I don't know where I picked it up, but when I'm nervous or excited or angry or if I just can't deal with whatever I'm feeling, these stupid questions burst out of me."

Stop. Take a breath.

The bark was still there. Ouch.

And once more.

"I'm nervous," I added. *"Soo* nervous." I bent over suddenly.

The scowl was gone. His head cocked sideways, and he stepped back, his hands stuffed in his hoodie. I was either back to the alien theme or he was looking at me like I was nuts. Which was still in the freak category.

I waved a hand in the air, puffing out. "I'm good. I'll be fine. Nothing to see here. Totally normal."

I felt them coming. More. They were going to burst out of me. Annnnnd...here we go.

"If you were guaranteed the truth, what question would you ask someone?"

I bent down farther, resting my forehead to the counter, but another question came out. It was mumbled. "Favorite curse word to use while having sex? Or biking? Or having sex on a bike?"

Fuck.

Damn.

Shit.

I'd just answered my own question, and I bit my lip.

It wasn't working.

I tried my cheek. *Ow!* And that wasn't working either.

"What do a mullet and a ferret have in common?"

GAH!

I bit down harder, and this time I tasted blood. I was almost hyperventilating again. If I went down a few more inches, I could just buckle to the ground, wrap my arms around my knees, and hope to disappear.

I'd started to think I should do that when I heard a soft chuckle.

"I would ask my brother something," he said. "I like the word *fuck* for anything, and having sex on a bike sounds fun to try. I can't think of anything they have in common except the words both have two of the same letters in the middle, both have six letters, and you could put a ferret on someone's head to look like a mullet."

I...had no idea what to do.

He'd answered my questions.

No one answered my questions.

I stayed frozen for a second before lifting my head. I gulped again.

"You don't think I'm a freak?"

"No, I do. You're crazy."

49

The corner of his mouth tugged up, and holy shit, my heart flopped over in my chest. There was the Reese Forster that was in *Person* magazine's Most Beautiful People issue. There was my fantasy for so many years.

"But I'm hoping you're harmless." He laughed softly, his hands pushing down on his hoodie so it stretched from his shoulders to accentuate his physique.

God.

This guy.

I had watched him running up and down the court so many times—I knew his body was lean and muscled. He was solid, but in front of me, he seemed larger than life, with bright hazel eyes. They had a golden ring of honey around the iris, and a smattering of blue and green.

Long eyelashes.

High and angular cheekbones.

A strong jawline that could cut paper, or glass—maybe not glass, but definitely something else. *Go back to the water*. Man, I had just envisioned him with droplets sliding down his face, lingering at the dip of his chin where it came to the most perfect square end. There was a slight scruff on his face. He hadn't shaved that day or the day before, giving him a very rough, slightly alarming, and so authoritative air.

I sighed to myself, my fingers curling around the counter.

I was ogling.

I didn't care.

After all the questions, this was nothing. The guy must've been used to it by now.

A slight growl vibrated out of him, and my gaze snapped up to his.

His hair. I was distracted again. It was the perfect short length and a dirty blond color. It matched the honey in his eyes.

In some ways, it wasn't fair.

No guy could measure against him. None.

"Would you stop fucking leering at me? I don't do camp groupies." He thrust a hand out, pointing behind me. "I want a ball. *Now*."

I snapped to attention, jerking around. I grabbed a ball and thrust it at him. "Here."

He took it and rotated swiftly on his feet, pushing the ball to the ground in a bounce as he stepped over it at the same time. He began dribbling as he went to the court—so smoothly, so naturally, it was like he didn't even realize he was doing it.

Legend.

L-e-g-e-n-d.

There was a sign-out sheet campers were supposed to use when they took equipment, but sorry, Keith. No camp policy for this guy, though I did scribble his name on the paper. My hand was trembling so much it looked like a chicken scratch.

Oh well.

It'd have to do.

He ignored me and began shooting hoops. He'd toss the ball up. It'd go through the basket, with a nice swishing sound, and he'd grab it off the first bounce to follow with a quick layup.

I was riveted.

My whole body had been shaking, but he kept going, and going, and going, and after what must've been an entire hour, I felt calm.

I almost wanted to freak out, realizing that, but nope.

Watching him play, the same motion over and over and over again, was soothing. He had such control every time he touched the ball. He never struggled. The ball answered his commands seamlessly, as if connected to him through a mental string.

The room was rippling with the power he had, but as I relaxed and lounged back against the wall, I began to pick up what else was coming off of him. And I felt anger. *His* anger. His bounces were hard and forceful. His shoulders were tense, so was his jaw as he kept his head bent down.

All pro players were phenomenal athletes, but when Reese was on the court, he was different. I should know. I watched him enough. He could move the ball around like it was magic, sending it through legs, outstretched arms, and behind his own back. There were times when he was in the Reese Zone, as the announcers liked to call it, when he almost toyed with his opponents. He could send off a quick round of sharp and abrasive dribbling, then suddenly, whoosh, that ball was either in the air or in the hands of his teammate and his defender had barely blinked.

I watched him for another hour, and he never slowed down.

Bounce, bounce, pivot, then up for a layup. Sometimes, he fell back and tossed it up in a pretty arc, what would be a teardrop shot or a floater. Other times, a hard hit against the backboard. Just over and over again.

A quick rebound.

Or back to the three-point line.

The free-throw line.

He just kept on.

After a third hour, he started to slow down.

Another player came in the side door, but he saw Reese playing, and after a second of watching him, he eased back out.

I didn't think it was coincidence that Juan Cartion came to stand outside another side door a few minutes later. He made no move to come inside. It was apparent he was there to watch his best friend, and when Reese switched from shooting hoops to walking up and down the court dribbling the ball in short, angry staccato beats, his friend left.

A normal person would've lost the ball in two seconds.

Reese never did.

My phone beeped.

Dazed, I grabbed it to see what the alert was.

Trent: Headed to my room. Where are you? I need to get to bed, early flight in the morning.

He wanted to come and say goodbye. I was weird about goodbyes. Just tack that on to the long list of what made me *special*, but it was what it was. I hated saying goodbye. Despised. Loathed. Strongly opposed. You name it, I was. There was a reason for it, and as I remembered and felt that pressure building in my chest, I shut it down.

It was ironic because that shut everything else off too.

Me: Damian called. Mind if I give you a goodbye hug through our phones? Can you feel it?

Damian was one of the few reasons Trent would believe I needed space.

I felt a burning in my throat. The bark had moved to the side.

I hit send, and there was a small pause.

Trent: Sounds good. Call me if you want to talk.

I pocketed the phone, knowing I wouldn't call, knowing he knew I wouldn't call, and knowing we both knew the next time we'd talk was when he came back at the end of this whole preseason training camp.

Turning off the light in the cage, I slid onto the stool behind the counter.

I sat and watched Reese Forster play, knowing this was a special moment in my life. I wanted to protect it, even if that meant lying to a friend.

I was okay with that, and if I explained it to Trent later, I thought he'd be okay with it too.

CHAPTER NINE

B *abe.*
Buzz.
I'm sorry.
Buzz.
Babe, forgive me.
Buzz.
Babe.
Buzz.
Babe.
Buzz.
Babe.
Buzz, buzz, buzz.

I swatted at a fly. It was waking me up, and it kept coming around. Finally, hearing another buzz, I bolted upright with my pillow in hand, and I swung. That sucker was going down.

But...

No fly.

I swung and the pillow hit me in the face. I ate cloth.

I had to sit for a minute and get my bearings, but when I heard another buzz, along with the words of Ricky Nelson's "Baby I'm Sorry," which I had programmed at an accidental brilliant moment. The song sounded different because I got the phone to sing it in an Australian accent. Genius, I tell you.

Without looking, I knew who the texts were from, and then I was wishing for the fly instead.

That song played every time Lucas texted, which meant he... I had no clue what it meant, actually. I hadn't heard a word from him since Newt broke the news to me and I'd left the next day with Trent.

I did the math, which was hard, and we were at the forty-eight-hour mark. So either Lucas just found out or the next girl had already dumped him.

I considered for a second, and my money was on the girl. I rolled over and picked up the phone.

Lucas: Why aren't you answering my texts?
Lucas: Where are you?
Lucas: Gramps said you came by. I missed you.
Lucas: I miss you now.
Lucas: You're still not answering—

He was covering his ass. There were twenty other texts from him, and I deleted all of them—without blinking, without a second thought, without reading. One by one, I wiped them clear, and once the screen was blank, a satisfied smile came to my face.

I lie back down, closing my eyes. I could get another twenty minutes of shut-eye.

BUZZ.

It was louder now that I was awake.

Groaning, I flipped the phone on and hit call. I was ready for him, expecting him to answer.

It rang, and rang, and then, *"This is the Luc-machine. Say your piece and I might listen..."*

He didn't answer and he'd literally just texted.

After the beep, I said, "Dude. You were fucking another girl. Your grandpa told me. We're done, and save your drool. You were the guy to help me get over someone ten times better than you. I used *you*, so whatever. We're through. You're not worth the time it took to call you." I started to hang up, but brought the phone back to my mouth. "Do not call, text, send smoke signals, think about me, or jerk off to me. Done, Luc-you-bet-your-ass-you're-an-*ass*. BYE, Felicia."

There.

55

I hung up, then wiped him from the phone and his number too.

Then I realized the last text hadn't been from him.

Trent: Hey. Call me later. Want to make sure you're okay.

Well... I sat and stared at it, and groaned. *Shit on me.*

Me: Sorry I flaked last night. I'm fine. How was your flight?

I studied my phone after that, looking at the history, and saw that Lucas had texted all day yesterday. They just all came flooding in at the same time because reception was iffy on this island.

Well...still didn't matter. He cheated. We were done.

A new text came in.

Unknown: Bitch.

That was Lucas.

I laughed, and once I started, I kept going.

I was tempted to tell him I'd met Reese Forster last night, just for some revenge, but it wasn't worth risking my NDA. He was the type to call Keith and tattle on me, or worse—show up so I would introduce him.

I groaned. I was too awake now. It was five in the morning. I'd gotten four hours of sleep. But in camp life, that was almost eight hours. Reese Forster had kept running drills until twelve-thirty. I could've kicked him out at midnight, but I hadn't had the heart.

I'd turned the light off in the cage, though, so when he was done, he must've thought I'd gone.

I was like a creepy statue against the wall, just to the side of the counter. If he had looked in and to his left, he would've seen me there. I'm sure that would've gone over well, but he hadn't. He put the ball on the counter, made sure it didn't fall off, and left, hitting the light switch as he went.

It had been dark, but a little bit of moonlight showed through the screen door, so I could see enough to take the ball and put it on the floor, then feel around for the door handle. My phone was in my pocket. I had been just leaving the cage, pulling my phone out to light the way, when I heard the screen door open again.

It was Forster.

I held still, not moving an inch.

He'd walked clear across the courts and checked the other screen door, shaking it and then locking it after he found it open.

He never turned the light on again, just rotated swiftly, retraced his steps, and locked the first door behind him.

The locks on the screen doors didn't really hold. If someone wanted to break in, they could've just ripped the door open with a bit of extra oomph. But still, his concern had me melting.

I didn't know where he was staying, but there was a good chance he was at the staff headquarters. They were the nicest place to stay, and Keith had closed it down for campers during this session. Forster was just about the best kind of camper there was, and if that's where he was going, he would've taken the same path as I needed to.

Stalking him in the dead of the night was a step this girl wasn't ready to take.

So I held back and sat on a bench just outside the gyms. After giving him a few minutes' head start, I let out a soft sigh and headed down the trail by myself.

If anyone tells you walking down a wooded path by yourself, at night, on an island with no lights is peaceful—they're lying to you. They're straight-up bullshitting you, because it wasn't. I felt like I'd spent half my life at this camp, and even I got freaked out. My phone's light was a small help, but not much. Visions of deer running at me, ready to spear my chest with their antlers or hoof me to death had me picking up my pace. Then there was the slight whiff of skunk. I was probably imagining it, but by then, I didn't need to add much more to get to full sprint. And because the path was made of wood chips, I was trying to run while picking up my feet so my toes wouldn't get caught up on anything.

My knees were rising almost to my chest, making my phone bounce so much that I about clipped myself in the chin with it.

I turned it off, but I could still imagine how ridiculous I would've looked to anyone wandering around with night-vision goggles.

And then I started thinking about the time people had snuck onto the island and we'd had to catch them and escort them back off. That had taken a coordinated effort by most of the staff, and tonight was just me.

So now I was running from deer, skunk, and any random island intruders.

I'd been out of breath by the time I got to my cabin, welcomed by the faint odor of fish.

That had been my night, and so far my morning was off to a bang-up start. After chilling myself to the bone because it was seriously cold at five in the morning, I dressed and stuffed a bag full of whatever I grabbed. I wouldn't have much time to run back here since Keith wanted the courts open almost all day. A few minutes later, after lacing up my sneakers, I hit the path again.

There was still not much light, but my absolute exhaustion pushed all my scary thoughts away. If a deer, skunk, or intruder tried to mess with me, they'd be the stupid one. I was also a little more rational this morning. Daylight tended to bring back the sanity, just a bit. And I was tired. Tired meant I wasn't a happy Charlie. I needed coffee before dealing with life, hence I'd chosen the best time for my call to the ex dipshit.

That cheered me a bit.

I was almost smiling when I got to the clearing between the gym courts and the main lounge. Keith had said he wanted it open at five am. I was thirty minutes late, but no one was here. I was pretty sure my job was safe. I unlocked the courts and flipped on all the lights.

The air was still crisp. I had slipped on a sweatshirt over my T-shirt and jean shorts, and shivering, I tugged the zipper up. It went up the side, all the way to my neck. I'd thought it was cute and trendy when I bought it, but it pinched my skin now, and I cringed. Oh well. I liked how it looked, so I was keeping it, even if it made me bleed.

I opened the cage, put Forster's ball up on the rack since I'd left it on the floor, and grabbed the list of inventory.

I started going through everything, but I was yawning so hard that it was making me tear up by the time I got to the relay equipment. That was three minutes later.

I needed coffee. I didn't care how distrustful Keith was. I was going to leave the courts unlocked (gasp, then hiss), and I was going to get coffee in the main lobby.

Putting a few basketballs outside the cage door, just in case someone showed up, I headed out. The cage was locked up. My bag was with it, hidden in the back with the hockey sticks, and I was just leaving through the back door when I more sensed them than saw them.

Reese Forster and Juan Cartion were jogging down the walking path.

All in gray, Reese had his hood up and head down, with sweatpants hanging low from his narrow hips. They ended around his calves. His shoes were neon yellow—the entire shoe, even his laces.

As the path broke out from the trees, Juan's head was up, and his eyes met mine.

They weren't anywhere close to me, but I still stepped back. My back hit the building behind me, and I stayed put, almost the exact same posture I'd taken last night when Forster brought his ball back to the cage.

Like last time, he never looked up.

He and his best friend ran right past me, going around to the front of the gym building and turning down the path that'd take them to the lake.

I'd swear I saw some amusement in Juan Cartion's gaze, but I wasn't sure, and after waiting another few seconds—as if they were going to magically run back—I smoothed a hand over my shirt. My heart was beating so fast.

This was ridiculous.

I couldn't keep almost having a heart attack every time I saw these guys. They were campers. I was staff.

Three weeks, or more like two and a half weeks.

I was on day two and almost pissing my pants at just the thought of seeing Reese Forster.

I needed a trick. Something to help me calm down.

I needed to think of him naked.

My pulse skyrocketed.

Yeah. That wasn't going to help.

I needed to... I went through some ideas.

Maybe I could just focus on his penis.

Another skip in my pulse. That wasn't helping, because I thought of why I would see his penis, and whoa boy—I got lightheaded.

Think of him vomiting.

Nope. I just wanted to help clean him up.

Think of him taking a piss.

And there was that penis again.

The same with taking a dump.

He was naked. He was squatting.

There might've been a smell, but there was his body in all its glory. I've seen pictures of him playing without his shirt. Goooorgeous.

I bit my lip, squelching a groan. *So* not helping.

Damian.

That hit me like a bat to my chest.

Everything was gone—the nerves, the flutters, the feeling of just feeling. Thinking of Damian took it all away.

I swallowed over that bark lump. It wasn't right, or it shouldn't have been, that just a memory could strip someone of everything.

But it worked.

CHAPTER TEN

Owen and Hadley had been running behind on making breakfast when I came in for my coffee. They had a sick kid, so they had to keep taking turns going back to the house to check on little Noah until Hadley's mom got there. They had one of the two houses on the island. Keith had the other. (*Boo, hiss*)

And speaking of Keith...

In another accidental-genius moment, I snagged a pair of radios and put one in the court and the other in the kitchen. Now I would hear if someone showed up, and like Owen and Hadley with their kid, I'd run out to check on the courts. Until then, I stayed in the kitchen to help with the food. The players were starting to trickle in, and I was behind the dish window again, waiting for Keith to show up for his coffee.

It was almost clockwork. Even after all these years.

Ten minutes till we started serving, he breezed in.

Khaki shorts. A green polo shirt. His Boss mug in hand. He filled it up, then entered the kitchen to talk to Owen. Seeing me, he stopped whatever he'd been about to say and blinked a few times.

I wasn't about to defend myself for not sitting in an empty gym when my two friends had a sick kid and needed help. He was beyond an asshole if he was going to light into me for that. After staring at me a couple more seconds, he turned back to Owen.

Clearing his throat, he asked, "How's the morning going?"

I tuned them out, going back to washing what dishes I already could.

I was on my third pan when I heard the players coming in.

The Damian effect was still with me. I'd felt it the whole morning since I'd let myself think of him, and it prevented my usual freak-out when the guys came in. I almost felt like a normal person. I was just standing here, doing dishes. No idiotic questions burst out of me like a backward fart, and I hadn't even felt the usual amount of anger toward Keith when he came in. That would change, but for now, I almost felt melancholy.

As if sensing he was safe, Reese Forster walked in with Juan Cartion right behind him and a couple other players too.

Normal Charlie would've categorized every single person. I would've taken note of what they were wearing, how they were walking, how I thought they might've smelled. All of it.

But melancholy Charlie only looked at him a moment before finishing my pan and putting it through the washer.

See? Normal.

I could do this.

Thoughts of the ex-soulmate who had shattered me were going to be my friend for the next three weeks.

These three weeks were going to suck.

I inhaled, feeling my lungs tremble, and swallowed over a couple knives in my throat. My hands shook slightly when I reached for the next round of dishes, but then I firmed everything. Whatever. I could do this.

It'd been a year. I should've dealt with the Damian trauma long before now anyway.

I'd have to look up nearby therapists at this rate—or write my book. *Shit.* I'd forgotten that was the main excuse for coming out here. Yes. Maybe I should plan to actually work on that thing.

I don't know why I looked up. Might've been the hairs on the back of my neck shifting. They didn't stand up. It wasn't that type of feeling that was trickling down my back, but it was an awareness.

I glanced up and that nice soft trickle ramped up in volume. I was scorched to the bone.

Reese Forster was staring at me.

He sat at a table a few yards away, and while his teammates were talking, he was looking right at me.

I paused with the dishes.

The whole thing only lasted a second or two, but the world melted away. I felt a pounding in my chest. Maybe it was my heart. Maybe it was Damian wanting to tear out of me. Whatever it was, I swallowed over that damn lump that seemed permanently lodged there, and I stopped what I was doing.

Until he looked away.

One of the guys spoke to him, and he turned to answer.

The spell was broken, but I felt the remnants still inside of me.

I was a mess—a very literal jumbled mess that had bones and skin keeping it together, but it really hit me at that moment. I mean, it had hit me at various times over the last year, and I was doing this whole denying routine to keep myself from falling apart, but in this moment, the reality of how destroyed I was inside became crystal clear.

I was nearing thirty. Three years away was really not that long.

I'd been fired from a job I kinda enjoyed doing, but also didn't really give two craps about at the same time. It was something that paid the bills and I hadn't hated it.

I was now doing dishes at my old childhood job, literally hiding from my life, and I had no idea how to move forward.

I snuck a look at Owen and Hadley. It made sense that they were here.

Owen had a plan. The normal kitchen staff were off, otherwise Owen was the one who usually ran things around here. Even Keith being here made sense. He was the director. Those were two respectable careers, and Hadley was here to support her husband. They had kids. She was a mom too. That was the most important job in the world.

Grant was head of the maintenance crew. That was a good job anywhere.

What the hell was I doing?

I had no kids. No boyfriend. No life.

I was trying to keep myself from becoming a gawking stalker. I mean, pathetic much? That was me.

The normal staff were usually college kids, doing a fun job during the summers while they went to school to get to the real careers they wanted in life. Even they had direction.

I was embarrassed.

"Charlie."

I literally jerked out of my thoughts, stepping backward and hitting the wall behind me. Two drying crates hung there crashed to the floor.

Keith had been making an announcement, but he stopped, and everyone looked at me.

I hissed, feeling the tears on my face.

Grant had been the one to say my name, his eyes now narrowing before he looked around us.

He stepped forward, shielding me from the rest of the room, except I looked around him. Reese Forster still had a direct line of sight to me, and he was staring like everyone else—except his jaw was clenched. His eyebrows pulled down, and he frowned.

Was he mad at me? Because I was crying?

Feeling an irrational burst of anger, I flipped him off.

The dish window hid most of me, but I raised my hand to my waist, with just the one finger showing. His eyes dropped to it and lingered.

I waved it from side to side until I realized what I was doing and tore myself away.

Then I did what I always did.

I went to the back of the kitchen and hid. What's one more embarrassing moment to pile on with all the others?

My heart raced and beat loudly in my ears as I bent down at the back sink to wash my hands. When that didn't help calm me, I cupped a handful of water and splashed it on my face.

That helped. A little. It disguised the tears anyway.

Owen and Hadley had been in the office, so they didn't know what happened. They were coming out now, and I heard Grant ask them, "Where'd Charlie go?"

Hadley answered, "I don't know. Why?"

I tensed, waiting for Grant to tell them. But he only said, "I had a question for her..." He saw me, and his voice trailed off. "Never mind."

He came over to stand next to the sink.

We waited in silence until Hadley grabbed what she had come out for and went back to Owen's office.

"You okay?" Grant asked in a low voice.

The answer was *no*, so I didn't answer. I couldn't bring myself to meet his gaze either. If I did, I was going to start crying, so I stared at a wall to the side of us.

When I trusted my voice not to crack, I said, "Thanks for covering for me."

He nodded. I caught the movement from the corner of my eye. "That's what we used to do."

He was right.

He'd been my best friend all those years ago.

I still couldn't say anything—I was doing everything I could not to cry—but I reached out and blindly grabbed for his hand. He held it out, shifting something to his other hand, and I squeezed it once.

"Thank you."

"We can talk later, if you want, but one of the Thunder's trainers was asking who's in charge of the courts. He's going to leave breakfast early to meet with you, go over what they might need from us. Can you handle that?"

Work. Distraction. I needed that like I needed air.

"Yesssss," I breathed out. Grabbing a paper towel, I wiped my face. "I'm going to go now."

"Get some food," he said again. "I remember how you used to not eat when you were upset." He started for the door. Then he stopped and looked back. "Oh. Hey. My fiancée is coming today. I'd like you to meet her."

"What's her name?"

"Sophia."

His voice got lighter when he said her name. So did his face. He relaxed, the tight lines around his mouth softening.

He loved her. He truly did, and he was happy.

He was worried about me, but she made him content. I saw it all in an instant because I knew him so well. That had never gone away, and despite the reason for me coming here, I was glad for it.

It was time to stop and face some of the people I had run from before.

I smiled. "I'm excited to meet her."

He nodded and was gone, and because I was feeling more myself, my eyes returned to Reese Forster. I should just embrace the stalker inside of me, right?

With a jolt, I found he was looking at me again.

As our gazes met and held, he reached forward. His gaze was almost smoldering. He grabbed his milk, his own middle finger splayed out on the side of the cup. Tipping it to his lips, he never broke eye contact, even when he put it back on the table.

I bit down, squelching a smile.

The ghost of a grin teased on his face too, and I had to bite down harder.

I shouldn't find that exciting, but I did.

And because I felt a question wanting to be blurted out, and knowing it was going to be highly inappropriate, I ripped my gaze from his.

I headed out.

Then I smiled.

CHAPTER ELEVEN

The balls were all there, in the same spot where I'd left them. They were good balls, trainable balls. I felt an odd amount of pride in these two inanimate objects and scooped them up. Cradling them as if they were *my* balls, I took them inside the cage.

The screen door creaked open and slammed shut a second later, and a guy walked around to the front of the cage, decked out in all white.

He had the swoosh symbols on his shoes, his pants, and his warm-up windrunner, and over his left chest was the Seattle Thunder lightning bolt. His hair was shaved on the sides with the top long and healthy, a sandy mix of browns. I wasn't even sure if he was blond or had brown hair. The length was pulled back into a messy bun—one I was jealous of.

He moved toward me briskly, as if it were his normal speed, but he was constantly being told to slow down for the rest of us mere mortals.

"Are you in charge of the courts? Charl—" He cut himself off, his head cocking to the side.

I would've bet money that he knew my name was Charlie, but he wanted to be the guy who called me Charlotte instead. That wasn't my name, but some men felt special, thinking they'd guessed the right name and called me that instead of the nickname everyone else used.

There's a reason it's used, and that's because I like it.

I finished for him, "ie."

He blinked. "Huh?"

"Charl-ie. That's my name."

"Right." His head lowered, but his eyes remained trained on me. His eyebrows pinched together as if he'd stepped into an invisible pile of poo, but he couldn't see it or smell it. He only had the feeling it was there. "Charlie. That's you?"

"That's me."

"You're a girl."

It came out accusatory.

I scowled. "You're a boy." This game was fun.

He frowned. "Yes?"

I nodded. "Yes."

He scratched behind his ear. "What's happening here?"

I was tempted to scratch behind my ear too, but I refrained. Barely. "Nothing. What's going on with you?"

His frown deepened. "You're..."

Here we go again. I almost sighed. "A girl. Yes."

"What?"

I relented. "You're Aiden?" And he was confused by *my* name?

"Aiden Marshall." He stuck his hand out. "I'm one of the trainers for the team," he said. "Keith mentioned you could be in charge of making sure the water is fully stocked."

He led me over to the screen door between the outdoor courts and the indoor area. "I was thinking of having a table here. Water. Sports drinks. Protein and energy drinks and snacks. Then towels. Keith said you could help with the towels too."

I was fairly certain Keith might've mentioned I was here to do their bidding, but I refrained from that comment too.

"How many do you need?"

"Anything we need to specially order, we'll already have, but if you could just make sure the tables are fully stocked. I was thinking around a hundred towels. Some of the players use a couple at a time."

"Just regular towels?" *Not heated?* I was already thinking of how we could get a steamer in here to hold the towels and how I could avoid that catching on fire.

"Yeah. Just hand towels. We brought some with us, but any you have on hand would be helpful. And ice baths. Do you guys have enough ice to supply for an ice bath?"

Oh shit. That would take large tubs. And ice, lots and lots of ice.

"I'll tell Grant about that. He's maintenance, so he'd be doing the ice baths for you guys."

Seriously, Keith? He told them we'd handle that? That sounded like an enormous pain in the ass, but it was just like him to offer.

"Grant." Aiden dipped his head forward. "You're right. I'll talk to Grant myself about the ice baths. We'll need a few tubs filled every day too."

Tubs. Got it.

I gave a bouncing nod and said, "You think a portable tub would make a good sled on a glacier?"

He stared at me.

"Never mind." I whipped around, intending to go for the screen door. A quick exit was always a good choice after one of *those* slipped out. Instead, I smacked into a chest.

Or I would've except, two strong hands grabbed my biceps and caught me.

It happened so quickly, not even half a second.

I saw the wall of muscle in front of me and closed my eyes. I opened them after being stopped and was an inch away.

Gulp.

I already knew. I knew because I was this guy's stalker, and that should've made me all giddy and euphoric. It didn't. Instead, dread surged in my gut like an Olympic runner taking off after the starting gun popped.

My eyes moved up and up and up, over a defined chest to strong biceps and where they met his broad shoulders. His throat had the slightest stubble, as did his chin. I looked over his perfectly formed mouth, up to his nose and landed right on those hazel eyes that I swore were smoldering. Again.

Reese Forster was touching me.

Red alert, red alert.

His hands flexed on my arms before he chuckled. "Again with the questions?"

"Questions?" Aiden looked between the two of us.

He hadn't dropped his hands.

He was still touching me.

I couldn't even formulate a response except what was exploding up from my toes, my legs, my groin, my stomach, my chest, my throat. "If scientists are able to add a rhino's horn to a horse through DNA manipulation, is that a real unicorn?"

Aiden made a gurgling sound, but to his credit, Reese didn't even blink.

He responded right away. "No. That'd be a horse with a rhino's horn."

"Whaaat is happening?"

Reese ignored Aiden, finally dropping his hands—and yes, he left tingles where he had touched me. His eyebrows dipped down. "You're a little odd, aren't you?"

I snorted. "Fantastically so." Somehow my hand found my hip in the most backward movement ever. I twirled and dipped it like it was an airplane going in for a landing. "You know me. Us camp groupies always have to keep you on your toes."

His eyes remained locked on mine.

I was such an idiot.

Aiden was almost gawking at us now.

Then Reese gave a little grunt and stepped back. "You're not a camp groupie. I was wrong. I'm sorry."

Little did he know...

The door that connected the gym to the concessions burst open behind Reese, and I heard the familiar *whisk-whisk-whisk* of Keith's khaki shorts before he bellowed out, "Charlie!"

I was right fucking here. I gritted my teeth.

Reese looked back.

Aiden stepped aside to see Keith too, and I stepped out from behind Reese.

"Oh!" Keith ground to a halt, that damn Boss mug in hand. He must've put hair product in his curls since breakfast because they looked wet. I'd bet my measly camp salary he was trying to impress the players, or the coaches.

Keith liked to pretend he was an expert on the sport.

To his credit, he did know quite a bit. He coached his daughters' basketball teams, and one time I had to help. I'd been slightly impressed with the way he blew his whistle. Until it became annoying. He blew the thing every five minutes.

"I'm Keith Gimpel." He stuck his hand out. "I run this place." His smooth-talker voice was on. He was hoping to impress Reese Forster now.

Reese just nodded at him and moved back a step, to the side. "Thank you for letting our team use your facilities."

Aiden stepped forward, shaking Keith's hand instead. "I'm Aiden, one of the team's trainers."

Reese stepped back again, as if Keith's presence repulsed him—or maybe that was my wishful thinking. Either way, Aiden moved forward again, engaging Keith in further conversation, and somehow, Aiden had Keith walking back into the concessions area a second later.

I was in awe.

I might need to be friends with this Aiden if he could handle Keith like that, because that's what they both just did. My boss got *served,* in the best way ever.

Reese had gone back to watching me, and I couldn't help myself. "That was awesome! It's like you have creepy-guy radar, and Aiden's your superhero," I gushed.

Reese winced. "I don't know if it's like that exactly." He lifted a nonchalant shoulder. "Your boss is a dick. I can tell."

Stalker mode: engaged. Again.

"I think I want to be your best friend."

I cringed, hearing those words before I could take them back, but a second later, Reese Forster laughed. It was small, brief, but it was there. And the sound flooded me with a warm, slightly gooey feeling.

"Let's just keep it at weird camp buds, and by that, I mean you give me a damn ball. Now."

That edge from last night was back in his voice. It was slight, but it was there, as if he'd been trying to hold it back.

I nodded, turning for the cage. That was the guy who'd showed up last night and practiced for four hours straight by himself, and with a vengeance—as if he needed to save the world with his basketball skills.

I felt honored he was even trying to hold back with me.

After handing over a ball, which Reese took in the same instant half-dribble, go-between-the-legs motion as he walked toward the court, the screen door slammed shut once again.

Please, not Keith. Please, not Keith.

Grant walked around the corner. "Hey—"

I shot my hands in the air and clapped them together. "It worked!"

I must've shouted, because Reese stopped dribbling. He and Grant both looked at me, but I didn't even care. At this point, both were aware of my quirks.

"Okay." Grant shook his head, rubbing his hand over the side of his face. "I'm not even asking. Did that trainer guy find you?"

"Yes. We need tubs."

"Tubs?" His eyebrows rose.

I nodded. "Tubs and other stuff. Water. Sports drinks. Towels." I indicated the spot behind him. "He wants a table set up there with all of that, and a second one outside. And he wants ice for the tubs."

"Oh. That doesn't sound so bad." He had twisted around, probably gauging what size table he'd need to get.

"No, no." I leaned forward and tugged on his sleeve.

He looked back.

I knew what he was thinking. "He doesn't want the tubs for drinks or food." Because that was a normal thing here. "He wants the tubs for the guys, for ice baths."

And now I waited.

"Are you kidding?" His eyebrows pulled together, matching the sides of his mouth. "Fucking ice baths?"

I smiled. "Keith told him we could do that."

He swore under his breath. "Goddamn fucking Keith. Where the hell are we going to find tubs that size? We've never offered that service before."

I had a feeling it was going to be a regular thing now. I said as much. "You know Keith will want to get more pro teams. He'll put images of them on the website."

Grant went back to growling because he knew I was right, and that meant it'd be on him to get it done. Finding tubs wouldn't really be a problem. Grant hated ice. His only use for ice was making drinks colder, but because winter retreats were offered here during the off-season, that meant he had a large hockey rink to maintain. Then there were polar bear plunges. Igloo making. Ice carving. And I got the newsletter—they were boasting a brand new ice carnival. All of those jobs fell on Grant's shoulders to maintain, and during a time when staff was cut in half and sometimes to a third of what he had during the summer.

He pulled his radio from his back and pressed the button. "Owen, you there?"

A crackle, then, "Owen here. What's up?"

"We got enough ice to fill up a couple of tubs for ice baths?"

More crackling.

Owen said, "For what?"

"Ice baths."

Crackle.

Crackle.

"Did you say ice paths?"

Grant swore.

The crackling intensified, and he swore some more.

He almost yelled into the radio, "Ice baths. B. B as in boy. Baths!"

"Psychopaths?"

"Goddamn!"

He wound up, ready to throw the radio over my head, but I lunged forward and grabbed it from him. He didn't even resist. He walked in a tight circle, his arms tucked across his chest and his head down.

I pressed the button. "Owen, ice soaks."

"Ooh! Yeah. We have enough. The machine is working fine."

I pressed it again. "Thank you." Let it go, then pressed it again. "Psychopath." I said to Grant, "He was messing with you."

Crackle.

Owen's laughter sounded over the radio a second later. "I was just having fun. We'll put out some buckets Grant can use. Owen, out."

"Fuck this." Grant started for the door, took one step, and twisted back to me. He took the radio in one hand, my arm in the other, and walked me out the door. "You're helping me."

A warm feeling exploded in me. I felt it shoot down my arms, and I couldn't have stopped my smile if I'd tried.

This was the old Grant, the old dynamic of someone pushing on his buttons for the fun of it. The fact that it had been Owen made it even funnier, and like those previous years, Grant was huffing and puffing, but he was going to get the job done.

And I was going along for the ride, even though I was supposed to stay and man the gym.

"The cage, dude," I said.

He growled. "Fuck that too." He shot a look over his shoulder at Reese, who'd lined up for a three-pointer. The ball swished as Grant added, "Keith's being paranoid if he thinks Reese Forster is going to steal a ball."

"But where are we going? Tubs won't have to be filled till after their practices."

A hard bounce sounded behind us.

Grant hit the screen door with the palm of his hand. "You can help me bring all the stuff up."

A second hard bounce.

We were out the door and walking for the main lodge when I felt a tingle in the back of my neck. I looked over my shoulder, and as Reese bounced the ball between his legs, I met his gaze.

A shiver ran all the way down my back.

I couldn't read him. His face was locked down into an impassive wall, and I had to reflect for a second. He'd been pissy, furious, bossy, commanding, and then suddenly he'd laughed at me. Now there was nothing. He was devoid of all emotion. His eyes were dead.

CHAPTER
TWELVE

"The team has to go to their first preseason game. They have to use Fairview's airport, so you're going to go with them, show them the way."

I blinked.

I saw the Boss mug first, then it moved from the opening in front of the cage's window and Keith appeared. He was hitching his khaki shorts up, his belly jutting out even farther than normal because he wasn't watching me. He was leaning against the cage, one of his legs crossed over the other, and he was watching the practice.

They'd been running drills for the last hour, with Reese and a few others sectioned off to the back corner. He was being fed basketballs as he was dribbling up to three at a time. He handled four at one point, but that was quickly shot off to the next person in line. They were taking turns, sending him the balls and he couldn't lose control over any of them. He was bent down, a wide grin on his face, his eyes lit up. So not like the other day, when there'd been no look at all. Since then, he hadn't looked at me. I was nonexistent.

Well. I was staff. There was a level of invisibility that came along with my position.

I wished that same power was extended to Keith, but alas he was my boss. What could a recently fired and recently dumped person do?

"You want me to do what?"

He waved his mug back to me, speaking distractedly, "You know how that airport is. The GPS always gets it wrong, so I told them I'd send a staff member with them. Trent's gone. Owen is needed here and Grant's got other things to do. You're up." Now he looked at me.

I wished he hadn't.

I knew he was trying to grin at me, he was even speaking neutral and like I was a regular person to him, but when his mouth lifted, it just came out as a sneer. I didn't think I'd be able to see him any other way.

He straightened up, readjusting his shorts. "I told Winston a staff person would direct them to the airport, so they know. They've chartered their own plane."

He and Winston. First name terms, huh?

Wait. "I'm riding with them?"

On their bus?

I was starting to hyperventilate and he hadn't even answered.

He was eyeing me, his eyebrows pinched together. "Yes. And you're representing the camp, so don't do anything nuts."

I wanted to snort for so many reasons. I refrained, chewing the inside of my cheek. But I did give him a half-salute. "Yes, sir."

"Good. They leave in about two hours. You'll go on the bus with them, and they'll park it there until they fly back."

Two hours later, I was told to wait in the entryway while all their equipment was first loaded. They left after eating, and one by one, they went past me.

Out the door. To the bus.

A few of the guys eyed me with interest. A couple winked. Two smiled. Then there were the blank stares, a couple disgusted looks, all until the end where Reese was bringing up the rear. Juan was in front of him, a coach walking next to Reese, his hand on his shoulder.

He was nodding to what the coach was saying, then he saw me, and his eyes sparked. He half-turned his head toward me, enough so the coach stopped talking, lifting his head too to see what caught Reese's attention. Seeing it was only good old me, the coach went right back to speaking, but Reese didn't look away. He eyed me the whole time as he passed, his head turning to watch me as Juan held the door open for him.

Noting the look, Juan took interest in me too. His own eyebrows pinching together, a slight frown marring his face.

And because they were the rear of the group, I waited a beat before I fell in line.

These guys were giants, all of them except their trainers, and even most of those guys were six feet and in amazing shape. Came with the job, I suppose.

This was my life.

I couldn't get over it.

I was walking behind the Seattle Thunder. I was going to ride on their bus with them, show them the way to get to the airport— wait.

Oh, shit.

I held up a hand. "Hold on!" I took off, back inside. "Owen!"

The door slammed shut behind me, then I heard it squeak as it was opened again.

"Where are you going?"

I was dying. That was Reese.

"I need directions."

His nostrils flared and his head moved back an inch. "You're supposed to be giving us directions."

"I know, but—" There was a fork in the road and I always went the wrong way, but instead of explaining that to Reese, I yelled for Owen. "Left or right at the fork?"

"Right!"

Hadley yelled, "He means left. He thought you said left, and he was saying right to the left. It's left."

I was confused.

A body stood next to me. I could feel Reese's heat coming off him, and his arm lifted. He had his phone out, was frowning at it. "Why's the GPS all fucked up out here?"

I gulped. "The signal out here is crap."

He grunted, putting his phone away. "Makes sense." He eyed me again, before nodding up at Owen who had come out from his office. "Why can't you come with us? Make sure we don't get lost."

So embarrassing, but then he stepped into my side.

My head whipped up, and I swear, he'd done it on purpose. His face was stiff, his lips pressed tight like he was holding back a grin, and he didn't look down at me. Then he did it again. He was doing it on purpose.

I tensed, standing to my fullest height of five six. And I had no idea what to do here.

Owen gave us both a grin, eyeing me with a slight wary look. "You know the way?"

I nodded. "It's left…"

"Right?" Reese added.

I clamped my mouth shut. My neck heating up.

Owen was skirting between the two of us, rolling his shoulder up and tugging on his neck. "At the fork, you go left."

Hadley yelled from behind the kitchen window, "That's right."

Reese started laughing.

I yelled back, "You can't see, but I'm flicking you off, Hadley."

"I'm twerking back at you."

"Yo!" A shout from behind us.

Reese and I both turned. The coach was there, a slight glare on his face. He was holding the door open, one foot inside. "What's the holdup?"

Reese turned around, stepping into me again. "Direction Girl needed to get directions."

"What?" His eyebrows shot up.

"No. I mean," I coughed and started forward, "there's a fork. I needed to remember which way to go. It's confusing sometimes."

Reese was close behind me. "She's *right*."

He was fucking with me.

The coach pushed the door open, stepping back and giving us space so both of us could pass him by. As I stepped outside, I moved to the side, giving Reese a good side-eye. "We go left."

His mouth twitched, but he ran a hand over it, hiding his expression. "You sure about that?"

My God. I had to think about it.

As he was looking down at me like that, like we were having our own secret, I almost faltered in my step. He was mesmerizing. "I...yes. I'm right." I blanched.

Reese started laughing.

I wasn't ready.

He'd been pissed the first night, confused after that, and guarded yesterday. This Reese was electrifying. I'd seen it earlier in their practice and had been half-swooning, but standing so close to him, having him giving me this attention—a jolt went through my entire body as the sound of his laugh washed over me. It took a moment to regroup.

"Yes. I'm right. It's left."

The coach sighed, moving ahead of us. "Just don't get us lost. We are on a time table here."

Then we were getting on, and a lot of eyes were focused on us. I gulped.

One head coach. Four assistant coaches. Two trainers. A few other extra staff and nineteen players were waiting for us. Only half were watching, but it didn't diminish the effect of being the center of their attention.

Reese started to take one of the open seats in the front, until their head coach grunted. "In the back, Forster."

He paused, mid-swing into the chair. "What?"

His coach was looking over some papers, jerked his hand toward the back. "Passing along the message. Cartion said you had to go back there." He looked up, his eyes all business. "I don't know why." Then the other coach was sitting behind me, and he focused on me. "You're the staff?"

Staff. I dipped my head down. "That's me."

Reese's grin was slow. "She needed to ask for directions."

"Shut up," I hissed under my breath, then was more mortified as three of the coaches looked over.

Winston Duty's eyes were narrowing the more he watched us. Then he motioned for an empty seat right behind the driver. "I'm starting to see why Cartion requested your presence in the back." He said to me, "That's for you. You'll be relaying directions to Pete."

Pete was fifty-three, grandfather to three little ones under the age of five, and he was tickled pink at being the team's driver. They employed him during the season, and not only was he deemed the team's greeter, but he was also their storyteller. Unofficially, of course.

By the time we were pulling into Fairview's tiny airport, where their plane seemed to take up half the tarmac, I learned about the time they traveled last year to Oregon and had a tire go out. I learned about the police officer names that came to assist them, and how Pete himself knew all of the first responders who attended their games in Seattle. Did I want to learn more about Washington itself?

I was turning that last request down, my head buzzing with all the information, names, dates, and little factoids like the fact that Pete's granddaughter was not actually named after Reese, the actress, but after their very own Reese Forster. Pete had a good laugh about that. It was always a source of confusion when people met his little granddaughter.

He kept talking, swinging the bus over into the parking lot.

A hand touched me from behind. Aiden leaned over, saying under his breath, "You can tune him out. Once he starts, he won't stop."

I half-glared at him. "You tell me *now*?" I motioned outside. "We just got here."

He chuckled, grabbing his bag as the bus stopped and Pete opened the door. Standing up, he patted me on the arm. "Pete does best when he's talking to someone, and from what I hear, you needed distracting. Least, that's what Forster said earlier."

Forster said?

He said what?

But Aiden was off the bus.

I was going to get off next, but one of the coaches said, "Stay put."

I stayed put.

I stayed put as all the coaches got off, the other trainer. Their other staff, and as each player trailed past me.

"Heard you almost got us lost."

I swallowed over a lump. That was Lestroy talking to me. He was teasing as he held his bag over his shoulder and added, "Thanks for not doing that."

Oh, God.

Garth Carzoni was next, winking. "I was rooting for the right, not the left. Glad you were correct."

Seat, swallow me now.

Matthew Crusty was up. He said to Carzoni as he passed me by, also winking, "I heard she's dyslexic and has to turn her hands around to get the L right."

A little gurgling sound came from me.

Juan spoke up, the next one passing me by, "That's why Reese went after her, making sure we didn't end up at that casino. Remember that one time?"

Crusky raised his arm, already outside. "Oh yeah. That one time."

Juan went down the stairs, but flashed me a grin over his shoulder. "Wish us luck, Staff Member."

Direction Girl to Staff Member. I wasn't sure if I'd been demoted or not.

Reese was the last one out except for one of their staff in the back of the bus.

He stopped at my seat, a backpack on and his hands resting on the straps. "They're hazing you, just a little bit."

Another gurgle escaped my throat.

"You guys don't get it." I had to blink a couple times. "This is—a wet dream for me."

But no randoms came out of me. I just now realized that, and as if reading my mind, Reese said, "Why do you think Pete was talking to you the whole time? I might've had a word with him earlier." Then he was moving past me.

"Wait."

All of them were going up into the plane. I was looking around. "Where is Pete?"

"He's on the plane. He wanted to get on first because his knee was giving him problems earlier. We'll have a bus waiting for us at the next airport to the stadium."

"But—"

Reese chuckled. "Have a good one, Direction Girl. We'll be back after we win." He didn't wink, but his smirk had enough punch behind it. I lost my train of thought for a second, until I clued back in that he was getting off and crossing the tarmac to get on that plane too.

They all had been, except one.

The last staff guy was holding a bag of garbage, coming back down the center aisle. I asked as he passed me by, "Do I have a ride home?"

He glanced up and shrugged. "I don't know, but you gotta get off the bus. I have to lock it for Pete."

I got off. He locked the bus, jogging over to the plane, and I was left standing there, my mouth hanging open. All the while as the plane closed up and took off, long after I saw it disappear into the air.

I'd been ditched, and I wasn't even sure who had ditched me.

Then the airport office door opened and a woman waved at me. "You Direction Girl?"

I groaned, heading over to her. "Yeah."

She smiled, laughing. "They told me to wait until the plane was long gone to tell you that I'm your ride back. Give me a minute to close up, then I'll drive you."

I didn't know if I should laugh or curse.

I did both.

CHAPTER
THIRTEEN

Two days later, they'd won their first preseason game and were back practicing.

Both gyms were filled and were in the middle of drills. The sound of bouncing basketballs, whistles, yelling, and the squeaks of shoes against the floor filled the courts.

And the smell of sweat.

I loved it.

I'd never enjoyed playing the sport myself, but my brother was a basketball star for our high school team. He was starting varsity in seventh grade, and growing up as Chance Manning's little sister had its benefits—but also its cons. One of the benefits, I was treated like royalty at every single basketball game. Another girl, whose brother was on the varsity team with Chance, told me she'd started being one of the team's managers. That was a loose title they'd given her because she showed up and took stats for their games. She'd asked if I wanted to do it with her, and the answer had been a resounding *hell yes*. The popular girls down front always had time for Chance's little sister, and the only better seating was actually with the team. That's where they put us managers.

So even to this day, a filled and active gym of basketball players made a part of me purr like a kitten.

I'd missed this, and I'd forgotten how much I missed this. Seems as if coming back to camp hadn't been the only part of my history I was revisiting, and I was okay with that too. I dropped the ball I'd been bouncing idly and whipped my head around.

Reese stood at the counter, sweat wetting his hair, his face, and his shirt. He held a basketball on his hip.

"What?"

My brain turned off. Reese Forster looked as if he'd stepped out of the shower. He didn't smell like it, but he looked like it.

My groin was inflamed. The Fourth of July decided to visit, and I groaned, biting my lip. So embarrassing.

"What'd you say?" I asked again, my voice a little raspy.

He nodded toward the screen door. "You and that guy from the other day. You're good friends."

It took a second, but Grant. It clicked then. The Tub Day.

And nope.

I was not going to let my weird brain go nuts with thoughts here. He was asking because he was curious. That's all. For no reason other than curiosity.

Right.

A monotone voice sounded through my brain: *Calm the fuck down.*

I swallowed, and just like that, I was calmer.

My normal response was to go into hyperdrive, but enough was enough. I needed to be a normal person. Reese (I wasn't using his last name any more) had asked a general question, because he was generally interested, and I could respond—like a generally *normal* person.

You'd think I'd be better after getting hazed. I wasn't. I was worse, in some ways.

I tucked some hair behind my ear. "I used to work here a long time ago, and he and I—"

Reese bounced the ball between his legs, once, catching it right away. "There was a thing?"

I was totally cool here.

"Yeah." I winced at myself. "I mean, no. We were best friends. That's it."

He dropped the ball again, starting to bounce it in front of him. "So there wasn't a thing?"

"Friends."

"So who did you have a thing with?" He was still bouncing, his head cocked to the side.

"What?" *Why is he asking about this?*

"Come on." He looked me up and down. "You're hot. You're trying to tell me you're single?"

I couldn't say I wasn't.

He kept on, "And you're working here as what? A gym court attendant?"

"Um." *Shit.* He wanted the deets on why this train wreck was still working at a camp.

All the Damian trauma, Grandpa Newt, and getting fired exploded in my chest in one big ball.

I let out a sigh.

"That's...stupidly tragic." What else could I say?

He caught the ball and stopped, staring hard at me. "Stupidly tragic?"

I clipped my head in a nod. "Would you like more water? I can get that for you."

Pretending like he'd *asked* for more water, I started walking away. I called over my shoulder, "I'll get you more water."

He stared at me the whole way as I went back out the door. I couldn't see him, but I felt him. And then I remembered: we had just filled the table with water an hour ago.

• • •

Reese kept his distance from me the rest of the day. I worked like a normal employee, with only minimal fangirling still going on inside of me, but not as much. The whole 'stupidly tragic' thing put a damper on my inner fangirl.

But he watched me, and I couldn't ignore the flutter going on in my stomach. And those weren't there because of my fanatical fan-ways. They were there and growing because of a different reason, one that was more like me woman and he man, that sort of way.

And that was bad.

I could do nuts. Crazy was a nice firm wall that I kept around myself, shielding people from getting too close, or from me connecting as a real human being kinda way. It was a good firm wall locked around me, and the more he was watching me, the more that wall was getting dents in it, and that was the bad part.

Really bad. Like seriously, I'm stupid—sign me up for another stint of therapy kind of bad.

I did not need to deal with anyone on a real basis. Lucas was the most I'd tried in a year, and we all know how that ended.

Reese Forster made Grandpa Newt not even a blip.

But, I was walking from the main lounge, after dinner when he fell in step beside me, and for some reason no one clued Reese Forster in on how bad of an idea he was to my senses.

"I didn't mean to freak you out earlier," he said.

I almost faltered in my stride, but caught myself and kept going. I needed to deal with this problem before I was put in a mental clinic.

"Tell me something gross about yourself."

"Why?"

We were rounding one of the outdoor courts. A couple of the other players were there, shooting hoops.

I figured, why not. "Because gross helps balance things out. I need balancing out. I'm starting to like you."

He grabbed my arm, jerking me to a stop.

His head inclined toward me. His eyes keen. "Say again."

I rolled my eyes. "Come on. You're a pro ball player. Women throwing themselves at you is not new. Why are you surprised by me?"

"It's not that." He gripped the back of his neck. "As a line, that was almost lame compared to some I've heard." An easy grin fell back in place and he let go of his neck, nodding to me. "You can do better."

This guy.

I—no words.

Then I blinked a few times, staring at him because he was right. I could do better, and that sort of thing wouldn't even phase him.

"Okay. Fine." I could do this.

This was weird.

I was still going with it. "Is your dick cold? Because I've got a warmer for it."

He didn't react, his face expressionless, then his smirk grew. "That's it? We're not at the Roxbury. Do better." His smirk was growing cocky.

Jesus. He did not realize the stalker he was fanning here.

Some of the bouncing from the court lessened. The guys were starting to watch us. One guy broke from their group, heading over. I saw it from the corner of my eye.

I coughed. "I don't know. How do girls usually hit on you?"

He shrugged. "Most just usually send me a nude in my messages. Or you know, practically being naked and just grabbing me."

"That works?"

His smirk was almost rakish now. "If I have an itch and she's got the warmer for my dick."

That was so crude. My warmer got hotter.

"Yeah. Well. I'm trying to warn you away from me."

He rolled his eyes. "You don't scare me. Besides, I thought you were funny." He relaxed, rolling his shoulders back.

"Reese," Juan called out, halfway to us. He shot out a ball. It bounced once and Reese caught it without looking away from me.

"You think I'm less funny now that I'm being honest?"

He flexed his hands around the ball. "Maybe I'm missing the questions?"

Juan stopped just shy of joining our group and conversation. He was waiting.

And I was waiting too. No one missed my questions. I didn't even miss my questions. I was waiting because I didn't know how to process this conversation. I narrowed my eyes at him. "Are you messing with me?"

There was another burning feeling in me, moving up, spreading over my stomach, my chest, rising all the way to my neck. It was a burning feeling that I hadn't felt in so long. I almost didn't recognize it.

"Is that another attempt? 'Cause that's lame too." He smirked. "Thought you weren't a camp groupie?"

Well...there was always going to be a fine line with that one, especially with him, only with him.

I closed my mouth and bit down hard. Juan Cartion was listening to our conversation, and not even hiding it. The Cruskinator was coming in too, his large hands on his hips.

I focused back on him, trying to ignore the other two and now a third was coming over. "We have an audience."

Reese's eyebrows pulled together, skimming a look over his teammates. "So?"

"So." I coughed, smiling and dipping my head down. My hands were almost shaking. "I should get the cage open. Excuse me."

I wasn't running. I honestly wasn't.

I wasn't hiding.

I wasn't avoiding.

I—just—I'd hid from life while I was with Damian, then hid for another year, and Lucas had been a crash and burn attempt at jump-starting my whole living again. This, though. This, with a minor conversation with Reese Forster (yes, I had to say his last name because his first name didn't put it into the best perspective) had me feeling things I'd almost forgotten could happen in me.

I felt normal, for a small moment.

I was a girl crushing on a guy, not a fangirl gawking over a celebrity, and it hit me hard in the chest. Right there, making that thing pumping and skipping a beat.

That was what I'd been afraid of.

CHAPTER FOURTEEN

I was normal again the next morning. So normal I was boring.
No fangirl. No creep or freak. Nothing. Not one iota.

Reese looked at me, and I barely reacted.

Reese asked me for a ball and I handed one over, just fine.
My hands only trembled a slight bit. See. Totally freaking so-blah
boring.

I could've put myself to sleep, I was that lame.

I was tragically normal.

That lasted until the afternoon.

Reese was in the hallway when I came out of the bathroom.
He was leaning against the wall, and his head lifted as I exited
the door. He pushed off from the wall and declared, "You're being
weird."

Holy shit. He finally knew me.

I grinned, not wanting to go back to the gyms. No one else
was in the hallway so I leaned back against the other wall. "Hate
to break it to you, but that's my norm."

"No. Not like this." He indicated me. "I can tell. You're off
from your usual weird shit." He scowled. "I don't like it."

I raised an eyebrow. "My usual weird shit?"

A smile ghosted over his face. "You don't think I didn't know
you were watching me that first night?"

Oh. I squirmed. This hallway suddenly got really hot.

"Or the next morning when I jogged past with Juan?"

I'd been a creeper both times, standing and hiding against the wall.

And really. I glanced at the back end of the hallway. Keith didn't believe in using an air conditioner for the indoor gym, said all the windows were enough for the ventilation, but maybe we needed to add more windows.

My voice came out strained. "You knew I was there those times?"

"One of the guys heard you freaking out the first night they got here, told me about it last night after he saw us talking by the courts. Figured I needed a warning."

I could've been a puddle by now.

"Oh, God."

A slight chuckle from him. "I don't give a shit about that. You about to start creeping outside my cabin window?"

Yes. Maybe. I mean, no.

"What cabin are you in?"

The corner of his mouth tugged upwards. "Yeah, right. I'm half-tempted to tell you. I want you back to how you were."

"How I was what?"

"Being weird." He raked me up and down. "You're being normal. I don't like it."

I frowned a little. "You're very vocal and demanding."

"I know what I want."

And apparently, he wanted me weird. Well, I could so out-weird him.

I mean—where'd that come from?

Now my eyebrows went up. "I don't get a lot of requests to go back to being crazy."

He grinned, but then shrugged and readjusted his leaning stance against the wall. His hands went into his pockets. "I don't know. Just doesn't feel right." Then that grin came back. It was teasing now. "Or maybe I thought I was getting my own ball girl for a second, and before you run with that one, I mean as in someone to retrieve my balls for me so I don't have to stop shooting hoops."

I almost cooed at him, all the embarrassment shifting to more comfortable terrain here. "That's cute. You want an errand girl."

"Yeah. Maybe." His eyes darkened.

"No, seriously. Think of it this way," I told him. "Now you don't have to be scared you'll find me in your bed one night with a knife and hot wax."

Someone walked past the hallway, then backtracked.

"Reese." It was Aiden. He was frowning at us. "Coach wants you back."

Reese nodded to him, and after a questioning look at me, Aiden returned to the courts.

I started to go back, but Reese caught my elbow.

I stiffened, my insides shrieking. Code Red, people! He was touching me!

Reese was saying over my internal tornado alarms, "Just tell me. Does it have to do with a guy?"

Oh.

Damian.

And just like that, the tornado alarms switched off. A whole different form of storm was tearing me up inside, one that was way too fucking real for this conversation.

I gentled my tone, but I needed to let him know I meant business. "Look." Fuck. I sighed, biting my lip. "Yes. It's part of the tragically stupid thing from before, but I don't even talk to my friends about it."

Technically, I didn't talk to anyone about it. The therapist had been a little over six months ago.

His hand was still on my elbow. He was leaning closer.

I gave him a little bit more. "It's taken a full year for me to get where I am now, so..."

He nodded, new understanding dawning in his eyes. He held his hands up, and I tried to ignore how I protested the loss of his touch.

He straightened away from me. "Back off?"

Something shifted.

I felt it. I saw that he felt it too, and I didn't think it was my delusional side imagining it. I nodded. "Back off."

"No need to say anything more."

He meant it, bypassing me.

He was almost to the courts when I followed him back into the gym. Someone tossed him the ball, and he was dribbling for his team within seconds, calling out the play as he went.

I stopped in my tracks, though.

God.

That look. His touch. The slight concern that I was just now realizing I had heard when he questioned me in the hallway. I didn't know how it happened, when it happened, but there was something there.

Something real.

His shirt was flapping in the wind, showcasing a good amount of skin and a tattoo running vertically under his arm, and my heart just did a backflip.

All those flutters exploded in my stomach.

My head spun. I wasn't quite sure what had happened, but I think, just maybe, someone had understood me without me saying a word about it?

Maybe?

I was in trouble, very real and serious trouble.

CHAPTER FIFTEEN

Over the rest of the week, I fell into a routine.

One could've argued that everyone had a routine, but mine was up at five to open the courts. The kitchen was next for coffee, then breakfast prep with Owen and Hadley. I'd start dishes when they began piling up, and do them throughout the meal. Most of the team still left everything at the tables, but after Reese started bringing his tray to the dish window, others followed suit.

I thanked each and every one in a polite, appropriately cheerful voice and a smile in my eyes—no extra weirdness or flaking out on my part. I was quite proud of myself.

After breakfast, I'd head back to the courts and man the equipment closet.

Aiden came up a few times with things he needed for the team, and I'd do whatever he asked. I was usually desperate to leave that equipment cage. A girl could only smell hot and sweaty ball players, hear the sound of basketballs bouncing and feet running up and down the court, and stare at nothing for so long before she's ready to combust.

The inner fan wanted to break out still. I was struggling at being completely rational. Still.

The other part of me would break out in heat whenever Reese came over and not because he was the celebrity superstar to me anymore, because he was a man. All man.

A few of the players had learned my name. I was no longer

Direction Girl or Staff Member, but Reese kept to his nods. He was polite.

A polite thank you here. A polite you're welcome there.

At times when I felt my inner craziness etch out of control, Damian would come to mind. And with the thought of him, the impending doom soon settled in, helping me bottom out all over again.

I felt like the underside of my stomach had a trap door, and the thought of him opened it. All my contents dropped to my feet, and the door would close, leaving me with nothing but a mess to clean up.

I'd operate that way until something caused a spark—usually Reese looksing at me—and then I'd start feeling a little buzz inside again.

After the first time when I realized I could use the Damian trick to calm myself, he had started sneaking into my head more and more. And I could handle that, sort of, but then the nightmares started.

I'd tossed and turned, and then the last few nights I'd jerked awake screaming.

That gave me a fright all on its own.

My time off was nonexistent, but that was okay with me.

The busier I was, the better, but I was tired because of it.

Still somehow that method had gotten me all the way to here: my first time off because the team had gone to another preseason game. Keith kept us busy the first time they were gone, with random projects around the island. This time, we got a full twenty-four hours off, and I was walking back to my cabin, unsure what I wanted to do.

I'd done nothing with the book I was going to write. That only brought more Damian gloom.

"Hey."

Oh, thank God. A distraction.

It was Grant.

"Heya back."

Be gone, stupid queasy stomach. I don't need to feel you. Please have work for me to do, Grant. I'll do almost anything at this point.

Almost. Let's not get crazy now.

He was walking toward me from the back of the main building. He slid his hands in his pockets and jerked his head back over his shoulder. "Owen and Hadley are heading into town, dinner and drinks. Want to come?"

He said dinner. I only heard drinks. "I'm down. Can we add the last D word?"

Grant laughed. "You know how those two are. Any excuse for some dancing. We can go to The Barn. They're actually playing a DJ these days."

"Really?"

I was impressed. The airport was small, but Fairview had a surprising number of bars and a couple nightclubs even. The Barn was in one of the smaller towns outside of Fairview. We were going even smaller.

I loved it.

Grant nodded. "It's Thursday, so there might be college students there."

"Just call me Mrs. Robinson."

Instead of the grin I expected, he grew more serious. He was quiet a beat. "You okay, Charlie?"

"As okay as I can be in Candyland." I shot him a grin, trying to up the ante here. "You know how I am with the Seattle Thunder."

He didn't fall for it again. I was losing my touch.

"I'm serious. I know you, remember?"

Oh God. We were going into Realityland. Nope. No way. Retreat.

My smile slipped, but I lifted a shoulder. "I'm as good as can be, I guess."

This was Grant. I had to give him something or he'd never let up. But I knew him too, and he loved gushing about people he loved.

"Is Sophia coming?"

See? There. His fiancée would do the trick.

And she did. His eyes lit up, and he launched into a story about how not only was she coming, but we'd be lucky if her Nana and *abuela* didn't show up themselves.

Grant filled me in on Sophia's dancing-loving family as we headed to my cabin. He didn't stop until we reached a fork in the path. I had to go left for my place, and he had to go right, because I assumed he had work in that part of the camp?

I gestured behind him. "Got a maintenance order or something?"

"What?" He looked. "Oh, yeah. One of the players was saying his toilet wasn't flushing. I'm excited to see." His chuckle was dry. "But yeah. Let's meet at the main lodge in an hour. I'll be sobercab too, so feel free to let loose."

Let loose. Did he not know me?

"Sounds like a plan."

He nodded, his eyes warming. "It'll be nice to hang out like real friends again."

I gave him a thumbs-up, but as soon as my back turned, my smile fell.

Friends were a commodity I hadn't had in so long. There'd been no friends from work. I'd faded away from all my friends during the Damian era, because it was too hard to see their normal lives when mine was slipping away daily. You can only talk about what's going on for so long. People like to say they'll be there for you, but there's a time stamp on that offer. What they really mean is that they're there for you over the next three days. If it takes longer than that, you're out of luck. You need to move forward, find new friends to confide in.

No one understood unless they were on the "outside" alongside me, because everyone on the "inside" was busy being normal and living a normal life.

So after it ended with Damian, it'd been just Lucas, and yeah, the rest is history from there. So, no friends for me. And now here I was, back where I had friends around me I'd considered family at one point.

Working was easy. I could do that without talking. Jokes?

Cheesy lines? I was the queen of those things. Want a random question? My need had simmered down, but I could pull one out if I needed.

But time outside of work, over food and with booze—that meant talking.

Normally, people love talking about themselves, so it's easy to distract them. But not these guys. Not Hadley, Owen, or Grant. And they knew my tricks.

Yep. Cold sweat.

I could already feel I was on the verge of a breakdown. Again.

But I was tired. Not sleeping tired, but bone tired—tired of being alone, tired of dodging and evading. As I stepped into my cabin, I felt tears starting to roll down my face.

Maybe I should actually tell them? I ran through the conversation.

I'd see pity on their faces. Hadley would start crying. Owen would roll his shoulder back because he'd be uncomfortable. And Grant, he'd be angry. I could only guess at why he'd be mad, but I knew he would be. That was his go-to emotion for situations like that.

I decided instead that I'd get drunk. Problem solved. I was always a happy drunk too, like a Labrador.

Labrador it was.

CHAPTER
SIXTEEN

I shouldn't have worried about deep and meaningful conversation. The Thunder's preseason game was on television, so we ended up taking our plates to the bar. We ate and watched the game—seemed the loyal thing to do. People were yelling and cheering, and I had a flare up of Crazy Charlie when Reese stole the ball at the end of the third quarter, followed up with a fouled shot that went in, and followed that up by sinking the free throws. And then he stole it again, but instead of running up for the layup—which would've been blocked, the guy had three extra inches on Reese—he backed up and laid out the prettiest, most smooth-sailing floater I'd ever seen.

Swish. Only net.

That was going to be played on ESPN for the rest of the night.

The bar broke out in groans, since they were playing our local state team but some had to cheer. It was so damn beautiful.

That seemed to set the tone for the rest of the game, and for us.

The Thunder stomped our team, but it was so pretty to watch. Reese dominated the floor. The announcers wondered aloud how the rest of the season would go, if this was an indication of the Thunder trying to make a point. They were one of the best teams for a reason. There was speculation about Reese's brother as well, about the consequences, and then a mention that the team was using an undisclosed location for their camp.

We all watched. We all heard, and we lifted our drinks for a toast. It wasn't high—more at chest level—and not a word was spoken, but after that, we were all in for partying. Owen ordered two rounds of shots. Hadley had two martinis, and we were lit.

And after meeting Sophia, then her family, I would've married her too.

We went to The Barn for dancing.

Hadley got another martini. I had another shot.

There was twerking. Running man. Sprinkler.

I grocery shopped. I changed a tire. I was a half of a unicorn dance. It was new. We'd just created it that night. I was the ass part, and Sophia's abuela was the head part. Sophia tried being the hooves, but she just didn't get it. When she swung her head back, I'd kick up my leg and throw some confetti in the air. Then we'd go back to prancing and pretending to kick people.

It was just what I needed. Tomorrow was going to kick my ass.

Even drunk, I could feel my sides hurting from all the laughing as we drove back.

Grant dropped Owen and Hadley off at their house. Sophia was snoring in the front, but they lived off the island, so it was just me. He drove to the village.

The path to my cabin wasn't driveable so he parked at the mouth of the trail.

"I'll walk you." Grant opened his door as I got out.

"No, no!" I nearly yelled. Looking around, some of the lights were on in the nearby cabins. "Those guys are back already?"

Grant looked around. "Yeah. I mean, Minneapolis is only four hours away. Their game ended around ten, and it's after three in the morning."

Oh fuck. That was true.

"I have to be up at five."

"We have the morning off, remember?" Grant nudged me because I'd started staring at one cabin in particular—the one Reese was staying in. The lights had been on, but they'd just turned off. Reese was in bed. Crawling into bed. Maybe shirtless. Probably shirtless. What guy wore a shirt to bed? He was definitely shirtless. And that tattoo. I remembered it. I'd been secretly salivating over it all week, and I say secretly because I was a reformed stalker.

Maybe not as reformed as I thought.

I hung my head. "I'm so messed up," I whispered to myself.

I wasn't talking the usual craziness. Though that was there, and I held it up like a shield, loving it and hugging it close because it kept so much real shit out. I meant Damian. I could feel him. He was sitting on my chest, pushing me down.

I felt tears on my face, which dammit, probably meant I was bawling.

"Charlie?" Grant edged closer.

Sophia's snore rose to a crescendo, and I realized what I'd just said.

I jerked away. "Sorry. I'm good. I—" I wasn't, but I wasn't looking at Grant. I was too embarrassed. "Thanks for the ride, Grant. I'll see you tomorrow."

"We're off till lunch."

I waved. "Okay. Thanks. See you for lunch."

Grant drove away, and there was a lone light left for the entire village. It cast just enough light for me to make it to my front steps.

That's when the dark shadow spoke. "You reek."

I screamed.

"Holy fuck! Shut up." The dark shadow moved at an unnatural speed, slamming a hand over my mouth.

It pressed in close, but I was still trying to get some air for more screeching. My heart was in my head, trying to burst out of my skull.

"It's me. Forster. Shut up."

OH! Oh, God. Oh God, oh God, oh God. Oh God, God, God, God.

Deep breath. I needed to calm, but holy fucking hell. I was having a hard time.

Shoving back from him, I hissed, "You scared the crap out of me." And on second thought, I felt my butt. I couldn't tell if my pants felt wet or not.

"No shit."

I couldn't see a thing, but I swear I could hear his eyes roll. I heard my screen door open, and he rattled the doorknob.

"You got a key?"

I moved forward, bumping into him so I could insert the key. No light meant you had to go with feel, and Keith had given me a crappy key. You had to insert it, then jerk it to the right just as you unlocked it, or the lock would get stuck. I was not going to explain that to Reese right now, when I was drunk, and he must've been...

I rounded back to him just as the door gave way. "What are you doing here? Why aren't you sleeping?" And who had turned that light off in his cabin?

He didn't say anything, just grunted and stepped inside. "Where's your light?"

Now that sane thought was fighting its way to the surface, I was having a moment. Reese Forster was in my cabin and asking where the light was. Did I want the light on? Of course I did. I might be deluded, but I wasn't a wanton hussy, or I was trying to tell myself I wasn't. Though with him, persuasion would go a long way.

"There's a string in the middle of the room. You gotta pull it."

I was not entering that fairway. With both of us standing in the middle of the room, swinging arms around, someone was bound to lose an eye.

A few more curses from him, he found it and yanked.

Light flooded the room. I was greeted by a pissed-off pro basketball player, who'd showered and was wearing sweatpants and a T-shirt that looked like it was made of the softest material on Earth. Seriously. Whoever made that shirt was a genius, because I wanted to touch it.

I was raising my hand to do just that when he shifted backward. "What are you doing?"

"Your shit looks so soft. I wanted—"

"My *shit*?"

"What?" I blinked. Huh?

"You said shit."

"Shirt." *Shit.* Um... I cocked my head. "What's going on here?"

"I asked what you were doing coming in so late. And you reek of booze. I couldn't sleep, and I heard you and your friend driving up, so I came down to wait for you. You walk like a tortoise."

"I'm drunk. And it's night." That made the perfect sense to me, and I remembered his earlier question. "I was a unicorn."

"I'm so fucking confused by you." He rubbed his forehead. "What are you talking about now? A unicorn?" "Me and the *abuela.*"

"*Abuela?*"

"I call her THE *abuela,* but I'm sure she goes by *Abuela* too."

"Who are you talking about?"

"Sophia's family. Her grandmother. And then there's Nana, *mija,* and lots of cousins, but the *abuela* and I were a dancing unicorn together. I threw confetti."

"I gathered." He nodded at me. "You're covered in glitter."

I shrugged. "From the confetti and the dancing."

"Where'd you get the confetti?"

Another shrug. "The world's greatest mystery. Where does confetti really come from?"

Suddenly his eyebrows went flat. "You guys went drinking."

"The booze oozing out of my pores indicates that. I thought we were past that."

"No. I thought you camp people stayed here all the time." He shook his head, rubbing his jaw as he looked around the room. "What kind of shithole do you stay in?"

He took in the fishing net that made up a chandelier, scanned the wall of fish hooks turned upside down. He wrinkled his nose. "This place smells too. Holy fuck." He took a good whiff. "What is that?"

"It's the old fishing cabin. I barely notice it now."

"Because it's on you."

"What?" *No!* "Take that back." I hit him in the arm.

"Who put you in here?"

"My boss."

"Your boss who's a dick?"

Best friends, this guy and me. I felt a good kick in the nether regions. Not good, though.

"You can't do things like that," I told him.

"Like what?"

"Like be on the same page as me." I motioned to my groin. "Makes the he-girl happy down there."

He groaned, but asked, "Your vagina is male? That's where you're going with that?"

Of course. Made perfect sense.

He rolled his eyes. "You can cut that shit. I've been watching you all week, and I know your deal."

That didn't sound good.

A knot was forming inside me. I felt its tentacles starting to wrap around. Okay. It was more of an octopus inside me, but it would harden and knot. All knots.

He sounded impatient as he picked up a bag of mine. "This whole crazy charade you're putting on is just that. It's a facade. You're not a real stalker. You're not even half a stalker."

"I am too."

He opened my bag, and I let him. I don't know why, but I did. He dumped out some papers I had stuffed in there and began looking around. He went into my bedroom and grabbed some of my shirts. Putting them into the bag, he reached for more clothing.

"It's an act," he informed me. "Yeah, you might have weird tendencies, and you might be a fan, but that's it. You're not a groupie. You're not a fanatic. If you were, I would've needed to kick you out of my cabin five times by now, and you've not once come over." He shoved more of my clothes into the bag. "I asked you one question, and you folded. Someone truly nuts would be convinced I was asking you to marry me. She'd have horrible boundaries, and you are really all about boundaries. Jesus. You told me to back off after one personal question. You closed up and flipped the switch. You're not even super friendly anymore."

He was done. My bag was so full he couldn't zip it closed.

I motioned him aside and took it, stuffing my underwear down so there was enough space to close the zipper. Then I handed it back to him.

He took it, staring at me. "I don't know your deal. I don't want you to know *my* deal, but sometime over the last week, I started to like you." He pointed at me. "And not like that. You're kinda cool, and I don't say that shit to anyone, so if you claim I said it tomorrow, I'll lie. Got it?"

I nodded. "Got it. I'm not cool."

"See? There's the annoying side of you." He started for the door. "Now come on."

"Where are you going?"

"Back to my cabin. Juan's there, but I'll have him bunk with Lestroy tomorrow."

"Okay." I waved. "Have a fun time with that."

He stood at the door, looking back to see I had not moved with the bag in his hands. "What? No." He threw the bag at me. "That's for you. You're not staying here. This place can't be healthy. The whole thing should be burned down."

"Don't tell Owen and Hadley."

"Why not?"

"They worked really hard at airing out the smell."

His eyes got big. "You mean it was worse?"

I was not usually the giving-in kind of girl, but I was tired.

Finding one of my other bags, I put in enough clothes for the night and some of my things from the bathroom.

When I had my phone and charger, I stood in front of him. "Ready to go."

He eyed my bag. "What's that for?"

"Clothes."

He held up his bag. "That's what this is for."

I took it from him and tossed it to the chair. "Thoughtful as you were, you packed all the wrong clothes. I don't actually wear half the stuff I brought with me."

"Jesus Christ." He grabbed my bag and shoved through the door. "Come on."

I went with him, my insides quivering in fear and aching with excitement.

The fish cabin had won this battle.

Juan Cartion was sleeping on the bottom bunk. His suitcases were open on the bunk above him, and that was the only bed open. They had one of the more private cabins, so Reese bunked on the couch and said I had to take his old bed.

I started to make a comment about not encouraging the he-girl, but he clamped his hand over my mouth and hissed in my ear about not being a smart-ass. I experienced a flurry of déjà vu moments, but did as he asked. I heard Juan snoring lightly, so I decided to be kind.

And I continued to be kind, even though I barely slept.

The sun had come up thirty minutes ago, and I'd waited this long before getting on my phone. Sound was off, the vibrate too, but I was doing some research. I had something to prove to Reese when he woke up.

That was all fine and dandy until Juan Cartion rolled over in his bed. His sheet slipped down to his waist, just barely covering his dick, and I watched as he stretched. His eyes stayed closed as his hand moved under the sheet to cup himself. He yawned as his hand moved, and I knew enough to know I had to announce my presence.

I coughed. "Morning."

His eyes flew open, and he launched in the air. "HOLY FUCK!"

A thud came from the main room. Reese was in the bedroom in half a second as Juan pressed against the wall with his sheet in front of him.

First horrified, then pissed, Juan lunged forward and grabbed the phone from my hands.

"What the fuck? You were recording me?"

Oh no!

"What the fuck?!" Reese glared at me.

"No." I scrambled to my feet. I was wearing a respectable tank and sleeping shorts, but Juan pressed back like I'd tried to brand him. He sucked in his breath, moving behind Reese to glare over his shoulder.

"I wasn't. I swear!" I motioned to my phone. "Look. I was on Google."

He examined my phone. "What is this shit? Types of stalkers?"

Reese's face switched, his eyes tight and his jaw clenched. He grabbed my phone, reading the screen. "Are you serious? You're supposed to be sleeping, and instead you're what? Looking up types of stalkers?"

Forgetting Juan, I took a step closer. "But look at the categories. I fall in, like, four of those. There's the rejected stalker, the resentful one, predatory, the one seeking intimacy, incompetent, or the morbidly infatuated one. I'm a whole bunch of those. I swear."

"You're nuts. That's what you are, but you're not a stalker. I have stalkers. You're not one of them." He shoved my phone at me, rolling his eyes. "Juan, let's switch."

Juan's eyes became saucers. "You're going to sleep in here with her?"

"Her dickhead of a boss put her in a place that should be condemned. It's not safe. Trust me. Just for a night. It was late. I was thinking you could bunk with Lestroy, or she can find a new place."

I folded my arms over my chest. I already knew how that'd go. "My boss won't put me anywhere else. It's the fishing cabin or the janitor's closet in the basement, and that main building is haunted."

Juan's eyes just remained saucers. "It is?!"

I was guessing. "I wouldn't be surprised, but that's the basement. I'm not sleeping down there."

He took a breath, suddenly looking more normal. He stepped away from Reese too.

"Shit. Okay." He grabbed his phone and some of his clothes and padded to the other room. A second later, he tossed Reese's pillow and blanket into the bedroom.

Scooping them up, Reese gave me a wary look. "We *are* going to be sleeping. We have this morning off. Then it's meetings the rest of the day and light hoops. It's a rest day for us too."

He said that like I was going to fight him on it.

I just shrugged, stepped into the bathroom for a moment, then slipped back into his bed.

I paused, seeing Reese's eyes closed. "You want me to sleep there?" I asked. "I mean, this is your bed. Right?"

He rolled over, shaking his head. "I was sleeping in the other room the whole time. Go to sleep, not-really-a-stalker girl. I'm tired."

Well... When he put it like that... I slipped under the covers and turned my back to him.

I fell asleep much more easily this time.

CHAPTER SEVENTEEN

Juan Cartion moved out.

I convinced Reese to let the fishing cabin go, because I didn't want to deal with what Keith would do afterward. He'd claim I seduced Reese Forster into taking up my fishing cabin cause, and I wasn't joking about the janitor's closet. I'd overheard him one time mentioning to the maintenance crew that if we needed an extra room for someone, a staff member could stay in that closet.

It was big enough for just a single bed to fit in there. The door would have to be turned so it opened the other way, and that person would have to climb on and off the bed to get into the hallway, then walk past the ghosts, the laundry, the maintenance office, and up two flights of stairs before using the bathroom the campers on the first floor used. The only pro for that room was that it was in the main building, which meant it was closer to midnight snacking.

But let's be honest.

Was I really feeling the impending need to find somewhere else to sleep? Not really.

The Thunder had practices and meetings and scrimmages over the next week, and I did my usual. I manned the gym, did breakfast prep, and did dishes for all the meals. More guys were bringing their trays up to the window now instead of making Owen go and get them from the table. Reese also came in and booted people out of the gym every night at midnight. Not that any guys were up there anyway, but every now and then, one might be doing late-night drills or just shooting the breeze. A few times one of the guys would take a phone call on the benches around the outdoor court. But it didn't matter. Reese would declare the gym closed. No one argued with their captain.

Then we'd walk back to his cabin and start the routine we'd developed.

I'd go to my cabin and get clothes. He'd be cleaned up by the time I got back, just leaving the bathroom and shower as I got in. Then it'd be my turn.

After that we'd sit in the living area. If he took the couch, I took the extra chair. Or vice versa. We'd work on whatever or read or listen to whatever until one of us got tired and went to bed. Going to bed and falling asleep weren't a hardship anymore.

I didn't question why I could sleep so easily with him across the room from me. I was just grateful to be getting around five hours of sleep per night. Reese woke the first few times I got up at five, but after two days of that, he was able to sleep through or just roll over and fall back asleep.

He did argue with me about not getting enough sleep, but I insisted I was getting up at five on my own. That was a battlefront I would die on, because he didn't know I was going to help Owen and Hadley with breakfast. He was already pissed at Keith about my cabin. I didn't need to give him more ammunition, at least until after camp, because a part of me was wondering how much damage a pissed-off NBA player could do to Keith? If anyone could get something done about Dickhead Boss, I would put money on Reese. Which made me feel bad, because he was a camper. He shouldn't have to worry about any of this. Nor should he have to put up with rooming with one of the staff because he was a decent human being.

"Why do you have a laptop if you never use it?"

Reese was lounging on the couch, wearing only shorts with rap blaring through headphones in his ears. No one was around at the gym, so he'd talked me into closing it early. And by talking me into it, I mean he took my keys and locked everything up, then stalked down the path to his cabin.

I hadn't argued. It was nice to feel like I had a night off. It was only around ten o'clock.

Or at least it had been nice until he asked that question.

I shifted in my seat, my phone in hand. I was stalking Lucas, looking at his new girlfriend because the douchebag hadn't wasted time. She was petite, with long brown hair and the largest almond eyes ever. She looked sweet.

I was tempted to slip into her DMs and see if Grandpa Newt had propositioned her, but I was resisting. Only one stalking target at a time. And I didn't know what to say to Reese, so I kept quiet, pretending to thumb up my music on my phone.

He grunted, then swung up from the couch. Reaching over, he picked up my headphones...which weren't plugged into my phone. Flinging them on my lap, he laid back down.

"If you don't want to tell me, fine. But at least try to lie better. For all your crazy facade, you suck at actually being crazy."

Oh. OH! Did he just challenge me?

I think not.

But as I was puffing up my chest, I knew he was right. I'd lost the will to be nuts. Even the random questions had stopped. I missed them.

"It's a therapy assignment."

I might've mumbled those words, my mouth tucked into the collar of my shirt. If he heard, he heard. If he didn't, he didn't. Just as long as he didn't kick me out of his cabin, because his was so much better than mine.

The lack-of-smell alone was worth it.

"What?" His eyebrows rose, and he lifted his head, his hand splayed out on his chest—his very nice and defined and muscled chest that was lean, with that tattoo that I hadn't yet brought myself to ask about because I couldn't read it. But damn, I wanted to. It was hot.

"Nothing." I tried to sink farther into the chair.

He wasn't having it.

He swung his feet back up and scooted to the edge of the couch. He reached over and plucked my phone from my hands, holding it hostage. His eyes dared me to even try to get it back.

"What'd you say?" he asked.

I knew my place. Professional athlete, I was not. I remained in my seat and only lifted my feet up, scooting my knees against me and wrapping my arms around them. I propped my chin on top and watched him. "You heard me."

He was giving me a new look. "You're in therapy?"

"I was." And damn. I just didn't have the energy to lie anymore. I held out my hand, palm up. "Come on."

He gave me my phone back, but cautiously. "Why were you in therapy?"

"Because..." I took the phone, my hand wrapping around it, but I only brought it back to my lap. My knees remained up, like they were a shield.

My throat burned. Was I actually going to tell him some of this?

This felt weird—too fast, too...too exposed.

Shit. I was going to tell him.

I was crapping my pants as the words formed on my tongue. "I was in a relationship with someone for a long time, and it was..." The burning increased in my chest. I felt an impossible weight there. "It was a hard relationship."

A lump formed in my throat.

Reese's eyes narrowed. "Did he hit you?"

I couldn't answer that. "It was—was he abusive? No. Did he hit me? Once, but it wasn't a normal situation. I—" *God*. I couldn't talk. I closed my eyes, pressed my forehead to the back of my knees, and inhaled. Once. And I counted.

5

4

3

2

1

Exhale. 5. 4. 3. 2. 1.

Inhale, and repeat.

It helped. Some of the pressure lifted, and I was able to look up again. I knew there were tears on my face, but for the life of me, I couldn't wipe them away.

"Have you ever been involved in a situation where you felt like the other person needed you so they could live?" I asked. "But you couldn't stay there because they were taking the oxygen you needed to breathe?"

A deep emotion shone from Reese—one I couldn't name, but I felt the air switch. He leaned back against the couch and dropped his head.

"Yeah." His voice was rough. "And it fucking sucks."

He got it.

I didn't even get it, but he got it.

I couldn't say anything for a while after that. So I just sat. I cried. I hid behind my knees.

And Reese waited. Or something. I didn't feel like he was waiting for me. He looked away, his eyes downcast. I had a feeling he was thinking about something else, or someone else.

"You know about my brother's shit?" he asked after a minute. "Why we're even here and not using our normal facilities?"

I nodded, looking up over the tops of my knees.

He still wasn't looking at me. "He was like that for me. But he didn't actually need me like that. He just made it seem like he did." He turned now, his gaze raw, looking right into me. "Was it the same for you?"

I wanted to say yes. That would be an easier battle to tackle. I couldn't, though.

"No. Not like that," I whispered

His eyes closed for a second. "Shit." A soft sigh. "I'm sorry for that."

"Me too."

The air was heavy. The room seemed to shrink around us.

Reese glanced around, and I felt a restless edge come from him. He checked his phone and scraped a hand over his jaw before standing.

"Come on." He put on some socks and shoes. Grabbing a shirt, he picked up the basketball he always seemed to have close by.

"Where are we going?"

I hadn't moved quickly enough. He tossed my shoes at the bottom of my chair, then took my phone and headphones out of my hands. He waited by the door as I pulled on my shoes.

"I need to turn my mind off, and I use two activities for that. We're going with the second option."

I wasn't asking about the first, but I did ask, "Hoops?"

He nodded. "Hoops."

The first night he'd been here flashed back to me, and I knew what the next couple hours were going to be like. I stood, and since it was a little chilly, I said, "I want to grab a sweatshirt from my cabin."

He dropped my phone and headphones on the couch, moving past me to the bedroom. Coming back out, he thrust a sweatshirt at me. "Here."

Picking up my phone and headphones again, he led the way out of the cabin.

We were heading down the trail when we passed a few of his teammates coming the other way.

I averted my gaze, pulling on his sweatshirt as he stopped.

"What's up, Forster?"

"Not much. Heading back to shoot some hoops."

I could feel their gazes.

Reese's sweatshirt swamped me, but it smelled like him. A hint of sand and pine mixed together. Tugging his sleeves down, I balled them up and pretended to look at them.

"We bus out at ten, right?"

Reese nodded. "Yeah. Breakfast is at nine."

That was news to me, though not the busing-out part. I knew they had another preseason game coming up.

Fists bumped between Reese and the others as they said their goodnights. We'd walked a few feet before someone murmured something, and the others began laughing.

The hairs on the back of my neck stood up. I knew that laugh was about me.

"They think we're fucking," Reese commented.

I smothered a "WHAT?" and let out a strangled chuckle instead. "Yeah. No shit." A second thought, "You think they'll tell your coaches about me staying in your cabin?" Because I hadn't said a word to the other staff. I didn't want to hear any of the lectures I'd get. Plus I knew Keith would relish the chance to fire me.

"Nah. And to be honest, I don't think the coaches would give a shit—as long as we show and do our jobs. And you're not underage." He laughed. "Juan told the guys about your cabin, but none of them are buying it. I figure it's easier to let them think that than tell them truth. Is that okay with you?"

I looked up. "What's the truth?"

He grinned, the look taking him from hot to HOT. "That you've become like an annoying gnat that I like for some reason." He raised an eyebrow. "How's that for the truth?"

Warmth flooded me. I could be a gnat.

We started forward again, and I kept his sleeves wrapped around my hands. "You could tell them the other truth."

"Yeah? What's that?"

"That I'm a stalker with polite boundaries."

He groaned. "Stop with the stalking bullshit." He swung, but his fist was more of a tap on my shoulder. It was a soft tap, one between friends.

Friends.

We'd become friends.

I was okay with that.

CHAPTER
EIGHTEEN

"I saw you last night."

Aw, shiitake.

I had to give Grant some credit for waiting ten minutes after the bus left to approach me.

He had stared at me for a full minute before grabbing his tray and going through the line for breakfast. Didn't take a genius to know something was up with him. Then once Owen handed him his omelet, he stared again for another thirty seconds through the main glass window.

A shiver had gone down my spine.

His eyes cut from me to Reese, who was eating with Juan, Lestroy, and Crusky.

For the most part, Reese and I acted like we didn't know each other during the day. He brought up his dishes. He signed out a ball if they needed an extra, but that was the extent of our back-and-forth—at least in front of the staff. Owen, Hadley, and Grant were never around in the evenings. They were all long gone to their homes, done with their hours for the day, so it was really only Reese's teammates who knew about the extra friendship between us.

Even if it was a gnat sort of friendship.

"Saw me doing what?" I countered.

Keith had already frolicked through the cafeteria, getting his usual coffee and having a "word" with the coaches. All the details had been ironed out, but he'd claimed he needed to know when they'd be back and if food needed to be prepared for them. We were nearing the end of their second week here.

"Something going on with you and Forster?"

Silence.

Hadley had been scraping the grill, but she stopped. Owen had been pulling the plate dispenser back over to me, but he stopped that too.

I let out a small sigh, reaching for a last bin to rinse. "What makes you say that?"

"Because it's the third night in a row I saw you walking back to the village with him."

There was nothing inappropriate about what we were doing. There was some gray area about me staying in his cabin, but nothing had happened. At all. But I felt some twinges of shame as previous accusations from Keith flared up in me.

I never did anything wrong back then either, but it never mattered. Keith always found some excuse to accuse me of something.

I waited a second before answering. Finishing the bin, I put it on the tray and loaded it into the machine, then turned to face Grant. He was in the doorway between me and the rest of the kitchen. Owen and Hadley were waiting behind him, both looking uncomfortable.

"What are you accusing me of?"

"Are you sleeping with him?"

Sophia had just entered the cafeteria, but she paused coming through the tables. There's no way she could've heard Grant, but she must have sensed the awkwardness in the atmosphere. Her gaze was searching. She found Grant first and then me, looking right at her.

Her eyes narrowed as she approached. "Grant?"

He looked, but turned back to me. "I asked you a question, Charlie. Are you sleeping with him?"

"Grant!" She sounded horrified.

I wasn't sleeping with him in the way he was asking, but saying no felt like I was hiding something. I didn't want to hide. It felt wrong.

"Charlie!" A second hiss from him.

"No, okay?"

His head tilted to the side. "Why'd you take so long to answer?"

I opened my mouth.

Hadley beat me to it, pushing past him. "Because maybe she wants to sleep with him. How about that? And she can if she wants."

Uh—what?

Little Hadley was all in his face, her two French braids bouncing from her energy.

"She's not a full-time staff member, and none of us are kids now. I have three little ones of my own. And really, who could blame her?"

"It's Reese Forster," Owen added. "I mean, if I swung that way, I'd want to as well."

That said *a lot* coming from Owen.

He adjusted his shoulder, rolling it back.

"You saw her walking with him back to the village. That's the same path she takes to her cabin. So what? She's allowed to talk to him." Sophia with another defense.

Guilt bloomed in me.

All three of them had spoken up for me. Gah. I had to come clean. I liked them all too much.

"Okay! Fine. You all can stop defending me because I...kinda, but not really lied just now." I squared my shoulders and shoved all the shame out of me, because I did not deserve it. "I'm not sleeping with him, but I am sleeping in his cabin."

Hadley wheeled to me, her mouth open.

"Damn," Owen breathed.

Sophia just blinked, looking shocked.

A flush was working up Grant's neck. "You're sleeping in his cabin?"

"He was waiting for me one night when I got back—just to talk. I don't know why, to be honest. He likes me as a gnat—his words, not mine." I held a hand up to halt anything incoming from them. "And it's not romantic at all. He was in the fishing cabin and almost puked from the smell." I gave Owen and Hadley an apologetic look. "You guys aired it out to the best you could, but the smell's come back. He made me sleep in his cabin that night. He's offered to demand that Keith find me somewhere else to sleep, but you all know he'll just put me in the janitor's closet downstairs. He doesn't give a shit about health codes for staff. So yeah, I've been sleeping in his cabin, but that's all. I swear."

Hadley's mouth had closed, and she rotated right back to Grant. "Happy now?" She looked over her shoulder to me. "And for the record, if I were you and I was single, I'd be sleeping with him by now." She moved past Grant with a *harrumph*. "And no one would be making me feel guilty about it. We're all too old for that."

Owen found my eyes. "We have a guest room you can use, if you want."

"That house is for you and your family. You can't be offering that room up for staff every time it's needed. That's your home."

"Offer's open anytime you need it, and we don't need to tell Keith either." He gave Grant a meaningful look before leaving, following Hadley because the last of the dishes were done.

They went to his office, and I heard the door open a second later as they left. Staff had the rest of the day off.

Grant was still silent.

Sophia cleared her throat. "I think Grant knows my thoughts on Keith, and I have a feeling he knows I stand with Hadley's thoughts on this matter as well." She spoke to me, with her eyes on her fiancé's back. "He'll realize he had no right to accuse you the way he did. And it's none of his business because you're not under contract like we are, and again, nothing illegal is going on."

Grant turned to her.

She shook her head. "It's not even unethical, Grant. Don't go there. They're adults. Both of them. That's it. And now, having said that..." She smiled at me. "We're having a group of people to the house tomorrow night to watch their game, if you'd like to come."

Grant said stiffly, "I was going to invite her."

"After the third degree? Really?" Her voice was dry. "I'm sure she would've felt so welcome." She looked back at me. "Please come. Grant will have his head out of his ass by then." She nodded, turned, and went back out the way she'd come.

Grant waited until the cafeteria door closed behind her, and his gaze swung back to me.

There was no apology in his eyes, though. He just seemed haunted, with an edge of anger, and his tone reflected both. "With all due respect to their opinions, they don't know you like I do."

Fuck. I looked away. I knew in that second that this was going to hurt. He wasn't coming at me in a disapproving way for my ethics. He was taking a personal angle.

Shit, shit, shit.

It had killed me to expose myself as much as I did with Reese the night before, and now here? With Grant? I wasn't sure I had the strength to hear this out, whatever he was going to send my way. Though, maybe I did deserve it?

He started low, quiet. "You were my best friend. Like, the bestest friend I've ever had. And yeah, I knew that kiss was a mistake. I knew it was going to scare you away, but I had to still try. I backed off after. I did."

I frowned. Why was he bringing this up? "The kiss?"

"Our kiss."

"Why are you..." I trailed off.

He jumped in, more insistent, "I knew I scared you away with that kiss. I don't want it to happen again, where you get with a guy, he hurts you, and we lose you all over again. I did it with our kiss, and then we completely lost you for years to Damian. And now I know things ended with you two, and you were still too scared to come to me. I..." He ground to a halt.

My eyes were wide. I could barely breathe. "Are you serious?"

His eyebrows bunched together. "I scared you away. It's because of me that you even started dating Damian."

120

He blamed—what? No. He couldn't, but he did. I saw it then.

He *blamed* himself for Damian, and for...I wasn't even sure what else.

I shook my head. "No. No! You didn't scare me away. That's not what happened."

His frown deepened. "It's not?"

"No! Not at all."

Oh boy. I would have to slide that door open once more and feel the Damian effects again. It was going to crush me, but he needed it. This wasn't my coworker in front of me, but a best friend I'd abandoned, and it was on me to make this right.

"I'm sorry."

"For what?" he asked.

"For leaving you—for leaving everyone, to be honest. I knew I'd hurt people. I just didn't know how much. I'm getting it now." And gah, that kiss. He blamed himself. "Grant, when you and I kissed, I knew there was nothing there."

His entire face twisted. "Nice."

"We were young, and I was a coward. I should've told you straight up right then and there, but you never pushed, and I didn't realize what you were going to think. You never scared me. I was okay. We kissed, and it was what it was. You were my best friend, and in a way, I think you still are, but I didn't run to Damian because of you. When we left the swing and I drove away, I decided to just let it lie. I was waiting to see if you pushed for something, and if you did, I was going to tell you then that there was nothing romantic between us. You and me kissing had no bearing on me falling in love with Damian. At all."

"It didn't? I didn't?"

We'd been so young, and I heard it in his voice again. That guy was in front of me, the one I'd thrown away.

"I am so sorry. When I fell for Damian, it was a whirlwind. He consumed everything in me, and I fell hard. I fell fast. We were—I could think something, and he knew it just by a look, or a twitch, or somehow he could feel it in the air. I don't know. It was unsettling at first, but I've never had someone know me the way he knew me and so fast." Pain sliced me right down the middle, my guts falling out. "He was my soulmate, and what happened with us—it wasn't a case of him cheating on me or abusing me. It wasn't like that, but it was tragic, and it was hard to walk away from. But I had to."

"A year, Charlie." He picked at the counter beside him. "You've been away from him and hurting for a full year. Why didn't you—I mean, you could've called. You could've emailed. Anything. I would've been there for you. What happened with you two? You're half the size you were back then. You were healthy and glowing, and you're like a shallow reflection of yourself. He did that to you. I don't care what you say. He did that to you."

"No."

"Yes! Stop defending him—"

"He has dementia!"

Oh—I bent over on a dry heave. I hadn't intended to say it out loud, not for a long time. But those words were out. I couldn't take them back.

How could I explain? The pitying looks, the confusion. Grant wouldn't understand. He would judge me—about leaving Damian, about not being humane and staying, no matter what. Ride or die. I cut and run instead.

"He what?"

Grant's words were soft, but still seething. The anger was still there.

I braced myself, because I knew it was coming at me.

"I can't," I choked out. "I can't do this. Excuse me."

I was empty.

I walked past Grant, tuning him out. He was saying something, but I was gone.

Suddenly I wasn't so grateful for a day off.

CHAPTER
NINETEEN

I rolled over the next morning and turned my phone on.

It had taken almost the whole day for me to get the Damian shame out of me. I'd gone to Reese's empty cabin and stayed most the day. Since the athletes were gone, we had no meals scheduled, so I'd heated some leftovers from the staff fridge. I hadn't seen anyone else when I walked back to the village, and since it was still nice out, I'd kept going. I'd walked the trails for another hour before returning to Reese's cabin, and then I did something I never thought I'd do.

I'd opened my laptop.

Lightning bolt!

Gasp. Shock. Yes, I actually did what my therapist suggested. I turned it on, brought up my music, plugged in my headphones, and I typed. Judah & the Lion were crooning in my ear. I didn't know what I'd typed—half the stuff was in red squiggles from being misspelled, but I felt better at the end. Enough that I saved the document, shoved the laptop aside, and curled up on Reese's bed to sleep the rest of the night.

It was still cold in the cabin, so it wasn't that late, but I was too lazy to get up and check the clock in the main area. I waited till my phone flashed on to check the time, but the buzzing started, and it kept going.

Buzz.

Buzz.

Buzz.

Buzz!

BUZZ!

BUZZZZZ!

I got it.

I hit silence on my phone, but still watched the alerts come through.

Wtf?

Where are you?

U okay?

Holy fuck, gnat.

Text me.

Why do I care? I care. Fuck's sake. Answer me.

Dude.

There was a whole list of them, all from the same number, and I had a feeling I now knew Reese's phone number.

I pulled up the last one and texted back.

Me: I'm here. Turned phone off last night.

My phone rang, vibrating alive in my hand within seconds.

"Don't tell me you were concerned about me?" I said in greeting. "How'd you get my number?"

He snorted. "Snagged it one night and I was bored. You're supposed to entertain me. You're slacking, Direction Girl."

Ah. I'd been demoted.

I lie back on the bed. My bladder was not happy with that decision, but who knew the next time a pro basketball player would be on the phone with me? Saying I was supposed to entertain him? My bladder could wait.

"Tell the truth. You'd rather I was your roommate than Juan."

He laughed. "Yeah. Maybe. He snores. You don't."

"Says you. Maybe I wait till you fall asleep and then zonk out, and I always wake up before you."

"You don't snore. I'm a light sleeper. I'd know."

"Yeah, yeah. Maybe I sneak over and put earplugs in your ears."

"I'd definitely wake up for that." He waited a beat, dropping his voice low. "For real, though. Are you okay?"

"Yeah." This was feelings territory. I liked Jokingland. Let's go back there. "You gonna replace me with a new ball girl? One that's a *real* ball girl?"

Another short laugh from him. "Nah. That's not the term I use for those girls."

"Right. Groupie."

"That or a one-use girl."

My eyes widened. "A one-use girl? Really? That's crass."

"So's fucking."

I could hear his smirk over the phone. Someone said his name in the background, and he responded, "Yeah. Be right there." A door closed, and he came back on the phone. "I gotta go. You're going to watch later?"

"Yep. A whole bunch of us are going to Grant and Sophia's."

"That's the good friend of yours, right?"

"Right."

He paused another beat. "Tell me straight. You okay or not?"

I had to smile. "Why? You worried about your gnat?"

"Maybe I'm a little concerned for my friend."

See! We *were* friends. "I've been promoted. Direction Girl, Gnat. Now Friend, but not your ball girl." And definitely not a one-use girl. Hell to the nah. I had more respect.

Maybe.

Well...

Okay, enough with that thinking. We were friends. Platonic, no fucking. But, "Hey, Reese?"

"Yeah?" He sounded distracted.

"Are you going to use a one-use girl tonight?"

There was silence on his end.

I shouldn't have asked, but I did, so I waited, my chest tight. I sat up, pressing the phone tightly against my ear.

"I was more hoping to call a certain gnat tonight."

My chest felt lighter. "Really?"

"Really."

He hung up after saying goodbye, and I sat there a full minute afterward, just holding the phone.

I took my phone out later on when I was waiting for Owen and Hadley to pick me up for dinner.

Me: Why is it llama and not lama?

Another one.

Me: Have you ever been propositioned by an ex's grandmother?

Me: Rate your teammates as shades, curtains, drapes, or blinds.

Me: Would you consider yourself a camel, a *lama*, or an alpaca? Or a goat? Goats are options too. Not sheep.

I was thinking of more when my phone buzzed.

Reese: What the fuck are you smoking?

I grinned.

Me: Boredom and emotional numbness.

Reese: You're not high?

Me: emoticon sad face, followed by emoticon thumbs-down

Reese: You didn't have to type that out. Could just do the actual emojis.

Me: But what's the fun there?

Reese: I gotta go. We're warming up.

Me: During your winning interview, give me an Easter egg.

Reese: I like your cockiness. And what do you want?

Me: Flick your ear, from behind.

Reese: Okay. Ur with good friends tonight, right?

Me: You're starting to more than care for me. Watch yourself, son.

Reese: Serious.

I sobered, because damn, the knot in my gut started to thaw.

Me: This was supposed to be an entertaining relationship. I entertain you. I am the gnat.

You're not supposed to care about the gnat.

Reese: I do what I want. And I'm being serious. If you're drinking tonight, you'll be safe right?

Me: That's not proper grammar.

Reese: This is texting. I don't give a shit. Answer me.

I sighed as I heard the sound of tires covering gravel from behind me.

Me: I'll be fine. Probably be bored even. Gotta go. My Uber just got here.

Hadley rolled her window down. She was on the passenger side, a bright smile on her face. "Hey! Ready for some margaritas?"

My phone buzzed again as I got inside. "Margaritas? I thought you were all about the martinis?"

Owen laughed as we pulled away.

"Not at Grant and Sophia's. Sophia makes *amazing* margaritas. You'll see. You'll love them too."

My phone kept going so I pulled it out.

Reese: So a llama isn't mistaken for a lama, which is also a Tibetan monk. Google.

Reese: I have actually. She pinched my ass and I offered her some Ensure.

Reese: Drapes: Juan. Nothing gets past him when he's playing defense. Shades: Carzoni because he does his job, but he's a softy inside. Curtains: Lestroy because he wears his heart on his sleeve so you can see through him at times. Blinds: Crusky because the Cruskinator is hard as nails, though sometimes his humor is sideways.

Reese: I'm THE goat. You figure out why.

I barked out a laugh, but covered my mouth quickly. Jesus. I hadn't expected him to answer, but he always did.

Hadley twisted around in her seat. "Is that..."

She bit her lip as I put my phone away. The smart-ass answers could come later, when I was buzzed with even more attitude.

"Yeah," I answered. "It was Reese."

She glanced to Owen.

Coughing, he rolled his shoulder back. "So, uh..." His voice was strained.

Hadley's wasn't. Her eyes were big, and her tone was gushing. "What's the deal with you two? Are you really not sleeping with him? Because, I mean—"

"Hadley."

"What?" She looked back at her husband. "Are we really going to ignore this? She's texting with Reese Forster! She was freaking out over him herself a week ago."

I snorted. "I still do."

"See?" Her grin was smug as she turned back to me. She leaned even closer. "Tell us everything. What's he really like? Is he nice? Is he a dick? Has he put the moves on you? Because you know, ball players can get laid."

Owen groaned. "We all know that, but..." He hesitated, looking at me in the rearview mirror.

They were curious. I would've been too, if I looked at it from the other side. But I wasn't on the other side now. And I was protective. Whatever kind of friendship Reese and I had, I needed it. He wasn't twisting my arm to know about Damian. I didn't feel obligated to apologize to him for skipping out on years of friendship, or to tear open my insides and show him how I was still devastated, still in pain, still not quite healing.

I didn't have to explain anything to him, and that's why I liked him. I mean, other than the obvious: his ball skills.

I sat back and shrugged. I needed to proceed with caution. I loved these two people. I owed them too, because they could've declared me dead to them, and they hadn't. But I couldn't give them what they wanted.

"He's cool. He's funny."

"Have you two, you know..."

"No, Hadley. There's been nothing like that. Just friends."

"But still." She sighed, moving to sit more forward in her seat, her profile to me. "Can you imagine being friends with someone that famous? I know we get celebrities here sometimes, but we're staff to them."

"Yeah." I understood.

"Some are so nice and down-to-earth, but we're not friends when they leave."

"It's their staff that aren't so nice sometimes," Owen added.

Owen and Hadley shared a laugh, and I knew what they meant. Reese and me, though, this wasn't just a camp friendship. It didn't feel like it.

But maybe it would be. Maybe when he left, and they entered their regular season, that'd be the end of us. I guess if that happened, then that's what happened.

Was I really in a place to demand otherwise? I mean, come on. I was a mess, a certifiable, fucked-in-the-head, slightly-crazy-and-I'm-not-joking-about-it sort of mess. Reese had become some form of weird name-calling glue that held me together.

Was this the beginning of healing?

Maybe?

God, I hoped so.

Either way, when we pulled in to Grant and Sophia's house, I was more than ready for some margaritas.

CHAPTER TWENTY

Three hours later, the screen door opened behind me. A beer and a package of smokes landed on the table, and Grant sat beside me.

I grunted as he yawned, then lit one up. "I forgot you smoked."

My stomach knotted. I knew why he'd come out, and the somersaults were going.

He breathed in, his arm resting on his knee. "Yeah. Just when I'm drinking." I felt his gaze. "If we were teens, I'd offer you one. You stopped, right?"

"I only had a few that one summer with you. And they were cigars."

I'd gone a whole summer thinking I was badass, sucking in, holding, then exhaling. I never actually inhaled the cigars, and I'd had no clue I was doing it wrong until a friend realized what I was doing. She'd laughed so hard that I gave up cigars after that.

My voice was hoarse now, from the yelling, cheering, laughing, drinking—just from all the hoopla I'd learned defined a party at Grant and Sophia's house.

"I think I'm in love with your fiancée and her family," I added.

He grinned, taking another drag, then lifting his beer. "I know. Why do you think I'm marrying her?"

I grinned, but I didn't look back to meet his gaze. We were side by side, and it felt right, like old times, though I was still certain he'd come out for a serious talk. And fuck me, but I was going to beat him to the punch.

"I don't want an apology."

There. Take that.

"Good." He put his beer down, coughing once. "'Cause you ain't getting one."

I gave him the side-eye now. "Excuse me?"

He grinned, then took another drag from his cigarette. "You heard me. This is what you reap. You don't let your friends in, and this is what you get. They can't know if you don't tell them shit."

I grunted. "Touché." And a second grunt. "Hadley and Owen were fawning over *him* in the car coming over here."

"As they will." A sip of beer. "They don't see it the way I see it."

I groaned. "I hate when you bait me."

He laughed softly. "Fine. I'll take the bait myself. How do I see it? Well..." He was quiet a moment. "Are you using him? How invested are you?"

"You're worried he'll hurt me?"

"I have reason to be worried."

Damian.

Dementia.

Early-onset dementia that was supposed to be so rare it never happened. But it did. It had happened to him.

I took Grant's cigarette. "I don't know what to tell you—"

He plucked it back out of my hands. I didn't even get the chance to bring it to my mouth.

He scowled. "What the fuck? I know you, Charlie. I *know* you. You're going to take a drag, then start coughing so much you're almost puking, and you'll run inside to the bathroom. Either way, you get out of this conversation, and I know that's the real goal for you." He pointed his cigarette at me before taking it to his mouth. "No smokes for you, and stop bullshitting me. Just tell me what I want to know, and we can be done with it." His eyes flicked upward. "And you know I'm sorry for being a dumbass earlier. I get you not wanting to talk about you-know-who, but just reassure this old bastard who used to be your best friend that you *are* talking to *someone* about him?"

I was quiet.

He sighed. "Charlie."

"I've mentioned the situation to Reese."

"Forster?" he scoffed.

"Yes. Him."

He was quiet again. "Shit. I'm trying not to be best-friend jealous here. Him? Really?"

I shrugged, my stomach settling back down. "To be honest, I didn't say much. Just that I'm going through something stupidly tragic."

Another beat. "It's not stupid. It's just tragic, plain and simple."

Oh whoa. I couldn't breathe, couldn't talk. I blinked back sudden tears. They'd come out of nowhere. I stuck out a blind hand for his cigarette.

He chuckled, swatting it back down. "Here. Drink this instead." He pushed his beer into my hand, and I guzzled it.

He sat back, and the air felt lighter somehow. He finished his cigarette. "I saw Superstar's interview. He flicked his ear." His shoulder nudged mine.

I'd beamed when Reese did that, and I knew Grant had noticed, though no one else did. Reese made the gesture so subtle, it looked like he was flicking off some sweat or an itch. But I saw it.

"That was for you, wasn't it? You used to do little signals all the time when we were young."

I laughed, the beer helping with my throat. "That's right. The good old..." I scratched my nose with my middle finger.

He laughed too. "Yeah, and this one." He made a circle with his thumb and finger, moving another finger through the hole.

"That's not that discreet."

"It is when you did it behind Keith's back."

I groaned. "He's such a dickhead."

"He is a dickhead, yes."

"How can you work there?" Scratch that. "How can you *still* work for him?"

He lifted a shoulder. "Patience. There's a plan in the works."

"Good. I support that wholeheartedly as long as it involves him getting fired in the end."

"You know..."

Oh no. He was back to his serious voice. I shook my head, standing up. "No. No more real talk. I've handled what I can for the night."

I was itching to shoot off twenty different questions to Reese—not because I was feeling uncomfortable, but because I wanted to see his responses. But I refrained, until after another beer.

Raising Grant's beer, I finished it. "That is one thing about your fiancée, though. She's not that perfect."

He harrumphed. "Says you."

I held the now-empty can out. "Her margaritas are too sugary. I need more beer."

A laugh, then he stood with me. Taking the can, he nodded. "Then beer you will have. Come on." He led the way. "We're off for a refill. I need one myself."

More than two hours later, after three more beers—don't judge me—and one slice of pizza then I finally sent off another round of questions. I had thought long and hard about them—and by that, I mean I gave it no thought.

Me: Octopus or bear?

Me: Why do people have to have the last word? What's the point?

Me: Why can't people vacation in their own homes? That's where all your stuff is.

Me: When global warming melts all the snow, will Antarctica have to change its name?

Me: Was I wrong for cheering in Aquaman when they tossed the trash back on the land?

Me: Stupidest advice you've ever gotten?

Me: What constitutes being nosy versus probing?

Me: Why do we call it a refrigerator and not a food-cooler?

Buzz.

Reese: Stop. Jesus, woman.

I giggled. Normally, I hated giggling, but in this instance, that's what it was. I'd just gotten back to his cabin, and I was curled up on the couch, my phone in hand and what I could only imagine looked like an unhinged smile on my face.

I was buzzed, gloriously—a let's-forget-reality kind of buzzed. It was the bestest.

The phone rang instead, and I hit accept. "When people work the midnight shift, are they nooners instead of a morning or night person?"

"Fuck's sakes. I'm tired, woman. Stop. Turn the brain off."

"Reese," I whispered. More laughter. A hiccup now.

"What?" But he knew. I could hear his smile. "Ah. You're buzzed."

"I am. Did you use a one-use girl tonight?"

"Who is that?" a voice asked from where he was.

"Sorry," he said to them. "It's a chick. Hold on." He was moving around. I heard a bunch of static sounds until a door closed, and his voice came back, dropping low, "Give me a second. I'm actually going to the lobby to have a conversation with you."

"I'm a chick? Why not ducklings? Little ducks? Too close to little dicks?"

He barked out a laugh, then smothered it. "Chill. Give me a second to regroup."

A ding.

"Are you on the elevator?"

"I am, and yes, there are people here." He said to them, "Nice night, huh?"

A woman laughed. A guy said something. Then I heard, "You're Reese Forster, aren't you?"

"No." I shot upright on the couch. "I've got him now. He's mine."

Reese snorted, but said to them, "I am." To me, "One second."

The elevator door dinged again, and I could hear Reese stop to take a selfie. He signed a couple things for them, and then the phone came back to his mouth. "Hold on. I'm moving somewhere more private." He asked someone else, "My roommate's sleeping, and I know you guys don't like people to hang out in the hallways. Is there somewhere I can take this call?"

A sudden burst of laughter and yelling came from where he was, in the background.

"Oh yes, Mr. Forster," someone said. "Of course. One moment, please."

It was another two minutes before I heard a door close and Reese said more clearly, "Okay. I'm in a back office that I'm pretty sure some dude was hoping to take a nap in for his thirty-minute break just now." He yawned. "And shit. Why am I talking to you at two in the morning?"

I forgot he was an hour ahead where he was. "Why would you not talk to me when I'm buzzed?" I felt a belch coming and stifled it. "I'm hilarious."

He laughed quietly. I heard creaking on his end. "Maybe. So entertain me, woman."

"Stop calling me woman. I have a name."

"Gnat."

"You call me a gnat again, and I'll start taking pictures of your dirty boxers. You have some here, you know."

"You wouldn't."

"Stop calling me a gnat. It's insulting."

"Okay, okay. I'm sorry. You're right. Just...names felt a bit personal, Miss Don't-Ask-Me-Any-Real-Questions. Thought a nickname, made in jest, was the right way to go."

"What do you usually call your female friends?"

He grunted. "I don't have female friends."

"Right. You have one-use girls?"

"Or multiple-use girls."

"That is disgusting."

He laughed. "Sorry. I don't really date, so I don't label anyone anything, but would you rather I say fuck buddies? I have a few of those."

I wasn't feeling a burning in my chest. Not at all. A gnat hadn't nestled there and started digging even deeper.

I scowled. "When's the last time you dated?"

"Really? We're going this route?"

"What?"

"Don't be a jealous chick. I don't like that."

"Don't call me a chick either."

"Shit!" He was silent a second.

I bit my lip. What was I doing?

"Are you seriously jealous?" He was quieter now.

Was I? "I don't know."

His voice was strained. "I thought we were friends. I mean... we are, aren't we?"

Had I just messed that up? I swallowed, pushed down a lump, and sagged back on his couch. "I have no idea. I mean, I'm a mess."

"Certifiable." He sounded relieved.

I relaxed, stretching my legs over the cushions. "You know about Stupid Tragic Guy, but you don't know about the ex-ex, the most recent ex."

"There was another guy?"

"I was using him to try to get over the tragic guy."

"It didn't work?"

"No."

"Let me guess. Did you get propositioned by his grandpa?"

"Yes!" I smiled. "You do pay attention to me."

"It was a shot in the dark." He was wry now, with a twinge of wariness. "Is this a problem for us?"

"There's an us?"

He was quiet again. One beat. Then, softer, "I thought there was. A friendship us."

"Friends."

"Are we doing it? The talk?" He was grinning. I couldn't see it. I couldn't hear it, but I could feel it.

"The talk?" I asked.

"Where we cement an actual friendship, where we move toward giving a shit about each other and have each others' backs, and it's not a big deal."

Friends. For real. "So that means I should stop calling you Reese Forster in my head, huh?"

He snorted. "Oh my God, tell me you don't do that."

I laughed. "I don't. Or I didn't. Today."

More laughter. "Fuck. You're whacked." A sigh. "So, when are you going to tell me about the ex-ex?"

"Never-never."

"You're a different duck, that's for sure." He seemed resigned to it.

"I know."

"But I like that."

I smiled once again, but just like that, my eyelids were getting heavy. "I know." The moment had passed. We were back to friendly and comfortable waters.

And I was still buzzed, but now the buzzed had moved to the buzz that makes you want to fall asleep, and fast.

I yawned.

A soft chuckle. "So, do you want me to answer those questions, or is this where we hang up and you pass out on my couch?"

I was nodding off. I yawned again into the phone, "Saftrabels. Congrassuladnsonurwn."

"Yeah. Okay." He laughed. "No idea what you just said. Good night, friend. I'll text you my responses in the morning."

But I didn't hear. I was asleep.

CHAPTER TWENTY-ONE

Reese: Octopus. BBC says they're smart. Bears could eat me, so there's that.

Reese: The point of having the last word is feeling like you won? I don't know. Conflict should be about resolution, not winning, or so my coach said, but he likes to yell. And get the last word in.

Reese: Makes sense to me, but I have someone to clean my place too.

Reese: Yes. It would have to change it to Warm Terrain and no longer Frozen Tundra.

Reese: Let's cheer again. Good measure.

Reese: Trust her when she says she's on birth control.

Reese: Are we talking anal or oral?

Reese: Not a goddamn clue. Let's make up our own word. That can be called Frozen Tundra instead.

I woke up to his responses, followed by one last one.

Reese: Night.

And then a few new ones that had come in this morning.

Reese: On the bus. Had breakfast. Want our flight number?

Reese: Why are you not answering? Still sleeping or am I getting the last word in?

**Reese: Fuck it, woman. Wake up. I'm bored.
Send me new questions.**

I laughed, rolling over, still on his couch, and typed back.

Me: I slept in. Awake now. Are you in the air?

I sent my response an hour after his last one, and when he didn't buzz back right away, I left my phone on the couch and got up for the day. After showering and dressing, I was heading out when my phone buzzed.

Trent: I'm coming back this week. The team canceled their last couple days, so I have free time. Want to do something fun? I've got nothing planned.

I frowned and called him.

"You're not with Owen and Hadley, are you?" he answered.

I needed to check on my fishing cabin, so I was heading that way. "No. Why?"

"Because I sent them texts too. What are you up to?"

"I'm heading to my cabin right now. What were you saying about canceling or something?"

"Yeah. I was scheduled to come in for a last motivational talk for them at the end of the week, but they've been changing the days a lot lately. The last change came in this morning. In three days they're done at camp."

"They're done?"

Reese hadn't said a word.

"Yeah, but the reason I texted is because I had them scheduled for later in the week. My manager moved things around in my schedule, but I still have those days off. So now, after flying in and doing their speech, I have four days clear. You want to do something?" He paused. "Hold on." His phone buzzed.

A second later, he came back on. "Uh, what's going on with you and Reese Forster?"

I stopped mid-stride. I was between the last cabin in Reese's village and my fishing cabin, a good five hundred feet ahead.

My stomach clenched. "Uh, what do you mean?"

And did his voice have a certain disapproval in it? Flashbacks of my father came to me. He'd tried to get me to leave Damian years before I did.

"I just got a text from Owen. They have time off from Keith, but he didn't know if you'd be able to or not. Something about being busy with Forster?"

Owen. Seriously.

"Nothing's going on. We've just become friends. That's all."

He was quiet a beat. "Friends? You and Reese Forster? The ball player, right?" His disbelief was evident.

I didn't know how to answer that one. Yes, to convince him, or yes, to defend myself?

I started forward again. I hadn't gone to my own cabin for two days, and the times before had been just to dash in, my nose plugged, as I grabbed what I could and dashed back out.

When I got to my cabin, I waited. I couldn't talk and not breathe at the same time, so I sat on the front porch, my feet dangling off the side, facing the lake. It was just beyond the tree line and a dip down to the edge, which was lined with rocks. The nice beach area was on the other side of the island. Still, it was pretty. The sun was shining, a sparkling line clearing right through the trees and making the water look like it was glistening.

I hadn't taken the time since coming here to appreciate the island. Most of my time had been spent avoiding things or being busy. Or with Reese. Sitting here, with Trent quiet for a moment, I took it all in.

A piece of me settled. Calm.

"I thought you went to camp to get away from another guy situation?" Trent said.

"Technically, I was fired and dumped, but let's be honest here. Lucas and his grandpa weren't really anything, and neither is Reese. Friends, Trent. Like you and me. Friends."

I might've been lying a tad bit, but that was between me and the fish smell.

"What were you thinking about doing?"

Shit. Not that I was making much money, but that meant I was losing four days of wages. That could've covered a weekend of laundry.

"I don't know. Some of the others aren't far away. I was thinking we could do a road trip. Janet mentioned having a new house. We could go there, see her. Dinner. You know, just spending time together. She has walking trails by her place too."

I glanced to the left of my cabin. There was a better walking trail right here.

"I don't know. You know I don't get along with Janet." She was one of the gossiping friends. I'd melted out of the scene so she couldn't talk shit about Damian. Though she didn't know that. So maybe the whole not getting along was more on my end, but her tongue could be razor sharp when she talked about her 'friends.' I'd heard more than I needed to. Why let myself be a target for her?

But Trent, he loved her. Trent loved everyone.

"Charlie." His voice dipped. We were going *real talk* here. All these people in my life, all they wanted to do was converse seriously about things. What was the fun in that? Could we not adult in other ways?

"You said yourself that you need to reconnect with people. Janet's the glue in the group. She's the only one who talks to everyone else, besides me. If you want to convey a message to the group or an apology, it's smart to go see her."

That made my decision. The words *apology* and *message* were enough. "You know, now that I'm remembering, I had a call from my last boss. She wanted me to come back and see her. Maybe I could get my job back."

"You're lying."

I was. I didn't care. "Have you really never heard Janet talk shit about people? You *do* know that's what she does."

"She's not that bad."

"Because you're a guy. She loves you. With girls, it's another thing. She'll talk shit about who you're dating, but she won't talk shit about you. If you have a vagina, you're fair game to her."

My phone buzzed, and pulling away from my ear, I saw a text.

Reese: Just landed. Coach said we're doing lunch there. I brought you a shirt from the airport.

"Hold on a second, Trent."

Me: What airport?

Reese: Congratulations. It says you've visited New York.

Me: Always wanted to be a New Yorker. One second. On the phone.

He buzzed through again, but I was speaking once more. "Hey."

Trent's voice twisted. "So you're going to lie and avoid more camp people?"

I sighed. "Janet and I were never close. And you don't get it. You don't know what I went through…"

"Because you won't tell me. I've been gone for two weeks, and you've not once called or even texted. I thought you wanted to change, reconnect with the group, but you're still avoiding us."

I tried to be gentle. "Look, seeing you, coming here, reconnecting with Owen, Hadley, Grant, and you—that's been huge for me. And it's all I can handle right now."

I didn't get why he was upset. When he'd gone through his divorce—the main reason he'd become a motivational speaker— Janet had ripped his ex to shreds. I mean, that'd been around the time I began leaving the group, but I'd seen the emails. She'd been vicious. Yeah, she'd been talking about his ex-wife, but Trent had loved her and married her. I knew he wouldn't have been okay with what she was saying.

He was silent, and I didn't know what else to say. "Maybe we can talk more when you get here? When do you arrive?"

"I'll be coming in tomorrow evening. You'll be free?"

"Depends on the time, but should be. I'm usually at the courts till I close down."

"Okay. I'll let you know when I'm supposed to arrive. Maybe we could go somewhere to talk?"

"Yeah. Sure."

I frowned as we hung up. The whole conversation had been odd, not really Trent-esque, but I decided to stop thinking about it. I'd just hear what he had to say tomorrow night. Until then, I stood and turned toward my cabin.

Grab and dash. Don't breathe.

I ran inside, and I swear the smell had worsened again. After grabbing pants, I had just enough time to grab the bag Reese originally packed for me. I had to gasp once, and I almost threw up. This cabin really did need to be condemned.

Thanks, Keith. Boss of the year.

I'd just deposited everything in Reese's cabin when my phone buzzed again.

Reese: At a gas station. You need anything?

Me: Booze allowed?

Reese: Done. Wine coolers?

I laughed.

Me: How about we do shots your last night here?

I waited, but there was a second before he texted back.

Reese: Shit. Just asked. Our last two preseason games are back home. We leave in three days.

I knew. And I tried to ignore how my stomach shriveled at the thought. Three days. Or more like two days. That's how much time I had with Reese.

Reese: I bought a bottle of vodka.

Vodka it would be then.

Me: Always wanted to be half-Russian.

He didn't respond, so I tucked my phone away and spent some time on my laptop. I needed to find a few jobs to apply for, maybe email someone about my apartment. Reese had his own Wi-Fi, and he'd left it behind, so I plugged that in. The camp's internet sucked. Since I'd be out of a job again in a few days, I figured it was time I headed back home to face the music.

If I didn't have any money coming in, I'd need to make some moves. New apartment, or *gasp*, make the dreaded call to see if I could bunk in my old room at my parents' house. Damian and I had broken up once before, and I had asked if I could move back home. My mom said I could stay for the summer, but I'd have to pay rent. Damian and I had gotten back together three hours later, so I'd never had to deal with her offer. Now things were different.

I had less money. Most of it had been used paying Damian's medical bills until his parents got involved, but no one knew. How do you tell family and friends that the person you thought was going to be your husband needed to put a note in the bathroom to remind him to brush his teeth? How do you do that and not have them look at your loved one in pity or look down on him? Because keeping your dignity is a thing. Sometimes it's the last thing you have in situations like that, and you might be surprised by how far you'd go to preserve a thing called pride.

God.

I had to take a breath.

My life was a mess. Everything about me was a mess.

Maybe Trent was right. Maybe it was time to start facing life again? I mean, I wasn't going to sign up for a Janet session. Not about that, but opening up? Telling people? I'd mentioned it to Reese. And Grant actually knew what Damian had. Both times, I hadn't gotten worse. Both times, I'd panicked, but I couldn't deny that I felt a tiny bit better afterward.

I took a breath.

I wasn't... I was.

I pulled out my phone and texted before I could stop myself.

Me: My ex had early-onset dementia. It ran in his family. His father got it super young, and he did too. It's why we ended things.

Me: And full disclosure, I'm gonna have a panic attack that I told you. I hope it's not too much for our new friendship. I'm turning off my phone. See you when you get back. You don't have to mention this if you don't want to deal with it. Totally okay with me.

There.

I turned my phone off before Reese could text back. Yes. I was being a coward now, but I hadn't been a moment before. That had to mean something.

I left my phone on his couch, turned off the laptop and his Wi-Fi, and went to the main lodge. The team would be arriving in a little over an hour, so Owen and Hadley would be setting up the food. I'd help.

I needed to stay busy or I was going to collapse.

CHAPTER TWENTY-TWO

I felt him before I heard him, when they arrived.

A hush came over the kitchen. Owen and Hadley stopped what they were doing, and Reese asked, "Where is she?"

I'd been in the back, putting away a mixing bowl.

Stepping around the corner, Reese saw me. His face clouded over, and he came into the kitchen.

Only staff was allowed back here, Reese didn't care. No one said a word as he crossed past Owen and Hadley and took my wrist. He tugged me to Owen's office and shut the door.

"I have to—"

"Don't even," he growled. He leaned back against the door, folding his arms over his chest. "You text me that and then shut off your phone? What are you? Twelve?"

I flushed. It *was* a bit immature. I picked at my shirt. "Adulting is hard."

"Tough shit." He pushed off from the door, stalking toward me.

I edged back, just a foot.

He lifted his hands, pausing mid-air, and I watched as a myriad of expressions flashed over his face. He fisted his hands, then unfisted them, then let out a harsh breath as he settled them on my shoulders.

His tone was gentle when he spoke. "You said he hit you once."

I was numb.

The feeling was spreading fast, coming up from my feet to my legs, my thighs, my stomach. It flared up my sternum, my chest. Through my shoulders. Down my arms. My fingers. Up to my neck, rising, rising until I looked at him.

I knew a tear fell.

"Once, yes."

"How bad was it?"

My voice was hoarse. "Does it matter? He wasn't in his right mind."

"It matters." His hands tightened on my shoulders, his fingers curving into my skin. "Please tell me the truth."

I looked away. I couldn't see whatever I was going to see in his eyes as I remembered this. I wouldn't be able to deal with it.

The words spilled, for the first time. "He beat the shit out of me."

He dragged in his air.

"It was the only time, but I'd started noticing little things. He wasn't in control of himself anymore."

"What happened?"

God. Really? My throat wasn't completely numb. It was hurting, squeezing, tightening.

"When I woke up, he was eating popcorn and laughing at *Impractical Jokers*. I got up, and he looked surprised. He didn't remember hurting me."

"Fucking hell." Reese hissed as he ripped himself away from me. His hands balled into fists, pressed at his sides, and he turned his back to me. He faced the door, his shoulders tightening.

"He was tore up about it, and he never hit me again, but there were other things. Small things sometimes. Big things toward the end. He stole groceries from a drive-up lane. He thought they were ours, but he'd already put our groceries in the trunk. Another time, he left the oven on during the night."

Reese's head raised up. His shoulders bulged.

"His short-term memory was getting bad. He would forget things he'd done the day before. One time he forgot my name.

147

Another time his own. Just for a moment—then he'd be back. He'd be normal again."

"How long?"

He turned back, a rawness in his eyes.

"How long what?" I could only get a whisper out now.

"How long did you take care of him until you got help?"

That question punched me, right in the diaphragm. He didn't know how much guilt came with that answer, how much shame, how much pain sliced through me. "He started showing symptoms three years in."

"Before what? How did the relationship end?"

I closed my eyes, shaking my head. "I can't, Reese. Don't make me tell you everything. I can't. Not yet."

He stepped closer. I could feel him, and he spoke so softly that it broke the rest of me apart. "How long did you have to breathe for him? Before you got help?"

I was crying.

I couldn't feel the tears, but I knew they were there.

I saw them falling to the floor, some hitting my shoes.

"Too long."

"How long were you guys together in total?"

I paused, not because it wasn't in me to answer, but because my vocal cords had frozen. One beat. Two. Three, and then I could speak again. "Seven years."

I'd had two years, two amazing years with my soulmate.

He cursed under his breath, then stepped close to me. His arms came around me, his hand cradling the back of my head, and at first I just stood there.

I had never spoken about what I went through.

I never said any of it out loud, just explained the bare minimum to his mother before they'd stepped in to help with him. I had to write out a list of behaviors and events for a lawyer once, but that'd been it. No one else knew—until now, until Reese. My parents. My siblings. My friends. No one. And in some ways, even I didn't know it all.

It was out now, though.

I had a bleak thought, standing in Reese's arms, that Trent had gotten what he wanted. Grant had gotten what he wanted. I was dealing with life again.

Then I crumbled.

Reese caught me. He held me, righting me so I didn't totally fall to the floor. He went with me, moving so we were sitting in a corner of the room, me between his legs. He folded his arms around me, and I broke apart, my sleeve stuffed in my mouth to quiet my tears.

CHAPTER TWENTY-THREE

I was still sitting in his arms, resting against his chest when I heard people leaving the dining area.

"You should go eat."

"Fuck eating." His chest rumbled from his words.

We heard a voice asking for Reese through the kitchen, then a tentative knock on the door.

"Reese?" It was Juan.

He opened the door, his head poking in and his eyes sweeping the room until he saw us. He didn't look surprised to see how we were, just pursed his lips together a second.

"Uh. Coach wants a word with you. We're having a meeting, then we're doing practice in an hour." His eyes flashed to mine, an apology flaring. "You got some keys on you? I can open the courts for you, if you want?"

Oh. That made me feel nice, but crappy. I shook my head, scrambling up. Every inch of me protested as I pulled away from Reese, but I had a job to do. No way would I let a camper, and a professional ball player at that, do my job for me.

"I got it. I'm okay. Minor meltdown on pause." It was a lame attempt at a joke, and it fell flat. No one laughed.

Reese stood behind me. "Coach is mad at me?"

"Uh..." Juan's gaze fell to me again. "I think he just wants clarification, if you know what I mean."

"Yeah. I got it." Reese's hand found my arm as he stepped around me. "Give me a second? I'll be right out."

Juan nodded. The door closed softly behind him.

Reese looked at me. "You okay?"

I nodded. "Totally."

He laughed. "You're a shitty liar."

I grinned, knowing it was crooked and more just an attempt. "You'd be the first to claim that."

"I doubt it."

I lifted my gaze, feeling the dried tears caking my face. I flinched, seeing his knowing gaze, feeling him in me, feeling how he knew I was so full of shit, feeling him know the storm I'd been through, just feeling him know me.

"Your coach wants to know about me?"

"Probably. He knows the team likes you, but me coming right in here and skipping a meal, that's going to raise eyebrows." He gave me a crooked grin. "Don't worry about it, though. I'll explain. It'll be fine. I don't have a $20-million endorsement deal in the works for nothing. As long as I show up and win, he's happy."

"What an understanding guy."

He smiled. "Think you can find me something quick to eat before I head over to smooth things out with him, just in case?"

"On it."

Owen and Hadley were quiet when we came back out, but Owen being Owen, he already had a plate ready. He indicated a tray on the counter: water, milk, silverware, even salt and pepper were on there.

"There you go. Owen's way ahead of us."

"Thanks, man." Reese nodded to Owen.

Owen cleared his throat, tugging one of his sleeves down, his shoulder rolling back. "No, thank you." He jerked his head toward me. "We, uh, we heard some of it."

Floor open up. Let me fall through. Please. Now.

Hadley was crying in the corner. She wiped at a tear. "I can't even imagine. Charlie..."

I couldn't. I just couldn't.

I should've gone to her, took her in my arms, whispered that it was okay, but I didn't have it in me. I wanted to disappear, and as if sensing what was going on with me, Reese took my arm once again.

"Maybe, uh, come with me? Yeah?" He looked at Owen, though, who nodded back. Owen was the one to go and take his wife in his arms.

He was the one to comfort her.

He was doing what I should've been doing, and Reese, he was being a friend. He pulled me with him, grabbing an extra apple on the way, and I knew that was for me and not him. He stuffed it into his pocket, his hand falling to mine.

He was leading me out, the cafeteria empty, when the back door opened.

Grant stepped in and saw us, his eyes falling to our hands.

Reese didn't stop. He only dipped his head to Grant, grunting, "What's up?" Then he tugged me the rest of the way through the cafeteria with him.

I was so beyond thankful for him because he wasn't letting me make decisions. He knew I wasn't ready to deal with the aftermath of what Owen and Hadley had just heard. He knew Grant would find out. He knew I wouldn't want to stand there, feeling completely exposed, all my insides out in the open for them to see. And he wasn't letting me stay and dwell.

He went into the camp office, where his coach was talking to Keith.

"Coach?"

Our hands came apart.

Keith's eyebrows bunched together. He was wearing an olive green polo shirt today, the same khaki shorts, though. Could he ever wear something else? I doubted it.

"Charlie?" Keith frowned at me.

Reese's coach cleared his throat, glancing between Keith and me. "Uh, yeah. Can we have a word? Keith, you have an office we could use real quick?"

Keith brightened and came around the desk. He picked up his Boss mug and held it out to me. "Charlie, wash this for me?"

Reese's jaw clenched. He took the mug and put it on the counter behind Keith. "Charlie's going with me to the gym. I asked her to open it early."

"Yeah?" Keith's smile was wide. "That's great. She does a good job. Don't you, girl? Oh hey. We're closing up early in three days, so you can make travel arrangements. I'll cut you a check at the end. It'll be a little short what I promised, but you did a good job—opening the gyms, taking inventory—a good job. I was just talking with Coach Winston, going over the last of the details."

I felt Reese's tension.

He jerked forward, but I grabbed the back of his sleeve. It wasn't a firm hold, just a reminder.

Coach Winston saw the motion and narrowed his eyes, but he didn't say anything.

Keith was clueless, as usual. He smiled, nodding. "Since you're here." He grabbed a piece of paper from the counter, holding out a pen. "Mind if I get your autograph? My son will be jealous when I show it to him later."

"You're kidding me, right?" Reese said, his eyes wide.

Keith's smile slipped.

Coach Winston stepped forward, moving between the two. "If you don't mind, Keith, I need to have a word with my player. We can do autographs later."

"Sure! That'd be great. I could grab some posters, get the whole team to sign them? We do auctions here. That could help support the camp a bit more."

"Uh-huh. Yeah. Sure." Coach Winston urged Reese outside. "Hallway." His eyes flashed.

Reese nodded, turning, his hand going to my hip and moving me ahead of him. Once outside, Coach said, "Upstairs. Your friend too."

I was in trouble. By Winston Duty.

The old Charlie came to life, just a little. She did a little somersault inside me.

We went upstairs, moving into one of the sitting rooms. Once inside, Reese's coach shut the door and shook his head. "Hell. That guy."

"Is he for real?" Reese asked. "He wants my fucking autograph, so his son gets jealous?"

"This place was recommended by a buddy of mine, but now I don't know."

"Keith is usually kept away from campers. Owen, he's the guy that's been in the kitchen this whole time? His job is usually handling campers. He's better at it."

Both looked at me.

Reese asked, "Why's he in the kitchen then?"

"Keith wanted to keep the staff at a minimum. It's protocol if celebrities are here, and you guys are special. Keith thinks he's a big basketball guy. He'd strut around like a rooster if more pro teams came here."

The two shared a look.

Yeah. I doubted that was going to happen.

"That's too bad," Coach Winston said. "I've talked with Owen a few times about meals for the team. He seems like a good man."

I nodded. "He is."

Reese gave me a small smile. "You mind giving us a minute?"

"Actually, I want to talk to both of you." He turned to Reese first. "She's been sleeping in your cabin?"

Reese explained about my cabin, about the fish smell, and about how my other option would be a janitor's closet. When he finished, the room was silent.

"Seriously?"

Reese nodded. "Are you really shocked after just hearing what he said?"

"This guy." Winston shook his head. "Fuck." He looked at me. "What about your friend? The motivational speaker guy? Where does he stay?"

"He'll stay in an extra room, but it's on the guys floor. Keith would never let me stay in a room with players on the same floor. He assumes I'd try to have sex with every single one of them."

His eyes got even bigger, his eyebrows even higher. "Are you joking?"

"I wish. He has a history of suggesting things like that."

He rubbed a hand over his jaw, stepping back. "This guy should not be the head of this camp. If I had known he was like this, we never would've come here." His eyes rested on Reese. "If the tabloids find out about her? About her staying in your cabin?"

"They won't."

"None of the staff will say anything," I said. "The few who know are good friends. Plus, we've all signed an NDA. That basically says we can't say anything about anything that happened here during the time you guys were here. We can't even say you guys were here in the first place."

Reese's coach continued rubbing his jaw. "Do the guys know?"

Reese nodded. "A few. They won't say anything."

A warning flashed in his coach's gaze. "If an incident happens? If we have to let someone go from the team? You know things can get dirty."

Reese grimaced, but he didn't respond.

"Goddamn." His coach shook his head again, gesturing to me. "She has to stay somewhere else."

"Where? You know what that guy is like. He'll put her in the janitor's closet." Reese cocked his head to the side. "Your place? You're rooming with the other coaches."

"We have an extra bed. You can stay with us. Leave her your cabin—"

I shook my head. "No. No way. I'm not putting a camper out of his own cabin. Juan already moved out because of me. I will figure it out. I promise."

"Where?" Reese demanded, both of them almost glaring at me.

"I'll—I don't know, but I'll figure it out. Even if I have to drive to town for a hotel, I'll do that. Or I can have Grant put a bed in Owen's office. That's easy. I'll do that."

Both of them were cursing.

"Owen offered me the guest bedroom in their house. It's three nights. I can stay there. It's no problem."

No way in hell was I putting Owen out. If they had invited me as a guest, if I was here as a visitor, not staff, if Keith wasn't such a dick and I knew he was banking on Owen and Hadley always offering up their guest bedroom—if any of those situations had been the case, I would've stayed there, but that wasn't how things were. But I was no longer Reese's problem. I knew that much too.

I would figure it out, even if I had to sleep in my car. It *was* camp. Maybe it was time I finally camped out? Problem solved. I could embrace my inner frozen tundra because end of October nights could get hella cold, but it wasn't their problem to fix.

"I promise," I said, a completely fake smile on my face.

They seemed to buy it, both nodding.

Phew.

And Reese said I couldn't lie.

CHAPTER TWENTY-FOUR

"You are really bad at lying."

Reese found me later that night, and he spoke up as I was bent over the back seat of my car. I screamed, whirling around before clamping a hand over my own mouth. I nearly dry heaved.

"You are a man," I hiss-whispered, speaking around my hand. Still in danger of dry-heaving here. "You're not supposed to sneak up on a woman, in a parking lot, at night. Never ever."

Everyone had gone to bed. I'd waited a full hour in Owen's office before making my move for my car. I could've carried a mattress to his office. They were lightweight enough, but there was something sketchy about sleeping in someone else's office and using the main bathroom everyone used—staff, campers, the random visitor, the mail guys, delivery service. Plus, I wasn't lying when I said the basement was haunted. I thought the kitchen was haunted too. There were weird noises when no one was supposed to be around. Spooky shit.

No way. I'd take my car.

Reese rolled his eyes. "You're not supposed to lie to me, and I knew you were lying. You're horrible at it." He motioned to his eye. "You do this little twitch up here. Do you not know that? Has no one told you that?"

I glared at him. "I've spent the better part of the last eight years with someone whose brain was slowly going. If Damian knew, he didn't remember to tell me."

The slight smirk vanished.

Reese straightened up. "Sorry. That was an asshole comment."

I waved it off. "It's fine." And I was back inside my car. I'd been in the process of spreading out a sleeping bag I'd grabbed from the lost-and-found. They were always laundered before going in there.

Reese moved around the car. The door across from me opened, and he grabbed the sleeping bag. "No way. You're not sleeping in your goddamn car."

"Stop cursing." I yanked it out of his hands. "And I am!"

"Why? Fuck the rules. Just sleep in my cabin. I'll stay in your cabin. I'm a man. I can handle it."

I snorted. "I had to go in there earlier, and I could barely manage to grab the bag you packed. I almost vomited. You try to sleep in there and your coach will be really pissed, because you'll be in the hospital. Trust me. Stay in your cabin. I can handle this. I might be sleeping in my car soon anyway, so I should start getting used to it."

Oh, crap.

I hadn't meant to say that.

He went still. "What are you talking about?"

"Nothing. I meant for the next three nights." Was it three, or two? I did the math. Two. Everyone was leaving on the third day, or now the second day.

"You're lying. Again." He reached inside, his arm span putting mine to shame. He grabbed my bag, my phone, and my keys. Shutting his door, he came around, hip-checked me out of the way, and shut my door. "Let's go." He locked my doors.

When I didn't start moving, he began guiding me forward. With his legs. His hips.

Good God.

He was muscled. It was surprising for how lean he was, but he was six-three and all muscle.

"How many miles do you ball players run in a game?"

We were moving past the cars.

He stepped to my side, my bag slung over his shoulder. "Is that one of your questions?"

"No. I'm actually curious."

He shrugged. "Maybe two miles? It's give or take per game."

Two miles per game? "How many games do you play per season?"

He grinned down at me. "We play eighty-two games per season. You want more stats?"

"Always." Did he not know me?

"Forty-one at home, forty-one away. We have five games this preseason. Our last two are at home."

We were walking behind the main lodge. There was no light to show us the way, but I knew it by heart. I didn't have a flashlight and normally, I'd have the random island invaders in my head, or a deer running at night, or a skunk even, but it wasn't happening now. Because of Reese.

He calmed me, and he was trusting me in return. We were halfway down the path, in complete darkness, before I realized the magnitude of what we were doing. I'd never walked a path in the middle of the night, with no moon shining through the trees, no flashlight, and not been freaked out.

I bit my lip. I wasn't about to jinx myself now.

"What'll your coach say?"

"I'll deal with him."

I started to look back, but yeah. No light. Total darkness. I could only see black where he was, so I veered close to him until our arms brushed. "Are you going to get in trouble?"

He sighed. "Why are you pushing this?"

The answer was immediate. "Because I don't want to be a burden."

He was quiet a second. "Why would you think you're being a burden?"

I bit my lip again, mashing them together. I tasted blood.

His voice was low. "Who made you feel like a burden?"

I remained silent.

"Charlie."

I had to grin at that. "That's the first time you've said my name."

"You serious?"

"Yeah. It's nice."

He let out a strangled sound. "I feel like a dumbass. Jesus. I was calling you a gnat. I'm sorry."

I shrugged, but remembered he couldn't see. "We were going with the theme. Remember, I was your stalker in the beginning."

"Don't start—"

"I was, Reese." That quieted him. "Damian liked you first, you know. I've always liked basketball. My two brothers played. One was a big star in school, and we weren't close, but I felt close to him then. I think that's when I really started loving the game. He didn't give me any attention—I was a gnat to him. I don't think he meant it in a bad way, but older brothers get caught up in being cool, you know? Except for basketball. I mean, I had to act a certain way. I could only say a couple things to him during a game, like hand him a water or give him a towel, but it meant something to me. I did stats, and he was the team's star on passing. That's why I started following you. Your passes are phenomenal. No one can match you in the league, and your ball handling skills are unprecedented. Anyway, I just wanted to tell you that before this—before you and I became friends—you were already more than just a basketball player to me. You connected me to a good memory from my brother, and the same with Damian. We'd watch your games together, and for some reason, he was always Damian during those times. I still had him. He'd slip away later on, but I always knew he was Damian for eighty-two games a year—the ones we could watch on television, I mean."

Reese was quiet. We walked a few feet, then, "Your brother didn't let you speak to him?"

More lip mashing.

I twisted the ends of my sleeves into balls, knotting them together.

"To give him credit, I was probably annoying—"

"No little sister is truly annoying. They're younger, and they just want to be loved. Unless they're spoiled brats. Then it's different. I have a feeling you weren't spoiled."

I wasn't. Ignored? Forgotten? Yes. Not spoiled. Definitely not that.

"Did your family help with Damian?"

It hurt to talk about it. My insides were being stretched until I felt they were going to break apart.

"I tried to tell them once, but they didn't want to understand it." My stomach twisted, remembering. "They wanted to think I was lying, making it up. My mom got on the internet and tried to look up proof that no one in their mid-twenties could get early-onset dementia, especially not something that progressed the way his did. So I stopped trying. It was too much work to try to convince them."

"That's shit."

Yeah. It was. "I think it's easier for people to deny something than learn and change."

"Still shit. Your family was shit for doing that to you." There was an extra edge in his tone. "And his family? Did they step up?"

Tears fell down my face.

He didn't know. He didn't see. I wasn't making a sound.

My voice was normal. "At the end. They took over conservatorship of him. He's completely reliant on them for everything now."

"Did they know before the end, though?"

My throat spasmed. My hands trembled. My knees almost buckled. But my voice—it was normal. Maybe I couldn't lie about some stuff, but other things, I didn't give a damn thing away. And for the moment, walking that dark path, I let myself fall apart, except the part he could hear.

"His dad had passed from dementia, and there was some violence that came with it before he went into a facility. Damian blamed his mom for letting it occur as long as it did, so there were problems between them. They didn't talk."

"Did you reach out to her?"

My voice dipped, a small chink in my armor. "Yes."

He paused. I knew he heard the small crack in my voice.

He asked, his voice low, "And he didn't want you to?"

The chink grew. "No."

"*I will never forgive you if you go to her about this. I'll never forget, even with my brain. I won't forget. It'll be the one thing I remember about you: that you betrayed me.*"

"She's your mom, Damian. She can help."

"*No, she can't! I don't want her to know.*"

Reese was quiet again. We walked a few more yards. My heart felt like it was down there with my feet, like I was walking on top of it.

I was whispering now, and Reese had to know I was faltering. "Sometimes the hardest part of having a disease, or having something happen to you, is acknowledging that it's happening. Once you do, your life is never the same. You're never normal again. Once you acknowledge it and ask for help, you're never the same person again. You cease to be you, and you become the you *with* the problem. He's no longer Damian. He's Damian who has dementia. Pride can sustain a person for a long time before they have to break."

I sank to the ground.

I couldn't go any farther, and I was cracked wide open again. I couldn't keep the sobs to myself anymore.

Reese sat beside me, his feet coming around both sides of me. His arms slipped under me and he scooped me up, pulling me onto his lap. So simple a movement, but it meant so much to me. He cradled me, his hand smoothing back some of my hair.

"Was he a good guy?"

I grabbed his shirt, fisting it. "He was the best kind of guy there was."

He got it. A small weight lifted. He understood. The dementia wasn't Damian. The disease didn't define who he was. So many didn't see that. They just saw the disease. And if they couldn't see the disease, they didn't think it existed.

Reese's arms closed around me, his forehead resting on my shoulder for a moment. "I wish my brother—I get you. I get what you went through, but Damian didn't want to suffocate you."

162

"No." I sniffled. "He did at the end. He couldn't help it. He was too far gone, too much in denial of what was happening to him."

"My brother thinks I owe him. My lifestyle should be his. Hell. He kinda looks like me, so he tells people he *is* me, and he gets all this treatment because of it. Penthouse suites. Comped meals at restaurants. He tries to get free shit. Women. I've had so many women claim I got them pregnant; then they realize it was my brother who fucked them, and suddenly, it was a false positive." His voice was laced with disdain. "He was using my name at a club, and a girl thought she was going to sleep with me. She found out during the act that he wasn't me. She tried to say no. He didn't stop. He just..." His arms tightened around me. His voice was anguished. "Didn't stop."

I felt hollow at times. I recognized the same in him.

I felt it, and I understood.

Letting go of my sleeves, I slid my hands over his arms, moving to face him. I twisted around, my forehead pressed into his shoulder as I tried to grip him back.

I wanted to soothe his pain, to shield him from the harm his brother could do, to take away the damage his brother had already done. I knew in that instant that these were the same feelings I'd had for Damian, all over again.

But this was different, because Reese didn't need me to breathe for him.

I just needed to sit alongside him.

He could breathe on his own.

After a beat, I lifted my head. "I know why we're friends."

He grunted, sliding his hand up my back, curling it around my shoulder. "Please, enlighten me. This should be good."

I paused, my hands falling to the bottom of his sweatshirt. I tugged on it. "You want serious or the joke response?"

His chest rose, pausing, and his forehead came down to rest on mine. "I think I need the joke now," he murmured. "That'd be helpful."

The joke. I could do that. I was good at that.

"Well, we're friends because we're both ridiculously good-looking."

He snorted, lifting his head. "Jesus. Are you kidding me?"

I shook my head. "Absolutely not. Ridiculously good-looking people are friends with other ridiculously good-looking people. It's a whole wavelength thing going on between them." Sitting back more on his lap, I rested my hands on his legs. "See? At some point, they'll always intersect, and that's where we are." I clasped my hands together. "We intersected."

"That is the stupidest thing I've ever heard. There are lots of good-looking people I am *not* friends with, and there are not-good-looking people I'm great friends with." He tugged on a tendril of my hair, pulling my head back a tiny bit before letting go to slide his hand down my back and tunnel up under my shirt.

His finger began tracing circles on my skin.

Goosebumps spread all over me. I ignored them.

They were weird. Odd. I couldn't handle having them, or the sensations that came from being in his arms, feeling his touch, feeling him all around me. Or the way his breath fanned over my shoulder, then my face because he was so close.

We were friends.

Friends didn't affect each other like this, hold each other like this.

But we were still friends, right?

I swallowed over a lump. "Which one am I?"

"What do you think?"

I could hear his smirk.

And I couldn't help myself. I reached up, my hands touching his face. I explored him. My fingertips moved over his jaw, feeling a slight stubble there, grazing its roughness, and I touched his mouth. He trembled, just slightly, but I followed the lips, and I was right.

He was smirking.

But it was disappearing under my touch.

I couldn't see him, but I felt the air changing. It was folding in around us.

I could smell him, the mixture of sand and pine filling me up, circling around me, pulling me in.

I was closing my eyes, giving in, when suddenly he asked, "What's the serious answer?"

"Why we're connected?"

"Yeah." His voice was rough, deepening. He felt what I was feeling, and before I knew it, I'd rocked forward on his lap.

He caught me, splaying his hand over my hip, and he leaned forward. I felt his breath warming my neck. Slowly, so slowly, he moved to pull on the end of my sleeve. He tugged, inch by inch, until a portion of my shoulder was bare to him.

If he dipped down, half an inch, his lips would be on me.

My heart sped up, and my breath quickened. My lungs constricted.

But the need—I ached, and I rocked forward once again.

He groaned under me, holding me even tighter, anchoring me to him.

I felt him hardening under me, and I couldn't stop myself. I had ceased to think. I couldn't remember what he'd asked in the first place, and I moved forward once more.

"Fuck," he gasped, his mouth slamming down on my shoulder. "Do you know what you're doing?"

I whispered, "No." But I moved again, rocking forward until I was full-on grinding on him.

I couldn't stop. Not if he asked. Not if I tried.

That wasn't true. I would have in both circumstances, but my body would've ached in protest. It was aching now because I wasn't moving harder, deeper. I just wanted more from him.

"Reese," I gasped. My fingers slipped under his sweatshirt, touching his stomach, beginning to explore there. "I..."

"You want this? Are you sure?"

I knew what he was asking. We were beyond the first kiss.

I gave in to maybe everything I shouldn't have. "Yes."

"Wait." He said it, but he was standing up.

I was still on him, and I started to slip.

He bent down as my feet touched the ground, saying in my ear, "Jump."

I jumped, and he caught me.

My legs went around his waist, my arms around his shoulders. Turning, he walked down the path.

Reese tightened his hold on me. "This was a bit different walking when you were leading me."

I laughed into his ear, then couldn't help myself. Leaning forward, I nibbled there, and he groaned. His hands shifted to my ass. His fingers flexed, digging in, and he bounced me a little.

"God, I love your ass."

My eyes widened. "Really?"

"Hell, yes." A low growl came from him. "Perfect size for me. A little meat, enough bounce, and I can't wait to really grab hold of it."

Damian had never talked to me like this.

I liked it.

Moving my head back, his breath was on me. I moved until the ends of our noses were touching. I could feel the outline of his mouth.

He was breathing harder, deeper.

"What are you doing?"

I smiled, softly. "Having fun."

"You start messing with me too much, and we'll be on our asses. As much as I might like this little exploration we've got going, I'm not fucking you on a wooded path."

I started to close in until he added, "And I'm not kissing you when I can't see you." I felt him smiling. His hand switched, grabbing my other ass cheek. "I like to watch. I like to see what my touch does to you. I like to feel your shivers. I like it all."

So damn hot. "God."

He chuckled, letting me dip down so I felt him between my legs. Then he helped me start to ride him right then and there, through his sweats and my jeans, but I could feel him, and I wanted him.

My hand dropped down to touch his waist. "I want you in me."

166

"Soon. So fucking soon." Both his hands moved to holding my ass.

With my legs locked around him, he moved me up and down, slow and sensual.

Sensations coursed everywhere through my body. I slipped my hand inside his sweats as an inferno raged within me.

He groaned into my ear. "You sure you want to do that?"

Even more so now. I bit my lip in anticipation as I found him. He was long and hard and thick. So goddamn thick. I almost came right then, knowing how he'd feel inside of me.

"Holy fuck, Reese."

He laughed in my ear. "Yeah. That's all for you."

It hit me: I was having fun.

Sex with Damian had been hot and intense, but not fun. I mean, there'd been moments, but my main memory now was that after a while, there'd been nothing. Five years of nothing, actually, and then I went to Lucas, who didn't know how to touch or kiss. He tried. I had to give him that, but his touch had made me want to close up. It didn't make me want him, or want this kind of touching.

With Reese, just a touch and I was burning up.

Feeling safe in his arms, I let my hand wander. I didn't think. No lights were on, even as we approached the cabins. The village lights were motion-activated, so if he stuck to the edge of the path, they wouldn't turn on. He did just that as my thumb grazed the tip of him.

He shuddered, nipping at my jawline. "Fucking hell, Charlie."

I loved the power I had over him, and I cupped him more firmly. I cradled his dick in my palm, and as he stepped up onto his patio, I began to stroke him. He had to stop, bending over to rest against the cabin wall a moment.

His cock grew even more under my touch.

I slid my hand over him, slowly, sensually, and his entire body was shaking under me.

"Fuck, fuck, fuck. You are killing me." He grunted, moving back as he opened the door.

He slammed the door shut, switched the light on, and had me against the wall—all in one instant. Then his mouth was on me, and the world exploded.

It'd been like this once with Damian. Our first kiss.

Maybe it was wrong, but somehow I couldn't stop thinking of him. My first kiss with Damian had been the same way. The world went away, exploding, and everything was right. Just right. But that's all I felt, all I remembered. For once, thinking of Damian didn't make me feel awful.

Reese cupped the side of my face, his thumb moving over my cheek and coming to rest on the side of my mouth. As he pulled back, his lips grew softer. It was just right. Pure. There was nothing holding me back.

No guilt. No pressure. No worry.

Just want and need and enjoyment.

I would enjoy this time with him—wherever it led, it would be what it would be.

And with that last thought, I gave in.

I kissed him back harder, more demanding, and he matched me. He could be commanding, then gentle, then tender, whispering grazes and caresses and making me quiver all over.

"Are you sure about this?" He paused, his eyes on mine.

I nodded. I had never been so sure, and it felt freeing. It felt powerful.

I slid my hand up his chest, around his neck, and pulled him down as I rose up to meet him. Because that was important to me, meeting him halfway. Fifty/fifty.

"God yes," I said.

For that night, I was his.

For that night, he would be mine.

CHAPTER TWENTY-FIVE

I woke the next morning and it took a second for everything to come back to me.

I was cramped back into the bed, and in a flash everything flooded in: The car. Reese. The wooded path at night. Crying. Falling apart. Him holding me. Then the *more*.

Feeling him.

Touching him.

Tasting him.

I looked over. He was sleeping on his stomach, his head tucked into his pillow, his arms crossed underneath it. The sheet had slipped down so the top of his ass was peeking out.

I scanned down that back, remembering how it had felt with him arched over me, thrusting inside of me. How I had raked my nails over him— I could see the marks today.

Shit, shit, shit. He had practice. Sometimes he was skins, sometimes not. They'd see what we'd done. Everyone would know.

I didn't think. I shoved him off the bed.

His eyes flew open. He barked, flinging his hand to catch himself, but he was on the floor. "What the fuck?!"

I leaned over the side of the bed. "Do you think you'll bruise?"

"What?" He sat up, scowling and grimacing. "Shit, woman. You're insane."

"I marked you last night. They'll know today."

He reached behind him, cringing, and my words began to penetrate. He cursed. "You're right." He blinked at me. "I'm going to have to fuck myself up, aren't I?"

"Just go on the walking trail and fall on your back a few times. That should cover it up."

"Shirtless?"

"You can say you went running and tripped?" I sat up on my knees, his shirt riding to the tops of my thighs.

I'd been a girl last night and decided his shirt was the only shirt I wanted to wear. The effect had been heady, for both of us, and he'd had me pinned underneath him a second later.

Eyeing my legs, he groaned. His head tipped back. "Shiiiiiiit. You're going to be the death of me." He got up, but grabbed for me.

"What are you doing?"

"I'll go and injure myself, but not before another quick one." He threw me over his shoulder—his back flexing with the minimal effort it took him—and slapped my ass, cradling my cheek to feel it jiggle. "We're taking a shower together."

"You're going to have to shower again."

"I don't care."

When the water was half-warm, he ducked in, taking both of us.

I shrieked, but he slid me down his body, and from there it was quick work. He'd said quickie, so the clothes were ripped off, he was more than hard for me as I wrapped my hand around him, readying him between my legs.

"Fuck." His arms dropped under my thighs, but he reached outside to the counter beside us.

"What are you doi—"

He brought a condom in, ripping it open with his teeth. Like teamwork, I took it and sheathed it over him.

"Fuck. Yeah." He grunted, bouncing me up and catching me by the ass. With my back against the wall, he lowered me. I sank down on him, and then he was in, he paused, his forehead resting just beside my face. We shared a grin as the water rained down on us.

"Ready?" he asked.

"Hmmmm." I'd barely answered before he was moving in me, stretching me, pushing in, pulling out, thrusting back in, rotating his hips to get me from all angles.

Good Lord.

I couldn't catch my breath. We were moving in a rhythm, and he felt so damn good.

"Reese!" I gasped.

His hands flexed on my hips. He dropped his mouth to my shoulder. "You're going to hate me."

"Wha—"

That was my warning, before he was out of me and setting me down on the tile. My feet had only just found their balance and he was turning me around.

"What are you doing?"

He was on his knees, pushing my ass cheeks apart, and then his mouth was there.

I gasped, feeling his mouth and his tongue stroking me. Exploring.

A silent scream began to build. I couldn't keep up with him, and then he was turning me again—to face him—and his mouth returned. He entered me once more, this time with his tongue, his hands holding my thighs apart. A new rhythm began, and I moaned, feeling my entire body slide toward bonelessness.

I was riding his face, and I had to grasp for the showerhead to hold me up.

Reese was relentless, determined to make me come, fast and hard, and with no regard for how that climax would rip me apart. I couldn't hold the scream in this time. It ripped from my throat, and he reached up, his hand clamping over my mouth to stifle the sound. He continued licking me as my trembling began to wane.

"Holy shit." I'd barely breathed out before he was standing again.

I just gave myself over to him, because he was manhandling me once more.

He turned me, pressed me into the shower wall, and angled my hips back. Still with the condom on, he surged inside of me, and I almost sighed from utter contentment. Falling back, my head rested against his shoulder as he pumped into me, one hand holding my hip and the other cupping my breast. He thrust over and over, in and out.

He was riding me now, and I was his.

He kissed my jaw, bending over me. His thumb grazed my nipple, then rolled around to caress my other breast.

I could only gasp. That was all the sound I could make as he brought me to another climax, flooding every inch of my body, and he wasn't far behind. He surged up, and I felt him coming inside of me.

"Fuck." Another kiss to my jaw, then my mouth, as he held me in place.

I couldn't think. I had no idea what had just happened.

He chuckled, the sound soothing and low in my ear as he squeezed me in a hug before pulling out.

"I can't walk."

"No problem." He held me, keeping me pinned against the wall as he reached for the shampoo and soap.

"Are you serious?"

He grinned as he turned me around, face to face again.

I shook my head, taking the shampoo from him. "You move me around like I'm a doll."

He swatted at my ass. "You are a doll. You barely weigh anything. You need more meat on you."

No one, ever, had told me that. My body warmed to it. Then I was putting the shampoo in his hair as he did the same to me. We shampooed, soaped each other, and when we stepped out, it was thirty minutes later.

After both of us finished washing up, he had another hard-on.

I eyed it as I left the bathroom, my teeth nice and brushed. "I'm not joking about your back. They can't know."

His hair was tousled, and I ached to slide my hands through it. But he ducked his head, running a towel over it briskly.

He turned so I could see his back, laying his last remaining towel around his neck. "Are they still bad?"

They weren't as bad, but they were still noticeable. "Yeah."

"Okay. I'll hook up with Aiden before practice, have him cover them with something."

"He'll know."

Reese winked at me. "He'll never tell."

I was struck speechless.

He proceeded to walk around naked, only the towel around his neck. I knew being naked didn't bother professional athletes, but it was still something to get used to.

When I walked out after him, a towel tucked around me, his eyes darkened.

"Why are you wearing that?" He reached for it, and sensing he was going to take it from me, I danced out of the way.

"Uh, no." I swatted at his hand. "Not all of us are so fancy free and comfortable being naked."

He grinned, rummaging in his bag. "You should be. Your body is nice and tight. You look good with clothes on, but you look hot naked." He whistled. "Anytime you're over and feel the itch to embrace being nude, you're more than welcome."

He waited for my reaction, side-eyeing me as he pulled out his clothes for the first part of the day. He was reaching for his shorts, but paused. "I forgot. We have meetings this morning. I'll still have Aiden put ointment on them, but they'll be gone by afternoon when we do drills. We'll be good."

That should've been a relief, but I was still caught on his casual mention of coming over to his place.

I sat on the bed Reese usually used, tucking my hands under my legs. "So... um..."

He stilled, watching me, a wary look in his eyes. "No."

"No?"

"No." He shook his head. "I recognize that look. It's the thinking look. Don't think. We're having fun, right? That's all. We're friends."

"We're friends who fucked." I remembered all the times. "A lot."

His mouth curved in a rakish grin. "And it was awesome. I'm hoping to do it again, and often, but I don't want to do the talk. I hate having the talks."

"The talks?"

He scoffed, pulling his pants on. He turned to find his socks and step into his shoes. "You know what I'm talking about."

"The talk," I repeated.

Then I remembered it was morning. He was getting ready to go to breakfast—breakfast I usually helped set up.

I shrieked, jumping to my feet. "I'm so late!"

"No one's using the courts."

"I help with the food. You know that."

"But you don't have to. You're not going to get in trouble for missing once."

I threw clothes in the air, grabbing for what I thought would fit. Somehow I ended up in shorts I wasn't sure were mine, a tank top that dipped too low over my cleavage, and I had no clue where my socks were, so I grabbed for my sandals.

"Nope."

I was about to dash out the door, my phone in hand when Reese caught me by the waist and pulled me back.

He tugged at my shirt. "You're not wearing that."

"What?" I looked down. "It's a bit much, but it's still cold. I'll cover up with a sweatshirt."

"I don't care. If you forget and take that off, people will see all this." He took my tank off, then flicked at some of the hickeys he'd left behind.

I'd forgotten.

Then I started laughing. "Hickeys. Could you have—"

Reese held back his grin as he handed me a different shirt. "Wear that. No one will see my handiwork, and no, I liked marking you." His gaze darkened as he watched me pull the shirt over my head, then down and over my bra. "There you go. Nice and covered." He swatted at my ass. "See you in about thirty minutes."

Thirty minutes. I stifled another shriek and hurried out of there.

It wasn't until I was almost to the main lodge that I looked at what shirt he'd given me. His.

CHAPTER TWENTY-SIX

I turned the shirt inside out, but even the tag in the back had a Seattle Thunder emblem on it. A lightning bolt.

Hadley and Owen were the only ones who saw it, and I caught the raised eyebrows, but that was it. Both kept silent except for one lone whistle from Hadley, which sounded at the same time Reese walked into the cafeteria. Juan was with him, and both looked over at me.

I busied myself with the dishes.

What do I do? Say hi? Look like a clinger already? Yes. My basic roots were fangirling and stalkerish, but I really wasn't that.

Work. I was here to do a job, so after I did a certain amount of dishes, I grabbed some toast and snuck out through Owen's office. I really loved that he had two entrances. The team was still eating when I popped into the office.

Ugh. *So* not a normal morning. I did not *ever* seek Keith out, but I had to today.

"Keith."

"Hmm?" He popped out from around the back office corner. His Boss mug was still on the counter. I've no doubt he never had it cleaned. He could've asked Owen to run it through for him, but that wasn't my concern this morning.

"Is the team using the gyms this morning?"

"Uh…" He had to think, his curly hair slightly damp from his shower. "No. They're doing meetings this morning."

Sweet. That meant a morning off.

I was slipping back out when he called my name. "Hey, Charlie! Wait. One sec."

Now wary, I eased back into the office, keeping the door open and one foot outside. "Yeah?"

He shifted, staring at me a moment. A cough. He tugged his collar around. "You're doing a good job, and I want you to know I've really appreciated all the extra help you've been doing around here. The board too."

He was being kind.

He was smiling at me, and it wasn't creeping me out.

But it was setting different alarms off in me, because this was not Keith. He wasn't kind. Ever.

"But?" I was readying myself.

He stroked his jaw, an uneasy guffaw leaving him. "Uh, but. Yes. But,.. I got a call from one of the board members last night, and I guess you weren't approved to be on staff during this time. We only have enough funds to cover your first two weeks here."

My first two weeks... That would've ended three days ago.

"Are you kidding? I'm not getting paid for this week?"

"Well, it's only been a couple days that you won't have been paid, and the team wasn't here, so technically, you shouldn't have been doing any work anyway. But yes." He moved closer to me, rolling his shoulders back, sucking his gut in. He began to tap on the counter, his nervous habit. "So what I'm saying is that—"

I was out of a job.

"I'll be manning the gyms for the next two days. I mean, it's really only today. They'll be leaving in the morning." He reached into his pocket and slid a check over to me. "Here you go. And we really do appreciate all the help you gave the kitchen too."

Really? I had no words. None at all, and because of that, I just stepped back, let the door slam shut, and I walked out. Unfuckingbelievable.

"You okay?"

Reese was coming out from the cafeteria.

I didn't look up. "No."

"Forster!" one of his teammates yelled.

I looked now. He stood in the hallway, concern etched over his face.

"Reese." His coach stepped up, putting a hand on his shoulder. "We gotta go. We have a meeting with the other coaches."

But he wasn't looking at Reese. He was watching me. There was a gravity in his gaze, but not the caution I saw last night.

I got it then.

This wasn't Keith. This wasn't the board. This was Reese's coach. He knew. Somehow he knew about us, and he was putting a stop to us in his way. He was pushing me out.

There was a warning in his gaze, his mouth thinning as if knowing I connected the pieces.

"Yeah. Okay." Reese was reluctant to go. He glanced back to me. "Charlie? You want to talk later?"

It felt final. All of this. The firing. Reese would be in meetings the rest of the morning. I could feel my bank account dipping lower every minute I stayed here. And I hadn't done anything I'd set out to do. Well, I'd written one night. But the reprieve from reality was gone. Whatever friendship I had with Reese, I'd have to see what happened, but I knew I couldn't stick around. I couldn't afford to stick around.

And I had a feeling Coach Winston would find a way to get me kicked off the island if I tried to.

"Yeah. Talk later." I attempted a smile.

It was enough to appease Reese, more because another two of his teammates were calling his name now. They all walked past us, heading outside and up to the meeting hall. Coach Winston waited until Reese was gone and the last of his team had filtered past us.

"If one of them knew, and if one of them was unhappy with our team, they could leak you and Reese to the tabloids. It'd be that easy. His name's already being put through the ringer because of his brother. We came here to protect him, and to keep him focused. I know he's a grown man, but he's *my* player. I have to look out for him." He paused a second. "You understand, don't you?"

I held up my check. "I came here for two reasons. One, because I'd just gotten fired, and two, to try to get my life back on track somehow because my dementia-boyfriend dumped me during one of his rare lucid moments. He kicked me out the apartment and his life, and I've been floundering ever since. That stopped here, because of Reese. And now I got fired again."

I looked at the dollar amount on the check and started laughing. It barely covered half a month's rent. It was less than what Keith first promised me.

"Here." I pressed it to his chest, passing him by. "I'm sure that's what you make in ten minutes. Have a couple coffees on me."

I'd gone a few steps outside before I had to stop and bend over.

I was going to throw up.

The world began to swim around me.

I was having a panic attack. I recognized the symptoms, and damn, these were a bitch.

I couldn't... I had to—one foot in front of the other. Breathe. Breathe. Breathe.

It hurt. I was moving against cement in the air, but I had to keep going.

I was dizzy and sweating, and when I glimpsed myself in the mirror back at Reese's cabin, I wasn't surprised. I looked like a ghost, but I didn't have time to stop and take shelter while this storm passed. I had to get out. Too much of life had taken a shit on me.

The amazing sex... I couldn't stay just for that. My pride was shredded. I just wanted to grab my stuff, get to my car, and leave. I'd send my goodbyes later.

I was running. I was doing it all over again, but my God, I had just been booted from my old place of employment—after being told I'd worked there three days for free. Keith was a dick, but he'd never made me feel unwelcome here. It took good ol' Coach Winston to do that.

I bit back tears as I filled my bag. Then I wavered. I did still have things in the fishing cabin, but I couldn't bring myself to go in there to pack it all up.

I was telling myself that as I walked the north path that wound around the lodge, bypassed all the buildings, and came out just beyond the parking lot. I told myself I didn't have the energy to explain to Owen and Hadley what had happened. They'd be angry. They'd rally around me, but for what?

I'd been dismissed because I was a liability to someone more powerful than all of us.

It felt like the world had stomped on me once again, but this time was different. I wasn't shattered by trying to hold Reese up. It wasn't that situation at all.

Unlocking my car, I tossed my bags in the back and got behind the wheel.

I had to reassess the situation.

I was exaggerating, reacting because of how final it all felt. That was it. That was all. This was not the end of the world.

I'd been fired. So what? I'd come here for the specific purpose of having a place to run away from my current life. Which I did. That'd been successful.

I'd wanted to reconnect with some of my old friends. Mission accomplished. I wouldn't text or email. I would call Owen and Hadley to say my goodbyes. I would call Grant—oh shit. Grant. I'd forgotten. And Trent! Trent was coming tonight. He was expecting to have dinner.

Then there was Reese.

I couldn't tell any of them why I was let go. It was because of Reese, and if I told them, they'd just have to look at me to know things had gone past friendship.

They would know.

They couldn't know.

I sat in my car, and I had no idea what to say to my friends.

I'd have to use Keith's excuse: the board hadn't approved my employment past the first two weeks. And in that case, the job was done. Whatever.

This was no big deal.

Right? I mean...

I came for a job, and it turned out that job was done. That was it. That was all.

I should've stayed and said goodbye in person. I'd left everyone, Reese too.

What do I do? How do I clean up this mess?

My phone buzzed. I tensed, but it wasn't who I thought it'd be. I almost started laughing.

Unknown: I have some of your stuff. Went to drop it off at your job, but the chick at the front said you don't work there any more. You got fired?

Of all the timing, *now* he texted me? Now?

I might still have been slightly hysterical, because I called him back.

"You got fired from that stank-ass place?" he said when he answered.

"Hi, Lucas. I'm fine. How are you?" I sighed. "You're right. Normal, pleasant greetings are a waste of time. Get right down to business. Yes, they fired me the same day your grandpa dumped me, and yes, I just got fired from the new job. I'm sitting outside a hotel, not sure what the hell to do anymore."

He was quiet for a moment. "You have enough for rent?"

"I have a small bit to cover a few months, but coming here wasn't such a good idea after all." I laughed, the sound so pitiful. "You take in homeless people? Because I don't know if my mom's going to let me stay at home rent-free this time. She wasn't really up for it last time."

"It's not my house. You know that."

Right. Of course. Why would he be decent?

The tears began. I mean, why even fight them? They were my old friends by now.

"Yeah, okay. You're right."

"Look. If Gramps didn't own it—but you know he's particular about who stays here and I—"

"So you have stuff of mine?"

"Oh. Yeah." He sounded stiff. "Just a couple things. Like some old sweatshirts. A Forster shirt. I know you loved it. A couple mugs. Nothing big."

"The same Reese Forster shirt your gramps was wearing when he propositioned me?"

"Uh..." His laugh was strangled. "I can't promise he cleaned it."

"Oh, for fuck's sakes. Just donate it to Goodwill. Hell. Maybe I can get it there at the rate I'm going."

"Uh..."

I heard someone call his name in the background, a female someone.

"Uh, I gotta go. You sure about donating? Tracy can drop it off at your place, if you're going to be around."

"Is that the new girlfriend?"

"Yeah. She's..." His voice lowered, getting closer to the phone. "She's not the one, you know."

"Right. Not the one you cheated on me with. She's even newer than that one."

"She's nice. Sweet." He chuckled. "I think you'd like her even."

I rolled my eyes. "Yeah. Sure. Maybe."

"So, um, when will you be around?"

It was close to ten by now. The drive back would take four hours. "I'll be there this evening. Anytime after six."

"Okay. I'll call you when she's headed over."

"Don't call." Never call again, in fact. "A text will do."

And after hanging up with him, I texted Owen, Hadley, Grant, and Trent all the same message.

Me: Keith said the board didn't have enough funds to pay me, so I packed up my stuff. I'm heading back to try to find a job. If you guys want, come and hang out! I love visitors. Sorry I didn't stick around to say goodbye. Hope you understand.

And to Reese.

Me: I was fired. I got the feeling your coach didn't want me around, so I'm heading back to my place. I need to look for a new job. Call later when you have time?

I didn't expect immediate responses from anyone, so I turned the engine back on, tossed my phone to the seat beside me, and raised the volume on the radio.

It was going to be a painful drive back.

CHAPTER TWENTY-SEVEN

B y that night, I'd come to two main conclusions.

I was the definition of a broke-ass bitch, and I'd been ambitious in thinking my friends would care about my most recent firing.

I had heard from no one. Not a one. My phone was silent the entire drive back, and through the entire evening since. The only text I got was when Luc-ass told me his new girlfriend was heading over with a box of my stuff.

I was ready to let loose, but when I opened the door, the sweetest petite little thing stood on the other side. Lucas was such a dick, because I knew that'd been his goal. He wanted to avoid me, and he knew I wouldn't be able to tear into her.

He was right. She was super sweet, and once she was gone, I had to face the music.

My friends' silence aside, I had just enough money to cover three months of rent. What had I been thinking accepting Trent's proposal to work at camp for the last few weeks? I hadn't been thinking. That's right—I'd been drinking. I was dumped and fired, all in the span of twenty-four hours. But reality was back, and I had to get my shit together.

If I didn't shape up, I had no idea where I could ship myself to.

My parents'? Someone's couch? My car?

It could be a new, sad drinking game. Take a drink wherever you end up, and then just get sauced because what's a better way to handle it?

Sighing, I opened my laptop and clicked on the classifieds.

Five job applications filled out later, I couldn't deny as I was getting ready for bed. I was hurt. I thought one of my friends would've texted—Reese at least. My phone was still blank when I climbed into bed. I turned it off, then on again, just making sure, but it showed the same thing: no incoming texts or calls, and it had worked earlier with Loser Ex, so it was working.

Still. Because I never liked to admit defeat, I texted Reese.

Me: No words? Are you mad at me?

I waited, and five minutes went by. Ten. I brushed a tear away at the twenty-minute mark.

One hour later, I had my answer.

He wasn't going to respond.

CHAPTER TWENTY-EIGHT

B*ANG! BANG! BANG!*
I fell out of bed, no joke.

I'd been starting to wake up. I was stretching and scooting to the end of the bed. Then BANG, BANG, BANG, and off I fell.

Hello, floor.

I winced, rubbing my elbow. That hurt, but then the banging on my door started again.

"You took my phone!" a voice yelled.

That was Reese and, oh shit—had I?

I hurried to the front door. My neighbors were hardcore Thunder fans. If they were home, they would recognize Reese's voice. They watched every one of his interviews on ESPN. I knew, because I could hear them blasting them from their computer at all hours of the day. I used to think I was dedicated, but they put me to shame.

Flinging open the door, I grabbed him. "Stop talking."

He was alone.

He was glaring, and he was pissed. Really pissed. His jaw was doing the clenching thing too.

"What?"

"You fucking left, that's what!"

Oh. He did care. I bit my lip to stop a grin from showing.

"I texted you what happened."

"Yeah." He scoffed, starting to go through my apartment.

Finding my bedroom, he went in and began pulling items out of my bag. I hadn't unpacked, like, at all. I still had on the clothes I'd left camp in. I just hadn't had it in me to take off his shirt, and he noticed, his scowl lessening, but then he pulled out a pair of shorts I hadn't realized I'd grabbed.

"A-ha." He pulled his phone out of the pocket and tried to turn it on. "It's dead."

Crap. I felt a pounding behind my temples and rubbed there. "Sorry. It must've been with the pile of my clothes. I was packing in a hurry." *And I was slightly hysterical at the time.* "Oops."

He didn't answer. Seeing my charger, he took my phone off and put his phone on. When it started charging, he turned back to me, his arms crossed over his chest.

"That crisis is averted. Now you want to tell me what the fuck happened?" His eyebrows went up. "Because I have news to share with you also—news about you."

"Me?"

"Yeah." He yawned. "But I need coffee first. Your friends showed up at my cabin, pounding on the door. Then I had to go and pound on Coach's door, and there was a fucking early-ass meeting this morning. I had to promise two extra charity events before Coach let me come here today and not leave with the team."

My head was spinning. "What are you talking about?"

Reese ignored me, going into my kitchen. My coffee pot wasn't on, so he began looking through my cupboards. "Where's your coffee?"

I moved him aside, ignoring the tingle at just feeling him again, being so close to him again, and pointed to the table. "Sit. I'll do this. You tell me what happened."

He went over and sat down. "You tell me first, because I think what I have to say is going to take longer."

I pulled out the coffee, put in a new filter. "Nothing really major. Keith told me the board hadn't approved me working there, so they only had the funds to cover me for two weeks. So, you know, I was fired. Then I came out and your coach was there. I thought maybe it was him behind it, which he confirmed when you left. He wanted me gone, and to be honest, I kinda understand why. He was protecting you."

"Yeah, well, he feels like a dumbass."

Pouring water into the machine, I hit brew and went to a chair across from Reese. Tugging my knees up, I hugged them to me. "What do you mean?"

"He told me in the afternoon what he'd done and wanted to apologize. The reason he did it was justified—we already knew that—but the way he did it was dickish. I went to my cabin to call you, saw your shit gone, and couldn't find my phone. I went to find your friends and discovered them having a little meeting in the kitchen guy's back office. They were upset."

I swallowed over a knot. "At me?"

"They didn't say that, but they asked if I'd be willing to speak about why you were staying in my cabin if they needed me. I told them I'd more than say a few things, and my coach too. After that, I decided just to wait till we were done, then try to bargain a deal with Coach to let me come here and get my phone."

The coffee was starting to brew.

"You said my friends came to your cabin in the middle of the night?"

He nodded. "They had to wait until another guy showed up, the speaker dude, but they'd convened the board and had them willing to do some form of emergency meeting about your boss."

"Keith?" I leaned forward.

The coffee was ready to pour, but I was on the edge of my seat. How had this all gone down when I wasn't there?! The laws of karma were not on my side.

"They were so mad about what he did to you, what he'd done to you the whole time you were there, that they got fed up."

I might've been wrong about karma.

"They called the board and there was a five-am video conference. They wanted to do it before your boss got in."

Reese's eyes flashed, and his jaw was like cement. He leaned forward, his gaze holding mine captive. "I sat there and I listened as your friends ran through a list of shitty things your boss had done, and not just these last two weeks, but for years. And you were the subject of several of the items. The fucker sexually harassed you? You mentioned him making comments, but nothing like what I heard. How he radioed you on the camp radio where everyone could hear, asking if you were making out with your boyfriend? How you walked into a meeting with another guy behind you, and he accused you both of screwing around in the woods? I listened to your friends explain to a room of old, white fat dudes how the 'boyfriend' had only held your hand once, and you'd only 'dated' for two days, and you'd literally just walked into the meeting at the same time as the other guy. And there was more."

His nostrils flared. Shoving back from his chair, he began to pace: around my living room, back to the kitchen, and around to the living room again. He kept moving, his hands unfisting and fisting in front of him.

"After they got through their sixteen-page fucking memo, complete with names and phone numbers and taped testimony from others, they got to me. I had to sit there and first deal with their fanning, which was fine, but then the leers. When I told them how you and I became friends, how I was at your cabin—fuck those leers. I could feel the dirtiness coming off of them. They didn't seem to care until I told them I'd gone into your cabin. That got their fucking attention. I went to grab the rest of your stuff. Juan tried too. We both got sick. That's what made them perk up. They seemed resigned to the shitty stuff your boss had already done, but they didn't start sweating until they heard that two pro ball players got sick from entering a cabin that *wasn't* condemned on their property."

Icy dread lined my spine. "Did you tell them about us?"

He snorted. "Hell no. All your credibility would've been gone. You'd have to be a goddamn nun, do charity events twenty-four seven, openly donate all of your earnings to God, and maybe *then* they might give you the benefit of the doubt. I'm sorry, but that sucks. That really fucking sucks."

I sank as far down on my chair as I could get. I was almost in a ball.

He didn't know. He couldn't understand what his words were

doing, how I never would've been believed, but now I was?

I pressed my forehead to my knees, feeling tears on my face once again.

I was so sick of it.

I was so sick of life, and that hadn't hit me until Reese laid it all out.

All of that I'd lived. All of that I still carried. All of that, alone, just on me.

I'd never told anyone, not Damian, not my family. Everyone had heard when it happened, but no one said a thing. Why would I have bothered to tell anyone else? Why would anyone believe me?

Until now.

Reese kept pacing. I could see him swinging his arms around from the corner of my eye. He was rolling his shoulders like he was warming up for a game.

"Coach spoke, and he backed up your claim about not having a place to sleep. He said he brought it up to your boss, and he'd said just what you told us he would. He'd have you stay in that janitor's closet. No one should sleep in a janitor's closet. And all the extra work you did? You worked from when you woke up, till I made you leave the gyms at night. You never got paid for all of that."

He snorted. "And you know what their first response was? That manning the gym courts wasn't extensive physical labor. That was their justification. That place sucks. Why in the world did you work there in the first place?"

He stopped now, waiting, focusing on me.

I lifted my head and rolled one shoulder back. "Because my friends were there. Because at one point, they were a second family to me."

His eyes swept over my face, and he cursed under his breath.

Crossing the room in two strides, he bent and picked me up.

I went willingly, my arms and legs wrapping around him, just like on that wooded path two nights ago. He carried me to the living room, sat us on the couch, and hugged me. His head burying in my neck.

"I don't have the words to take away what happened to you, but I can tell you what happened because of your friends rallying around you."

I sat back, wanting to see him when he told me.

He tucked a strand of my hair behind my ear. "Your boss was canned. I spoke up, saying I'd only consider coming back to your camp if your friend Owen took that dickhead's spot. Coach backed me up on that, just saying we'd consider it. I'm not saying they hired him based on our recommendations, but I think it helped a little."

"So you're saying…"

"Your friend Owen is the new director at that place. And they hired your friend Grant to take Owen's spot. I don't know what it was, because he was in the kitchen the whole time I was there, but they all seemed happy about it. They made another move to hire you as their head of publicity. Apparently you're good at that stuff?"

I frowned. I was? "If I am, that's news to me. What'd they say?"

"They approved it, and I told them what my publicist makes and not to take that position for granted. You could do a lot with publicity, so I guess if you want it, you have a job with them?"

"What'd they say the salary would be?"

Really? Was I going to be picky?

"I don't know. I just know your friend suggested you, and they approved offering you a job. I had to promise all your friends tickets to the next local game for them to let me come see you first."

"What?" I shoved back from him, already turning for the door.

"Relax." He chuckled, his hands moving down my back, pulling me close. "I got the night. They'll show up in the morning, when I go to the airport. I worked it out with them."

This was all happening so fast.

Still on his lap, I leaned back, dazed. "I went to bed last night worried about a job and a place to live, and now all of this? If they offer me a job, I'll have to move there, but even staying in Fairview, the rent will be cheaper than anything here in the city."

I couldn't believe it.

And Reese was here. And he wasn't mad at me, just irritated, then mad *for* me.

I started crying.

Big surprise there.

"What? This is all good, right?" He brought his thumbs to my face, wiping tears away.

"I think it's just a conditioned response. Anything happens, and it was the questions. Now it's this. I'm evolving."

I think...

But I was laughing and smiling, and I couldn't believe it. "Am I going to wake up and all of this will be gone?"

Reese smirked, bringing his palm up to my face, wiping the last tear away. "Nah, but can we skip some of the other formalities, because I only have the rest of the day and night with you...if you know what I mean."

I nodded, and he picked me up.

He took me to bed.

CHAPTER
TWENTY-NINE

Later that evening, after the bed, the shower, the couch, and back to the bed, we ordered pizza. The delivery guy left after a full-out gushing moment over Reese, who had answered the door before I could offer to get it first. He'd paid for the pizza, signed an autograph, and declined a selfie before I came out of the bedroom fully dressed. Only going around in shorts had its benefits—one was getting the door first.

After we began eating, which I insisted we do at the table, I asked a question. "How'd you know something was going on yesterday?"

He picked up a slice, folding it and lounging back in his chair. His legs kicked out under the table. "I guessed something was up, but I figured I couldn't do anything till you came to see me. You never did, so I asked Coach. He told me what happened—oh, and I have that check for you. When he looked at it, he felt bad, said no one should earn that little after working morning to night like he knew you did."

He gazed over his pizza at me, his grin wolfish. "You're a hot chick who knows basketball. Okay, that's not that rare, but you're a girl who gets noticed. We all saw you doing dishes when we came in for breakfast, and you closed the courts at night. You're a hard worker, and you never complained about it."

"I still can't believe what you said happened." I'd checked my phone. There'd only been a call for a job interview. "Are you sure? My friends are really coming tomorrow?"

He nodded, biting into his pizza. He chewed. He swallowed. "Trust me. It wasn't just four tickets I gave away. Two of the guys wanted another for a date. That made six tickets, plus one for you because there's no way your friends are coming and you aren't. I made them promise that part, even if they had to drag you there."

"You really think I wouldn't want to go to your game?"

He snorted, grabbing his water bottle. "By now, who knows with you. You didn't want your friends to know about our friendship. We're fucking, and you're aghast at anyone knowing. I had no clue what you'd do if I invited you to a game."

"I *am* a basketball fanatic." I pointed toward my bedroom. "You gave me a shirt to wear, and a sweatshirt. If you think you're getting either of those back, think again, buddy." I snorted and couldn't dim my grin. "It's like you don't know me."

Sex, food, and feeling wanted went a long way toward making this person happy.

I stared at Reese, really seeing him. He was here. He'd come after me. He'd fought for me. He screwed me six ways to Sunday, and oh so amazingly. Yeah. I'm pretty sure I was glowing at this point.

He stared back, his gaze growing somber. Putting his bottle back on the table, he twisted the cap on it and cleared his throat. That was his signal. We were going serious.

"I know I put off having the talk, but I didn't realize you'd hightail it out of there two hours later. Based on our history..." He adjusted in his seat, squirming. "Maybe we should have the talk."

Oh boy.

Deep breaths.

A whole new churning started in my gut.

He opened his mouth, but I stopped him. I had to go first, especially with this one.

"You know I have baggage. Caregiving for someone who wanted to deny he was losing his mind, that's a lot. For me. For the next guy. For anyone." I pulled my knees up again, pressing them against my chest. "I went to camp a little out of my mind—I'll be honest. I think I've been out of my mind for a while. But at some point these last few weeks, I started talking about Damian. Not just to you, though you got the most, but to the others too. Grant knows. Now Owen and Hadley do too. No one knew what I was going through for all those years. Damian wouldn't let me tell anyone. We had to pretend everything was normal, when it was so *not* normal, and I slipped away. Little by little. Every day. I'm just now starting to feel like a person again. You're part of the reason for that, but..."

I was so stupid. I knew it, but I had to say this.

"I can't be anything right now. I can be a friend, but anything more? I can't take that on. I will never lose myself to a guy again, ever. And I don't know what you're going to say, but that's what I had to say first."

He stared at me long and hard before scooting his chair back so he could lean his elbows on his knees. "I will tell you this. I like our friendship."

"I do too."

"And I really like fucking you."

I grinned. "I do too." But then my smile dimmed. "But not if you're dipping in others." That was a deal breaker for me.

He lowered his head. "Got it. Okay, I will not screw anyone, except when I see you. Then I'll screw you."

I nodded. Such crude words, but that was what we needed. Those words held no emotional attachment, and the only attachment I could handle was what we were spelling out right now.

"So..." I sat up, lowering my feet back to the ground. "Still friends?"

His head bounced up and down once. He laid his hand out on the table for me, palm up.

"And we have sex when we see each other?"

He nodded again. "And neither of us does that with anyone else. It has to go both ways. I'm all about female sexual equality, so I know you ladies get as horny as we do." He wiggled his fingers at me. "Deal?"

I started to reach for his hand, but paused. "Should we be ironing out how often we see each other? How often we talk to each other?"

He stood abruptly. "Shake my damn hand, woman. Friends is friends. We talk as much as we can, and we see each other as much as we can."

"Deal." I reached over and slapped his hand.

"Oh no!" He caught my hand, reaching out and lifting me clear of the table and into his arms.

It was exhilarating and terrifying at the same time. He made me feel like I could soar, but he could drop me so fast.

"Christ, you make me work to get in your pants." But he was grinning as his mouth found mine. He took me back to the bedroom, and once we got there, he laid me down on the bed, holding himself above me. "You have to promise I can fly you out, because I'm going to be traveling a lot. During season, it's nuts. I won't get here that often."

I framed his face. "You're so cute, acting like I'm not a basketball groupie."

A twisted laugh ripped from him, but his eyes were back to darkening. "You are definitely not a groupie." His hand moved down my side, slipping under my shirt and smoothing up to cup my breast. His thumb rubbed over my nipple. "I know you like to joke about that stuff, but do me a favor? Stop with the bad talk. Stop calling yourself a stalker, groupie, and whatever else you think is funny but is just a put-down. Only I can use those as endearments. Got it?"

I stilled, swallowing. He watched me, affection warming his eyes, but there was more—an emotion that had my pulse spiking because I didn't want to name it, or feel it, but it was there.

As I whispered a yes, his mouth found mine.

I closed my eyes, giving myself over to him, and I tried to forget what I'd seen. Because if I didn't, I couldn't stay with him. I'd just ruin everything.

Instead of thinking, I wound my arms around his neck. I opened my legs as he settled over me, and I pushed down his shorts.

Condom on, he slid inside me moments later.
I forgot everything else.

CHAPTER THIRTY

Reese's alarm went off at four, and just as he rolled out of bed, I caught his arm.

"Hey, go back to sleep."

"No." My eyelids couldn't open. I was seriously tired, but I was determined. "Cancel your driver. I'll take you to the airport."

"No. Go to sleep. I'll just slip out." He bent down, pressing a kiss to the side of my mouth. "For real. It's ungodly to be up at this hour. Rest till your friends get here."

Did he not... He didn't. It was official. I needed to introduce myself again.

I growled, lightly shoved his head away, and swung my feet down. I was at least sitting now, but yeah—eyes still not open. Around a yawn, I tried to be fiercer. "I said I'd drive you. Airporaaaaah," I yawned, "is five minutes from here." Okay. I just needed to rub my eyes a little, and then they'd open.

He chuckled, bending close again. He placed another soft kiss on my forehead before he pushed his finger there, easing me back down. "Go to bed, psycho. I have a driver coming."

"No."

I was determined.

Pride. Stubbornness. All of my superhero qualities.

There. I got my eyes open, and whoa—it was so dark out. He was right. No one should be up at this time, but he was, so I was. He still wavered over me. I pushed him aside and scooted to the bathroom first.

"Are you for real?" His exasperation was evident.

"Yes," I yelled over, peeing. A quick wash. Teeth. I splashed my face a little, then I opened the door and waved him in. "Go. Get ready. I'll put on coffee. You canceled your driver, right?"

He growled as he grabbed for his phone.

I pulled on clothes. I wasn't even looking, but it might not have been a coincidence when I grabbed one of his sweatshirts. I had a problem, a sweatshirt problem. Pretty sure I could've started a support group, because I know I wasn't alone.

Slipping some shoes on, I got the coffee going, and had a cup ready for him when he was done. Keys. Phone. Purse. I was set. Black leggings on, his sweatshirt over, and my hair up in a messy bun, I was sure I was the epitome of beauty. *Not.* I didn't care. The coffee gave me points.

He came out, all ready, saw me, and shook his head.

Giving him the biggest smile I could muster, I handed over his coffee and dangled my keys. "Let's go."

My neighbor was coming home from his night shift at a factory. He was trudging down the hallway when he saw us, lifted a hand in greeting, then stopped. His head shot upright and his shoulders stiffened.

He rotated swiftly on his heels, his eyes wide and bulging. He held up a hand. "Is that—"

"No." Lying. Another superhero quality of mine. "It's late, Bill. That's my brother."

Reese squashed a laugh and nodded to the guy. "What's up." It wasn't a question, but a greeting, and he hustled me past my neighbor.

I gave Reese a look as we went to my underground parking spot. "He's going to hammer me later. He'll know he wasn't seeing things."

"He's a fan?"

"The biggest."

Reese smirked, meeting my gaze over the top of my car. "Bigger than you?"

We were entering cheesy couple territory here. We needed to scale it back.

"I have a cardboard cutout of you," I told him. "In my closet."

He froze. "You're joking."

I was, but now I had to buy one. "Wouldn't you like to think that." Settling into my chair, I felt better—more familiar terrain again. "But the funny thing is, next time you come, you won't know if I was serious or if I bought him after I told you."

Reese just rolled his eyes, putting the coffees in the cup holders for both of us.

He was looking around as I pulled out of the lot. "This is actually a nice place."

"The underground parking is nice. The apartment building itself is okay. Nothing great." I didn't tell him how the lights in the laundry room would dim, so if I used those machines, I had to prop the door open with a rock. Or how I'd only do my clothes between seven in the morning and nine. Nine was the latest. After that, people were stirring, and there were a few neighbors I wasn't so sure about.

Reese whistled as I pulled up to departures seven minutes later. "You weren't kidding. That's close."

"And you've barely had your coffee."

He yawned now, blinking a few times. "I'll grab some inside. You can have it."

I parked, but didn't shut off the engine.

"Do not get out," he warned.

I grinned. "Wasn't planning on it. We really don't need to go to that level, with the hugging, would we kiss or not... Too many strings, *friend*."

He smiled back, but his eyes had started to smolder a bit. He leaned over, dropping his voice, "I'll answer one of those questions." His lips caught mine in a good, firm kiss, one that sent my senses spiraling and stole just the slightest bit of oxygen from my lungs.

I might've needed to gather my bearings as he pulled back and grabbed his bag from the back. Before he turned, he gave me a second kiss, this one lighter. "Go home. Go to bed," he said as he reached for the door. "Text me when you park, and again when you're inside your place. Humor me. I'm a friend. I can care."

He was starting to leave, but I tugged on his shirt.

He paused, looking back.

"And after that?" I asked.

"We're friends. Let's play it by ear."

Our gazes held, a shared reminder of the other details in our agreement. I saw his darkening, so I let go. "Okey-dokey. Hope you don't get mauled."

He laughed. "It's too early for that."

But we both knew the truth. It could happen.

As if reading my mind, he amended, "It's usually not that bad. If it is—and I don't think it will be—airport security is good with celebrities here. They've got a special room and everything. Plus..." He reached in his bag and pulled out a baseball hat, dragging it low over his eyes and flicking up his hood. "This is pretty incognito."

His height wasn't, but I decided to pick my battles. "I'll expect twenty questions by the time you land."

He laughed. "Don't think so. I'm going to be sleeping that whole time, but I'll text you updates just to annoy you." He got out, but bent back down, his tone more serious. "Do me a favor? Only take that job if you want it. Don't take it because you feel desperate. I can loan you money, if anything."

That wiped all joking aside. "Reese." Dammit. "I'll never lose myself in a guy again. Ever."

"Yeah, but before you didn't have a friend who could loan you money until you got to a place where you *could* pick something that actually made you happy." His eyes flashed a warning. "Now you do. Just think about it. It's a loan. I'd give one to another friend in the same spot."

I rolled my eyes.

He chuckled. "Drive safe. I liked screwing you. Let's do it again and *soon*."

"I changed my mind. Get mauled!"

I could hear his laugh as he shut the door and headed inside, his bag over his shoulder. Only a couple guys squinted at him, their heads cocked to the side. He was right. His incognito look really was incognito, but he was still frustrating.

And I was hoping for the *soon* too.

Driving back, my phone kept buzzing.

Reese: Checking in.

Reese: I had to check my bag. It's too big for a carry-on.

Reese: Two autographs.

Reese: Going up the escalator now.

Reese: At the security line. The guards are cool. They promised not to be angry when Thunder beats the Coyotes.

Reese: Through security.

He knew I couldn't answer. I was driving.

Reese: I'm at gate A6.

Reese: This is a nice airport. I always forget till I get here.

Reese: I upgraded to first class.

Reese: Coach wants to make sure I get back in time for meetings this morning.

Reese: Still not boarding. Just letting you know.

After parking, I grabbed my phone.

Me: It's supposed to be questions. Like, if I asked security if I could put a body in my bag, could I still check it? Questions like that. You're not following the rules.

Reese: Fuck the rules. These are my rules.

Reese: You do questions. I do updates. Deal with it.

Reese: Except now. Are you back at your place?

Me: Yes. Walking upstairs now.

Reese: No updates from you. Well. Yes. Tell me when you get in your place.

I turned down my hallway. Bill's door opened and his head popped out. His hair was scruffed up like he'd been trying for a Mohawk. "No bullshit. Was that him?"

I was about to break a fellow Reese Forster fan's heart. "It was my brother."

He glared. "You're not fucking with me?"

"No."

"Oh."

That was it.

His head went back in, and he slammed his door shut.

Immediately Mrs. Rings yelled from her apartment across the hall. "STOP SLAMMING THE DOORS! EVERYONE FUCKING SHUT IT!"

And her parrot a second later.

"STOP SLAMMING FUCKING SHUT IT!"

And then, "SHUT IT, BORIS!"

And her parrot again, "EVERYONE FUCK IT AND GO TO SLEEP!"

My phone kept buzzing. I didn't read them, just typed back.

Me: In my place. I lied to Bill, broke my heart to do it.

Reese: He'll get over it. There'll be other chances for you to lie again.

Reese: They're letting me board early. For this time, there's a lot of ball supporters here.

Me: The life of a celebrity. Poor you.

Reese: Image of me giving you the middle finger.

Me: Image of my big toe.

Reese: What the fuck is that?

Me: Now you won't be able to stop wondering. Okay. I'm going back to bed.

Reese: Turn your phone off so I can keep sending you updates while you sleep.

Me: Shouldn't you try to sleep too?

Reese: Yeah, but in case I can't. Your friends said they'd just show up and bang on your door anyway, so sleep. For real. Turn your phone off.

Me: It's like you care about me. Friend.

Reese: Don't do that. But I care about certain activities with you. How about that? Better?

I laughed, and something settled in me. I wasn't going to question it. It'd been with me since we woke up—an uneasiness sitting on my stomach.

This might've been a good feeling, but I was scared to feel it. Even while we were doing the jokes, the teasing, using the crude words, that feeling wouldn't dislodge.

Whatever it was, it was there, and I knew when it left, I would miss it.

I typed back.

Me: Turning phone off. I care about fucking you too.

But I didn't turn my phone off. I silenced it, left it on, and propped it so it was facing me.

The screen lit up as his texts came in, and that unsettled feeling became more permanent.

CHAPTER
THIRTY-ONE

It was two weeks later and I still hadn't made a decision. Shortly after Reese left, Trent, Grant, Owen, and Hadley had all shown up at my apartment. Things went down just as Reese said they would.

My friends gave me their dramatic interpretation of the events that had happened after I left camp, and also brought me a job offer. It was a part-time head of promotions position. I would be given an allowance for moving, but that was it.

I wasn't sure what to say.

Was I desperate enough to take something like that to tide me over. I could hear Reese's words in my head. The salary wasn't great—I really needed full-time work, but could I be too picky? I'd had a couple job interviews since I got back, but no one had called me for a second one. And I'd applied at a bunch of places. I was open to all sorts of possibilities. My degree was in social work, but I'd never used it. I took what jobs I could get.

Eye doctor's office receptionist. Guest services coordinator at a hospital. Research assistant. My last job was data management. I'd liked that one the best, except for the boss and, you know, being fired because she mistook me for her husband's mistress. There's that. But the pay hadn't been bad, and I'd enjoyed looking at numbers all day.

I was a closet nerd, until Reese found out.

He kept asking for a pic of me in a skirt and wire-rimmed glasses. I'd succumbed once as I walked past an eyeglasses kiosk in the mall, but I itched my nose with my middle finger in the photo. The sales guy thought it was hilarious—until I handed him back the glasses and tossed a "thank you" over my shoulder. He'd been dropping hints about when he got off work and asking what kind of food I liked. I booked it before the proposition could happen.

The text I'd gotten back from Reese was an image of him pulling his shorts away from his waist.

Reese: Are we doing this?

Me: Is that growing? Can't tell. Your boxer briefs are in the way.

Reese: I have a game tonight or I'd be buying you a plane ticket right now.

That was the typical back-and-forth with us.

My friends had spent the rest of the weekend at my place, and they'd even talked me into having lunch with Janet and her new husband. I'd sworn each of them to silence about Reese. If Janet found that out, friends from when I'd gone to camp as a child would come out of the woodwork. I also made sure they were tight-lipped about Damian. I was better about talking about that situation, but I still didn't care to go there with Janet.

I'd also returned to my therapist.

She was surprised by my willingness to open up, but we were peeling away one painful layer at a time. Turns out I suffered from something called caregiver's toxic guilt.

It was a mouthful to type and say, so I kept that to myself as well. Just easier. My friends knew I was going through a level of guilt they couldn't understand, so they had refrained from asking too many questions.

Reese was the only one who brought Damian up these days, and it was just every so often and always a roundabout question—like what other teams Damian had liked. He was never direct or demanding, but he'd bring Damian's name up until I peeled another layer back and gave him some details about the past. Once I'd done that, he'd change the topic.

Touch and go. That's what we were.

But it'd been two weeks of that: texting, phone calls, pictures, jokes, memes, crude gifs.

Until today. Today was game day. The Seattle Thunder was in town to play the Coyotes for the regular season.

Trent was flying in, and he'd said he was bringing a date with him. Owen and Hadley had already arrived, and we were in the car to go pick them up.

When it had slipped at Janet's two weeks ago that they were coming back for the game, she and her husband mentioned they were going to try to get tickets. I'd looked down at my lap because I knew a few pointed looks were likely coming my way, but nope—I wasn't interested in assisting with that in any way. Janet had never made my life any easier, and she hadn't kept in contact with me. She'd been the easiest to stop talking to because we'd never really talked in the first place. So no, I wasn't going to ask Reese for another set of tickets. It burned my ego to allow the ones he had offered up in the *first* place. I kept wanting to pay him back, but he hadn't paid for them. He said each player had a few they could use each game, but he never used them so he had a surplus.

We were all supposed to do dinner together later tonight, though, and I wasn't sure how I'd handle that situation.

Reese had to travel back with the team, but they weren't flying back till the morning. That was also a touchy subject I was putting off until later. Trent and his date were going to sleep at my place. Grant, Sophia, Owen, and Hadley were all staying at Janet's.

Where I was sleeping, I wasn't sure yet.

"What's holding you back?" Grant asked as we pulled up to Arrivals.

He meant what was holding me back from taking the job offer at the camp. Lack of money was one, but also, I wasn't sure I wanted to upend everything and move there. The only place to live near camp was a small town. It was a whole different culture.

I could've said all those words, but there was another reason. Damian.

Fuck it. What'd it matter if I told them the truth?

"Damian is here."

Cue the nerves now.

But the car went quiet.

Finally, Grant cleared his throat. "We don't know what to say to you. It's obvious you don't want to talk about him. We get that, but we have no clue how to handle this. Do we ask questions? Do we not? What do we say to make you feel like we're here for you, but not pry because we know it's a touchy subject. You loved the guy, and his mind was slipping, but we have no clue what even transpired. So..."

"Grant," Sophia warned.

"You have to take the lead when you bring him up," he said, sounding strained. "We don't know."

Hadley leaned forward, her hand touching my arm. "But we love you, and we're here for you."

Grant coughed from the driver's seat, pulling forward into a line moving at a slow pace. "Yeah. That sentiment." He frowned, ducking his head to see the passengers lined up on the curb. "Trent flew Delta, right? This is the right baggage claim?"

Just then, Trent and a woman came out, both pulling suitcases.

He saw us at the same time we saw them, and the entire group started laughing at his immediate frown.

We pulled up, and I opened the side door, but he just shook his head.

"Are you guys serious? The camp van?"

Hadley and I were laughing as we jumped out to hug Trent, and then hug the girl.

"Oh." She blinked, and her arms jerked up. "Hi there."

But our hugs were quick. We were already done and climbing into the farthest back seat.

Sophia got out and was a more gracious hostess. She hugged Trent first, then greeted the girl. Grant came around to hug Trent and shake the girl's hand as Owen collected their suitcases, putting them in the back.

Trent was still scowling at the van, rolling his eyes.

"Stow it," Grant said. "We figure it's good marketing, and we all came down together anyway."

"Right." Trent poked his head in, glaring at me. "You could've warned me I was getting the camp van greeting at the airport."

I shrugged. "It's how we roll. You should know that."

He grunted in response, but his scowl faded. "It's good to see you guys." His hand came to his date's back. "Guys, this is Lauren. Lauren, the official camp greeting. All except Charlie, in the Thunder jersey."

"Hi." She smiled as she climbed in and took the middle seat. "Hi, everyone." A pause. "What are your names again?"

We went around, but her dazed look never diminished. She was a deer in headlights.

Grant pulled the van back into the driving lane. "We all work at camp."

"Still?" Her hand came to rest on Trent's arm. "Or you used to work with Trenton?"

Trenton?

Hadley and I shared a look of delight.

Trent noticed, turning back to us. "Not a word."

Hadley squeaked.

I scooted down in my seat, whispering under my breath, "Trenton. I love it."

Trenton was in love. I could tell.

Lauren was exquisite—long, flowing black hair, lips like a doll's, and dark almond eyes. I was tempted to ask if she was a model, but decided to wait until Sophia had warmed her up, which she was doing.

Trent brought a date! He brought a date to a camp social gathering. That was serious.

Right? Right. I felt it was.

Owen leaned forward from the other side of Hadley. He and Sophia had somehow become the appointed hosts of the group.

"Hey." Grant raised his voice. "Are we going straight to the game or swinging back to Charlie's? What's the plan?"

Trent looked back at me. "We have time to drop our stuff off? Maybe clean up a little?"

"Oh, yeah. I guess it depends on how long we want to wait for concessions, but yeah, we have time."

It was an hour before the game. There was plenty of time.

"I'd like to wash up a little, maybe not leave our suitcases at the arena, you know?"

"Say no more." Grant flipped on the turn signal, veering toward the next exit for my apartment.

My phone buzzed.

Reese: You wearing my jersey?

Me: Coyotes.

Reese: I'm calling to take away your ticket—just yours. Not your friends'.

I bit the inside of my cheeks. Every time my phone buzzed, I knew everyone was wondering if it was Reese or someone else.

I loved that Trent had brought Lauren, but I was highly uncomfortable. We were going to Reese's game. I was wearing his jersey—one I'd bought that he didn't know I'd bought—and we were using his tickets for the game. Janet couldn't get tickets anywhere near where we were sitting, and I was already feeling that pressure. Reese was doing dinner with us, and my friends were in town for the whole weekend, but I wanted tonight with Reese.

I just didn't know how to maneuver all of those moving pieces.

Maybe it was unrealistic, but I didn't want Janet to know about him or Lauren to spill the beans, if she found out too. And I didn't know if Trent had told her where he got the tickets or not.

And then part of me felt I was stressing too much. I should just let it all lay how it was going to lay, but I was coming off quite a few years where I hadn't told *anyone* what was going on with me.

Habits were hard to break.

People knowing my business gave them reason to form opinions, spread gossip. I was sweating just thinking of all the talk that'd rip through the group about Reese and me.

"Hey." Hadley leaned close. "No stressing, okay? We all took a pact. No one will say a word."

I loved her. I truly loved her.

My chest felt lighter.

"What about dinner? How do we do that?"

She gave an easygoing shrug. "We'll figure it out. We're prepared to handle Janet for you. Don't worry. If you want him to come with us, he's welcome. If you want to have your time with him, just give me a wink and a motion and I'll cover. It's really no problem. Are you staying with him tonight?"

I glanced up at Trent, half-turned to face Lauren, and he glanced back.

"You can just give me an extra key," he said. "We can work it out. If you want to sneak in, I'll make sure Lauren and I are in the guest room. We can do this. I mean, we understand."

My face felt flushed. "We're not even..." Yeah. How did I have that conversation with them? "We're just friends."

Trent smirked.

Hadley snorted. "Right. No boning there."

"Hadley!"

"We might work at a camp, but we're not backward hicks or something. I do have three children."

The back of my neck was sweating. "This is just a lot to handle. I'm used to being a hermit and taking care of someone who some days remembered me and other days didn't."

My second reference to Damian.

They were coming easier and easier.

My therapist would be so proud, and I waited, but the instant, white-hot panic that always hit me after I mentioned Damian didn't come.

It *was* getting easier.

Reese: Easter egg request?

It was like he knew me. Finally, finally.

Me: Sexy librarian look. I want the glasses.

Reese: You serious?

Me: Absolutely. You'll get banged tonight if you do.

Reese: Not to be cocky, but I'm going to bang anyways.

Reese: K. Gotta go. Head to the players' exit when you're done. Or I'll check my phone once we're done. Think Juan wants to do dinner with us.

Me: Us?

**Reese: Whoever. Are we doing your friends too?
Or just you, me, and Juan. I don't care.**

**Reese: Or I can tell Juan to do his own thing. You
decide.**

It was all up to me. What a disconcerting thought.

I didn't text him back. The game, then the players' exit after
that.

But one thought was seeming more and more appealing:
There was beer at the concession stands.

CHAPTER THIRTY-TWO

I loved going to basketball games. Like, *loved* loved, obsessed-over loved, and I was such a sports fanatic that it wasn't just basketball games. Football, hockey, baseball—men's, women's, kids. I didn't care. I'd go to a fifth-grade football game if I were invited. I couldn't explain why, but it never mattered.

As soon as I got to my seat and got comfortable, I was ready to go.

An excited buzz started to build as we entered the arena, and once we got to our seats, I felt ready to explode. Nerves. Excitement. Anxiety. All of it had rolled together, and I felt like I was bouncing inside of myself, only being held together because of my skin.

"Trenton said you had a friend who got these tickets for us?" Lauren leaned over Hadley to ask me. She was so beautiful, even a little birthmark over her lip winked at me from her confusion. "Does your friend work at the Target Center? These are really good seats."

I swallowed.

Hadley leaned forward, an easy smile on her face. "It's someone who knows someone who knows someone. It was that sort of deal. I don't think it'll happen again."

"Ahh." Lauren leaned back in her seat. "I got it." She laughed. "I thought for a second Charlie knew one of the players or something."

Hadley didn't respond. I pretended I hadn't heard, and as Hadley patted Lauren's hand, we shared a look. We were close to where the players would come in from the locker rooms, so that was adding to the whole messiness inside me. I kept thinking a player would step out, see me, and point saying, "SHE'S OVER HERE!"

I know, I know.

I was a bit much.

But really. I had some anxiety.

Hadley checked her phone. "Owen's bringing beer."

"Thank GOD!"

Lauren frowned at me.

After the guys got back, the dance music started. The teams were coming out.

When the announcer's voice began booming, the Thunder began running in.

Hadley gripped my hand. "OH MY GOD!"

The Cruskinator went by.

Lestroy.

I could name each and every one of them, and not just because of camp.

One saw us and stopped. "Hey!" He waved. "It's nice to see you guys again." He saw me. "Oh yeah," he said with a laugh before he hit the guy next to him, jogging on.

Still others passed by.

A couple of the coaches.

Aiden was with them.

Juan.

Then...

When I turned, Reese was staring at me, a smirk on his face.

I couldn't hold it in. A secret grin showed, and he answered it with one of his own.

Juan pounded his arm, waving to me too before they jogged the rest of the way.

I was not going to look around, but I knew the people around us were watching me. I scooted low in my seat and folded my head in, now wondering if his jersey was too obvious?

Then, fuck it. I was here to support him. Half the women in this arena had his number on their backs, so I sat back up and started cheering with the rest of the crowd.

Hadley was up and dancing. She and Owen were doing their dances the way only they could. He pretended to smack her ass as she waved her arms in the air.

Lauren looked at them, her eyebrows high until Trenton leaned in and whispered something in her ear. Her confusion cleared, and her cheeks pinked. She drew closer to his side, and soon both of them were moving to the music.

Once the game actually began, it was pandemonium—the way a game should always be. Everything happening inside of me came out, and I was yelling with the rest of them. We were in Thunder territory, but I liked the Coyotes too. It hurt when they fell behind, when Reese stole one, two, three balls, made his free throws, and had at least one beautiful teardrop shot.

He really was having one of his best years. They'd won all their other games but one, and they seemed to be on the fast track for the NBA Finals, but that was a long way off. They were currently rated number two in their conference.

And it wasn't just Reese.

Juan was on the court almost the whole time, leading the team in rebounds and tying with Reese for assists. Lestroy led with three-pointers, and the Cruskinator dominated under the basket.

Thunder led 72-63 at the half, and after a quick dash to the bathroom, I sat down for the first time since the game began.

"Holy shit." Hadley fanned herself. "We need to come to these games more often. They're a workout."

The Coyotes mascot was throwing shirts into the crowd across from us. On our side, the dancers were tossing little basketballs.

Lauren leaned over a bit after the guys went for the concession stands, her eyes a little wide. "This is so exciting! This game is amazing." She pretended to scowl at us. "You guys never told me you knew some of the Thunder team."

We'd signed NDAs. None of us could say a word.

Hadley just smiled, the way she usually did. "There's a reason we can't talk about it."

"Oh!" Lauren smiled. "I got it. Say no more. But did you guys meet Reese Forster? He looked over here like he knew you. Does he?"

Right then and there, I decided I was keeping Reese to myself tonight.

Hadley coughed. "Again…"

"Oh." Lauren sat back, waving her hand and trying to air out her shirt. "Say no more. I got it." She giggled, results of the beer. "I might ask Trenton later, though."

The guys were coming back, more goodies in hand and a beer for me. Owen handed it over before sitting back down.

I'd just had a sip when Grant came around to kneel beside me. "Hey. So did you decide about tonight?"

I lowered my voice and flicked my eyes behind me. "Trent's girlfriend seems kinda keen on Forster so…"

"Okay." He bobbed his head. "You can make plans with him after the game, I'm guessing?"

"Yeah."

"Good. We ran into Janet up there. She might come down and visit a bit, but we'll make up some excuse for you about dinner. I think Hads had something planned. She thought about it all on the way down. And about Trent and his girl?"

I lifted a shoulder, shaking my head. "I don't know. I have to talk to Reese, see what he says about tonight."

"Well, I was going to suggest, do you want Sophia and me to switch with Trent and Lauren? They can take the second guest room at Janet's and we'll stay at your place? It makes sense, in a way. Trent's a lot closer to Janet than I am. I was always loyal to you. Plus, Hadley's friends with her too. And you and I are closer, you know."

I nodded, loving this new plan. "Yes. Then we don't have to hide or dart into a hotel room."

"Good." He squeezed my shoulder, standing back up. "I'll talk to Trent about everything, and we'll sort it out. If for any reason it doesn't go down like that, one of us will let you know. You can have your time, and tomorrow then?"

"He's flying back with the team, so I'm free as of tomorrow morning."

He knelt back down, looping his arms over his knees. "Janet asked about you, wondering if you're mad at her or something. I think she's trying to figure out how we got these tickets."

I groaned. "Can Hadley make up something there too?"

He grinned. "We'll cover, but just so you know for tomorrow. She invited all of us over to her place for dinner."

"When are you heading back to camp?"

"That's kinda up to you. I mean, we're in off-season, so we don't actually have to go back till Monday. Are you free Monday morning? Should we plan to go back that day? Or we can go back tomorrow after Janet's."

I was happy they were here, which was not something I would have imagined myself thinking even three months ago. A lot could change when you started letting yourself live.

"Whatever you guys want. I'm easy. I don't have a job."

"Speaking of." He gave me a serious look.

"AHH! YOU GUYS ARE ON THE KISS CAM!" someone screeched behind us, trying to push our heads together.

I jerked, whipping my eyes up to the jumbotron, and there we were, my profile to the camera.

I paled.

Grant stiffened.

And Hadley acted.

She yelled, then grabbed my face and whipped me around to her. Her lips mashed to mine, and after a second of shock, a cheer rose up around us. People clapped and laughed.

Owen surged to his feet, pointing at us. "She's my wife!"

Trent bit his lip, trying to keep from laughing.

I just held my hands up and shook my head. "She kissed me."

"She's not my girlfriend. My girl's on the other side," Grant announced to anyone who would listen.

Sophia was dying in her seat, almost on the floor, her arms hugging her sides. And Lauren? She was back to being confused.

The camera had moved on, but it zoomed back again. This time it found Owen and Hadley. Husband and wife kissed, and another cheer rose up. The camera came back to me, but I shook my head. "I'm alone," I mouthed.

A guy yelled from above us, "I'll kiss you!"

Grant tapped my shoulder. "I'm going to get back. It's unsafe being here. We'll talk later."

The players came back out, there was more dancing music, and the next half didn't disappoint.

Juan fouled out, leaving the court to a chorus of boos.

Reese led the charge, and it wasn't really a surprise when his team won at the end, 109-85.

CHAPTER THIRTY-THREE

I got my Easter egg during Reese's last interview, right before he jogged off the court. He asked to wear the interviewer's glasses. It was all a joke, but the guy loved it, and I had a feeling that clip would be played on YouTube quite a bit.

As he ran into the tunnel, I saw him looking for me.

Once our gazes caught, I held up my phone. He dipped his head once and kept running. I knew people saw the exchange. There was no way they couldn't have. I ducked my head as I noticed a few cameras pointing my way.

Hadley touched my arm. "You want a hat? Owen brought one he didn't wear."

"Maybe that's a good idea."

I pulled my hair around my face, tugged the hat down low, and tried not to look up until we'd left our seats. There were two guys following me, one holding a camera in front of him.

We were nearing a bathroom, and I grabbed Hadley's hand, ducking inside, then circling around a group. The exit was at the other end. The guys were waiting outside the second door, trying to look inside. I held back. When a big surge of people went past them, I moved us into the middle. Hadley was right with me.

She laughed, her beer breath blasting me as she twisted to look behind us. "Who was it?"

"I don't know, but they were following me."

"I hate to say it, but if you and Reese do become something, that's going to happen more and more. People watch him like a hawk."

I nodded and squeezed her hand. "Let's just get through the 'we're friends who bone' stage. I'll worry about that later."

She laughed, patting my arm. "Sounds good to me."

A guy pointed at us. "Hey. It's the lesbian chicks." He turned and yelled at us, "You guys are hot. Keep kissing."

His friends thought he was so funny. One added, "Yeah. Always keep kissing. Without clothes."

Hadley flicked her eyes up. "Is it wrong to want to dump beers right on their crotches?"

"Then step back and yell, 'Oh! Who smells like piss?'"

We were both laughing when I remembered I wasn't supposed to be leaving with them. "Shit. I have to go somewhere else." I pulled my phone back out, but Reese hadn't texted yet. I began backing away. "I might have to go that way?"

We had separated from the group, so I was torn. I was good with directions. Hadley wasn't. She could get lost in a Super Target, and since I didn't see Trent or Grant or any of the others ahead, I decided to take Hadley to where we first came in, then make my exit to wherever Reese told me to go. He probably needed time to shower.

My phone buzzed.

Reese: Leaving from the main floor exit, in the back. Go out where you were sitting, and go left. Keep going left until door 16. Take that down a floor, and you'll see a group gathering. Press is here, by the way. If you want, you could come to the hotel and we'll meet there?

I was still with Hadley, so that worked best.

Me: Which hotel? That's perfect.

Reese: Hotel Ivy.

Me: Sounds good.

Reese: Wait. Fuck.

Me: What?

Reese: If we're doing this, why don't I just come to your apartment?

Me: Sounds even better. I'll have my friends drop me off.

Reese: Sorry. I didn't realize how many press would be here. Hot kiss cam, by the way.

He sent me a picture of Hadley and me. Kissing.

Me: Her lips are super sweet. You should be jealous.

Reese: Jealous is not the word.

I barked out a laugh, then saw Hadley watching me. I sent one last text.

Me: Leaving now. See you as soon as you can get to my place.

"Look." Hadley motioned behind us.

The two guys from before had spotted us. They were following again.

Hadley walked next to me, close enough to nudge me with her arm. "Maybe they're following us because of us, not you and Reese?"

It was a thought.

I squeezed her hand, and for some reason, I enjoyed holding it during that moment. She felt safe, reassuring.

"Let's just find the rest. Change of plans."

Reese texted me just as we saw the group lingering at the door.

Reese: Coach let me go early. He's got a soft spot for you. I'm leaving straight from here. I'll shower at your place. I have clothes with me. If I go back to the hotel, it's going to take forever to leave again.

Me: Okay. We're walking out now.

Hadley went to Owen's arms, and Grant moved toward me. I explained about the two guys, who Grant immediately spotted and began scowling at. Then I let him know about the change of plans.

Trent migrated over. "That's fine," he said. "But things will get tricky because we're dropping you off and have to grab our stuff. What if, you know..." He gestured to where Lauren was standing, far enough away not to hear us, but close enough to know he'd mentioned her in some way. Her eyes narrowed.

At this point, I was done with all the planning and evading. "It will be what it'll be."

Grant snorted. "Yeah. No." He rotated to Trent. "She can stay in the car. You and I can grab your suitcases."

"And if she insists on coming up?"

"Oh my God." I was done with all of this. "Let's just see where the chips fall, okay? Two guys following me is enough for me to deal with."

"Well, let's go now," Grant said. "See if we can hurry and be out of there before he shows up."

With a plan in place, we all surged out to where we'd parked. Hadley and Sophia yelped from surprise, and Lauren hurried to keep pace, throwing suspicious looks my way. Our way. Her eyes lingered where Trent and Grant had closed ranks around me.

My phone buzzed again.

Reese: I'll be out of here in twenty.

I showed Grant and Trent the text. Both nodded.

"Then we'll be out of there in twenty, just to be safe," Grant confirmed.

I loved my friends. Why had I ever stopped hanging out with them?

I didn't want them to feel rushed, but that's what we were all doing. Rushing.

Walking through the parking lot to the van took ten minutes. Getting out of the parking lot was another twenty minutes itself.

Reese buzzed me as we pulled onto the street, and we still had to maneuver through the traffic.

Reese: Almost to your place.

Grant was driving, so Trent looked back at me. I just gave him a resigned look.

Me: We're still trying to get there. Post game traffic is a bitch. How are you getting there faster than us?

Reese: Left from the back way. We have roads cleared for us. I'll wait till you get there.

Me: Juan?

Reese: Told him to take a hike. I just want you tonight.

Me: Friendship boning.
Reese: FF. Friendship fucking.

That was one phrase for it, but every time we talked on the phone and during our text exchanges, something else was there. It was building, growing. It was becoming more and more cemented inside of me.

When we pulled up, an SUV was pulling away, and there, about to open the door, was Reese.

Lauren jerked forward, gripping the seat in front of her. "Is that—oh my God!"

Wearing Thunder warm-ups and a Thunder sweatshirt, a cap pulled low and his hood up, Reese was still easy to recognize. He saw our van and paused, then turned toward us, raising his hand.

"Hey, strangers." He smirked and bent down to see inside. "Oh, wow. You have a full vehicle." Angling his head, he saw me and his smirk grew. "All the way in the back. That's my little psycho."

I flushed.

The rest of the van started laughing.

Lauren's eyes were saucers. "How do you—you know—" She looked at me and then at Reese. "What is happening right now?"

He took pity on her. "Hi. I'm Reese. I know these crazy people." He nodded. "And I'm liking the vehicle digs. I should get something like this. I can get a driver to take me around. More branding for the team. Right?"

I was done waiting for someone to get out first.

I started forward, and Trent opened the door for me.

Lauren began to climb out, but he held her back. "Maybe we should park and all come in then?" he suggested to Grant.

I almost sagged from thankfulness. They were giving us just a moment of privacy.

Reese moved, and as if we'd practiced it, he held his arms out and I jumped into them.

I barely registered Hadley's surprised gasp, or the fact that Trent shut the door behind me. I was just focused on Reese's arms and the way he carried me, like I was a doll again, inside the building, away from any more prying eyes.

Once inside, he walked right to the elevator. "I'm assuming they're coming up?"

I took him in. He hadn't showered, so the tips of his hair were still wet, pressed under his hat, and he reeked, but he'd just run maybe two miles and scored forty-two points. That made up for any smell. I was also eager to get in that shower with him.

Once the elevator door closed, Reese's mouth was on mine.

"*Fuck*," he breathed out, his lips opening mine. "I have missed this." His hand slid down to my waist, lifting my jersey and stroking up my naked back. "You taste so good. Smell fucking good. I want your friends to go away forever. Right now."

I wanted the same, but I didn't have a joke. We had three more floors to go, so I tugged his mouth back to mine.

He set me down on my feet once we got to my floor, but his hands didn't move off me. Not as we walked down the hall or as I unlocked the door, and once it was shut? It was the elevator 2.0 except a whole lot more insistent.

Reese was on me.

He hoisted me up, and my legs wound around him. He rocked into me, groaning into my ear. He caught the lobe in his teeth and murmured, "Once they're gone, we are boning long and hard. I'm so glad I chose to come here first."

I moaned, searching for his mouth, and we didn't part until we heard feet shuffling outside, then a knock. Someone rang the doorbell.

Grant called through the door, "Yeah, we can hear you guys. Let us in before the rest of the hallway does too."

Reese buried his head in my neck, smothering a laugh.

I was beyond embarrassed. My entire neck was red. I could feel my face heating, and as I reached for the door, Reese kissed me on the neck, saying, "I'm going to wash super fast."

"Wait—"

But he'd already ducked into my bathroom.

Not the guest bathroom in the hallway, but mine. In my bedroom.

I was so screwed.

Smoothing my hair, I opened the door and cleared my throat. "Heya, guys."

Grant came in first. Knowing eyes. "Nice."

Sophia followed with a thumbs-up. "Doing great!"

Owen rolled his shoulder. "Sorry. Tried to stall as long as we could."

Hadley was beaming and bouncing up and down. "I have to pee. It's my fault." She darted around the others, grabbing the bathroom first.

Trent and Lauren brought up the rear.

"Sorry," Trent mouthed.

, I lifted my shoulder. It was what it was.

Lauren's eyes hadn't diminished in size, and she was giving me a whole different look than before, as if seeing me anew.

I didn't like it.

My bedroom door was closed, but we could hear the sounds of the shower.

Grant sat at the table. "Got some booze?"

Owen sat next to him. "Or food?"

Lauren's hand gripped Trent's tightly. "Are we staying here?" she asked in a loud whisper.

Trent's eyes met mine. I shook my head. No way, not after her reaction.

He mouthed Janet's name.

I held up my hand. It wouldn't matter. She'd see Janet anyway.

As if we'd had a whole telepathic conversation, he sighed and said, "No. We're staying at Janet's."

"Yeah." Grant spoke up, raising his hand. "I'm not trying to be a dick, but in the spirit of protecting my friend, you can't say shit to Janet."

It took a moment before Lauren realized he was talking to her. When she did, she looked around. Everyone was watching her. No one was laughing. Or grinning. Or looking any way other than deadly serious.

The door opened behind me. Hadley stepped forward, not her usual happy self. She charged right up to Lauren and said softly, but so damned clearly, "Janet cannot keep her mouth shut. You tell her one thing, and she'll tell forty others by the end of the night. You want us to protect you when she rips you to shreds—because it'll happen—you do us a solid now." She motioned to me. "Don't say a word about Charlie and Reese. Charlie isn't hanging out with us because she has a friend in from out of town. That's it. You don't know who the friend is. She was someone from college. That's all you say to her."

She stepped back, all sunny-like now. "Do we have martinis here?"

Lauren turned to Trent. "Excuse me?"

Trent groaned. "Thanks, Hads. I was going to ease into the whole thing about Janet being a gossip."

Hadley and Sophia both made exasperated sounds.

Hadley went to sit on Owen's lap. "Right. There's no way to ease into that conversation. We love Janet. We accept her for who she is, but we also know when to keep our mouths shut. This is one of those situations."

The shower turned off.

A different headache began forming at the base of my neck.

Janet. I'd have to see her tomorrow. She'd not been subtle, wanting to know all about Damian the last time I saw her. I had escaped without much slipping, but it was hard under pressure.

The door opened. Feet padded down the hall. I smelled him at the same time I felt his warmth, then an arm curved around me, pulling me back into a very strong chest.

He propped his chin on top of my head. "The whole gang's here, with a new friend. Trent, you got a girlfriend you never mentioned?"

In some ways, it was the best icebreaker.

Everyone relaxed, and Trent shook his head. "Right. I'm the one with the gir—"

"We're friends," I cut him off.

"Who bone," Reese added.

"Reese!"

I tried to turn in his arms, but he tightened his hold. His laugh reverberated near my ear, as everyone else laughed.

He started rocking me from side to side. "So what's the news with the camp upsets?"

"What?" Lauren asked. It was about the only thing she had left to say.

Trent chuckled, putting his arm around her shoulders. She whispered something to him, and he responded, moving his mouth to her ear.

"It's good," Owen said. He nodded to me. "Mostly waiting for Charlie to make her decision."

Reese knew I hadn't decided. He'd reminded me of his offer a few times. I felt his attention now and looked up. "Nothing's changed. I'm still thinking it over."

He swallowed, some of the carefree demeanor I'd noticed he kept when my friends were around slipping a little.

He squeezed me tighter, saying just over my ear, "Yeah."

Grant frowned. So did Trent. Owen looked away, adjusting his shoulder.

Hadley and Sophia both seemed to sober.

Lauren was the only one unaffected, for once.

Grant broke the tension. "So." His eyes moved between us. "You don't want her to take the job?"

Reese shifted, coming out from behind me, but he kept his arm on my shoulder. "Would you? Knowing what she's gone through, where she currently is, and knowing she might be working with you guys, but she'll be working for that board?" His smirk was hard. "No offense, but your board still sucks. I was not impressed with them."

Lauren looked completely lost.

Owen's mouth tightened.

"Right." Grant's gaze found mine.

Okay. Yeah. This was on me.

I broke free from Reese, hooking my hands in my sleeves. "It's my decision. I have to decide on a few things, you know that."

"But what about money?" Grant asked. "I mean, you wouldn't be making a ton, but rent and stuff is way cheaper in Fairview than here."

I moved into the kitchen. "Again, it's my decision. And I've not made it yet."

"You said yourself you can't afford to stay here much longer..." Grant followed me.

I turned. "And that's my business!"

Reese moved to stand in the kitchen doorway, resting his shoulder against the frame, but his eyes were not nearly so relaxed.

I hadn't told him the extent of my financial issues, but at this point, who really cared since he'd already aired some of his thoughts in front of the group.

I gestured to him. "And it's none of your business either." And another screw-it moment. "The real truth, for anyone who wants to know, comes down to Damian. He's still here. He's still someone I care about. And yes, one day I need to go and visit him."

I needed alcohol.

Going to the fridge, I yanked the door open.

Reaching inside for the wine, I said—more to it than anyone else, "You don't stop loving someone even if they've forgotten you."

No one said a thing.

Then, from the living room, Lauren whispered, "Who is Damian?"

That was it. I took the wine and went to my bedroom, shutting the door. Maybe it wasn't that big of a deal to anyone else. I tried to tell myself that. They all cared about me in their ways, but I cared about their opinions—each one, and they were varied.

Reese didn't want me in a place that would hurt me again, and with the board, that was a fair assessment. He also didn't want me to take a job because I had to. Grant, Owen, Hadley, and Sophia, they just wanted me there. They wanted to work with me every day, but they were each making more than I would. They had each other as well, and working there was their full-time job. They wouldn't have to supplement with a second wage.

Maybe if Damian couldn't—yeah. I wasn't going there. Not yet, but my hosting duties were done for the night. I uncorked the wine, sat down by the bed, and took a swallow.

Rosé all day, or in my case, the rest of the night.

CHAPTER THIRTY-FOUR

I heard them leave.

Hadley knocked on the door a few minutes later and poked her head inside. "We're heading to Janet's. You want Owen and me to stay here tonight instead of Grant and Sophia?"

I shook my head. "No. I'm fine. Let's stick to the original Grant plan. I'm sorry for being dramatic."

"It's okay." Her smile slipped. "My grandpa had Alzheimer's, but to lose Owen to it? That's not how it's supposed to go, you know? Not that it's supposed to ever happen, but you know what I mean."

Maybe. Regardless of circumstances, I didn't think the sting ever went away—whether it was parent, grandparent, or in my case, someone who was supposed to be my husband.

"We'll see you tomorrow then?"

I nodded, gripping that wine bottle so tightly. "Sounds good."

Grant stopped behind her, saying over her head, "Sophia and I will be back later tonight. That okay?"

I nodded again. "Sounds good. We'll see you later on."

His eyes were hooded, and he dipped his head before heading out.

Hadley gave me a small wave, disappearing after him.

Then Reese was in the doorway, and he let out a long breath of air. "I feel like I fucked up earlier."

I shook my head, as he came into the room, but I didn't need to worry about moving. He came over and deposited me on his lap, sitting on the floor.

He tugged the wine bottle out of my hand, taking a drink and handing it back.

I took it back. "I messed up. I got emotional."

"Seems like you have a right." He brushed my hair back, resting his head against the mattress. "I don't think any of us can imagine what you're going through."

"You can."

He shook his head, pursing his lips together. "Not even a little bit. My brother's an asshole to the umpteenth degree. He's in jail right now, and he's mad he can't get anyone to post his bail. He's pissed that I won't take his calls and my lawyers are fielding everything from him. Now, if my mom decides to use her money to post for him, that's on her. All I can do is protect myself against them. That's not the same situation as yours at all."

But he was wrong. For both of us, there was a hole where our family was supposed to be. Damian had created mine. His brother had created his.

I settled back against him. "Loved ones aren't supposed to go away, whether it's their choice or not. That's not how life is supposed to be."

He ran a hand down from my face, cupping my cheek before falling away. "You're not close to your family?"

"It's not that there's anything really wrong with them. It's just... They couldn't support me while I was losing Damian, and that put a wedge between us. I don't know how to make that right, especially when they won't acknowledge it."

"They know you guys broke up, right?"

"No. I had no reason to tell them."

He cursed softly, hugging me close. "You shouldn't go through that alone."

I tipped my head back. "But I'm not. Not anymore."

A look flashed in his depths.

Raw. Tender. It was the way he'd looked at me last time when we were having sex, and I turned away from it. I wasn't ready to see it. After a moment I shifted up, raising my hand to his face. My thumb grazed his chiseled jawline, the dip around his mouth, the rough stubble that told me he'd shaved last night, and then finally, I traced his lips. His breathing grew shallow, and his hand moved more insistently behind me, molding over my hip.

He turned me to face him more directly, sliding his hand under my leg.

My breasts pressed against his chest, our foreheads resting together.

Our lips so close, a tantalizing temptation. He licked his, his eyes never moving from mine.

"If we do this, it's not going to not mean anything," he whispered.

I swallowed over a lump. I knew what he was saying—a question not in question form. But I couldn't stop it anymore.

The calling. The texts. The jokes. The concern. Him being here, making me a priority. And him just being him—I couldn't go back. I was too far gone by now.

"I know."

He cupped the side of my face, his palm resting against my skin. "It's going to mean something."

He was giving me an out.

I could pull away, slip off his lap, walk out of the room.

But really? Could I?

A door opened inside of me, letting everything out. It flooded me, going through every vein in my body, warming me, filling me with something akin to lightness, hope...happiness.

I was already gone.

So I gave him my answer, closing the distance and pressing my lips to his. I held there and whispered back, "It's meant something for a while."

That was all he needed.

His hand moved to the back of my neck, and his mouth opened over mine. Flames licked my body, teasing me, making me shiver all over. As his mouth slid down my chin, my throat, I let my head tip back. My hair fell free, the ends resting on my back because he had moved my shirt up to pull it free. I lifted my arms, goosebumps breaking out as he took me in. A primal desire flared in his eyes.

His hands slid underneath my bra straps, and his mouth found my shoulder as he unclipped my bra. It fell away, and he drew it away from me, using it to further torment me.

His mouth found mine again, coaxing me open, and his tongue slid inside. He did a slow and sensual sweep, claiming me.

A rumble started in me, vibrating me, making me headier with need.

"You're so beautiful," he murmured, his mouth moving back down my throat. He arched over me, one of his hands cupping my breast as his mouth closed over the other. He sucked me, a nuzzle, a nibble, still so damned slow and torturous. I could only hold on to him, falling back against his arm, now anchored firmly behind me.

"Fuck, Charlie," he growled, biting just slightly on my nipple.

We continued exploring, my hands sliding down his arms, over his chest, around and down his back. Every place my hands went, he shivered under their touch.

I was writhing now, panting for him.

His hand moved to my pants, and I bit my lip, keeping a cry inside.

I needed him inside of me.

His fingers slipped into my underwear and found me. "Christ," he hissed, his mouth nipping my throat again. "You're so wet."

I rolled my hips back and forth, feeling him, and then feeling his fingers as they dipped inside.

"Reese," I gasped as I started to ride his hand. "Please." An ache.

"Go."

I held on to his shoulders, and his hand moved down to my back. He urged me on. "Ride me. Come on. Come, Charlie. Come for me."

He sat back, his gaze molten as he took me in, his hand gripping my thigh and moving with me. I rode him as his fingers thrust in and out, moving inside of me until the climax started. I came on his fingers, my entire body jerking. I couldn't move for a second after, and he held me, hugging me to his chest.

He chuckled softly in my ear before he started pressing kisses to my shoulder, my forehead, my cheek. He dipped, finding my lips, and then moved down to my throat again. With each kiss, he was warming me, growing more insistent.

I could feel him. He was still hard. His fingers slid out, but he was right there, pressing up against me. Still in his pants, he rasped next to my ear, "I need to be inside of you. Right now."

"A condom?"

"In my bag."

I was clean. I was on birth control, which he knew. I looked up at him. "Are you clean?"

He nodded, but I still saw hesitation on his face. He told me once he never went raw. And I understood why. He was a professional athlete. Wrapping it up was vital for them, but I didn't care right now.

All logic had fled my mind, and I reached down for him, tunneling through his pants to find him.

He hissed, his hips jerking up at my touch.

I wrapped my hand around him, giving a slight squeeze, just enough to torment him. Then I began stroking. I wasn't timid about it. I had a good grip, and I knew just the way to touch him to make him go mindless with desire—the same way he had made me feel.

Cursing, his mouth dropped over mine. "Can we do this bare? I need to feel you."

I paused. It was my decision now.

I couldn't say anything, but I couldn't stop touching him either.

He grabbed my hand, pausing me. "Charlie, I need to know." His hand went to my hair, taking ahold of the back of my head, and moving my mouth against his. "What do you want? I'm clean. I know you are too. It's your decision."

The temptation was strong. But... "Are you sure?"

"God, baby." His tongue moved over me. "I am so fucking sure."

Lust skyrocketed through me, and I was nodding before I realized I was nodding.

He lifted me up, and we both clawed to get my pants off, until I was bare. As he lowered me down, I yanked at his pants until he stood before me.

Firm. Thick.

Mine.

I grabbed his cock and moved over him. One adjustment, and I sank down on him.

"*Fuck*," he hissed through his teeth as his eyes clamped shut a second. His hand flexed over my ass. "You feel so damned good."

I was almost shattering apart, just feeling him surge up inside me.

The sensations. The pleasure. They slammed through me, almost violently from the abruptness and so quickly after I'd already peaked. Then he began moving over me, his mouth tasting mine, and I went with him.

Together.

Our hips rolling back and forth.

His hand cupping my breast, holding me, squeezing, his hips digging up.

He was hitting my wall.

A savage growl ripped from him, and he picked me up, shifted us to the bed, and was between my legs once more. He grabbed my waist and plunged back inside.

I could only hold on.

Pleasure seeped into every inch of me, coating my insides. My second climax barreled through me, even more powerful than the first, and I was a trembling mess as he pushed in one last time, his hips rotating, grinding to touch every angle inside, and then he jerked, coming inside of me.

He groaned, collapsing on top of me, his body relaxed.

CHAPTER THIRTY-FIVE

We'd taken a shower together and dressed in lounging clothes. Reese pulled on the same sweats he'd worn after his first shower, but I wore leggings and the sweatshirt he'd given me at camp. We'd ordered food in, and the delivery guy had just dropped off our salads, plus two sandwiches for Reese. I'd answered the door this time, preferring to keep Reese to myself, just for a bit longer.

Grant and Sophia were coming back.

I didn't know when, but I guessed we had another hour, maybe two depending on how long everyone decided to talk after dinner.

Reese asked, "When are you hoping to see Damian?"

I paused in spearing some lettuce with my fork. "Are you serious?"

He put a forkful of salad into his mouth, nodding. "Yeah." Swallowing, then taking a drink of water, he put the bottle back down on the table. "That's a big deal."

I felt a heaviness settle over my shoulders. It weighed me down, but I knew this was the time. This was the moment I would say it all.

It wasn't even about Reese. It was about me. I finally could, for some reason, so I needed to. If I didn't now, I didn't know the next time the words would come to me, because sometimes grief closes you up and doesn't let you open. Sometimes grief controls you, and not the other way around.

I set my fork down and scooted all the way back in my chair, assuming my normal position: feet up on the chair, arms wrapped around my knees. But I didn't hide my face. I watched Reese right over the top of my knees, resignation taking over me.

"When you fall in love with someone, you're not supposed to lose them right away. That's tragic. I mean, normal breakups—like if someone cheated or lied, I don't know. Those would be easier, but when it's something inside a person that takes them away, little by little, each day a tiny bit more, it paralyzes you."

I had to take a breath.

And then, I found I could continue.

"Damian never wanted to accept what was happening to him. He wanted to deny it. He wanted to remain normal, but every day he had to make a small adjustment to keep the lie going for himself. Suddenly he couldn't drive during busy times because it was *too dangerous*, not because it confused him. Not because one time he forgot how to get home, and he had to call me."

"Where are you?"

"I don't know."

"We were three years in. Seven months before the wedding, he forgot my name. He stared at me with this blank look. He was terrified. I thought he was terrified about the wedding, and I teased him about it. I'd had to ask him three times to send the save-the-dates. I thought he kept forgetting them in his car because of cold feet."

It hadn't been cold feet.

"We lied to everyone. I told everyone he was stressed at his job, and that he wanted to put the wedding off one more year. Everyone... I don't even know what my family said to my extended family. My sister was panicked, wondering if everything was okay, but I couldn't tell her. Because I knew my world was falling apart, but even then I didn't really understand. And I was stubborn. I knew something was happening, but I didn't want to accept it. I didn't want to lose him, not just yet. So I held on, and I lied too. I denied too. It's easier than fully walking away, because what are you walking away from? Your future? Someone who was going to be your husband? The guy you thought would be an amazing father to your future children? The guy who could light up the room with one laugh, one look, one touch. He was mine, and then he wasn't. The disease took him, but not right away. At first we all became roommates: Damian, me, the disease. It slowly ate at him, and he kept refusing to go in. Kept saying they couldn't even diagnose him if it was what we thought it was, that it was pointless. That—"

I couldn't speak. My throat was scraping against itself. I could taste the blood.

"And that's when I lost myself."

"Damian ..." I'd whispered once in bed.

He'd rolled over and stared at me. Then flatly said, "Get out."

"He was so cold at times. Everything was about keeping his lie going. All he thought about was 'what-ifs.' What if he had done this—then maybe he wouldn't have this happening to him. What if he had done that, and maybe it wouldn't have happened. If he'd eaten healthier. If he never drank, and he rarely drank anyway. If he'd only had a certain healthy drink. If he'd spent time with—I don't even know. I thought at times he was trying to learn what he could do to prevent it from getting worse. But that wasn't what he was doing. He was thinking back on his life, thinking back on what he could've done to have lived better. A more fulfilling life—that's what he told me one time. He yelled at me that I didn't fulfill him. That he didn't want me. That he had never wanted me. That he had never been attracted to me, and he'd had to force himself to kiss me."

I choked up, pressing the back of my hand to my mouth.

"Guys want it-girls," he said. He refused to look at me, sitting on the edge of the bed. "You're not an it-girl. You're too nice. But every guy wants her, just ask them."

My voice was hoarse. "He tried to break up with me so many times, but I never went. He broke me down, though. Little by little. And I don't know if he did it on purpose, but the end result was that I was a shell. I had nothing in me to fight him on things, to insist we call his mother, to force him to go see the doctors, to say what was happening wasn't normal. I just gave in. He threw temper tantrums. He told me how disappointed he was. And I took it."

I managed to look up for a moment. "That was my mistake. I took it until I couldn't stay in our house anymore. And once I walked out of the door, I couldn't bring myself to go back. My body wouldn't let me."

"Jesus."

"But I had to go back. By then he was dangerous to himself. He used to turn the oven on and leave it. He drank hot water once, not even stopping himself until he'd swallowed a good mouthful. He went a whole month forgetting to use soap to wash himself, or shampoo for his hair. He was using my facial cleanser."

"What was the breaking point?" Reese asked.

I almost laughed. "It should've been when he beat the shit out of me, right? It wasn't. No."

I'd come down the stairs one night and there was a blizzard going on outside. Windchill was -25 degrees.

"He left the door open one time. I shut it, not thinking about it, and went back to bed."

I shuddered, the memory haunting me.

"I bolted upright thirty minutes later. I knew—he hadn't just left the door open. When he went outside, he never closed the door, but he rarely went outside anymore. The door wasn't closed...because he was out there."

Reese drew in a harsh breath. "What happened?"

"911, what's your emergency?"

"DAMIAN!" I could hear myself, the wind. I could feel the biting cold.

"They found him two blocks from the house."

I couldn't feel my mouth.

I couldn't feel my hands.

I couldn't feel my legs.

"He almost froze to death, and it was my fault."

"No—" Reese began.

"It was!" I bit out. "It was. I was the caregiver. Me. Not him. I should've taken control long before then. He told me over and over again that I had to take him how he was or it was over with us. He threatened me every goddamn time I tried to say something, but I should've done it anyway. I should've called his bluff. I should've broken up with him if he wouldn't listen to me. I *should've* called his mother as soon as the first symptoms started, but I didn't. I didn't because I didn't want to lose him, but I lost him anyway. He was already gone. That first time he forgot my name? He looked terrified, but it wasn't because he couldn't remember me. It was because he thought a stranger had broken into his house. He was terrified *of me*. That's the day I lost him; I just never wanted to accept it." I shoved up from my chair.

I got two feet before Reese caught me. His hand took mine, and he folded me into him. "Charlie. Charlie," he whispered, wiping my face.

Tears. Of course. When were they not there?

"Jesus, Charlie. I'm so sorry." He hugged me as I stood frozen. There.

I heard the click. It had happened once before. And it just happened again.

I felt everything shutting down, turning off.

I closed up.

Nothing could hurt me.

I was a stone-cold statue, whether I wanted to be or not.

CHAPTER
THIRTY-SIX

I sat on my bed.

Reese's phone was going off, and he'd been on it for the last hour, almost since the moment I went robot-style. I caught a few names, but he was trying to keep his voice muffled. I knew he was talking to Juan at one point, then his coach. Who knew who else. People had started calling him. Otherwise I would've been worried he was trying to plan a feelings intervention for me.

"Okay," he said. "I'll be there in the morning. Thanks, Coach."

The front door opened.

Grant and Sophia were back.

They came in laughing just as Reese went back down the hallway. I could see them from my room.

"Hey!" Grant burped. "Sorry, man. We had to Uber here."

Sophia bumped into him, trying to take her shoes off. "Too much wine. So much wine."

Grant caught her, steadying her, and then she helped balance him while he took his shoes off. They were a good team. Perfect for each other.

I could feel Reese looking at me. I could feel his concern. It was in the air. I could almost smell it. And me, nothing. Just nothing.

I was back to that shell I'd always been.

This was a mistake. All of it—opening up. Letting Trent come over in the first place. Going to camp. Being with Reese. I sucked in a shuddering breath...falling for Reese. All of it was a mistake. If it happened again? If Reese ever looked at me and told me he didn't want me? If his mind started to go? What was I doing?

He was a pro basketball player.

He wouldn't want to be with me. Not for long.

We were friends. Fuck friends. Screw friends.

It didn't mean anything.

His going bare? That meant nothing. That was just for heightened pleasure. That's all. Nothing else.

"How was your night?" Grant asked. "Should I even ask?" He slapped Reese on the shoulder.

Reese was turned toward me. His hand ran through his hair. "Charlie."

"No." That word wrenched itself from me. Just no. No to anything more. I couldn't take any more of anything. "No."

"I think you should tell your friends."

"No!"

Grant frowned. "What's going on? Tell us what?"

"Charlie, she, uh..."

I was off the bed the next second and pushing Reese back. "It's not for you to say anything."

"You spilled all of that to me, and you've been in lockdown mode since. You don't think I recognize the signs? My brother's an alcoholic. That's why he does all the shit he does. That's why I enabled him for years, but don't think I don't get phone calls from him that break my heart. I do. And I get it—some of it. I get what you went through. But going locked-down right now? Not the answer. You can't open up, then shut off right afterward. That's not how you get better—"

"Fuck you!"

I didn't know why I'd said it. I just wanted him to shut up. I wanted him to stop. He didn't understand. No one could.

But his words had made a dent. I felt them sinking in, burrowing inside of me.

His brother was an alcoholic? What did that even mean?

"You enabled him?"

"Yeah. Like you enabled Damian."

I shook my head, bowing until I was almost a ball, just barely standing on my feet. It wasn't the same. "I didn't enable—"

Gentle hands found my shoulders. He lifted my head, then groaned at whatever he saw and just lifted me up. "You did enable him, but you didn't know you were enabling him."

He ran his hand through my hair, down my back. He was holding me like a child, but maybe it was appropriate. I was acting like one.

"You didn't do anything wrong," he whispered into my neck, pressing a kiss there.

Grant coughed, clearing his throat. "Um... I'll give you guys some time, yeah?"

Reese took me back to my bed, but got up again with me still in his arms. He crossed the room as Grant shut the door. He left the bathroom light on, the door ajar, and he hit the lights in the bedroom. The room was cast into darkness, a soft glow from the bathroom shining in.

It helped. I don't know how, but it helped. It lifted some of the whatever-the-hell-I-was-feeling off me, just slightly. There was still so much there. Almost too much.

He flipped on my fan next, giving us a modicum of privacy so we could speak freely.

Then he settled on my bed, resting against my headboard, with me on curled up on his lap. He tipped my head back so I could meet his gaze, and he tucked my hair behind my ears.

"I idolized my brother. He was the star in the family. Charismatic. He always had a girlfriend—and always one of the hot ones. For a guy, that says something. He was popular. There's about five years between us, so I was young enough not to see the signs growing up. Drinking, partying. I thought that was normal, and he was the star athlete, right? Then things changed. I was starting varsity as an eighth grader when it was his senior year. He rode the bench during the first few games. Suddenly basketball wasn't his thing. Suddenly he didn't want anything to do with the game. Football, though. He boasted how he wished I had played varsity on his team. He would've destroyed me, hazed me. And baseball. He let me know that if I made varsity baseball, I'd better watch out for his pitching hand. So I heeded his warnings. I stayed with basketball. I didn't even try for baseball, even on my own grade's team. I didn't want any issue with him."

His voice grew thick, strained. His arms tightened around me. "I thought things would be fine. They weren't. He didn't want us at his baseball games, said there could only be one kid who got Mom and Dad's attention in the family. They went to my basketball games, so if they did go to his baseball games, he wouldn't see them there. It was a brainwashing/mind-fuck thing on a whole other level, because he wanted them there. He just wanted them to feel like shit because they supported me his senior year. It worked."

His tone turned gravelly.

"His drinking was worse that year. He crashed his car, but our parents just felt so guilty. They felt bad for him. I realize that now—that they knew I was going to be something and Roman wasn't. Or he wasn't going to be a star athlete, and that had always been his thing. He'd banked on a professional career."

He sighed.

"He got a scholarship to school. Joined a fraternity. My parents thought everything would be fine. He was out of the house. Had a new girlfriend. Then the drinking got worse. He was skipping classes, skipping football practice. He had his second car crash that year, and this one smashed his leg. He was off the team. His grades were so bad, he lost his place in the fraternity. So he came home. And he kept drinking. And it got worse. Worse and worse and worse, to the point where his friends still in high school threatened me *for* him."

I gasped.

He kept going. I didn't think he'd heard me.

"His leg healed, but it almost didn't matter. He got his first DUI a month after he was driving again. He went to rehab. Thirty days in and out. Then to a sober living home. But as soon as he could start drinking, he was. I was a freshman in high school, then a sophomore during all of this, and he started getting hired for jobs because they liked having Reese Forster's brother working at their establishment. If it was a bar, they threw parties for him. If they were retail, they used my name on their banners, saying 'Come in on game day! 50% off in honor of Roman's little brother, Reese Forster.'"

He began grinding his teeth. I could hear the clicking sound.

"He burned his way through all the jobs in town—and I didn't grow up in a small place. It was a suburb of a bigger city. Didn't matter. By the time I was a senior, Roman was a full-blown alcoholic. Cops knew him by name. He'd had so many probation officers. I was removed from the house when I was a senior, because he kept going back. My parents kept taking him back. Parents' guilt, it's fucking powerful. But my coach noticed bruising on me from where Roman had 'wrestled' with me, which was really when he would try to beat the shit out of me, laughing as he did it. Social worker came in and surveyed the situation, because by then our parents were slipping too. My mom gave up. She just stayed in her bedroom all the time. My dad started joining Roman with the drinking. And I was sent out of there. Best goddamn time of my life."

"Reese." Somewhere in there, my wall had fallen. I turned toward him and put my hand on his face, turning him to me.

He gave me the saddest, the most haunting smile, and it broke me wide open. My tears were falling, for him, for me, for Damian, for his family.

I bent forward and rested my forehead to his chin. "I am so sorry."

He rested his cheek against the top of my head. "My brother lost his license that summer and went to rehab again. He'd gone so many times, but this time was longer. He stayed in for six months. I paid for everything, and no, I wasn't taking bribes or anything. I sold my car to pay for his rehab. I hoped—I really did—that he'd come out and be the big brother I wanted. And he was, for three weeks. He came to see me at school. He stayed with me even. He was the greatest brother. I'd never known this guy. We had a great time, and then he went back home to get a job. Three days with our dad, and he was drinking again. I went back a few times to try to help Mom, but she wasn't having it. She was so firmly in denial that I let her go too. All three of them. My high school coach had been in talks with my college coaches, so they all had a meeting with me. They laid it out. Let go of your family and keep moving forward to where they thought I could go, or let my family back in and never go anywhere. Alcoholism doesn't just affect the one person. It affects everyone."

He looked at me now, his eyes so piercing. "I get your denial. I get that you didn't want to lose Damian. I get all of it. The difference between my situation and yours? I had help. I had people in my corner ready to support me, but if they hadn't been there, I don't know where I would be. And yeah, I get you wanting to put a wall up, but it ain't happening."

He laid me down and loomed over me.

His hands traced my face. "Not on *my* watch. Not while I'm in your corner."

He paused, his eyes growing tender. "Got it?"

He'd used a hammer. Each word he'd said was a strike, a dent, a chip away. With his last word, the wall fell.

I crumbled. "Got it."

Then his mouth was on mine, and after we checked to make sure Grant and Sophia were sleeping (both snoring), he locked the door and turned my fan up even louder.

Once again he moved inside of me.

No condom. Just him. Me. Nothing between us.

I was fairly certain this felt like making love.

CHAPTER THIRTY-SEVEN

We'd missed the friendship bus, Reese and I. The train. The subway. The entire freaking airport. We were so far off base from friends who fuck, or whatever we were supposed to be to keep out the emotional attachments that I didn't know how we'd recover

I rolled over, knowing his alarm would go off in three minutes.

I wasn't sure I wanted to recover.

His face was turned toward me. His long eyelashes resting against his cheek.

One arm was up under his pillow, and his other draped over my waist.

Maybe he felt my gaze, but his eyes opened. When I saw he was watching me, a slight twitch to his top lip, I spoke.

"Would you still like me if I wasn't funny anymore? If I resorted to lame jokes I stole from a Laffy Taffy, would you look at me differently?"

I propped my head on my hand.

"Can I have your entire wardrobe?"

"Do you think Grant and Sophia boned last night?"

"Are we still friends?"

A pause, then, "Does dementia run in your family?"

His eyes shifted, growing more alert with each of my questions. He moved, his hand sliding around my shoulders at the same time his alarm went off. Reaching over me, he turned it off.

Lying on his side, his head on the pillow next to mine, he smiled. It was slow and tender, but only one thing would make it the best smile I'd ever seen.

Reaching behind me, I opened the drawer on my nightstand and pulled out two pieces of gum. I offered him one. "To preserve the romance."

He snorted, but popped it in. "There." He breathed on me. "Better?"

"Minty fresh." I put mine in too. The only thing I needed now was to ignore my bladder. I knew Reese. He would answer my questions.

"I never liked you because you were funny. I started liking you because you were nuts, but you really weren't, if that makes sense."

I grinned. "It doesn't, which makes me feel like it does."

He smiled again. "I think Laffy Taffy jokes are the best, so every now and then maybe? Let's not overdo it. No to the wardrobe, since I need it, and we can't do a switch. No. I don't think they boned. I think Grant thought about it, wished he could, but was too drunk to get it up."

"Ew."

He ignored that. "Yes, we're still friends." His finger moved up, tracing the side of my face, pushing some hair from my mouth. "I think we can save time and acknowledge we're more than friends." He caught my look. "More than friends who bone even."

"Oh."

"And no, dementia does not run in my family. My grandfather was an alcoholic, so's Roman, and I think my dad pretends to be so he doesn't have to deal with life. But I don't drink, so you don't have to worry about that—you know, if we remain more than friends who bone."

It was like my heart was made of flower petals. Each one opened, beginning to collect, build, blossom. His last words were the last petal falling into place, completing the heart.

Cheesy, but the perfect description. It fell into place, all of it.

"I think I like you," I whispered.

Reese moved closer, his forehead resting against mine. "You have a cardboard cutout of me. I think you've liked me for a long time."

I barked out a laugh. "I was messing with you. I don't have a cardboard cutout."

"If we keep with our more-than-friends-who-bone theme, I'll get you one for Valentine's Day." He lifted me up and rolled to his back, holding me over him, his hands under my arms.

"Deal." I nodded. "I feel like I'm your new puppy."

"Christ." He draped me over his chest, and nuzzled against the top of my head. "I have a flight to catch."

"You do." My hand traced his chest, because I could, because I was already missing him. Catching on his boxer's waistband, I slid my finger underneath, moving across his stomach and then smoothing my hand back up to his bicep.

"We have a game tomorrow." His hips nudged mine, jostling me a little. "Would you come?"

An argument could've been made that I already had, but I knew we weren't joking anymore. Lifting my head, I peered at him. "What are you asking?"

He smoothed his hands down my back, resting on my hips. "Spend the day with your friends, and then fly out tomorrow morning. Come to my game."

"Are you serious?"

He nodded, his eyes somber. "Come see me. Home games are the best. Spend the week. I can show you my city."

My heart lurched upward, and I went with the motion. Sitting up, my legs falling to either side of him, I rested my hands on his chest. "We're *so* far past the friends-who-bone-who-can't-bone-anyone-else, aren't we?"

"I think we have been since we started." He watched me, steadily. "I think we were *before* we started."

My heart lurched again. "You're okay with that?"

He could have any girl, any number of girls. Why would he want someone with baggage the size of the Atlantic? Who couldn't communicate except through random outbursts of fuckery questions. Who longed to return to her hermit status, but knew being social was healing and something she wanted in the long run.

"I have problems."

He pressed his lips together, sighing. "So do I."

"Not like mine."

"Want to do this? A battle of who has the worst problems? I could put together a good argument that centers around high-pressure versus low-pressure situations?"

My eyes grew wide. Damn. That was a good counter.

"If you're okay with it, then I am," I said. "Or I will be."

"You sure?"

"Are you sure?"

"Are you repeating everything I say?"

"Are *you* repeating everything *I* say?"

He paused, then seemed to surrender. "You're right. You have the bigger problems." His top lip curved up. "Satisfied?"

"The mostest."

Satisfaction spread through me, warming me, tickling me, and not because I'd won our stupid argument.

I was happy.

In that moment, in his arms, with the slightest glow of light behind us, as he asked me to visit him, as we decided we were *more than*, I was happy.

And that should've scared me to death, but it didn't. That's how far gone I was. I'd even take a Valentine's cardboard cutout of him and gush over it every day.

"Okay."

"Okay?"

I nodded. "Okay."

He held up his hand, his pinkie extended, and I met it with mine. We pinkie swore on it.

Then he grabbed me, rolled me under him, and almost missed his flight.

CHAPTER THIRTY-EIGHT

G rant took me to the airport the next morning. Sophia was still sleeping. Hell, everyone was still sleeping. Reese had gotten me a ticket for the first flight out.

It was four-thirty in the morning, but score—he'd upgraded me to first class. I was looking forward to settling in the land of extra leg space and free booze, except this morning it'd be constant coffee.

I hoped.

They did that, right?

I'm digressing.

Airport. Me. Grant. And my nerves. There were so many.

I pressed my hand to my chest, willing some of those nerves away. It wasn't working. They just slammed back against my chest. I felt them mocking me. Who got taunted by her own nerves? Me.

Grant pulled the car to the curb. Since it was so early, there weren't as many travelers here. The pressure to dump and dash wasn't as high as it usually was. Grant put the car in park and leaned back in his seat.

He watched me. "You okay?"

The nerves were now pointing and laughing. I jerked my head in a stiff nod. "Yep. Totally great. Super*b*." I popped the B.

A faint grin showed, then he yawned. "It's early. Why'd he get you a ticket this early?"

I laughed. "Right. Like I'm going to complain."

"Touché."

"Besides." I reached for my coffee. I needed to inhale it before going through security. "He said something about this way he can pick me up and not have to send a driver."

"Fair enough."

We were both joking. Reese had bought me a freaking ticket. It could have eight layovers, and I wouldn't care. The gesture was kind and giving and just Reese—or the way he was with me.

"I still can't believe you're dating Reese Forster."

"We're just—"

Grant rolled his eyes. "Say what you want. I know what I heard last night, and that, my friend, was a couple talk, fight, and makeup. You and him. You guys aren't just friends." He leaned forward. "He's flying you to freaking Seattle. That says a lot. Friends don't do that, or at least not after seeing you twenty-four hours ago. You know it."

Yeah. He had a point.

I was still going to fight it. "Friends."

He scoffed. "Yeah. You and me. We're friends. You and him, not friends, not like that."

"You and I kissed."

He snorted. "Which you told me meant nothing—thanks for the ego boost."

"Now you have Sophia."

"Yeah." I could hear his fondness. "I do. Now I have Sophia." His eyes focused on me again. "And you have us too."

I nodded. I knew he was serious. And he was still looking at me.

"We're going to be gone by the time you come back," he said. "Do me a favor?"

"Yeah?"

"Don't disappear for five years, or six years, or however long it was. Please. You really are a dear friend."

My throat swelled with an onslaught of emotions. "I know. I won't," I rasped out.

"Promise?"

Oh, man. More throat burning. I looked away, tugging at the ends of my sleeves. "I told Reese about Damian, about those years. I told him some of the bad stuff. There was good too, but yeah—if I was going to hide and lock down, it would've happened last night."

"That's what we walked in on?"

I nodded.

"He broke through?"

Gah. Those three words were everything.

I whispered, "He broke through."

"Then I'm indebted to him. But if he breaks your heart, I'm going to troll all the Seattle Thunder social media sites."

I looked back at him, flicking away a tear. It was only one. Progress. "As a good friend should."

He grunted. "Damn straight."

After a hug goodbye, I went inside, and not long after that I was through security and heading for my gate.

The flight was just as I'd predicted: the extra leg space was heavenly. And it might've been the reason I was buzzed off of coffee when we landed in Seattle. I only had a carry-on with me, so no stop needed in baggage claim. When I stepped outside, I wasn't quite ready for the entire-building mural staring back at me.

Reese. Juan. Three more players in the background. *Seattle Thunder* painted in big bold letters—but it was the look in Reese's eyes that drew me in. I mean, yeah, the chiseled jaw and his hair in a small fauxhawk—which was hot on him—but it was the eyes. They were piercing my soul.

Or the chest.

The arms. The narrow hips. The way he was turned sideways and I could see his ass and—*honk!*

A silver truck had parked in front of me. The driver had leaned over to the passenger side, and those same eyes were smirking at me.

Busted. He knew I'd been checking him out.

I had ovaries. I was supposed to.

When he hopped out, he had on the same disguise as yesterday: a ball cap pulled low over his eyes and a hood over that, but his six-three frame was drawing looks. The curse of the professional athlete. Their build alone had people speculating who they were.

He came over, grabbed my carry-on, and said, "I'll kiss you in the truck."

Right.

Two ladies were gawking, and a guy was starting to head over, camera in hand.

Reese hooked a hand in the back of my pants and pulled me to the passenger side of his truck. I climbed in as he rounded to his side, he put my bag in the back seat, and we were off. The guy had almost gotten to us, his camera in front of his face now.

Reese hit the accelerator, reaching over and tugging me so I wasn't looking out anymore. He ducked forward as well.

We got down the ramp and he'd hit the signal to merge onto the interstate when his hand finally fell away.

"I think he recognized my truck."

"I didn't think that was such a problem for you?"

"It's not." His lips tightened a moment. "Usually. It's gotten worse since my brother's shit happened. He got someone to post bail—a sports fan of mine—and now a new story has hit the blogs. He promised the fan they'd get to meet me, and you know how that went down. The woman is furious and blasting my name all over the gossip sites."

His jaw had clenched. His hands were tight on the steering wheel, and I heard the slight growl under his words.

This was the reason they'd come to our camp. This was the reason he'd needed to shoot hoops for hours on end that first night. His anger was back.

As Reese turned the steering wheel to exit, I glimpsed his bicep bulging through his sweatshirt. There was a rigidness there that hadn't been present in Minnesota.

I reacted without thinking, catching his hand and pulling it to my lap.

He glanced over, but didn't pull away or say anything.

I began to rub at the base of his thumb. It was rock hard.

He bit out a groan. "Jesus, that feels good."

"That's all stress."

Another grunt. "Tell me about it." His eyes fluttered a second, and he seemed to shake himself loose. "Wait. No. Tell me about it. Tell me about your flight. Your dinner. How's the infamous Janet? Am I ever going to meet her?" He managed a crooked smile.

I filled him in: A caffeine buzz. Okay. Same. And no.

His laugh was a low baritone. "That's it? You're not going into any more detail?"

I shook my head. "Nope. My turn of being the center of attention was, like, five states ago. We're in your territory now." I kept rubbing over his thumb. "Fill me in on what's going on with your brother."

His hand jerked, but he kept it in mine. "It's a shit show. That's all I can say."

"So tell me."

He cursed, pulling his hand away and rubbing it over his jaw. "I don't really want to talk about it, to be honest."

I tried not to feel dejected. I was mostly failing. "I told you about my stuff."

"And I told you mine."

"You gave me the bulletproof version. The stuff that's in the past and not affecting you." I eyed his hand, but he switched his grip on the wheel, his left hand going to his leg now. "What's affecting you now?" I murmured.

"Charlie." He gentled his voice. "I don't want to be a dick, but I spent all fucking evening on the phone with people about Roman. You're here." His hand covered mine again, squeezing. "And I didn't kiss you at the airport." He glanced over, his eyes darting to my mouth. "I'm more pissed about the camera guy now."

He was lying.

I recognized the signs. Distraction. Smoothing things over. A more cheerful tone. Bullshitology 101, and I'd become damned good at it.

Feeling a pang in my chest, I said, "Look, full transparency? You're full of shit."

His head whipped back to mine, just for a second before returning to the road.

I didn't touch his hand, and he didn't move it away.

"You pushed through my walls. You dug inside when I didn't want to talk, and then you poured out your baggage. We chose to be more than friends. That means real conversations like this."

My chest tightened as I flashed back to Damian's temper. My teeth began to grind together. "I won't be anything with a guy unless he gives as much as I do. That's my rule. And yeah, that's friendship too, I guess, but most definitely a guy I'm fucking. You open up, at least a little, and we're good. I opened up last time. Remember?"

Damian would've turned the tables, made me the bad guy for pushing. He'd be the victim... I felt like a rock, entirely on edge as I waited for Reese to blast me. My eyes were closed, my nails digging in my jeans when he let out a soft curse.

His hand took mine, tugging it to his lap. "Fuck. Is that what he did to you?"

"What?" My voice had gone hoarse.

"I was a dick, and a second later your entire body froze up. You said your piece, and now it's like you're expecting me to start beating you or something."

He was right.

I knew he was right. I had thought it too, prepared for it, but hearing it come out of someone else, that was different. The impact was smack in the middle of my chest.

"I..."

"Did he?" His question was biting.

I flinched.

"Hey." His hand squeezed mine, let go, squeezed again. Over and over. "I'm sorry. I didn't mean that the way it came out. Just..." He was fighting for control. "You're right. You're completely right, and I was being an asshole. You called me out on it, and I like that you did that. But...fuck. Did he hurt you because you did that to him?"

Tears dripped down my cheeks.

I was really sick of feeling this way.

"He didn't physically hurt me, but yes. I'd call him on things, and he'd twist it. I was always the wrong one, until I just stopped talking."

He wore me down. That was the truth, and that gaping hole was back inside of me.

I tugged my hand away, turned to the window, and pulled my feet up on the seat—folding in on myself, my go-to. If I could've gone into a fetal position, I would've.

"Hey. Hey." Reese reached over, taking an exit. His hand touched my leg, softly rubbing back and forth. "I'm sorry, okay? My brother shit? It's just that: a shit show. I'm sorry for being short."

"I don't care if you're short. Honestly. Just..."

We were back here. I was pushing, or prompting, and scared to do that. But that's what was normal, right? Or was I wrong?

I started laughing, wiping away the tears. "I don't know how to do this, whatever this is." I motioned between us. "I went from a seven-year relationship to a three-month regret. Now I'm here, and..." It wasn't the same, so not the same. "Is this healthy?"

Reese slowed at the intersection, taking a right. We were pulling away from the city, moving onto a road that wound along the shoreline. It was gorgeous. Trees. Long stems of grass sticking up in the air. White tree limbs on the ground. Rocks.

I thought Minnesota was pretty, but this was different. It has a more majestic, grander feel to it. Larger.

"My house isn't too far ahead," Reese said. "Traffic normally sucks here, but we got lucky today."

"That's nice."

We'd been on the interstate for most of the trip, but now on the smaller roads, I felt a calm settling into my bones. It didn't make sense, though I wasn't going to fight it or try to explain. Watching the ocean, the waves rippling over the surface, I was struck by the vastness.

"We have lakes where I live. They're pretty and calming, but they're small."

"Yeah?"

"Yeah." I wasn't at all sure what I was saying. "You know there are boundaries. Your danger is more from drowning, not being pulled away by an undercurrent and taken out to sea."

But despite the danger, there was something freeing about driving along the shore. And just like that, I knew I wasn't talking about the different bodies of water.

Damian was a lake. He had made me feel trapped. Caged in.

Reese was this shoreline, the edge of something new, something freeing.

"You okay?" He slowed the truck, turning onto another road. We moved away from the shoreline to drive past houses now.

"Yeah." The word caught in my throat. "So. Roman..." My voice squeaked, and I smoothed my one hand down my leg. "You share now."

He grinned, glancing over. "Need a subject change?"

"Drastically."

"Fair enough." He inclined his head. "But we're almost to my place, and you'll see for yourself."

"What?" Did he mean...?

"No!" He must've read my thoughts. "No, no. I'd never let my brother into my place, but I have to warn you that once we get to the house, you'll have a front-row seat to the Roman Show. One of my lawyers is coming over, my agent, my manager, a rep from the team. We have a game today, so they're all coming over for a powwow on how to handle everything. Roman's supposedly trying to come to the game tonight."

"No."

Another jaw clench. "Yes."

Then we were slowing. He reached over, touched a button, and a wrought-iron gate started to open.

I was dumbstruck—fitting, because I'd forgotten who exactly Reese was. I knew, but I didn't know. And him being rich was one thing I'd definitely forgotten.

I was looking at a three-building lot. Five-stall garage to one side. The main house was a giant square with arched posts around the door. Another building sat to the other side, a smaller one, and

I could see the bright blue of a pool just beyond, nestled among lush green lawns.

Reese pulled up in front of the main house, saw me, and snorted. "Come on. And you've got drool coming down the side of your mouth."

Drooling. He wasn't exaggerating.

"Coming."

And I think I really was, which was awkward. I walked to the door, my legs pressed together, a grimace on my face.

• • •

Once inside, Reese hauled me up, his mouth on mine. And—oh! *Oh.*

Lust and pleasure trailed down my spine, making me shiver, and he wasted no time. Carrying me straight through his house, he took me to his bedroom, and we were writhing naked in no time. He entered me—a hurried, desperate edge to him that I hadn't felt at my place or at camp—and then it was lights out. My mind stopped working.

"God." He dropped a kiss to my bare shoulder after we'd both climaxed. "I really love being in you." He thrust one last time before sliding back out and collapsing to his back.

I... Yep. No words.

A speeding horse had come along, plucked me up, and taken me on a twisted pathway over a mountain's edge. Exhilarated and *worked over* completely—that's how I was feeling.

"Reese." I was blind. The orgasm had taken my sight. I threw my arm out, patting for his hand until he chuckled and took it. "You broke the he-girl. My spine. I can't see. I'm wrecked."

There was a buzzing in the house, and he groaned as he sat up. "Hey." He tapped my chin.

I opened my eyes—that's why I couldn't see. And I grinned up at him, knowing my smile was akin to a wasted sailor's. "Hey there."

He gave a short chuckle before he grew serious. The buzzer sounded again. He looked over his shoulder, but turned back to me. "I'll bring your carry-on up here, but take your time coming down. These guys are..." He sighed.

Buzz.

BUZZ!

He ran a hand through his hair, scooting to the edge of his bed. The sheet pooled over his waist, but I appreciated the corded muscles in his back.

He stood and looked back down at me.

His jaw was back to clenching, and my heart sank.

"Look—"

BUZZZZZZZ!

He ignored it, bending down so his hands rested on both sides of me, an apology already in his eyes. "Meeting you at camp and the time with you afterward has helped me. It distracted me from what's happening now." His eyes softened, and he smoothed his thumb down the side of my cheek, leaving a trail of tingles. "I don't know how to say this, except that a guy's gotta..."

He paused again, took another breath. His eyes flashed, a hardness replacing the gentleness before. "Being a pro athlete, you're a professional. You have to be. This is my day at the office, and along with that comes lines I won't cross, people I won't let in, and I put up harsh boundaries sometimes. It's a high-pressure living, and that means sometimes I'll be hard, but not with you. Whatever you see from me down there, I'll never be like that with you. I want you to know that."

I nodded, speechless, as he twisted around. The buzzer was a constant now, and he pulled on some pants, cursing as he went out of the room.

I was dazed, from all of this.

He had kissed me like he was starving, then shoved inside like he was dehydrated. I loved it—every bit of it—but the warning? That had fallen to the pit of my stomach. What kind of guys were they that had come over?

He brought my carry-on upstairs just before his door opened and we heard someone holler, "Reese?"

There'd been no time to talk, and he'd disappeared after running a hand over his face.

I showered, marveling at his bathroom, then got dressed. It was an hour later when I was ready, and three more voices had joined the conversation downstairs. I couldn't make out their words, but I could hear them. There was some shouting, curses, and low murmuring too.

"I don't give a shit!" Reese barked as I left the room.

His bedroom was on the second floor. At the end of the hallway, stairs covered in white carpet swept down to the front door. I could tell they'd gathered in a room off to the side— probably the living room.

And here I was, not sure what to do.

I opted for going back to his bed. After making it, I lie down and dug in my bag for my phone and headphones. Barns Courtney had a new single out. I must've dozed, because when I came to, Reese was standing over me, a weird smile on his face.

"Hey." I pulled the headphones off, sitting up.

A guy stood in the doorway, his eyebrows pinched together and a firm scowl on his face. He was trim, maybe around six feet, in khaki dress pants and a blazer. A Seattle Thunder pin was attached to his lapel.

"Who the fuck is this?" he asked.

Reese ignored him, saying to me, "You fell asleep?"

"Reese." The guy stepped in the room.

Still ignoring him. "I have to go to the gym. Juan's girlfriend is coming over to pick you up. She'll take you to the game. You can hang with her until after."

Jeez. I was being inducted to the girlfriend circle already? Not intimidated at all here.

"Okay." I sounded cool and calm, not lying whatsoever.

Reese saw right through me. "You'll like her. She's like your friend Hadley."

That eased a few of the knots.

The guy took another step, his hands clutching the ends of his jacket. "Reese!"

"What?" Reese looked behind him, a scowl on his face now.

There was the guy I first met. He'd warned me. He went from kind to dick in two seconds flat.

It was wrong to be turned on, right? A burst of flutters started in my chest.

The guy pointed at me, his finger jabbing in the air. "Who the hell is this girl? Was she here the whole time?"

Reese was cold. "It's none of your business."

"She could've overheard everything. Has she signed an NDA?"

Reese's back was tense. He took a step away from the bed, partially blocking me from the guy's view. "When have I fucked up?"

The guy was quiet. "Your brother—"

"That's Roman. When have *I* fucked up?"

"You haven't."

"Then why are you acting like I just fucked up?"

The guy eased back a step, his tone a mild bark now. "Your judgment could be impaired—"

Slap! Right to my face. The guy's invisible hand left an imprint.

"—and you've never had one of your women—"

A second slap, followed by a *pow.*

"—here before when we have business going on. It's my job to look out for you."

"Yeah. Look out for me, not assume I've completely lost my mind." Reese jerked his head toward the door. "I'll be right out. Got it?"

There was a moment of silence. Then I heard the guy succumb. "Fine."

He left, disappeared down the hallway, and the front door slammed shut a beat after.

Reese didn't look at me, not at first. He stared at the door, letting out a soft, "Fuck," before turning back. Regret flared over his face. "I'm not even going to address that guy, because honestly, you're going to get more reactions like that. I'm sorry."

I gulped. "It's fine."

"It's not." His face was tormented. "And I won't be around to block it all." He sat by me, his eyes tracing my face. "Just stay close to Marie. She'll be here in an hour. She talked about coming early to get to know you a little."

I was getting a wake-up call here. That guy's reaction, the camera guy, the mural outside of the airport. Yeah. It wasn't time for jokes, though I winced. There should always be room for jokes, but okay. Serious again.

I sat up, touching Reese's leg. "Hey. I got it. You don't have to worry about me."

"I'm not sure what to say here, because I don't want to keep you a secret, but..."

Yes. Invisible writing on the wall. I could read it. I reached, my fingers sliding through his. I gave him a reassuring squeeze. Our roles were switching. The significance wasn't lost on me.

"I'll be fine. I'm not a girl who's going to get upset you're not telling people about whatever we are."

His eyes flashed.

I grinned. "I mean, I know we're having great sex, but well, you know what I mean."

He groaned, leaning down and capturing my mouth. "You're more than a screw. You know that, right?"

I almost preened. "The best words ever. Put that on a Valentine's Day card."

A grimace, then a chuckle. "Shit. I'm sorry. I..." He leaned back, tilting his head to the side. "We don't use the big words."

"Because of me. Because of my baggage." I squeezed his hand. "So if you think I'm a chick who wants to shout it to the tabloids or anyone that we're whatever—"

He laughed. "We've progressed. Screwing to whatever."

I lifted a shoulder. "—then you never really knew me." I waved a hand around. "All of this is a lot, but I've got too much damage in me to start getting ideas. You can relax. I'm here to whatever you and hang out. That's it. But if Juan's girlfriend isn't cool, I might ditch the game."

His eyes widened. "Are you serious?"

"No." I flashed a grin. "But I might ditch her and watch from the aisle somewhere."

He groaned, bending down to rest his forehead to mine. His hands cupped my face. "Don't do that. Marie's cool, and you'll hurt her feelings. Then Juan will get mad at me because Marie's very picky about who she befriends."

That made her more appealing. I perked up. "Yeah?"

"Yeah." He pressed a kiss to my forehead just as a honking sound came from outside. "Jesus Christ. I'm going to kill that guy."

"Go." I shooed him. "Get out of here."

He backed toward the door. "Marie knows the code to lock everything up, and stick with her after the game. We'll meet up with you guys." He turned to jog down the stairs.

I scrambled to my knees. "Good luck!"

"Thanks," he shouted.

Then the door shut again, and I could hear voices outside.

I couldn't help myself. I went to the window, watching Reese get in the passenger side of a very expensive-looking car. I had no clue what kind it was, but it screamed money. The gate opened, and the car sped off.

Then it was me, and the realization of the world I'd stepped into hit me hard.

I was fairly certain I'd just crapped my pants.

CHAPTER THIRTY-NINE

Reese lied to me.

Marie was nothing like Hadley.

I mean, height and weight she was petite like Hadley, but she had black hair, a lip ring, and had a solid amount of makeup on her face. Also, her arms were crossed over her chest and she was inspecting me like I was an ant under her shoe.

"What are your intentions with Reese?"

That wasn't even her first question. She'd started off the interrogation Monty Python-style with "What is your name? What is your favorite color?" And we'd progressed from there. I was past the first molehill of questions and she now circled me as I sat at Reese's kitchen table.

"Uh, my intentions?" I shrugged. "Besides phenomenal sex?"

She kept circling, those arms still crossed tight. "You know what I mean. You're a funny one, I see."

I was tempted to snort, but I'd done that after the first four questions. She got tired of it, growling, "You're not taking this seriously." I'd been refraining since.

I sighed instead. More appropriate.

"Okay." I was having déjà vu. This was the third time my cards had needed to be laid out, and I stood.

Marie paused in her circling.

I mirrored her, folding my arms over my chest. "I get that you're being protective of Reese, but if you think I'm going to lay out all my innermost secrets to you, a stranger, you can walk right back out. Reese invited me here. He said you'd hang out with me until he was done, but I have no problem buying a scalped ticket and going to see his game by myself."

She sneered. "It'll be in the nosebleeds."

"I don't give a shit. I'm going with the pure intention of being able to say yes, I was there to support him when he asks about the game. I don't like lying, but I'm also not going to let you interrogate me anymore. The first ten minutes were out of respect because Juan is a nice guy. The next ten minutes were for my entertainment, but these last five minutes, the arrow went real quick to not enjoying this anymore."

"Reese never asks me to take care of someone for him. Ever."

"Then maybe you should trust him? I don't know what to tell you."

Her eyes were almost slits. She tipped her chin up. "You hurt him, and I will sic a private investigator on you. I'll ask him to expose your weakness, and whatever that is, I'll exploit it. I don't care. Reese is a damned good guy."

"Why do you think I'm here?"

She cocked her head. "Because he's rich, and famous, and hot?"

"I don't care if he's rich. The famous thing actually freaks me out, and yeah, the last part is nice. I'll give you one of those."

"Are you an actress?"

I snorted.

A small growl escaped her closed mouth.

I amended, "Sorry, but no. I was recently fired from two jobs, and I'm a mess right now, but despite all of that, Reese still invited me out here."

"Are you a mode—"

I almost snorted again.

She amended this time. "You don't have the height for that." Suspicion still hung heavy. "One last question and I'll ease up."

"Okay?"

"Will you let me go through your purse?"

A purse. Ooooooh fuck.

I paled. "I knew I forgot something."

"What?"

But it was no problem. I had transferred all my stuff to my carry-on. A purse wasn't needed. Relief weakened my knees after a small heart attack.

"I would, if I'd remembered it. I took everything out and put it in my carry-on for easier access. I hate carrying two bags, so I was going to stuff my purse in my carry-on too. But it's at my apartment right now."

Her eyebrows went up into her forehead. "You don't have a purse?"

"No."

"And you only brought a carry-on with you?"

A slow nod from me.

She relaxed suddenly, her arms falling to her sides and her shoulders rolling backward. "Girl, you could've said that and saved us a whole lot of time."

"Why?"

"Because no chick who only brings a carry-on to see fucking Reese Forster is out to use him. No high-maintenance chick would forget a purse." She flicked her hair over her shoulder, pivoting and going into the kitchen. She reached for a bottle of tequila and poured two shots for us. "Here." She pushed one to me. "We could've been drinking this whole time."

I migrated to the counter. "I don't want to argue with your theory, but I don't quite get it either." I picked up the shot and held it. "But here's to an interrogation-free game? I'm hoping."

She grinned, the first time her ice façade had cracked. She toasted me with her shot, before tossing it back. "Damn. I need one more."

"Are you driving to the game?"

"Let's do an Uber. The guys will drive us home later."

She flashed me a grin, and my heart stopped. It took her from terrifying to stunning. She was a short little minx, sassy scary, though.

"And you can't really blame me. I've been with Juan for four years. Reese is like family. He's a godparent to our son."

"You have a son with Juan?"

She nodded, smiling in pride. "And two little girls too."

This was *so* not the world I came from.

She must've sensed my thoughts, because she held up that finger again. "And don't be calling me Juan's baby-momma, because it's not like that."

I frowned.

"You're from the Midwest?"

Wary now. "Yeah?"

"You conservative and shit?"

"Huh?"

"You know. Looking down on me because Juan and I are shacked up, three kids together, and no ring?" She had lowered her head, giving me a side-eye I knew I'd never be able to mimic.

I was about to break one of my rules. "I lived with a guy for seven years. No kids, but no ring either." And even though she hadn't asked, I added, "And yes, my dad disapproved, but I didn't care. And by the way, I've never used the term *baby-momma* in my life. I've only heard it on movies and television."

"You serious?"

"Yeah. You gonna look down on me now?"

We took a moment, eyeing each other. Her side-eye was still perfection, but I was trying. I felt like a bobbing ostrich, though.

Then she sighed, every inch of her loosening up. "Okay. I got you. I think." She paused a second. "You must have baggage?"

My lips were sealed.

She grunted, nodding to herself. "Yeah." She threw back the second shot and grabbed two beers after that. "Definite baggage."

She slid one of the beers to me, and I took it. I was so far out of my depth, I was just going to go with it. She said drink the beer, I'd double-fist it.

Later, after we'd both settled down and called a truce, she grinned at me from the back of our Uber.

"I should probably tell you right now that I'm into girls too, and damn—Reese has good taste."

Awwww...

A whole chunk of thawing ice fell off my chest. "If you hadn't won me over with the shot glasses that look like tampons, that would've done it." I patted the tampon in my pocket.

At least for the time being, I had a feeling Reese was right. Marie and I were going to get along just fine.

CHAPTER FORTY

"That's Shelly. She's Crusky's current girlfriend, but don't make eye contact for too long or she'll start thinking we're talking about his wife."

"Huh?"

We were three beers in, and four shots. We'd also eaten a slice of pizza, so I was pretty sure that absorbed one of the beers. Saying I was more than tipsy would've been... What was I saying again?

I burped. "Crusky has a wife *and* a girlfriend?"

He was no longer the Cruskinator to my inner fangirl, but Crusky. I was talking like I knew him, which I didn't, not really. He teased me once, though.

And I was talking to myself again.

I focused on what Marie was saying, blinking a few times because that seemed to help.

"—going through a divorce, but the wife is fighting it and it's taking foooorever."

Marie nudged me with her shoulder, leaning in from where we were standing. The game hadn't even started. She'd brought us up to this box area because family could come up here, but it was really just to grab a few free drinks and food. She asked if I wanted to stay. The other choice was a pair of regular tickets. I opted for a fill-up, then the seats down below.

"Can't say I blame you. It's dangerous being up here."

I hadn't known what she was referring to, but when more people came into the box, I got it then. Wives. Families. I

269

recognized the guy who'd barked at me at Reese's and ducked when he looked back at me. Marie was shorter than me, but a little heavier. I hunched farther down.

She stopped talking about Crusky's love life and frowned at me. Moving her hotdog out of the way to see me, she asked, "What are you doing?"

"Hiding."

The guy moved, frowning at me, and I turned my head—because I was two again. If I couldn't see him, he couldn't see me.

"Marie?"

Fuck. Damn. Incoming.

"Hey, Stan!"

Why'd she have to sound so friendly? Marie was my new ally. Right? Wrong. I was just visiting. Of course she'd cozy up to him.

"Hello..." He sounded stiff, and I couldn't avoid this any longer.

I turned, standing tall again, and locked eyes with him. He wasn't as hostile as before, his eyebrows were still pinched, confusion clouding his eyes more than anything else.

He put a hand out. "You are?"

Okay. Fine. He was playing this game.

I gave him a big smile. I loved games like this. Fitting my hand in his, I gave it a firm pump. "I'm Marie's friend."

She looked down, her shoulders shaking, trying to smother her laughter. She was failing so miserably.

"Right." He sighed and pulled his hand away. "What's your name?"

"What's yours?"

Déjà vu again. This was a Keith 2.0 moment, except this guy was a lot younger. He didn't look too much older than Reese.

"What?"

Marie entered the fray. "This is Stan. He's Reese's manager."

"Ah."

I didn't care. I should have, but I didn't. Reese and I were not a permanent thing. And even if we became—nope, I was not thinking that way. Stress, expectations, all the normal worries about relationships were starting to weigh me down, and that wasn't Reese and me. I wouldn't let that happen. We were fun and carefree. *Free*, being the key term there.

I plastered a smile on my face, nodding again. I was tempted to bow, but refrained. "It's nice meeting you."

I made a point of turning to look out at the gym. The team's cheerleaders were on the court, doing a dance for the crowd. Thunder was waving his arms around.

I could feel Marie and Stan exchange a look, but it wasn't happening. I wouldn't get pulled in, get a label put on me, and then have to endure another round of suspicious questions. He and Marie had both put me through the wringer, but then she'd introduced me to tampon-shot-disguising tubes and told me I was hot, so I was a little in love with her.

They still hadn't started talking, so I looked back. "Excuse me. I'm going to go to the bathroom."

Stan's entire face was twisted in a question mark.

Marie coughed. "Oh. Okay." She finished her hotdog, wiping her face with a napkin. "We gotta go out for the restroom. You want anything else?"

I had a full beer in hand, and my own hotdog was starting to feel unsettled. "Nope. I'm good." I smacked my groin. "Just gotta pee."

Stan's head reared back, and Marie's eyebrows shot up.

She seemed transfixed, so I led the way—around a few groups of women who looked like they could be supermodels, and men I knew had to be in positions of power and wealth to even be in that box. Once outside, I was grateful. Marie had been following, but I looked back through the door, and she'd been caught by one of those groups of people.

The door closed.

I waited against the opposite wall.

The door opened, and two guys came out. Marie caught my gaze and held up her hand. One minute.

I nodded, settling in.

But then the door opened again and Reese's manager stepped out. He had turned to look down the hall, so seeing me across from him drew him up short. He straightened up, smoothing out his collar and adjusting the Thunder pin before stepping toward me.

"Can we talk?"

"Why?"

He cringed. "You're...not what I expected, I'll admit."

The appropriate thing would be to ask what he meant. I did nothing.

His response to me cooled. "I'd imagine you wouldn't want to make a bad impression on Reese's manager since I've worked for him since the second he turned pro."

Seriously? "After how you talked to me at his house? You laid the groundwork first. And—" My fourth lay-your-cards-down moment. "—I'm not permanent."

"What?"

The door opened behind him, and it was Marie. She crossed the hallway, standing to the side of Stan.

"I get that you guys want to protect him, but it's not him you have to protect. We became friends, oddly enough, and that's all I'm going to say. You want information, you ask him. You want my name, you ask him. You want to know my intentions, you ask him. I have no problem walking away from this. Like I told Reese before, I could ditch and watch his game from the aisle because that's the type of girl I am. Whatever girls you're used to, that's not me. Promise."

They were both quiet.

"I don't like you," Stan announced.

"I think I love you," Marie countered.

Yeah. Okay then.

I stepped away from the wall. "I'm going to go find a bathroom. I can meet you at the seats?"

The door opened and a woman stepped out, calling Marie's name. I was going to give her an option to sit with me, or stay in there. It would be up to her, but I saw the conflict flash over her face. Her mouth tightened a second.

"Hey." I infused my voice with warmth. I was being so fake, but I was selling it. "You called me low-maintenance earlier. Well,

I really am. I'm a true sports fan, so if you want to watch with your friend in there, I have no problem sitting by myself. I'm totally okay with it."

"The fuck are you talking about?" She looked back. "I'll be right there, Tawnia." She looked back to me. "I was right." She dipped her forehead to me, walking backward with her beer. "Baggage. Lots of it."

I had to give her that one. "More than you could imagine." I nodded behind her. "Go. Talk. I'll be at the seats."

She rolled her eyes. "You and me. We're getting drunk later, and you're gonna tell me something about you." She dug in her pocket with her free hand and handed over one of the tickets. "I'll see you there later."

I ignored Stan. So did she, going back inside.

I went in search of a bathroom, knowing I'd just crashed and burned in my first brush with Reese's world. I hoped he wouldn't hold it against me.

• • •

Reese or Juan, whichever of them had done it, got us regular seats, so I wasn't close to the court. That didn't quell the excitement in me when the players came out and the game started. The whole lights dimming, announcer booming their introductions raised everything up a notch.

Marie never came to the seats, and I didn't think I'd be allowed back up to that box if I went to search for her. We hadn't exchanged phone numbers, and I was glad I'd remembered to grab my usual items when we left Reese's place.

Though, shit—I didn't know his physical address, and I wasn't about to go find Marie to ask her. I'd figure it out. I had money with me. My phone. My wallet. I was an able-bodied person, so I settled back and enjoyed the game.

Reese didn't lead in scoring, but he did with three-pointers. Having a girlfriend and a wife must've worked for Crusky, because he got most of the foul shots, and he made all except two of them.

After the ball sank on his last one, tying up the score, I was on my feet along with everyone else.

I loved this game—the fast pace of it, how a steal could flip everything upside down, how fouls were necessary to stall, but could work in the other team's favor. The way you have to have teamwork to get anywhere. This game couldn't be won by one person—there were exceptions, but that was rare. It was beautiful with high-arching shots, edgy with quick ball work, surprising the way a shot would go through that shouldn't have or how an assist could get past a wall of bodies that should've stopped it. And it was rough with shoving under the basket.

It was ruthless, but so captivating, and I was back at my high school gym, watching my brother throw up a winning shot. It was the end of the fourth. Three seconds on the clock, which could get stalled out to twelve seconds, plus a time out.

Adrenaline bounced around inside of me.

I was on my feet yelling, and I didn't give a thought what happened with Marie. If I'd been a long-term thing, if things had been serious with Reese and me, then maybe. But I wasn't. We meant something, but that was all I could deal with.

I did keep an eye out for Marie on the off chance I saw her on the way out.

I sent Reese a text, letting him know I got separated from Marie. But he never replied, so after waiting a while, I decided to take things into my own hands. I headed out, calling an Uber, and I looked up a hotel on the north end of Seattle. It was a 3-star, so I was hoping I could get a room if worse came to worst.

For now, I got out and headed for the hotel's bar.

Then I waited, an empty sensation settling on my chest.

CHAPTER FORTY-ONE

REESE

"What do you mean she's missing?"

Marie held her hands up, arms wide, and panicked— right here in the team waiting room at the stadium. She'd been on the verge of panic since she first came to me, telling me Charlie wasn't in the seats when she went to sit with her.

"I don't know. I gave her the tickets. Candace kept asking me questions, so I couldn't get away as fast as I wanted, and when I got there, she wasn't there. We didn't exchange numbers, and I kept asking you for her number, but you weren't answering either."

"Fuck!" I threw my head back, raking my hand through my hair.

I'd showered after the game, knowing Juan wanted us to go to his place for a low-key party. But I was fucking agitated. Roman had been here. Word had gotten to me. I'd tried to have him banned from the stadium, but there was only so much security could do. He'd gotten in and was live-tweeting the game until they'd found him and escorted him out.

"I forgot my phone at the house. Stan was being a dick—"

"Hey!"

I didn't even look. "You were, asshole. No wonder she ditched. She said she would."

Juan was laughing, shaking his head.

"Thanks, man."

"Hey." He lounged back on a couch and spread his arms on both sides of him. "Your girl, she was a trip at camp, and she's still being trippy. She's hilarious."

Marie sat down, perched on the edge until he wrapped a hand around her shoulder. Juan tugged her back.

"I like her," she said. "Go find her, and make sure she's fine."

That was the plan—but fucking hell. That meant a drive to my place. Post-game traffic sucked getting anywhere.

"Where would she have gone?" Stan asked.

I whipped around to my manager. "*Now?* Now you want to be helpful? And why are you here? Roman's been kicked out. My order of protection was served to him. Your job is done."

He tugged his blazer shut, smoothing it down. "You just had a game. Your new girlfriend is missing, and I feel like I had a hand in it."

Juan kept laughing, the sound getting louder.

Marie was giggling with him. "It's not that funny." She let out another giggle.

I gave her a look. "You sure you didn't go to the wrong seats?"

She hiccupped, shooting upright. "What are you saying?"

"How much have you had to drink?"

"Oh, dude." Juan groaned.

Marie was on her feet, advancing to me. "Are you kidding? Do you know what I put your girl through? I railed her ass up and down and sideways, and then I flipped her over, and she took it. All of it, until she put me in my place... I forgot why I started with that." Her fight left her quickly.

Juan tugged her back down next to him.

"I might've drunk too much tonight," she admitted.

"It was a good game, wasn't it?"

She turned to Juan. "Yeah, baby. You were amazing."

They began nuzzling each other.

"You guys are all fucking worthless to me."

I wanted to do violence—to someone, my manager, Roman, anyone at this point. Charlie was alone. She wouldn't have been allowed to stay in the stadium this long. Security would've kicked her out. We were waiting out the traffic in the team's waiting room, and I couldn't do a damn thing. I needed to get home, get my phone, and then get her ass back. Now. Five hours ago. Yesterday even.

The panic almost choked me.

"You really like her, huh?"

I didn't respond to Marie.

"I'm sure she's fine."

"She doesn't know where I live. I picked her up from the airport just this morning."

I was helpless. And I hated feeling helpless. She couldn't have just asked a stadium employee where to wait for players, because how many people tried that route? It was an unofficial rule. If a player wanted someone to know where they were, they told them how to get there. Too many fans had tried before, and everyone had been on alert anyway because of Roman.

"Relax."

"You fucking relax, Juan!" I snapped. "She doesn't know anyone in the city. Put yourself in her shoes."

He quieted, then shrugged. "I'd just hole up at a bar and wait it out. Eventually you'll get back to her."

But shit happened. All the fucking time.

I'd ditched girls before. And if she went on social media and searched, I knew she could pull up a few. But none of them were like her. They were the one-use girls. A screw. No promises given. They'd known what was happening, and while most were fine with it, there were always a few who wanted more, expected more.

This life, knowing how Charlie handled pressure—a part of me couldn't stop worrying she'd decided to ditch me. If I went to the airport, would I find her there, trying to go through security? Or what if she'd already gotten through security?

What a great fucking start to whatever we were doing.

I growled and punched a plastic ball. It shot across the room. Ignoring everyone's looks, I started pacing.

"It's the only thing I could hit." I couldn't damage my hands.

Juan was laughing. Again.

"Shut the fuck up, Juan, or I'm going to punch you."

He laughed harder.

"Okay." Stan came over. "I'll talk to security, see if they can find her on the cameras. If she left the way everyone leaves, maybe we can see the car she left in? How about that?"

"You can do that?"

"I'm your manager. Trust me. I can pull a few strings."

"Then why are you fucking offering now? The game ended an hour ago."

He shot up his hands, but turned and left.

And I just kept wanting to do violence.

Roman. Charlie missing. My phone at my house.

I wanted to do more than violence. I hated this feeling. It was clawing up in me, rising, filling me, and I couldn't work it out.

"Reese."

"What?"

Marie lifted her head from Juan's shoulder, somber. "She said she wasn't permanent."

I frowned. "What's that mean?"

She shrugged, settling back into Juan's side. "She was saying it to Stan when I walked up to them. I don't think she knows I overheard her."

Not permanent?

Foreboding filled me. The fuck?

CHAPTER FORTY-TWO

CHARLIE

I 'll be honest.

I wasn't too sure about my relationship with Seattle.

Two business guys eyed me from across the room at the hotel bar. I had my back to them, and I was trying to shred every napkin within reach manically to scare them away, but they didn't seem to be taking the hint. Their smirks only grew the longer I stayed. I'd gotten three dirty looks from the staff, so I ordered a drink. The waters weren't doing it for them, but I was feeling quite sober now, so I figured one drink was fine. I could nurse it, keep my wits about me, and decide what time to give up on Reese.

He'd ditched me.

It was almost three hours after the game, and still no text.

I wished I had some willpower, but I didn't.

Me: Ever think saltwater and freshwater have a conversation and ask which one is better?

Me: A follow-up: Would you outlaw pervy old business guys or celebrate them? Have a day just for them?

Me: I'm trying to look crazy to scare off two guys. Shredding my napkins and laughing like a hyena isn't working. Suggestions?

Me: If they approach, I'm going to start talking to my barstool.

I had more in me, but the server was coming back around. I'd been nursing my drink for the last hour. He stopped, eyed the pile of napkin pieces and asked, "Want more napkins?"

I burped. "God, yes."

Shit. I should've been louder. The guys hadn't heard me.

ESPN was on. They'd moved past talking about the game and talking about Reese, and were on to the daily highlights. It was early in the season, but there were other sports going on too. Why couldn't they talk about one of them?

Oh. Right.

Reese. Seattle.

Made sense.

I needed to add this to the *con* list regarding my relationship with Seattle. Dating one of the city's celebrated pro athletes after he'd ditched you? Most definitely a con.

My phone buzzed, and I considered heralding it in the air and yelling, "Hallelujah!"

The business guys were past drunk by now. They probably wouldn't have even heard, but I tried to slow down how quickly I checked my phone.

I wasn't desperate or anything.

I opened the screen, and my lungs deflated. It was a text from Grant.

Grant: That game was awesome tonight. Caught it on TV. How's the trip? How's your man?

Right. It was just past nine there.

I didn't have it in me to text him back, but I would in the morning. I might need tips on how to get my carry-on back from Reese. *Buzz!*

Another Grant one, I assumed, reaching to read it, but no!

Reese: HOLY FUCK! I left my phone at my house. Traffic fucking sucks. I'm coming to get you. Where are you?

My hand shook. My throat trembled. Really? Had he really?

Then...whatever. I still needed to get my carry-on, no matter what.

I took a picture of the napkin the server had just put on my table. It was still intact and the logo hadn't been shredded. I sent that picture, no words with it.

I slammed my drink and agreed to another when the server almost immediately offered.

Feeling ditched, whether it was real or not, sucks balls.

Two drinks later, a flash of brake lights illuminated the hotel's windows as a car paused, then went to park.

I knew who it was. It was another expensive-looking car, just like his manager A-hole's.

Another knot to swallow.

Reese was so out of my league. I had one job offer on the table, and really, if I didn't take it, I'd be homeless.

What'd Reese see in me? The charm of my random questions? Really?

Humor could only go so far. What was I doing?

Marie had ditched me. Then I'd had this three-hour whatever-it-was.

Even though this all seemed a miscommunication, I couldn't ignore the hurt swimming in my gut. The pain sliced me, thinking Reese had decided he was done with me. And sorry, but those thoughts do exist when you're sitting in a bar for three hours and that phone won't buzz back.

It was a wake-up call.

If he could hurt me with just this small blip, what would he do if I really let him in?

One more time.

One more night.

That's what I'd give Reese. I'd fly back tomorrow, I'd take the camp job, and I'd learn to love it. That's where I belonged—with Owen and Hadley, Grant and Sophia, even with Trenton coming to visit. Maybe a dinner with Janet too.

I was still reminding myself of that, ignoring the piercing stabbing in my chest, when Reese came in. No ball cap on. No hood over his head. He was dressed in jeans and a regular-looking shirt.

Bad move, pal.

"That's Reese Forster!" one of the pervs exclaimed, and not quietly.

"What? No."

Someone else, "What's Forster doing here?"

"Yeah." A pounding sound. A barstool scratched across the floor.

As Reese saw me, his eyebrows pulled together, his face clouded over, and he looked beyond me.

The two business guys had forgotten me. They zoomed past, and man, I caught a whiff. They were more loaded than I thought.

"Hey, man!" The first one held out his hand. "I need to shake your hand. When you went head-to-head against Zorskianova tonight, it was amazing ball work." The guy was salivating.

I had my first flicker of pity. Been there, done that too.

He and his friend fawned over Reese, and the other table of customers approached—a quieter couple and another female friend with them. They asked for autographs, then pictures. The staff came next, all while Reese was ten feet from me.

I sat and watched, finishing my last drink.

Once that was done, another two hotel staff had come to get autographs, and hotel customers were coming out from their rooms. Word had gotten out somehow, so I silently paid for my drinks, and began to walk outside.

"Oh—okay. It was nice to meet you all." Reese saw me going, scribbled the last autograph, and pushed it toward the guy waiting. "I gotta go."

"But... Come on, one more?" a lady asked. She'd just stepped into the bar, her shirt barely covering her rack. One guess what she really wanted.

"I can't. Sorry, guys."

I was almost to the front door, and I could hear Reese coming up behind me. People were grumbling, and a few called out good-natured goodbyes and congratulations. Then Reese was next to me.

His hand came to the small of my back.

I sucked in a breath, tensing, but I didn't pull away.

One more night.

"Hey." His hand had been cautious, but when I didn't jerk away, it pressed more firmly against me, anchoring me to him. "I'm really sorry. I left my phone at the house—"

"Let's just go."

His hand left my back. "You're mad."

I shook my head. "No."

I was, but I was trying to tell myself I shouldn't be. It had been a mishap. Simple.

Tell that to the baggage that was rising up in me, threatening to choke me. That shit wasn't rational.

Falling in beside me, he hunched his shoulders forward. "I can understand why you're mad, but it was all a mistake. Really. Marie said you went to the wrong seats, but I'm pretty certain she was the one who messed up—if she even went to the seats. Stan told me she was taking shots the whole time in the box, and I'm sorry about her. Marie's usually really cool. Her doing that doesn't make sense—but again, that wasn't me."

We were almost to his car.

"Hey," he said more firmly. He caught my hand and pulled me to a stop.

I glanced back and saw a crowd had formed at the hotel's entrance. A couple girls had followed us to the parking lot.

He stepped in, his hands coming to my face, but I stepped back. "Let's do this at your house?"

It wasn't really a question, more a strong suggestion. I turned, going to the passenger door.

He studied me a second before pulling out his keys. He went to the driver's side, but paused before opening the door. "You *are* pissed."

I looked away.

He sounded truly sorry. And it tugged at my heartstrings, but I'd decided.

His world was too much, too big, too powerful—too everything. I was just now surviving the one I'd left. How could I handle his? Even just for the small time we were anything?

I couldn't. That was the answer. There was no way I was getting around that answer, no matter how much I was already yearning for his touch, and how much my insides were splitting open at the idea of flying home tomorrow and never returning.

I sighed. "I'm not, actually." And because he wouldn't leave it alone, I gave him my heart. "I'm hurt. I'm sad. I want to be in your arms, and I'm scared. I'm all of that."

His eyes narrowed, and he seemed to come to some conclusion. He opened his door. "Please don't shut me out because of this. I know he hurt you. But this, this was an accident. Bad timing. Bad events that made me forget my phone. Any other time, when my brother wasn't being a nightmare, I would never let any of this happen. Do you believe me?"

I didn't answer. I didn't want to lie anymore.

He didn't push for another response, but he took my hand for the whole drive back, and I let him.

Who was I kidding?

I clung to him. I didn't think I could ever let go.

His phone kept buzzing as we drove. I glimpsed Stan's name one time when I looked over, and after Reese parked in the garage, he read through the texts. Cursing softly, he sent out a flurry of responses, then turned his phone off and shoved it into his pocket.

He took the keys out of the ignition. "You ready?"

There was a bittersweet taste in my mouth as I nodded.

Reese lingered, his eyes falling to my mouth. "Juan mentioned drinks later this week. You up for that?"

He knew something was up, and he was casting out a tentative net, seeing how long I was planning to stick around. Or maybe not. Maybe he really was asking for drinks. I'd already lied to him once tonight.

"I thought I was flying back tomorrow?"

His eyes darkened, and he rested his head against his headrest. "I was hoping to change your mind."

"Don't you have an away game on Wednesday?"

"We won't fly out till that morning."

"You have practice tomorrow?"

"I gotta put some time in tomorrow."

I should fly out. I should stick to the original plan, but... Even now, after just holding his hand for the last thirty minutes, I was having a hard time giving it up.

This was supposed to be fun. This was supposed to be just an odd friendship. When did all these emotions get involved? And fuck, but I couldn't bring myself to make the hard decision.

One more day. Two more. Then that was it. A week.

I nodded. "Okay. You have a game in New York on Friday?"

"Yeah. Wanna come? I'll fly you out."

I could tell he didn't think I'd take him up on that offer, and as a sad smile stretched over my face, he saw it for what it was.

"Yeah. Okay. I'll change your flight for Friday morning?"

I nodded, not saying a word because his lips were on mine, and then I was wrapped up in all the sensations, all the good feelings, all the feelings I shouldn't be feeling at all.

He groaned, pulling away to rest his forehead against mine. "Thank you for coming, even though it was a shit show tonight."

What was I supposed to say? I shook my head, laughing lightly. "Thank YOU, you mean. You paid for the tickets. I just came and..." His hand moved to my legs, dipping between them, and I narrated as I did it: "I just spread 'em wide."

He barked out a laugh, his mouth coming back to mine, harder, rougher, more demanding. "Come on."

He came around the front to my side, bent down, and tossed me over his shoulder.

"Reese!"

"Hush, woman. Now's not the time for words." His hand was firm on my ass, squeezing a good handful. "God, I love this ass."

He carried me inside, tossing his keys onto the table, then kept on going, all the way up the stairs and to his bedroom. The windows were open, a sheer curtain covering them, but his gate gave us some privacy. We could hear the sounds of the ocean, a few cars on the road going past, but then silence.

I was surprised at how peaceful it was. Leaving the light off, Reese lowered me to the bed.

"I thought Seattle was supposed to be loud?" I remarked as I stretched out.

He knelt over me, the bed dipping under his weight. "It is, and it is in the city. I'm far enough out that we're good. Plus, my neighborhood's particularly quiet."

A world I'd never live in, but it was a nice visit. Reese bent, and his mouth came to mine. This was all just a nice visit.

Not permanent.

I had to remember that. I couldn't get caught up.

Reese's mouth moved down my throat as he undressed me, and I undressed him.

I realized I'd been wrong. I'd thought the ocean was freeing, but it wasn't. It was dangerous. His shirt came off, and I ran my hands down his chest, feeling how he shivered under my touch.

Yes. So much more dangerous.

CHAPTER FORTY-THREE

I was up, enjoying my first official coffee from Seattle (shame on me for missing it yesterday) when the text came through. Reese had been gone when I got up. He'd woken me to whisper he'd be back around three, so I zonked back out and woke late in the morning.

We'd stayed up till five, a schedule Reese said he couldn't keep up on a regular basis, but it was a one-off for us, and it'd been worth it.

Every inch of me had been worked over, kissed, worshiped. My vagina felt like it had played a double-header, and I almost groaned when I got into his shower and had the time to appreciate what I was seeing. He had a steamer shower.

Take me now—that's what I felt as I put the timer on, and it was twenty minutes of gloriousness.

I was tempted to take my coffee back up for another round, because damn, the coffee was amazing too.

Any girl Reese chose could get spoiled by this life. I could see why Marie and A-hole Manager were protective.

Reese: You asked if salt and freshwater could have a conversation and determine who's better? I can see it. Saltwater would win. It's fiercer. It has whales. Come on.

Reese: And no I wouldn't outlaw pervy old business guys. Celebrate them for sure.

Reese: If you ever need to scare off scary dudes again, I'd say up the hyena laugh while you shred *their* napkins. Side note, were those the two who came up to me first last night?

Reese: Yes. Talking to your barstool would be a good tool to scare them off too. Barstools can have the best conversations.

Reese: Want food? I'll bring Mediterranean on the way back.

I was laughing, but I flicked something annoying away from my eye too. Rational thought had returned, and there was an ache in my chest. The hole Damian had put there still remained, and I had a feeling some Reese was filtering in there too.

He was being kind. My God, he was so nice, and I was being what? Dramatic? Overreactive? I was the annoying girl people rolled their eyes at—but they didn't get it. I was just now starting to stand. If I kept falling, sinking more and more into the Reese tsunami, he would spit me out broken in pieces. When did self-preservation kick in?

When did I need to harden my walls so they weren't completely ripped from me?

I had no answer, because I knew he'd come back. He'd have food with him. That smile would cause my heart to do flip-flops. He'd look at me, smile at me, say my name, and my body would ignite in a happy flame. All the buzzing my phone did from him, that's what he did to me.

He made me buzz. My heart. My mind. My soul—my inner comedian was gagging at the cheesiness, but it was true. I was a goner, and I was slipping further away each moment Reese was in my world.

My phone went off again.

Grant: You never answered last night. Everything okay? You're not doing a disappearing act, are you?

I took a deep breath, feeling an instant kick start of nerves, and I forced myself to take the first steps. It was now or I didn't think I'd ever do it, but I really had no choice.

Me: Things are good. It's fun, and I'll take the job.

My phone rang right away. Grant.

I accepted his call, taking the coffee out to Reese's patio—where, dear Lord, the view was amazing. My knees almost buckled in shock. The waves rolled in and out from the shore.

"Hey." My voice had gone hoarse for a beat.

"You okay?"

"Yeah. Hi."

He was silent a second. "What's wrong?"

"Nothing." I sat down on a patio lounger, coffee on the table in front of me, and I snuggled down, getting comfortable.

"Are you sure about the job? Ball Wonder okay with it?"

I grinned at the nickname. "Ball Wonder doesn't really have a say. We're friends—"

"Oh my God, shut the fuck up with that!"

I laughed. "Yeah, yeah. You know what I mean."

"No. I don't, actually. Listen, tell me to stay in my lane, but he seemed to have reservations about you taking the job. And he's not messing around. He cares about you. You sure about saying yes?"

"Don't you want me there?"

"Hell yes, I want you here. Sophia and Hadley will be over the moon, but I want to make sure you're not doing it because your back is up against a wall. I know you. I know you're probably making yourself feel like you are, but you aren't. Forster seemed serious about making sure you didn't take a job out of desperation."

I wanted to scoff at him, but I couldn't. That made all of this even shittier.

He waited a beat, then asked, "What's going on, Charlie? For real."

So many years of silence.

My first instinct was to say nothing, but I had to remember, Damian had wanted me to be quiet. He'd wanted me to hide in our pretend world where nothing real was happening, where his mind wasn't slowly being taken away from us.

Fuck him. Fuck being silent.

"I won't recover after Reese."

There it was, the ugly truth. My voice trembled. "Walking away from Damian was the hardest thing I've ever done, and when something bad happens—because it will—I won't be able to stand up again after Reese. It'll be too much."

Now it was his turn to be silent. I heard a soft sigh.

"Then come home. I'll drive down and pick you up at the airport."

There. Just like that.

I was crying, but I needed to hear this. I needed one other person to give me permission to walk away from someone else.

"Okay."

"But you're wrong, Charlie. Walking away from Damian wasn't the hardest thing. Loving him and staying was the hardest thing you did. You stayed. Remember that."

No. I left.

Everyone leaves, eventually.

Right?

"I'll fly back on Friday," I told Grant. "And that'll be it. That'll be the end."

CHAPTER FORTY-FOUR

"I'm back!" Reese walked into the kitchen and set a bag on the table. "I grabbed some salads, but I have to warn you, I'm starving. I might need to eat something else too." He tossed his keys and wallet on the counter, then came over to where I was standing by the sink.

His arms wrapped around me and he grinned. "I have to say," he murmured, dipping closer, "it's really nice to see you here."

He caught my lips with his, and a dizzying spell rushed through me. I went with him as his head began to lift, going to my tiptoes, and just as he was going to pull clear, I clasped him by the back of his neck.

"No," I said, keeping him right where he was.

Maybe it was because of my decision, or maybe it was because I agreed with him—it was really fucking nice to have him come home to me, like we were married. But for whatever reason, need pulsated through me. Demanding need. I needed him. Now. Five minutes ago. My hands turned frenzied.

"Yeah?" He paused, his mouth still on mine, his body arched over me as he leaned against the counters beside me.

"God, yeah." I moaned, yanking him against me, and after that, it was a mess of limbs, desperation, and hunger.

I was starving for *him*.

I couldn't let him go. I just couldn't, so I turned my brain off. I had to or I would start crying because I was already aching at the thought of what Friday would mean.

"Shit." He kissed my throat, his hands moving more urgently on me.

He grasped under my thighs and lifted me, moving me toward a spot on the counter that had more space. He pulled off my shirt and kissed down my chest, finding my breast, but I wasn't the only one getting undressed.

Yanking on his shirt, he pulled back to help me. He tossed it to the floor and was back on me.

"I seriously will never get tired of this." He caught me in a whirlwind kiss before returning to my breast. "God, do you know how much I love your body? The way you smell, taste, move for me. You've made me fucking addicted to you." He pushed his cock against me, still in his sweatpants.

A growl moved up my throat as I reached for his pants. "I want these off. Now." I couldn't help myself as I reached for his dick and took hold of it.

He froze over me. "Fuuuuuuuck, Charlie."

Fevered. Blind. I moved according to my needs, not thinking at all as I wrapped my legs around his waist. I pressed down and rolled my hips around, grinding on him slowly and goddamn deliciously.

I fell back on the counter, stretching out. My legs kept hold of him, and I just wanted more and more and more.

Reese held himself immobile, letting me do what I wanted, until finally a primal sound came from him. "Okay." He grasped my hip and took hold of my pants. Shoving a hand inside, he grunted. "You're having your fun. So am I." He plunged two fingers inside of me.

I gasped, arching my back.

His mouth came down to my nipple, his tongue rolling around it.

We'd had sex before. We'd screwed, fucked, had fun, as Reese said. We'd had slow sex, feelings sex, and yes, there'd been times it was akin to making love. This, this was different. There was a raw urgency in me, and I knew it had awakened in Reese too.

As if this would be our last time, or perhaps my body was trying to claim him before I left.

It was almost rough and ugly in a way, but I needed to be owned by him. I needed to own him. Feeling that rise up in me, I sat up, released his dick, and shoved his pants down.

His eyes met mine, hungry, smoldering, dark. He continued thrusting his fingers inside of me, and I bucked against his hand. He lifted his other to cup the side of my face. His hold was tender, such a contradiction, and I gasped, freezing in his hold. Tears spilled from my eyes.

He wiped one away with his thumb, a question coming to his eyes, but I leaned in.

Touching my lips to his, gently, I whispered, "Fuck me hard. I don't want to see by the time you're done."

His eyes searched mine, and a hard and feral look slammed over his face. His nostrils flared, and he gripped me once again, but this time, he lifted me and turned me around.

Bending me over the counter, he yanked my hips up and back, and he leaned over me, "Like this?"

"Yesssssssssss," I breathed.

He stripped me bare, ripping my underwear off along with his clothes, and I felt him against every inch of me from behind. He leaned over me once again, one hand resting on the counter beside my head, the other on my hip as he lined up at my entrance.

"Like this?"

"Yes," I panted.

He thrust inside.

I cried out, but I couldn't help myself. As he pushed all the way in, I was shoving right back. We fucked hard and rough and brazen, and I almost wanted to be punished. But what Reese was doing to my body was not that. It was so far from that. I began crying toward the end as he slowed and began to pepper kisses down my spine, as his hand curled around my thigh, caressing down to my ass, then roaming back up to cup my breast from underneath me.

His touch felt almost loving, and that wasn't what I wanted at all—but maybe I did? Maybe this wasn't only what I wanted from him?

He held still, inside me, both of us gasping. "What is this?" he asked quietly.

I sniffled, unable to quiet myself.

"Charlie." More insistent.

A thrust, hard.

"Answer me," he grated, sliding out and back in once more. "What am I doing here?"

I couldn't talk. The tears were choking me, but the pleasure had me paralyzed. Such a fucking contrast, because that's what I was—a big fucking mix of insanity.

"Charlie." Another firm plunge, and I cried out because it felt so fucking good.

I lifted my head, sitting up as much as I could.

He caught me, like I knew he would. His hand came to my breast, anchoring me there, and he dipped his head to my shoulder, placing a delicate kiss.

"Answer me," he whispered.

I could hear his yearning. My heart spiked up in response.

I couldn't hold it in. "I'm leaving on Friday."

His hand flexed over my ass. "Yeah?" A groan left him, and he moved inside of me again. "I knew that. What else is going on?"

"Are you seriously questioning me while we're fucking?" I looked up over my shoulder.

His eyes twinkled, and he smirked, moving inside of me once again. This time, he pressed all the way in, rotating his hips, and I moaned, my eyes fluttering closed from the torment.

"Answer me and I'll finish." He grinned. "Maybe."

A spew of curses left me, but fuck, it felt so good. "You fucker."

"You asked for this." He slid back to my entrance, then shoved in, his entire body bending over mine so we were lined up from waist to face.

I looked back and his eyes were right there. We stared deep. I could almost see into him, just as I felt him inside of me. His eyes softened, then grew fierce again.

His lips nipped mine, and he groaned against my mouth, "Why do I feel like this is the last time I'll hold you?"

Fresh tears spilled.

He felt them, tasted them, and pulled back. "Charlie?" His cock quivered inside of me.

I gasped. "When I go on Friday, that's it for me. I'm done."

He went still. Every inch of him turned to stone, and a wall slammed over his face.

"The fuck?"

He didn't pull out of me, and I almost sagged from relief. I needed him to finish. I needed him to claim me once more.

"Why?"

I flinched at how cold he sounded. My head hung down. "Because I care too much. Because when you leave me, I won't recover." I willed myself to meet his eyes. "It took everything in me to leave Damian. I can't—if you walked away from me, I'd never get back up again. You can destroy me."

I'd cut myself open for him, revealed everything in me.

Taking a second, his forehead fell to my shoulder, and he cursed under his breath. But then he began moving in me again. His cock was almost stroking me. His hand slid around to rub my clit, pressing, holding, circling, teasing. As he brought me toward my climax, I felt his lips on my shoulder, then the back of my neck. I bent over for him again, my hands fisting on the counter.

I knew what he was doing. "You too," I yelled. "Don't you goddamn make me come and you don't."

I lifted my head, intent flashing in my eyes. "If you don't, I'll be on my knees in front of you."

He paused, holding my gaze, and I tried not to flinch at the wall I saw in him. But then he shuddered. He took my hips and brought both of us to climax.

We erupted together.

I fell against the counter, too weak to move, as we both trembled from the aftermath.

"If you're going to go, why wait till Friday?"

I winced. His voice was devoid of anything humane.

"I'll take you to the airport today."

Then he pulled out, and walked out, leaving me lying there. Alone.

CHAPTER FORTY-FIVE

I don't know what I did after Reese walked away from me.
I don't know how I got to the airport, or even packed the few items I had with me.

I don't remember the flight back to Minneapolis.

For the next two weeks, I wouldn't remember hardly anything.

I texted Grant when I landed.

Me: I'm at the airport. Can you pick me up?

Grant: What?! I'm at camp.

Me: Okay.

Grant: I'm coming. Are you okay?

Me: No.

Grant: Don't go home. I have no clue what's going on, but my gut is telling me not to let you be alone. I'm sending Janet.

I didn't argue. That said everything. I *do* remember that.

Me: Okay.

I sat on a bench near the curb, my suitcase beside me, staring at nothing.

A car rolled to a stop before me. The window went down and I heard, "Charlie?"

I looked up.

It was Janet.

A little while later, we were at her house. I followed her inside, and she put her purse and keys on the counter by the door.

She took off her coat, watching me. "Do you need anything? A drink maybe?"

I almost laughed at that. "God, yes."

Her husband was in the living room, and he paused the television. ESPN was on, and I froze, a numb feeling spreading through me as I forced myself to look at the screen. But they weren't talking about Reese. His name wasn't in the captions. They weren't playing highlights of his game.

They had remembered there were other sports and teams out there.

• • •

"She hasn't said much?"

"No. What's wrong with her? She's freaking me out." .

Grant had arrived and was talking to Janet in the entryway. They were using hushed tones, but they still carried to the kitchen and even the living room.

Janet's husband gave me a pitying smile. "She's not the greatest on tact," he said quietly.

I shrugged. I'd known her longer than he had. It was understood.

"I want to help, but I have no idea what to say to her. Did she break up with Damian again? Why am I always in the dark?" Janet hissed.

• • •

We were in the car. Grant and me.

City lights passed by, looming over us on the interstate. He cleared his throat. I could feel his worry when he looked over. "So, you're okay with what we're doing, right? I mean, you seem out of it."

No. What were we doing?

But I only nodded and pressed my hands into my lap. "Of course."

"Really?"

• • •

I found out later that Grant and I had packed half of my apartment the day he came.

There were reasons everything was moving fast, but I didn't understand it. I just went with it. Who was I to argue?

I'd turned in my notice with the lease office and asked Lucas to grab the rest of my stuff. It was supposed to go into storage until I could come get it later.

I saw the text conversation with Lucas. He hadn't wanted to help me until I threatened him with a sex tape Newt had sent me early in our dating relationship. It was of Newt. There was nothing illegal about it, but the idea of getting a video sent by your ex's grand-whatever was just all sorts of gross.

Luc-ass said he'd have everything packed up and moved by the next day.

I didn't tell him, but I was going to release the tape anyway. I was just waiting for the right day.

The internet needed to know about the likes of Newt.

• • •

"You're okay staying here until you find a place?"

Bless Sophia's heart. She had no idea how to make things right for me.

It was past the weekend now. Time was coming back to me. I was starting to adjust to this new life, but I was a zombie.

Still numb.

But I knew I was five days post-Reese.

He would've had his away game, then gone to New York.

"Did he win?" I asked Sophia.

She swallowed. She knew who I meant.

"They lost their Wednesday game, but won against New York."

Good.

That was good.

• • •

"We have a retreat this weekend," Owen was saying to Grant.

We were at a staff meeting, going over budget and planning. Why was I there? They still didn't quite trust me to be alone.

A month had gone by.

Nothing felt better.

I'd left him because of that, right? Didn't I?

Things were supposed to feel better by now. Be better.

Why did I feel so wrong?

"I think I fucked up," I said to no one in particular.

• • •

I was packing again, throwing things into my bag in a mad rush.

I had an audience at the door.

Hadley took a breath. "Oh boy."

Grant frowned. He rarely *didn't* frown when he saw me now. "Are you sure this is a smart idea?"

Owen flinched in pain, rotating his shoulder over and over again.

Sophia leaned forward, her eyes bright and shining from unshed tears. "We can call Trent. He said he was doing some traveling this weekend. Maybe he could meet you? So you have a friend there, unless you want one of us to come along?"

"No." I was firm. I'd made up my mind.

"Oh boy," Hadley said again.

"Charlie. I don't know..." Sophia began.

Grant cursed, stepping into the room. "This is not a smart idea. Remember what you said to me? You wouldn't recover? Now you're going to him. Charlie, I don't think—"

I whirled to them. "I don't care!"

I stopped, my chest heaving.

Time and thought and me—all of it slammed back into place at once, and suddenly I was in my room at Grant and Sophia's house. My friends were standing in the hallway, scared to come and talk me down, but also worried about letting me go.

They were terrified—of me, but for me.

And that was on me.

I had done this. To myself. To them. Me. No one else.

"I fucked up," the words regurgitated from me, full of disdain for myself. "I've made a mess of everything. And I'm better. I'm okay, but I have to do this. You guys don't have to worry about me. I promise. I *will* be okay. I just—I have to do this before I move on."

"But going and seeing him. I mean—"

I cut Hadley off this time. "I have to let him go. I never did before. I need to do it this time or I'll never be able to move on. I have to do this."

I zipped up my bag, pulled it onto my back, and faced them.

No one moved aside.

I let out a sigh. "I'm really okay. I promise."

I wasn't, but I would be.

That was a promise.

CHAPTER FORTY-SIX

I woke the next morning in a hotel.

I felt *damn* good, and there was a sadness with it because I couldn't remember the last time I'd felt like this—like I knew what I wanted in life, I knew what I needed to do, and I was filled with hope. With Damian, I'd lost hope.

That's the saddest part of grieving someone—whether they're still with you or not, whether it's a relationship or not. You're fighting to keep hope, but when the last of that string is cut, that's where you get lost.

That's where I'd been for too many years, but not anymore.

I knew. In all the madness and confusion and wackiness, clarity had come to me, and once I got it, it was a ray of sun breaking through the clouds. I clung to it, and the longer it stayed with me, the stronger I got.

This. This was what I needed to do first. I got out of my car and went inside the Silver Shores Assisted Living facility.

Damian's mom met me at the door. Her hair was cut short, a dirty blonde similar to Damian's when we'd first started dating. She had the same angular, long face, and the same blue eyes. She watched me cautiously, which stopped me in my tracks.

Jesus.

Damian had lost some of his looks as the dementia progressed. He'd lost the muscle definition, and the freshness of youth I hadn't started to appreciate until later in life. His hair was greasy half the time, and uncombed the other.

But seeing his mother now, a wave of memories flooded me.

"Hi. I'm Damian, and I suck at hitting on women, but I still wanted to come over and try with you. So consider this my lame pick-up line." He had smiled, holding his hand out in the middle of a busy bar, as if we were meeting in a boardroom.

His eyes had twinkled.

Sandy brown hair in a crew cut, a golden tan from the summer months, and a form that showed he lifted weights on the regular—I'd been taken aback. Not by him, not by the simple pick-up line, but because he'd laughed after he held his hand out.

That laugh.

I heard it again now. Like an intoxicating bell, light and breezy, and like sunshine after enduring four months of a gloomy winter.

I breathed in the memory and blinked back tears, because I missed him.

"I'm going to warn you." He'd smiled down at me on our first date. *"You're going to fall in love with me."*

"I am, huh?"

"I'm scarily intoxicating. You'll see." He'd winked before coming around to open my door for me.

A year into our relationship he'd told me, *"I will never hurt you. I will love you forever. You and me, we'll conquer the world."*

"Charlie?"

Brenda approached, her hands coming out of her pockets. She jerked forward, as if unsure then suddenly going for it. This wasn't the Brenda I remembered. She'd been smooth and confident when Damian and I first started dating. There'd always been a sadness about her, and Damian had pulled away from her when his first symptoms started. When she finally learned the truth, she'd just seemed resigned, like she knew that phone call was going to come one day.

Thinking on it now, she probably had.

"Hi. Yeah. Wow." I fitted my hand in hers, feeling her shaking, just like me.

She laughed, finishing my thought. "Long time, huh?"

"Yeah."

Yeah. I sighed.

We were in a nursing home. He was too young to be here.

"Damian mentioned you the other day."

This was so fucking painful. My throat swelled. "Yeah?"

He could still remember me?

How many good days did he have?

How bad were the bad days?

How far had he slipped?

Would I recognize him?

Stop. Pause. Take a breath.

The lobby had two different directions. A front desk sat at the hallway leading to the left, and a beeping came from behind the desk. But the right side was quiet. It led to a longer carpeted hallway.

Brenda headed for the right side, and without me asking, she'd answered the main question. *How was Damian?*

"We were able to get him in here—at first they were hesitant about taking him since, you know, he's so young, but I got him in about six months ago. It took a while for everything to be approved, but so far, I think he's enjoying it. He always did joke that he was an old soul."

"I should just move into a senior community," he'd once told me.

"Why?"

"Because that's just how I am. I never thought I'd have kids. I hate loud sounds. I'm not a partier. I don't know. Give me my sports network and my dog, and I'm happy."

That'd been early on in our relationship, before I'd thought about kids. He mentioned one time he'd have kids if I wanted. I believed him, but he never yearned for a family of his own.

"Do they allow pets here?" I asked his mom.

Her smile lightened, and she walked with an easier gait. "Oh yes. And that was a big thing we got this year too. He has a therapy dog, and I do think Mickey has helped. He gets Damian out of the apartment and walking around. He can still...you know."

I didn't. "What?"

She faltered, wiping at the corner of her eye before looking away briefly. "He can still go outside on his own. They..." She paused, her shoulders rising as she filled her lungs. "They have an alarm on him. I guess he wandered once, but since he's had Mickey, he's doing better. Mickey guides him back."

"I want to own a kennel and take care of eight dogs. More even." He had laughed, as we were the couple who went to the dog park without a dog.

His hand had found mine, and I'd heard the longing in his voice. *"Someday, Charlie. I know we can't afford a dog now, but one day. And I'm not joking. Dogs over people, man. Dogs don't leave you."*

I stopped walking as the memory blasted me inside, knives cutting me.

He had known. Somehow, he had known.

Brenda was still going, her voice lighter, and she pointed to a television room as we went past. "AJ comes to visit every weekend. Whenever the football games are on, those two are cackling like little girls together. One time they watched in here and a few of the other guys came to watch with them. It's a sight to see. Damian, AJ, and four older gentlemen. They all get along like best friends. Damian enjoys giving the older guys dating advice, because—"

She stopped, realized I wasn't following, and turned back. "A few of the older ones are dating, you see..."

AJ.

"AJ comes to see him?" I choked out.

Understanding dawned, and she nodded, biting her bottom lip. "Yeah. I reached out after you two broke up, and he's been helping."

His childhood best friend. The two had a falling-out, and that's when I came into the picture.

"He talked about AJ, but I never met him."

"Yeah. He, uh..." She drew closer, nodding her head. "AJ talked to me a little about their argument. I think... I think Damian knew what was coming for him. AJ had just gotten married. Angie was pregnant, and I think it was hard for Damian to see that. Then he found you, and to be totally honest, I think he wanted to keep you all for himself, for as long as possible."

Damian 's mom was back in his life. He had the dog he'd always wanted. His childhood best friend was back in his life.

I was the one gone.

"I'm so sorry." The dam broke. I didn't even try to wipe my tears. It would've been pointless. "I'm so sorry I left him—"

"Oh, honey." She caught me, her arms wrapping tightly around me. "No, no. Don't think like that. You—it's different for you than me, different than even with AJ. He's my son. I had a husband. I had a family. And Damian's my family—that'll never change. The same with AJ. He has a family."

She was trying to make me feel better, but it didn't matter.

She was losing a son. AJ was losing a best friend.

"Hey!" She was more forceful, as if reading my mind. She caught my face in her hands and looked me in the eyes. "You are mourning. I know how much you loved him, and when you see him, it's going to be a different grief. Because he's still here, but he's not the same Damian."

More tears. They were choking me, damming up in my throat.

"He was going to be my husband."

"I know," she crooned. "I know, honey."

"I wanted him to be the father of my children."

"Oh, Charlie. I know. I'm so sorry." She pulled me in, rocking me as if were a child. Her hand cradled the back of my head. "Damian knew this was coming, but he was living life as if it wasn't going to happen. He loved you. I know he did. But I don't want you to feel bad about not being here. Sometimes you have to step back, you have to heal, so then you can come back and be here for him. Because he's not the same Damian you knew."

"Is he..." I looked at her, my hands fisting her shirt, holding on like she was a lifejacket. "What's he like now?"

"Happy." She laughed, for the first time. She wiped some of her tears. "Sometimes they get happy and sometimes they don't. He's happy. I mean, that's the typical day for him. There are days when he's not, when he knows he's slipping, and those days are hard."

She went on, walking with me down the hall.

He got along with the other residents. They took care of him, doting on him like he was one of their grandchildren. And he had them watch movies, gave them stats on sports to impress their grandchildren.

I smiled at that. "He always did love sports so much."

"Yeah." Her arm linked with mine. "Sports and his dog. He always used to say that's what he needed to be happy."

Hearing my memory coming from her broke me again.

I felt a crack down the middle as I remembered the first time we'd kissed, how he'd felt like home, how I'd wondered if that was normal. Our first date—how it'd been uncomfortable until I made a joke about farting and he'd countered with a poop joke. We'd both laughed when the neighboring tables gave us looks of disgust.

I thought about the first time we'd told people we were dating—how proudly he had stood with me, holding my hand.

I remembered when I came home to a bouquet of roses on the table, how he'd stood to the side and waited until I saw the ring on one of the stems. How he was on his knees when I looked back.

I'd gotten two and a half years with him. Those years had been good. Laughter. Love. Kindness.

"He made me a sandwich one day and left it at my door." I felt myself grinning. "He texted me while I was at the gym, and I was annoyed that I had to leave early to get the sandwich because he was worried my neighbor's dogs would get it. That was before he had a key to my place."

But then I'd realized how he took the time to make the sandwich, how he'd put a Hershey's kiss in the bag with it, along with strawberries because he knew I loved both. It'd been the first of a long line of thoughtful little gestures he did for me.

He'd left a handwritten quote on my bedside table every morning for a full year.

He used to buy me chocolate muffins to share from my favorite deli.

If I was ready to go to sleep and he wasn't, he'd watch television, but he'd watch it with no volume. He never wanted to wake me up.

"He drove me to work, and he'd pick me up if he could."

"Yeah." Brenda nodded, her hip brushing against mine. "He'd come home during his lunch breaks to check on me. He bought me puzzles. He always knew I loved them. Now we do a puzzle here every Sunday together."

A new wave of grief broke over me.

She was in her sixties, doing a puzzle with her son who was thirty-one.

As if sensing my feelings, Brenda stopped and gazed at me. "It'll get better. The first visit is the hardest. You're going to cry probably the whole time, and when you leave, and maybe for a few days after. But it will get better. You're grieving the family you didn't get a chance to have. Not just him, but you're grieving a part of yourself. It always gets better. Time moves along, and the hole you have for him may always be there, but you'll grow layers around it. It'll begin to heal."

A hole. Check.

Layers around it? Maybe.

But getting better?

We turned the last corner, and she opened the door to Damian's apartment. He sat in his living room, the television on, and as I entered, I remembered the day and the time. I knew, before walking in, that he'd be watching Reese's basketball game, and I also remembered that I always got Damian during those games.

As he turned to look at me, I saw recognition and a bright smile broke over his face. Inside me, something clicked back into place.

This was family.

Brenda was right. It would get better. It already had.

CHAPTER
FORTY-SEVEN

Five days ago, I'd sat next to my ex, listening to him tell me Reese Forster's stats, hearing the old ribbing he used to give me about my crush on Reese. I'd sat there with tears welling up, but I never let them fall. Not in front of Damian. The tears weren't for the teasing—far from it. And they weren't even from the pain of seeing where Damian was in his disease.

The tears were good tears, finally.

I hadn't realized how empty I'd been without him.

I'd gone back two more times through the week, meeting AJ for the first time and getting closer to Brenda. And I met Mickey, who was adorable. A German Shepherd, whose first priority was always Damian —always checking on him, watching him. It wasn't until Damian sat down that Mickey was off-duty. He hadn't been brought up as a typical service dog. He had training specifically for dementia, and while I hated the terminology—because Damian wasn't Damian with dementia to me. He was just Damian—I understood the training was needed.

A few times Damian started to get up and do something, and Mickey sensed it, whining, pressing him back down. One point he prepared to leave the apartment, but Mickey blocked him, and AJ called his name. Then Damian remembered we were there. His eyes lit up, a smile spread over his face, and he came back for another round of Reese Forster stats.

Going to see him had been a goodbye in my heart.

Not a goodbye forever, because I could never do that, but a goodbye to him being my romantic partner. Maybe if I were older, if we'd had kids, things would be different. I would've stayed at his side, held his hand, kissed his cheek, and known he was my soulmate for life.

But I was too young.

He tried to send me away so many times because of this reason, so I could still have a husband, perhaps children. I got it. I got it then, but I never accepted it. I hadn't wanted to lose him either.

At one point, one of the other residents had tried to classify my relationship with Damian.

I wouldn't have it.

I wasn't his sister. I wasn't his best friend any longer. I was family. That was it.

And now, I was back to traveling.

A part of me felt whole again. I was getting there, and I had one more piece to fix. Reese.

"Why are you going to Chicago?" my seatmate asked once they announced we were starting our descent. He'd kept to himself the whole time, headphones plugged into his phone, but after going to the bathroom, he didn't immediately tug the headphones back on.

I'd been slouching down, but I sat up now, stretching my arms and back. "I'm, uh... I'm seeing a friend."

He nodded. "Yeah, yeah. Good friend?"

He was in a business suit, and I because I didn't want to talk about the details, I gestured to him. "You're going for work?"

"What?" He looked down and laughed. "Oh. No. I travel so much, I forgot. Nah. Not this time. A friend of mine has box seats to the Chasers game tomorrow. I'm flying in to see him, catch the game, and then I'm off to Japan after that."

Really.

I swallowed tightly. "The Chasers?" My stomach twisted up.

"Yep. Yep. They're playing the Seattle Thunder, who seem to be the fucking team to beat this year. I kinda miss the old days when Johnston played, you know? He would've shut Forster down hard."

I couldn't help myself. "But Forster, Cartion, *and* Crusky?"

He sighed, resigning himself. "I know." He settled into his seat. "Thunder's stacked this year. They don't usually have so many heavy hitters. Chasers are hurting. They need to plan better for their team, but we can get there. I know it. Give us another year, and Thunder wouldn't stand a chance."

"That's your opinion." I waited.

He registered the dig and looked over, his eyes wide. "You must be a Thunder fan?"

"Kinda."

"Not Coyotes? We flew from Minneapolis."

"Not this year."

He groaned. "God, you're one of those."

I knew where he was going, but I wanted him to say it. I wanted him to squirm as he said it.

I blinked my eyes, so wide and pure. "I don't know what you're talking about."

"Right." He snorted, facing forward again as the flight attendant came with the garbage bag. "You're a fair-weather fan. Those are the worst." He side-eyed me, smirking. "No offense."

I snorted right back, clipping my seatbelt in place. The descent would still take a while, but I wasn't going anywhere. "I've always been a Thunder fan, and I've always been a Forster fan. Don't underestimate the Reese, man. He's going to be the GOAT one day."

He groaned, and a couple of the other passengers glanced over. He waved at me. "Sorry. She just told me Forster's going to be the GOAT one day."

A guy a few rows back yelled, "Reese Forster? You kidding? The guy can't rebound for the life of him. He's gotta depend on his teammates."

Yeah. *Oh-kay*, my seatbelt was off, and I twisted around. I rested an arm against the back of my seat so I could properly see my target. It was a bigger guy who, no surprise, had a Chasers ball cap on.

"Excuse me? What are you talking about that he can't rebound? Who cares? He's not on the inside. Wanna know what he does excel at?"

"Everything else?" said a woman from the other aisle. She and her friend started laughing together.

"And he doesn't look too bad, either," her friend added as they collapsed in laughter.

I had to pause, fighting back a grin, before finishing, "He led in scoring five out of the last seven games. He's led in steals most always. His balls skills are close to Stephen Halorry, another legend in the league, and his floater balls can come in damned handy—and yes, they can win an entire game. Thank you."

I was not done.

Raising a finger, I continued. "No, he doesn't lead in rebounds, but that's why they have Crusky, or Lestroy even. And no, he doesn't lead in three-pointers, but seriously, he's really good at those too. He's the youngest captain that team has ever had, and that's a feat all by itself."

I needed a breath. My face was getting hot.

And once I stopped, I started noticing the looks.

A few guys wanted to argue, but the guy beside me was just smiling. Leering, slightly. He leaned forward. "You wanna go on a date, honey? I think I could get tickets to the *Chasers* game."

I couldn't stop myself. My retort came before I knew I was going to say it. "Oh, fuck you."

Half the plane erupted in laughter.

I sat back, and one of the middle-aged ladies waved at me. "You go, girl. You put those men in their place. They ain't used to girls knowing about sports."

As I put my seatbelt back on, I noticed my neighbor eyeing me. "What?"

"I'm not hitting on you—I have a girlfriend in New York—but do you wanna go to the game? I'm sure my friend would have room for one more. I didn't know you were that big of a fan."

I wanted to huff, but only because I was still feeling spicy. Instead, I shook my head. "I think I'm already going with the friend I'm flying in to see."

"Okay. Well, if I see you, I'll give you a shout."

"Same here."

The fight drained from me once we landed, and I headed for the exit. My seat neighbor ended up keeping pace with me. We both had only carry-ons, so once we were outside, I waved Trent down and turned to him. "You got a ride coming?"

"Yeah..." But he was looking at Trent, his eyes narrowed.

Then, as Trent's SUV pulled over and he got out to meet me, my neighbor's eyes went wide. "Fuck, man. I thought we were meeting at the game tomorrow?"

Uh...back up. Screeching brake sounds.

Trent stopped, and his shocked gaze jumped between the two of us. He scratched the back of his head. "Um. Huh?"

"Give me a hug, man. It's good to see you. I don't know how you—" He stopped, catching on that Trent was staring just as hard at me. "Oooh." He motioned between us. "You two know each other?"

It was clicking in place now.

Of all the ironies.

I gestured to Trent. "This is the friend with the box seats?"

When my plane neighbor nodded, I turned to Trent. "You have box seats?"

He coughed, his face pinking. "I, uh, kinda know the team."

Oh. Duh!

Oh my God.

I wanted to smack myself in the forehead.

Then Trent and my seatmate were shaking hands and hugging. I learned his name was Dwayne—Trent introduced us.

"Charlie, huh?" He released my hand, stepping back and frowning. "That's an unusual name for a girl."

I glared at him, but he grinned. "Sorry. Had to see if some of that fight was still in you."

I grunted, putting my bag in the back since Trent was now enamored with Dwayne. Going to the back seat, I opened the door and hollered at them, "Let's do all this on the ride."

Other cars were starting to honk. We'd exhausted the thirty seconds we could use to greet each other, throw our suitcases in the vehicle, and take off.

Both guys laughed, and Dwayne nodded to me as he sat in the front passenger seat. "This is nice. Thanks for letting me have it."

I just grunted again. There was another potential problem in the future, and I waited till Trent was inside and we had pulled out to the main road before bringing it up.

"Is it the box with the team girlfriends and family?"

He met my gaze in the rearview mirror. "Maybe?"

I groaned. "Trent."

"I thought—"

"No. Can we get regular tickets? I don't want to deal with his manager and a few other people." Ahem. *Marie.* But mainly Stan.

"I'm sorry. You said you wanted to come down and see—"

I coughed, shooting a meaningful look toward his friend.

Trent caught it, amending, "—the game, and I did a recent speaking event with them. Just was natural to reach out, but I can change it."

"No way!" Dwayne protested. "I was looking forward to the box."

Turned out Dwayne and Trent knew each other because they both traveled a ton. Trent had been booked for a speaking event with the company Dwayne worked for, and the two saw each other on a plane not long after that. They'd been fast comrades at heart. Dwayne mentioned he was flying in from Alaska, and because it made sense for both of them, Trent invited him to the ball game.

I was content to listen to them talk, but I knew Trent was concerned about me. He kept looking back in the mirror, and I gave him a small wave. I was fine. He could talk with his friend, who told him what hotel he'd booked. Then he asked a question that had me listening closely.

"You still dating that model?"

Trent started coughing. "Uh..." *Cough!* "What?" Another cough. A sputter to follow, "How'd you know about that?"

"All the guys know. What's her name?" He was snapping his fingers, trying to remember.

I couldn't hold back my Cheshire Cat smile, offering, "Lauren?"

"Yeah! Thanks." He said to Trent, "Lauren."

"How do you know about Lauren?" He shot me a dark look. "And not a word from you, thank you."

"Consider it box tickets payback."

Dwayne frowned at me as he spoke. "Yeah. My buddy knows her. Small world, right? He follows her on Instagram and said there was a picture of you two. He remembered you from that work thing and showed me. She tagged you and everything, said you were her *beau*."

Dwayne was teasing when he used the word, but Trent shifted in his seat. The back of his neck had grown a little redder.

For once, it wasn't my life.

For once, it wasn't my romance or lack of romantic life.

For once, I wasn't the center of attention.

I leaned forward, propping my chin on my hand. "Yes. Let's hear more about this Lauren." I winked at Trent, who just scowled.

"Um, how about you, Charlie?" he asked under his breath. "Seeing anyone new lately?"

Dwayne's gaze jumped between us, his smile not dimming.

I retreated back to my seat, but after Dwayne kept on, talking about how hot Lauren was, Trent looked at me in the rearview mirror. I pretended I had a carton of—what was this? It was huge. I had to really work to get my arms around it, and then what was inside? Popcorn? Hmmm. Delicious. But wait, it needed more butter.

I was lathering it on when Trent said, "Not funny, Charlie. Your days of being a comedian are over."

I held up a kernel of popcorn. "Don't make me start with my questions again. It's a problem. They can come back." I popped that invisible kernel into my mouth and rubbed my stomach. It was delicious.

"You're messed up." But he was trying not to smile.

Dwayne had stopped his gushing over Lauren to watch the two of us. "You guys are good friends, huh?" He nodded to me.

"You missed it, man. She gave a guy his ass on the plane after she took offense at a rib against Forster." His eyes sparked.

I pretended there was a platter in front of me. I served it to Trent.

He just grumbled, "So funny, Charlie."

I was throwing the popcorn at him now. "Watch it. I heckle too."

He coughed. "So. Forster, huh?"

"Yeah." I leaned forward. "Where'd that popcorn go? I might need a vacuum to clean this mess back here."

Trent burst out laughing but then cursed, veering into the next lane and hitting the turn signal as he eased onto the exit. "Shit. Sorry, guys. I wasn't paying attention." He asked Dwayne, "You're at the Hilton?"

"Yeppers. I always stay there."

We got off the ramp and pulled into the hotel's front parking area. Trent got out, talking with Dwayne for a bit longer, and I moved to the front seat. They must've mentioned me because I saw Trent motioning to me a couple times before Dwayne nodded. Then they clasped hands and did that chest bump that's somehow a hug for men.

Trent climbed back into his seat and sighed. "So. How drunk you want to get tonight?"

No question. "Wasted."

"On it."

CHAPTER
FORTY-EIGHT

I was dumbfounded, and speechless.

That rarely happened.

We were standing outside a nightclub, the entire exterior all in black except one word in neon pink, *Whisper*. A line of people lingered outside, there were two bouncers at the door, and I gave Trent a look.

"Really?"

He laughed, moving ahead. "Come on. You said you wanted to get drunk, and I have an 'in' here."

Well, okay then. We went to the head of the line and—why was I surprised?—the bouncers knew Trent, nodding and grunting hellos as they opened the door for us. As we entered, a server approached, tray of shots at the ready.

She offered, but Trent leaned over and yelled over the blaring hip-hop music, "Lauren around?"

Now this made sense.

Now I knew why we'd been allowed to skip the line.

The girl nodded and motioned down a hallway. She gave Trent more instructions, and then we were off.

As we went, I noticed the inside of the club was a mind fuck. It had been created to look exactly like the outside—the same curb and street, just different cars. And instead of one of the buildings across the road, there was a stage for dancing. The DJ booth was set high up, above a streetlight, which acted as a podium bridge.

People were dancing and milling around underneath the DJ, and couches lined one end of the room. Boxes with tables lined the wall on the second floor. As we walked past, I saw the doors open on a few of the boxes, and they looked a lot like the building doors that we'd walked past on the way from Trent's car.

The "street" wasn't the dance floor. It was the walkway for everyone to get from place to place.

Suddenly Trent grabbed my hand and pulled us onto one of the "sidewalks" that led to a seating area. "I see Lauren," he told me. "Come on."

We were weaving around couches when Lauren spotted us. She was dancing on one of the tables in between the couches.

I was speechless, again.

Lauren was a go-go dancer. But it made sense. She was gorgeous.

Wearing silver sequin underwear (for real, that was all) and a black corset, she had coordinating silver streaks in her hair. She squealed as she jumped down from her table, throwing her arms around Trent. There was some heavy petting for ten full seconds. I counted, right after making sure my gaze was anywhere but on them.

"Sorry."

I felt a soft touch on my arm. I turned back.

Lauren flashed me an apologetic smile, leaning in close. "I found out about the party a few days ago, so when I mentioned it to Trent, he thought it'd be a good chance for you." She moved back, inclining her head. "I reserved a table just for you guys. You'll be close when they arrive."

Dread lined my insides.

No time for jokes here. This was serious, and I locked eyes with Trent, raising one eyebrow, all villain-in-a-movie like.

Okay. Who was I kidding? Jokes made the world go round. There was always room for at least one.

He flushed, giving me a closed-mouth smile, and there he was: his hands in his pockets, his shoulders slumping like a self-conscious little schoolboy. Not today, *Stan*.

Lauren led the way.

Trent started to follow, but I grabbed his arm. My grip was cement. He didn't even look at me. He took my hand, lifting it from his arm like it was cotton candy.

He spoke, even as his eyes continued to follow his girlfriend. "Just hear me out when we get to our table. Okay?"

He didn't wait for an answer. The asshat took off, knowing I had two choices: follow so I could get all the information, or leave, having only a gut feeling about what was going on here.

I followed. There was a little Veronica Mars in me.

As I wound through the couches behind them, I knew there could be only one reason Trent would lie to me—or I should say one *person*. One person who I knew was already in Chicago with us, and who I'd originally come to see anyway. But that was different—my timetable.

And anyway, this person was someone who wouldn't go out the night before a game, who was the epitome of professional because pro athletes had to be.

So there had to be another reason Trent had brought me here. Right?

Lauren was weaving around, taking us down a back hallway with the same decor as the main area of the club. It looked like an alley. Murals on the walls had been painted to give us a 3D image of the fire escape stairs that hung off the sides of apartment buildings. When we went past a door, a cityscape was painted on it as if we were passing a street.

Lauren opened the one with a San Diego cityscape.

We had our own box. A large booth in black leather lined the back wall, and a small table sat in the middle, with champagne already waiting for us. There was a large chandelier hanging above, and it was a little quieter here.

Lauren went straight for the champagne, picking it up and opening it. "You guys ready for a fun night?"

I harrumphed. Why, I had no idea. I just felt it.

Trent threw me a look, turning to face me. "I don't get why you're mad. You came to Chicago to talk to Reese. I figure instead of waiting an entire night where you're going to feel nervous—and I know you, you'd be trying to talk yourself out of seeing him—what does it hurt to catch him when he's not guarded?"

Because he didn't know Reese.

But really, did I?

I did.

The realization flared strong in me, growing firm. I *did* know Reese. I might not know all his idiosyncrasies, but I knew his favorite color. I knew what his brother was like. I knew he slept on the left side of the bed.

I knew he was kind, and loving, and sensual, and could fuck amazingly.

I knew he had never yelled at me, not once. He'd growled once or twice, but that was in the beginning and at the end. The latter had been deserved.

I knew he took the time to answer my questions, no matter how many I sent him.

I knew he answered my call after he was already in bed, in a hotel with a roommate, and when he probably needed his sleep. He took the time to leave the room, go down an elevator with strangers, and seek out a place to talk to me because I was tipsy and wanted to chat.

I knew he cared enough to tell me to have fun, but then worried whether I was going to be alone or not.

I knew he cared enough to be nice to my camp friends, to speak on my behalf to the board, to help get my nemesis fired.

I knew he didn't want me to take a job just because I was up against a wall. He wanted to help so I only took a job if I truly wanted it.

He'd asked me not only to come to Seattle for him, but also to New York.

I knew I wasn't a one-use girl to him. Or I hadn't been.

And I knew even though he hated what his brother did, he actually did care, and he'd help his brother if the circumstances were right.

But one thing I didn't know was his stance on second chances. Would he give me one?

"But why would he come here tonight? He has a game tomorrow."

Lauren handed me a glass of champagne. "It's a birthday party. One of the trainers, Aaron or something?"

"Aiden?"

"Yeah. Aiden. It's his birthday, and the reservation came through that they're only using the private suite above for a little bit tonight. They should be arriving soon, and we have another party holding it at midnight. They'll be gone by then. It's like a quick dip, in and out."

It was almost nine. That made sense.

But knowing didn't help, because a whole new fresh batch of nerves pounced on me. Good Lord. I contemplated my champagne—down it like the princess trucker I could be or shove it aside and head for the toilet? Both reactions assaulted me at the same time.

Eyeing me, Lauren leaned close again. "You going to be okay?"

"That's a loaded question."

She moved back and shrugged. "Okay, but they're here." She nodded behind my shoulder, and I turned.

They were like gods.

There was no other way to describe it.

Coming in, one by one and in pairs, they were heads over the rest of us. All eyes in the club went to them. A few mouths dropped. Some frowned, confused. Others scrambled for their phones and a frenzy began as they walked underneath the DJ booth bridge and toward us.

Lauren nudged me, her head dipping toward what seemed like a throne room looking out over the entire club. It was like a huge black box sticking out from the wall, with one side open and stairs leading up to it. I couldn't see all the way in, but I knew similar black leather couches likely lined the inside of it.

A team of servers, clad in the same clothing as Lauren, led the way. Three of them carried bottles with sparklers coming out of them. A few others brought up the rear with more alcohol. It was all a show, but damn, it worked.

I named the guys as they filed past us, walking up the stairs and taking their deserved seats over the club. Terry Bartlonguesen. Matthew Crusky. Brad Michems. Carzoni.

I recognized Aiden. Lestroy had his arm around him, and Aiden was laughing.

Some wore sharp business suits. Others were just dressed up, with pants to impress and custom-tailored shirts.

One by one they came. Almost the entire team was here.

I waited, the lump in my throat doubling as each player went past, not sparing us a look. We were within eyesight, but not in their way. Our booth was set back against the wall, whereas theirs was front and center, meant to be noticed, meant to be worshiped.

A few more trailed in.

Then, I felt a new frenzy begin on the nightclub pathway. People were migrating over from the dance floor, and I knew.

More people came running back, their phones raised, so at first I didn't see them. The lights were blinding against the dark and neon colors inside the club. Then a small clearing opened, and I could see both Juan and Reese...and Stan?

Fucking Stan.

I started growling. He was another Keith the Boss to me, but the effect was momentary because once I saw Reese, I couldn't look away.

Tingles shot through me.

A buzz started low, simmering and building the closer he got. And at the same time, the lump in my throat moved down, choking me until I pushed it down to fall with a thud to the bottom of my stomach.

My mouth dried.

He looked so good.

Faded jeans, a black shirt, the silver-tinted sunglasses, and a Thunder ball cap pulled low over his head, I'd never seen Reese more a celebrity than just now. His head was down, and there was a girl on his arm. I almost fell back when I saw her.

God.

Her little hands clung to his arm. She was hurrying to keep up.

Juan and Stan were talking, moving at a more sedate pace toward the private box. Reese edged ahead of them, an urgency in his gait, as if he just wanted to get away. The girl teetered behind on her heels. It was like he'd forgotten she was there.

She wore a bikini top with a ripped jeans miniskirt that barely covered her ass. As she stretched to catch up with Reese, I caught a glimpse of something lacy underneath. Her hair was blown out and her makeup was heavy.

Skank.

Okay. In fairness to her, she might not have been one. You never knew—but then she stuck her hand in one of Reese's back pockets. She was definitely a skank.

Pretty sure I was showing my front teeth as I growled. It was savage. I was scaring even myself.

"Down, girl." Trent pulled me to sit. He laughed in my ear, sitting next to me. "The girl's not with him. He doesn't even really know she's there."

Yeah.

He was up the stairs, looking for a seat.

Trent was right.

Maybe.

Probably.

Reese looked like he really didn't know she was there, and then he sat down on the far end of the box, facing our direction—and she climbed right onto his lap.

I started to surge to my feet.

Trent clamped a hand on my arm, holding me in place. "Stop. Stop. She doesn't mean anything."

I knew that. She was a fucking one-use girl, but that didn't matter.

Reese was mine.

I leaned back against the seat. "I can't do this. I can't sit here and watch him get mauled."

"Well..." Trent kept his hand on my arm. "I don't think you can get to him right now, so you're going to have to. Try not to watch?"

A gurgling laugh erupted from me. Yeah, right.

He patted my arm. "Or focus on what you want to say? You're here now. He's here. Lauren's done working for the night, so she's hanging out with us. We'll keep an eye out for you. If he goes to the bathroom, you can move in."

Lauren leaned over Trent, her boobs almost coming out of her corset top. "Completely. A few of my girls here know about the situation, and they're all in to help set this up. Knowing someone who's dating Reese Forster is a story no one wants to miss out on—what we can tell the grandbabies one day when Reese is in the hall of fame." She raised her glass in the air. "And if anything, it's an adventure."

An adventure. Right. It was my goddamn heart.

But they were right. I had no other options here. *I mean, I could send him a text...*

Fuuuck.

I was doing it before I even fully comprehended I'd made the decision to do it.

Me: What should I wear if I were going to go to a nightclub?

Me: A fucking bikini top? Maybe just a bra around my crotch? Or only a thong?

It was go-time now. I unleashed it all.

I was typing the next as I watched him pull out his phone. He frowned at it, reading.

Me: Or maybe just sunglasses? The silver kind.

His mouth pressed down in a firm line, but he edged the girl off his lap, waving her away. One of the other guys snapped her up, and she went happily to his lap. Juan and Stan were settled in the box by now. Both gave Reese a look, but when he leaned forward and started to type, they moved to the other side of the booth where the others were. Reese remained sitting off on his own.

A part of me was glad to see that. *Good. Stay like that, because you're all mine.*

Oh, yes. My inner crazy stalker fangirl was back, but now she was possessive. I was all *sorts* of possessive.

I wasn't walking this time.

A bitter taste soured my mouth as I kicked myself.

Me: I never should've walked. I'm sorry. But...

Me: What are your thoughts on second chances? Providing it's not to an alcoholic brother who uses your name for stuff he doesn't deserve?

My phone buzzed back.

Reese: Where are you?

I grinned, slinking down in our box. He wasn't even looking around the club.

Reese: Are you in Chicago?

Me: What about ex fucking? Positions on that? Pun intended.

Reese: Where the *fuck* are you?

Me: Pun intended?

Me: I'm just saying yes for you. Good one.

Me: Answer my questions.

My body had heated up. A throb started between my legs, and I moved in my seat. I didn't know what the end result would be, but I knew the chances of meeting up and having a quick fuck were extremely high. Whether he'd still want to talk to me afterwards was another matter.

I held off, watching him stare at the phone. He wasn't responding, but he wasn't putting the phone away.

Me: Answer me and I'll answer you.

He shook his head, but returned to typing.

Reese: Fuck. You.

Ouch.

Still.

Me: So you're saying there's a chance?

A slight grin from him. He typed again.

Reese: Where are you? I'll come to you.

Me: So you can 'fuck. me.'??

Reese: Yes.

A whole burst of shivers moved down my spine, setting every cell on vibrate. I groaned, biting my lip.

Me: What are your thoughts on a girl who was so messed up she could barely look at herself in the mirror?

Me: Who hated herself so much because she was leaving behind someone who could no longer be next to her because a disease was eating him away, slowly, every goddamn day? What are your thoughts on that girl?

Me: Who still cries at the thought of losing the guy she thought she was going to marry one day? But knows he'll never come back and she still has to go through that grieving process?

Me: Who isn't in love with him, but knows she'll always care for him because she respected him that much, respected the relationship she thought she would have with him? Because he was actually a really great guy before the fucking disease TOOK HIM AWAY FROM HER?!

Me: She never got a say. He didn't.

Me: They were happy one day, then poof, he couldn't remember her the next for a few minutes. How's that right? How's that something we're supposed to just take? Move on with life?

Me: Well. It doesn't happen. There are feelings and thoughts and dreams and lives that are plucked away from us and we HAVE NO FUCKING SAY IN THE MATTER!

Me: Sorry. Calmer now.

Me: Still glad we became friends?

Me: Still glad we had sex?

Me: Still glad you put up with me enough so we were more than friends, more than fuck friends?

Me: What are your thoughts on a girl who was so filled with shame that it took her an entire year to start living again? To hope to live again? To want to live again?

Reese: Where.

Me: Or about a girl who realized because she hadn't dealt with her baggage, she might've royally fucked up her chances at being with another guy who could make her happy? Who could make her live again?

Me: Or...

My hands were shaking. My stomach was going to empty out, and I was about to be sitting here texting with him and crapping my pants all at the same time. But I took a deep inhale and typed it to him.

Me: What are your thoughts on a girl who sends you random questions because she's too scared to tell you the one simple truth?

Me: That she fell in love with you.

Me: And she's now pissing herself, knowing she'll have new baggage over losing out on someone she doesn't deserve, but she's hoping he'll give her one more chance?

Me: Because she's a lot more sane. Promise.

Me: Because she really is working on herself now and she's just really hurting and sad, but she has love in her to give and she knows if you can just put up with the void inside of her that may never go away, she's hoping you'll deem her worthy enough for a second chance?

Me: I'm talking about me, by the way. Just making that clear, because talking in third person probably doesn't help sell the whole 'I'm more sane here' premise.

Damn!

I sent another flurry of texts because I couldn't stop myself.

Me: And beware with your rejection. I'm a reformed stalker, but the reform could be temporary.

Reese: Are.
Me: What would happen if a camel was born with three humps? Deformity or evolution?

I was faintly aware of Trent's phone buzzing beside me. I kept on. I was committed now. Good luck on knowing when I'd stop.

Me: Thoughts on ending poaching worldwide?
Me: Rugby or football?
Me: American football or the real football?
Me: Favorite book? Besides your playbook.
Me: Why are manatees so cute?
Reese: You?!
Me: Who'd win in an ocean selfie contest? Dolphin or manatee?
Me: Seahorses don't look anything like real horses. Discuss.
Me: Who really puts together the DSM? Do we actually need all those volumes?
Me: What do you think—

A hand rested over mine, stopping my text in mid-type.

"What?"

I was almost desperate to get these questions out, but Trent wasn't looking at me. He nodded toward the front of our box. "Look."

I did, my insides a hurricane, tsunami, and let's throw in a few tornadoes. All were happening. All at once, and they were inflicting horrific damage, but there he was. Standing just at our entrance, his glasses still on and a firm scowl fixed on those so-kissable lips.

I held the phone up once more.

Me: Can you even see with those sunglasses?

He read the text, shaking his head, and I saw a crack. His top lip curved up, but it was flat the next second. He shoved his phone into his pocket, took mine, and grabbed my hand.

"Let's go," he said.

Trent tossed him a set of keys. Reese caught them, giving him a nod.

Then we were leaving.

CHAPTER FORTY-NINE

He walked me down the hallway.
Hand in hand.

His face forward.

He wasn't looking at me, and I couldn't help myself. The texting had unleashed something in me.

"You had a girl on your lap."

I didn't mean it to come out accusing—no, no, I totally did. Let's be honest here. I was seeing green and red at the same time. It was Christmas in the nightclub.

Reese's hand tightened over mine. He spared me a brief glance, and then his phone was out and he was using his other hand to type on it.

"She grabbed me when we came in. I let her stay because I thought the guys would leave me alone then. Chicks on laps usually do that, unless they're hoping for a share."

Oh. God. What I could do with that one from him.

I gulped, only asking with a bite, "Do you usually share?"

He stopped. I almost slammed into him from the abruptness, and he rotated around.

"No," he clipped out, taking the sunglasses off and shoving them into his pocket. "Do you?"

I reared my head back. "Are you kidding me? I would never not be texting then. *Everyone* would be getting the texts."

He grinned, just slightly, and it made my heart flip over.

He shook his head, starting forward again as his phone flashed. "You are truly insane."

I snorted. "That's been established. Long ago. Keep up."

We were at the front of the club. He paused before stepping out. A few people had gone past us in the hallway, and only a couple had stopped to look back at him, but it was different now. He was going out into an open area, and beyond that, there were more people. If the press knew almost the entire Seattle Thunder team was at Whisper, they'd for sure be camped outside.

He cursed.

I *tsk*ed him, grinning from the side of my mouth, because— another truth bomb here—I was feeling a little maniacal. "Where's the hood? It's like you don't know how to do this whole celebrity thing."

He laughed shortly, but mostly ignored me, staring out. He checked his phone again.

"What are you doing?"

He showed me. "I called a driver."

The dot was getting close. We were going to make a mad dash. I was thrilled.

I pushed the phone back at his chest. "I know I joke about being crazy, and there's a little truth in there, but I can turn on the Crazy if you need it. People stay away from Crazy, unless they are too, and no one's going to out themselves as that level of Crazy here. I can raise the bar if you need me to."

He stared down at me, and it finally happened.

He'd been all hard and ice and monotone, a wall over his face, but at my suggestion, some of it melted away. A small grin tugged at his mouth, and he placed a hand on the small of my back.

He pulled me against him, just for a second, and murmured into my ear, "Keep the maniacal crazy till later, because you're right. I want to fuck. you. tonight." His mouth closed over my ear, and I swooned, my knees buckling.

Flames burst inside of me, and I sagged against him.

He continued his kissing, moving down my neck to my shoulder, and his hand joined the exploration. It fit right under my shirt, and then tunneled under my jeans. He grabbed a good portion of my ass before going even farther, and I squeaked, feeling his fingers go somewhere I was not ready for.

"Holy shit!" I jumped, dancing away.

My breath was shallow, and I knew I was flushed. All sorts of flushing here.

He was on me. Literally.

His eyes smoldered, and he dipped his head to stare at me eye-to-eye. He backed me up against the wall, guiding me until I had nowhere to go and the club melted away, the world with it.

When it was only the two of us, he said, so softly, "I do not scare. Stop using the crazy card on me, because it's not working. I've seen crazy. Remember? You are hurting. You are sad. You are broken, but you are not crazy. You may feel that way at times, but you're not. Trust me. So stop saying it."

Oh—whoa.

He took my breath away.

I reached for him, my hands running up his arms, over his shoulders, curving around his neck, and just as we both felt his phone buzz, his eyes trained on my lips and he groaned.

Moving quickly, his mouth was on mine, and he sealed everything with that kiss.

I would do anything he wanted.

Everything. Anything. Nothing.

Whatever he wanted, because I just wanted him. I wanted to feel him, be in his arms, be able to speak the words to him that so far I only had enough courage to text.

But more than anything, I just wanted to be with him in whatever way he was going to allow that.

Fireworks continued exploding in me as he groaned and his lips nipped at mine. "Our car is here. Ready?" He took my hand again.

He turned, his shoulders rolling back. He was preparing too, slipping his glasses back on.

I—yeah... Where was I? That was about my mindset right now.

But then he tugged on me, and we were going.

I followed him.

We walked out through the club's main entrance, and I was aware of flashes of light all around us. A few people gasped Reese's name, and then we were outside on the street and more camera flashes were going off.

Someone had definitely called the press. It wasn't a barrage, but enough to disorient me.

Reese ignored everyone and herded us both into the car.

When he gave the directions to Trent's apartment, I looked at him.

"It's not a great idea to bring girls to the hotel. Trent offered his place. Said he'd stay at his girlfriend's."

Well. Okay, then. It was all settled.

We were about to have it out. The driver didn't seem to care who was in his back seat, but I still didn't want to talk about anything until we got to Trent's.

The drive wasn't long—a little over twenty minutes. Reese kept a hand on the small of my back as I got out, and then stepped out beside me.

"You were here earlier?" he asked.

I nodded. "We came for a bit, ate, changed, and went back out." I led the way inside.

Trent didn't have a doorman, so I held my hands out for the keys. Reese handed them over, and for being in Chicago, I was surprised not to see anyone else out in the lobby on a Thursday night.

We stepped into the elevator, and I asked, "Are you going to get in trouble for not sleeping there?"

Reese shook his head, rubbing a hand over his jaw. He looked tired, softening lines around his mouth and bags under his eyes. Taking off his hat, he ran his hand briskly through his hair before shoving it back on, squashing it. He leaned back against the elevator wall.

"Coach knows about Aiden's party. We're fine. I mean, we're all adults. We gotta meet at eleven for meetings, but I'm fine till then."

The elevator dinged, and we stepped out onto Trent's floor.

Reese stayed right behind me, his hand on my hip. "I thought your buddy lived in Minneapolis?"

"No. He moved down here for college and just stayed, but he travels a lot for his job." Speaking of, I opened the door and asked, "How'd you know where we were?"

He grunted, shutting the door, flipping the locks, and stepping around me.

That wasn't a good sign.

Dropping his hat and sunglasses on the counter, he went to the fridge. He grabbed a water, and tossed one to me. "Drink that."

I caught it, holding it a second. "Excuse me?"

He motioned to my phone and me. "I don't want to talk to drunk Charlie tonight. You're acting fine, but I don't care about how you're acting. I want you sober. I want to get shit dealt with, because I'm sick of this absence crap."

Absence crap.

My heart soared.

I opened my water and took a drink. "You really do care, don't you?"

He rolled his eyes. "Spare me."

I laughed and capped the water again.

"Really? All that texting was you sober?"

I touched my chest. "It's like you don't actually know me."

"Oh..." He let out a myriad of curses, his head tipping back. "Not with this bullshit. Come on, Charlie. I want to deal with you, not just another chick playing fucking mind games." He tossed his phone on the counter, his water next to it. Stepping back, he folded his arms and fixed me with a glare. "You said a lot of heavy stuff in those texts. Say it again to me—face to face, not behind your little phone keyboard. Give me a chance to actually respond this time."

Man.

Goodness.

He wanted to go there.

I looked away, holding on to the counter behind me. I kept my head down, but I started. I had to. For him—and fuck my chest that felt like I was taking a cigarette to it from the inside.

"Everything in those texts, I meant."

"Really?"

Ooh... I was trying not to, but... "Yeah. I mean, I often wonder who'd win a selfie contest? A manatee or a dolphi—"

"Stop joking! This is serious." His chest heaved. "At least it is to me."

I quieted.

Then, staring at me, he raked a hand through his hair. "You know—shit. Yeah. Okay. You laid out your heart. I read those texts. I can't imagine what you're going through with Damian. But what I can say is that you shouldn't be ashamed of trying to keep living. Never be ashamed of that. I doubt he would want you to feel that either. You shouldn't feel guilty about wanting to keep living. I mean, my God, there are no words. There's nothing I can say to make that okay, or even try to what—hold your hand through it? I have no clue. All I know is that when you left, I hated it. I watched you walk away from me at the airport, and I wanted to fucking go nuts. You joke, but that's what I was feeling. I had you..."

His eyes blazed. His nostrils flared. He jerked forward, coming to me and stopping a few feet away. There was no one else, just him and me.

I couldn't look away. I was captive to what he was saying, the way he was looking. My fingertips curled around the countertop behind me.

"I know the hell it is going through life with two alcoholics in the family and a mother who gave up long ago. I can understand that suffering, but I don't have the words to help you with Damian. I wish I did. I wish I could shovel a bunch of money at his doctors and they'd make it go away, but not with this disease. I can't do anything except care for you and hurt with you, that's all."

Yep. Tears. Again.

Shocker.

I was steadfastly ignoring them.

He'd stopped—maybe for air or maybe because it was my turn—so with a tight chest, I started. My head was firmly directed to the floor. I'd really lose it if I had to see him when I said these things.

"I fell in love with you, and not the stalker way. The real way." I laughed. "I think it might've started when you called me a camp groupie. I'm weird like that, or maybe when you answered the first round of questions I asked you. Then a bit more when I stepped out of the bathroom and you were there, waiting for me. You told me you didn't like 'it,' and that meant something to me."

I risked a look. He was rolling his eyes, but I spoke again, drawing his attention back to me. "You saw me. Most don't. You were right. I use the crazy as a shtick, and it's not right. I mean, I'm being really unfair because I know no one's really *crazy*. There is no crazy. People have struggles, or imbalances, but they're not really nuts like I use it. But it kept people away for the longest time. Until you. You saw through it, and you started to like me anyway."

His arms fell to his side, and his eyes became softer.

"We were friends, and I really loved being friends with you, but I was still trying not to feel anything or let anyone in. I couldn't. I thought I would shatter, because if you let people in, they can hurt you. I was raw—still am, to be honest. But you got in there, and I started not only wanting to be around you all the time, but looking forward to seeing you, to texting you, to just hearing your voice. The calls. The texts. That's all just because I'm desperate for some attention from you."

My voice broke off.

In one sense, this was embarrassing. In another sense, I was exposing myself again and bracing for what he'd say in return. But most of all, I was saying what I meant, and deep down I knew I would handle whatever came back from it.

That was freeing.

It was needed.

This. This was a part of moving on. I couldn't explain it, but I felt it. I knew it.

I looked up again, unshed tears pooling in my eyes. "I fell in love with you, but I am still really messed up, and I am still really exposed, and I am... I am like a toothless saw that had all its jagged edges fall out, and you have to put them back in. Glue them. I don't know how you do it—buy a new saw? Though since I'm the broken one, I hope you don't do that. Anyway, a toothless saw, that's me."

I smiled, my lips curled over to blanket my teeth. "Like this. I'm like a shark with no teeth."

"Shut up." He moaned, his head swaying from side to side. "You are unbelievable. You sent me all these really deep texts, and now you're joking about being a toothless shark while you're professing your love? Really?"

I said it simply. "I love you, and I'm telling you, and I don't have much more to expose, because what I have, I've already shown. The rest is self-preservation, in case you decide to walk out of here. I'll crumble, but I'm really hoping that doesn't happen."

More because I really love basketball, and if you leave me, I'll have to stop watching ball, and that'll hurt too.

It'll be like a second dumping all over again.

So please, please, please, don't walk out and leave me behind.

Please don't—

I looked up. He stepped closer, his head tilted to the right.

I eyed his hands. They were at his side.

I wanted them on me. Once he reached for me, he could make the world go away. All the hurt and sadness, all that was stripped away under his touch, but he didn't lift them to me.

"The correct usage of crazy aside, you are a complete ball of psychosis at times."

That's what he said.

My chest filled with warmth.

He laughed, a self-deprecating edge to it. "Having said that, you were like an itch. I needed to scratch it, and the more I did, the more it grew until it took me over completely."

He began to scratch at his chest idly. "It was on the outside at first, then on the inside. I felt like I was being tickled constantly. I liked it, but it was odd at the same time, and then suddenly one day, I found myself wondering about you. I wanted to know what you were doing, how you were. I mean, you were thirteen feet away in a ball cage, but I still had the thoughts. They just built and built, and you started to fucking take over. All my brother shit, that got pushed aside. You and basketball. That was what I thought about, and it was nice—a nice break from everything else. And somewhere along the line I began worrying about you, caring about you, doing things to make you feel better, to make sure you were okay. Then we started screwing and I thought, *Okay, this will get her out of my system.* It was the opposite. You started to consume me, and I hated it. I loathed it, but I couldn't do anything about it. It's like you decided to take over everything inside my body, move in, and be content to live with me for the rest of time, and I had no say about it."

He scowled at me. "It was really fucking annoying. Now you're in there, and I give a shit. And I want you around me all the time. And I loved that your boss got canned, and I loved fucking you away from camp. And then I had to leave, and I just wanted to be back with you. I didn't care where it was. Here, I mean, not really *here*. We're in Chicago, but you know what I mean. If I'm on the road or in Seattle or at your place—wherever you are. I just want to be around you, and I want to make you happy, and I don't ever, ever want you to walk away from me again."

He stepped closer, within touching distance. His eyes were so fierce, shooting daggers at me. "Got it? You're all about being exposed and shit—well, you're not alone. I love you, and I have no idea what to do with this. I don't say pretty words or make fucking declarations. I like you. I love you. I want to always be with you, and that's that. Right? Isn't that good enough?"

He was almost shouting at me.

I loved it.

I lapped it all up like a cat getting cream for the first time. Yes, sir. More, sir. I'll drool for it.

He laughed at me. "You're beaming."

I was.

I loved to beam.

Standing up on my tiptoes, I raised my arms for him. He stepped in, folding his around me, and his head bent to my neck. I kissed his jawline, his cheek, the corner of his mouth, and I whispered against his lips, "You're annoyed at how much you love me. That's the most romantic thing anyone's ever said."

He barked a laugh. "I doubt it. I bet Damian said all sorts of nice things to you."

He did, but he said not-so-nice things to me too.

"Your net worth outweighs his. How about that?"

Another bark from him, then his hands shifted to grip my ass, and he began nuzzling my neck. "God." He pressed a lingering kiss to my throat. "I really fucking love you."

"I really fucking love you too."

He kissed me. My lips molded to his, my body melting.

Then he lifted his head. "Don't ever leave me. Okay?"

I sobered at that question and leaned backward. My hands rested on his biceps. "Same. Got it?" I held up my pinkie.

He stared at me as a wicked grin curved on his face. "Really?"

I raised it higher. "Got it?"

"You and me?" He wrapped his pinkie around mine, everything in him gentle. He smoothed his hand through my hair, the touch loving, and he let out a soft sigh. "I about died when I got your texts tonight."

I tightened my pinkie around his. "Really? How so?"

He laughed again, his hand breaking away, but curving around my back and sweeping up under my shirt. His head bent. I felt his lips tasting my neck, tantalizing, caressing and licking.

"Just almost shit my pants thinking what you'd think seeing that girl. I didn't touch her, but I didn't stop her from touching me." He looked at me, earnest. "I've not touched anyone since you. I swear. You've ruined me. I've realized it's either you or no one."

I smoothed my hand up his arm, twining my fingers around the back of his neck, and I leaned back to smile at him. Dazzling.

"Oh, Reese. You're trying to tell me an NBA player wouldn't eventually have sex with all those girls who throw themselves at you guys? You're right. I believe in the Easter Bunny too."

His hands squeezed my sides, and his mouth found mine. "It's true. I don't care what you say."

Then his tongue danced with mine, and soon we were doing more than kissing. Soon no more words were needed, except that I really loved the way he professed his love as he slid inside of me that night—and afterwards, and before we fell asleep, and again and again and again.

Breaking News

Roman Forster, the older brother of Seattle Thunder player Reese Forster, has died. Medical personnel found his body early this morning after responding to a 911 call from his hotel room. Sources indicate he died from an overdose.

Roman Forster had been recently released on bail for pending sexual assault charges. Though estranged from his younger brother, Reese Forster, Roman had indicated in interviews that he wished to make amends. A source close to the family reports that a history of alcoholism and addiction has played a part in their estrangement. It's also reported that Reese Forster is estranged from his mother and father.

A spokesperson for Reese Forster had no comment when we reached out.

The Seattle Thunder is scheduled to play the Chicago Chasers this evening. It's not been reported whether Forster will be playing.

We'll be following this story as more details develop.

CHAPTER FIFTY

The call came at three that morning.

They asked Reese where he was, and told him to stay put.

The first knock came thirty minutes later, and Stan and Juan came into Trent's apartment. Unshed tears glistened in Juan's eyes, though Stan barely blinked when they walked past me. I saw him wiping his eyes in the kitchen corner later on.

The phone rang over and over after that. Stan took some of the calls. Juan talked to the coach, but after an hour of being beside Reese, Juan bunked down in Trent's guest bedroom.

Reese couldn't take time off, so they made the best decision they could. I found extra bedding for Stan, who said he'd sleep on the couch. I changed the bedding in Trent's guest room as well, but Juan insisted on having us use Trent's main room. He said we might need privacy and the bathroom was attached. Plus, this was my friend's place, so that was that. We lie in bed until Reese's alarm went off.

He turned it off, but didn't move.

I didn't have to ask if he'd gotten any sleep. He hadn't. We'd both lain in bed, and I'd held him as tears slipped down his face.

A soft knock came an hour later, and Juan stuck his head in. There were heavy bags under his eyes. "I'm heading back to be with the team. Coach called, said you weren't answering your phone. You want anything special from us?"

Reese sat up on the edge of the bed and leaned forward, his head in his hands. "Nah. Thanks, man."

"Yeah." Juan's gaze met mine over Reese's head. "You need anything?"

I shook my head, my hand resting on Reese's back, moving up and down, comforting. "I'll call if I think of anything."

"Uh..." He cleared his throat. "I heard the team is moving hotels tonight. The lobby was flooded with fans, so I'll grab all your stuff. Marie said she was flying in. She'll handle it all, bring your stuff wherever you end up."

"Have Marie give it to Stan. I'm sure we'll fly out of here tonight. He'll make sure it's all on the plane."

"I'll do that."

"Thanks, man. Means a lot."

My eyes closed. Reese's voice was hoarse, and I could feel the emotion in him. I blinked back a tear of my own, my strokes growing firmer as I rubbed over Reese's back.

Someone knocked on the apartment door.

Reese looked up.

Juan glanced over his shoulder.

We heard muted footsteps, then the door opening and low murmurs.

Juan looked back. "It's Coach."

Reese sighed, running a hand over his face. "Tell him I'll be out. Gotta dress quick."

"Will do."

After Reese got up and went in the bathroom, Juan said to me, "You'll take care of him?"

"Always."

He nodded. "Roman was a pain in the ass," he whispered, "but Reese loved him. You love family whether they're kind or not to you."

Then he shut the door behind him, and I could hear him talking to someone on the other side.

Waiting for Reese, I slipped out of bed and grabbed some clothes—his sweatshirt, some leggings, and a pair of ballet slippers I'd grabbed at the last second. I sat on the edge of the bed until it was evident Reese wasn't coming out anytime soon.

I crossed to the bathroom, knocking. I tried the handle. "Reese?"

He didn't answer.

Opening the door, my heart broke. There was no other way to say it. He sat on the floor in his sweatpants by the toilet. His knees were up as he did his best to curl himself into a ball. His head was in his hands, and I didn't think.

Going to him, I said his name once, sliding to my knees and moving right between his legs.

A sob left him, but he opened his arms. Crawling into his lap, I straddled his waist and wound my arms around him, pulling him close.

His hands balled into fists at my sides, and he cried.

There were no words. Not like this, when it's raw and new and has the power to change you forever. Nothing could take it away or soothe it, and the only thing I could offer was knowing he wasn't alone.

I brushed his hair back, kissing his forehead and whispering over and over, "I'm so sorry. I'm so sorry."

Eventually I felt a presence behind us.

Twisting my head just enough, I saw Coach Winston at the door, looking utterly broken. Reese seemed oblivious. His tears kept falling, his head buried against me, and I just kept soothing him. I was doing the best I could.

Coach nodded to me and mouthed, "Thank you."

I nodded back, just the smallest of motions, and he eased back. I heard the bedroom door click shut softly, and I assumed he would talk to Stan about whatever needed to be said to Reese.

Thirty minutes later, Reese pulled himself together, his eyes red-rimmed and still sniffling. He dressed for the day, putting on the suit Juan had brought with him the night before. I didn't know what all happened on the day of a game, but figured there were team things he needed to attend to.

He stepped into the hall, and I was right behind him. Stan straightened in the hallway. He had dressed in a suit as well.

He noted our clasped hands and cleared his throat. "I'll make sure Charlie's in a room close by for you."

Reese's voice was raspy. "Thanks."

And just like that, we gathered the rest of our stuff and headed out. I took Trent's keys with me. Going downstairs, no one said a word in the elevator, but an SUV was waiting for us.

This was Stan's doing.

On the drive to the stadium, he informed Reese, "I've chartered a private jet. A car will take us straight to the airport after your game. Your coaches are aware of everything. They're on board for you to take the weekend. You'll be expected back to the arena Monday morning for your game that evening."

Reese nodded.

"Your mother identified the body this morning, and she reached out about funeral planning. She'd like you to pay for everything."

Reese's hand tightened over mine. "Of course."

Stan paused, then coughed. "The timing was good—shit." He looked down. "I'm sorry. That was a bad choice of words..."

"Roman went to rehab twelve times."

I looked over. Stan stopped talking.

Reese was gazing out the window, his hand still holding mine.

"And he wasn't alone in that hotel room. Two girls were with him. One already reached out, asking for money to keep quiet."

Stan's eyes closed for a beat. "I didn't know that."

Reese's voice was devoid of emotion. He kept looking out the window. "She reached out via my Instagram. My social media team sent it to my publicist. Monica's waiting for my decision."

"I can—" Stan's voice was strangled and thick at the same time. "I can handle it all, if you want?"

"No."

So sad.

So empty.

But so firm at the same time.

Reese sounded sure as he said, "No. I don't care what they come out and say. It's no secret what Roman was like. I've never paid to have anyone keep quiet about him. I'm not going to start now."

Stan winced, looking down at his lap for a second. He looked up at me first, then Reese. "The medical examiner's report says overdose, but some media outlets are reporting it was suicide. How do you want me to handle that?"

Reese turned to look at him now, his eyes hollow, his face gaunt. "How do you usually handle it? I've never spoken out about Roman. Won't start now, not about this. Why would I change now that he's dead?" He raised our clasped hands and pressed a kiss to the back of mine before turning once more to the window. "He's at peace now, Stan."

Agony ripped through me, and tears came to my eyes. I held them back, but my chest felt a crushing weight, as it had over and over since that phone call.

"I gave up on a relationship with my brother long ago, but I didn't stop caring," Reese added. "That's the part that was hard—still loving him when I couldn't do anything to help him. He tried a couple other times."

Stan's eyes widened.

Reese kept on, not seeing his manager's reaction, "It was earlier in my career, when I was in college, so it never hit the news. No one cared about Roman Forster back then, but it was only two times. He wasn't bad all the time, or struggling all the time. He went in waves. He had some good times when he was doing well, when rehab stuck for a bit. But then he'd fall back down. He's better now, though. He's not hurting anymore."

A car honked outside.

A sprinkle of rain sounded on the top of our vehicle.

We drove a few more blocks.

"What should I tell your mother?" Stan asked.

"Tell her I'll pay." Reese's hand squeezed mine so tight as he looked over at his manager. "But only if Dad goes to a six-month rehab and she's checked into a mental health facility. I won't pay for shit if they both don't agree, and they go today."

Stan's face went white. "What about Roman's funeral?"

Reese went back to that window, his hand easing on mine, but not letting go. "They get committed, but they'll need permission to leave for his funeral, and only his funeral. They go to the church, to his burial site, and then back into wherever they go. No time afterward for 'coffee hour.' I won't do anything if those steps aren't taken today. And if she thinks about going to a tabloid and selling some story that I won't pay for anything, let her know I *will* respond, and I will be giving my terms to the public." He laughed, bitter and empty. "She always hated what people thought of her. If anything, that's the only threat that'll work on them both."

"Okay."

We pulled into a back parking lot for the stadium.

Stan had his phone out as the doors opened and we got out. "One of our lawyers is with her. I'll relay your terms, and I'll give the word to start the process. We'll get them both into facilities today. Don't worry about that. I'll take care of it."

"Thank you," Reese said.

Stadium employees greeted us just inside the door. A photographer and camera crew were there, but no one paid them any attention. When Reese turned down the hallway, Stan caught me and held me back.

The phone to his ear, he said under his breath, "He's gotta be with the team now. There'll be some press interviews, just one, but he needs to focus on the game as much as possible."

"What do I do?"

"There's a family lobby here. I'll show you where, and I'll get a pass for you. You can come and go as you want. Reese needs to know you're close by, but I know him. He won't reach out for you until after the game. He'll try to put everything out of his mind as much as possible right now."

I nodded. I could do that.

Be here. On call.

I could more than do that.

• • •

Trent called. Owen called. Grant called. I talked to Sophia and Hadley as well.

I asked Stan at one point if I could get Trent a pass to come in and stay with me. So two hours into me being here, Trent came to sit next to me.

We didn't talk much.

I texted with Reese a few times, checking on him, but I knew he needed to focus.

The afternoon stretched into evening, and someone from their team came to get me. Reese had requested to see me an hour before going onto the court.

Trent had gone up to the box by then. He said his friend and my airplane buddy Dwayne was there, and he didn't know anything about what had happened. Someone had taken a picture of Reese kissing me the night before, but my face wasn't visible, and in light of Roman's death, Stan got that story killed right away. I hadn't even known about it until Trent mentioned seeing it in an early alert, then nothing after that.

I was taken to a room. People were everywhere, lining the hallway, and someone mentioned the locker room wasn't too far away.

Stan came in minutes later and motioned to the door. "Reese just wants a minute with you. He'll be coming shortly, but then to fill you in on everything, he'll return to the locker room, and after that, they'll go out to play the game."

"Trent said there was a picture of us?"

Stan grimaced, tugging at his collar. "Yeah. I bought the story and killed it. People are already curious about you. It's been pushed off because of Roman's death, but word's spreading. Two bloggers are claiming they have video of you two conversing at the Coyotes game. Is that true?"

I knew who he was talking about, and unease began to trickle in. "Not talking or anything. Reese was going off the court. I held my phone up and he nodded. That was it. Those guys followed me after that, but I lost 'em and left the game with my friends."

"And these friends? If they're tracked down, what are they going to say?"

"Nothing." I felt slapped by his accusation, but the jaded look in his eyes was just resignation.

"Everyone has a price."

"Not these guys." My head rose higher. "Not me either."

He stared at me, hard, unblinking, and then a wall slid away. He cringed. "I, uh, I have to apologize for something."

More unease. Alarms began to sound.

"That last game you were at, in Washington, that whole mess was because of me."

Say what?

I lowered my head, my eyes still on him. "Repeat that."

He studied me a moment. "Marie didn't ditch you. She was so intoxicated that I switched her ticket. I stayed in the box, and she left twenty minutes later. She thought you'd ditched her until she saw how irate Reese was about it all." A vein stuck out from his neck. He was so stiff. "And Reese didn't forget his phone. I purposely took it out of his bag and put it on the counter, after I knew he wouldn't return to the house."

My teeth were grinding. I was seeing pink. Not red, just pink for now.

"Why?"

"I wanted to see how you would respond."

This fucker. "And did I pass?"

He flinched, a flash of regret passing over him before his features turned back to stone. "It was...eye opening. If you'd wanted Reese for his money or fame, you would've stayed at the stadium. I apologize for the damage I inflicted. I didn't realize how deeply he cared for you. I do now, and I can tell you I will never do anything to get between you. I am four years older than Reese. In many ways, I feel like I'm his older brother. Taking care of him has always been my job, and knowing how much he cares for you, you are now a part of that world. Now..." He drew upright, adjusting his suit jacket and smoothing out his sleeves. "Because I am not actually a big talker, this is probably the longest conversation you'll have with me, but I am in your corner. That will never change."

He started for the door.

"And if I hurt him? What then?" I called, stopping him.

He didn't even look at me, just reached for the handle and opened the door. "You won't. I can tell you love him too."

Then he was gone, and I wanted to curse at the door.
What a fuckhead, who I kinda liked now.

CHAPTER
FIFTY-ONE

There's a stillness in the air after someone's died. You feel it, knowing something had changed drastically, but yet the world around you keeps moving forward because while you know it, they don't. It's an odd dichotomy, and standing in that room, waiting for Reese to come in, I noticed everything.

The quietness in the room.

The distant roar of the crowd through the walls. People going past in the hallway. The smell of popcorn, hotdogs, and whatever else mixed together for the heady aroma and yet, down below where I stood only a faint trace of it mingled down here.

There were also hushed tones. Quiet footsteps.

And nerves. My nerves.

I was in that room by myself, knowing Reese was going to step in, knowing he loved me and I loved him and knowing how big of a responsibility that was now. In that stadium, twenty thousand people were waiting to watch him play and most of those probably knew of his loss. Some would care; some wouldn't. Some would just want to watch a fucking good game.

I was nervous.

My heart was breaking.

And I just wanted to see Reese, one last time before he had to go out there for his job.

The door opened. My heart jerked, but it was a female staff member. Seeing me, she pressed a finger to her ear and said,

349

"She's ready." She disappeared and a second later, she was back, but opening the door.

Reese walked in, decked out in his warm-up gear.

A burst of sensations exploded in me, filling me up. My throat swelled for a second, but without looking around, he came right to me.

I held my arms open and he stepped in, folding his body around me. I heard the distant sound of the door closing, and it was just him and me in that room. Not a word was said. My heart swelled up too, beating hard, beating strong.

He buried his head into the crook of my shoulder and neck. I felt his body shudder.

A few seconds...

Thirty...

A minute...

Eighty-seven seconds...

He felt good against me. Firm. Strong. And his arms tightened.

We were at a minute and forty seconds now.

Two minutes.

Another.

Three and thirty.

Then, a soft knock on the door, and he lifted his head up.

It opened as he stepped back, the same girl from before looked in. "It's time, Mr. Forster."

His hand was still on my hip. It tightened, flexing against my skin, and his shoulders rose up and down in an exhale. His head folded down. "Okay." His hand fell away, but I caught it. It kept moving, his fingertips grazing mine.

With a last look, his eyes haunted in a brief flash, before he looked back to the staff and he closed it all off again. His shoulders went back up. His head straightened. And his walk was more confident.

He was back in game mode.

And me, I was fighting back tears, for him.

CHAPTER FIFTY-TWO

"Are you ready?"

Stan. I hated him in the beginning, but now I was starting to rely on the dickwad. He'd come back after Reese left and after the team had gone out to start warming up.

Now he guided me up to the family and friends' suite. He walked beside me. A few people recognized him, their eyes enlarging, but he swept past as if he didn't see them. He kept a hand behind, not touching me, but still there as if he were guiding and protecting me all at once. A couple people frowned when they saw me. I don't know what that was about, but when we got to the suite, we paused outside.

Last time I was in a similar room, I wanted to hide and run away. That wouldn't happen this time. Word would've gotten out. Plus, I knew Trent and Dwayne were in there. He'd left me earlier to meet him, so giving Stan a small nod, he stepped forward and opened the door. He held it for me, but I couldn't bring myself to go in first. I waved at him, motioning for him to lead instead, and he dipped his head, doing as I asked.

I didn't need to be worried.

I knew that as soon as I stepped inside and Marie was there, her arms around me, tears on her face. "Charlie. Oh my God. How are you?" She pulled back, framing my face with her hands, her eyes so earnest. "Do you need anything? I packed up all of Reese's things and gave them to Stan." She glanced at him.

He stepped close, coughing. "Yes. That's all been taken care of."

My tongue was firm in the back of my throat, weighing me down. I—I didn't know quite how to respond, but it didn't seem to matter. Marie was hugging me again, then stepping back and wiping her tears away. "I can't imagine. Okay." She was scanning my face, reading me. "You're a little overwhelmed, I can see it." She squeezed my hands before stepping even farther back. "What do you need? Booze? A shoulder?"

I was scanning the room. Half the room was watching us, some of the women were whispering to each other, then starting to come over.

"I had two friends coming today..." I started to say.

"I got you. There are two guys in the corner. They were talking to the manager." She pointed behind me. "Is that them?"

They were positioned at a corner table, in another suite that was connected to this one. Dwayne had a beer in hand, nodding to the conversation and watching the teams below. Trent was conversing with another man in a business suit. The suit guy was the one talking, his hands in the air, but Trent glanced back. His eyes caught me, and a look flashed in them. He said something to the suit guy, turning to come for me.

"That's them, yeah."

"Got it." Marie patted my arm. "You go over to them, and I'll grab you something to eat and drink, hmmm?"

But she hadn't gone a step before a woman stepped in. "Are you Reese Forster's girlfriend?"

A gargle left me. I didn't know how to respond, not at first. Then a calmness settled over me and I held my hand out. "Yes. I'm Charlie."

She introduced herself. It was Lestroy's wife.

"If you ever need anything, let me know. Marie has my number." She was kind, and giving. She was there for me, but I knew it was her way of reaching out, being there for Reese. This was all for Reese.

And after she stepped back, another came forward. Crusky's girlfriend.

Then another.

And another.

A few of the men came over, introduced themselves. Condolences were said over and over until my mind was a blur.

I couldn't remember faces, or names, or even what they said. But I remembered the sentiment.

They were being kind.

That went a long way with me.

By the time the last one who came over had stepped away, the lights in the gym were dimming for the announcer's introductions. Trent was next to me, his hand on my arm. "We have seats in the corner. Ready?"

I had caught Trent and Marie introducing themselves from the corner of my eye during my line of people. Stan appeared when we went over. There was no surprise from Trent so I assumed they knew each other. Dwayne was watching me, his eyebrow slightly raised, but he kept sipping his beer. He was eyeing Marie at one point until Trent nudged him and leaned in to whisper something. Dwayne jackknifed toward the window again, and stayed there.

From what I'd been told, I didn't think an official announcement had been made over the game's intercom system about Roman's death. I mean, people knew, but it wasn't something that needed to be announced.

But then the lights cut for the Seattle Thunder's entrance, and the personal phone camera lights blinked on. But they weren't the usual color. They were a pastel blue—the team color.

Someone gasped in the suite, and I blinked back tears.

I heard someone ask in a whisper, "Did you know they were doing this?"

Her friend replied, "No."

Trent leaned over to me. "They were handing filters out in the entrance to everyone."

The stadium was an ocean of blinking blue lights. An awareness spread through me. I knew, I just knew that this was for Reese, because of Roman's death. The fans were trying to give him their support in their way.

My hand went out to the window, and I spread my fingers, pressing my palm there. It was my gesture to Reese, though I knew he wouldn't see it.

I caught movement beside me and looked over. Trent was giving Dwayne a filter, and they both raised their phones, holding the blue in front of the light.

A few others in the suite were doing the same.

When Reese's name was announced and he jogged out onto the court, a roar sounded through the entire stadium. Those blue lights waved around, and everyone was in a frenzy.

The camera zoomed in on Reese, and he wiped away a tear, blinking to stop the rest. He dipped his head to the crowd, then turned to look where I was.

My hand hadn't left the glass, and I leaned forward.

The entire arena was Seattle Strong for Reese that night.

CHAPTER
FIFTY-THREE

Once the game ended, we remained in the suite. Most of the others filtered out right away, but a few remained. Marie was standing point guard for me. It was too much. The game had been emotionally exhausting.

Reese played and he played with his whole heart, but there'd been a few camera cuts to him when he'd been caught blinking back some tears. Every time I wanted to go to him. Every time I wanted to take away his pain. Every time I could do nothing.

Our small crew remained in the corner. I hadn't even gotten up for the bathroom, not once during the game.

Stan was either talking on his phone or checking his phone.

Dwayne had no idea my relation to Reese still. Bless his heart. He was blissfully drunk, sitting between Marie and Trent. He hadn't witnessed the line of hugs I received when I came in, and I don't think he let his beer run empty the whole game. If I were asked, I'd have to say that Dwayne had the best time this game.

Trent nudged me with his arm, showing me his phone. "Look."

He had ESPN pulled up and my heart stopped in my chest. It was a picture of me, from the beginning of the game when I placed my hand against the window. The headline read, "Forster's New Girlfriend There in Time of Need." I gulped, grabbing the phone.

"How did they—" But I was scrolling, reading the article.

Stan leaned over. "The word's out. I wasn't able to stem all of the articles popping up. If ESPN found out, it's a loss. They know."

I didn't know how to process this.

Handing it back to Trent, I scooted back in my chair and pulled my feet up, folding my arms around my knees. My go-to position when I want to hide.

Trent was eyeing me, pocketing his phone. He shared a look with Stan, then Marie.

"How are you doing, hon?" Marie switched seats with Trent.

I shook my head. "It doesn't matter. All that, it's whatever. I'll deal, process it later. I just want to be there for Reese right now."

He'd been there for me.

He made me want to live again.

It was my turn now.

"Yeah. That makes sense."

Trent was standing, almost hovering over us. I tipped my head back. "Have the others texted during the game?"

He was reading his phone again. It wouldn't stop buzzing now. A deep frown pulled at his mouth, and he itched an idle hand over his forehead. "Shit." Soft, under his breath. He raised wary eyes to me. "Janet's husband was watching. He saw your picture."

So she knew.

I lifted up a shoulder. My feelings had thawed toward her since she'd been there for me that day.

He kept reading more texts as they were coming in. A grunt, then a grin. "Most are just the gang, expressing concern for how you're doing, how Reese is doing."

Dwayne's head jerked around. "Forster?" He belched, a hand pressing to his chest. "Oh. Sorry." His cheeks pinked. "I think I'm fairly drunk."

Marie laughed. Even Stan grinned at that.

I eyed Dwayne. "Fairly?"

His eyes were almost swimming around from all the booze.

An embarrassed grin appeared. "By fairly, I mean that I am very intoxicated. I should get a cab for the hotel."

Trent shot him a look, putting his phone away. "Nah, man. I'll take you. My car is here anyways."

Dwayne stood up, then began to fall again. Trent grabbed his arm, steadying him up. That grin turned grateful and he patted Trent on the arm. "Thanks. You're a good friend."

Trent asked me, "Are you—I mean—do you need anything? I could—"

Stan finished up on his phone at that moment, a look of finality settling down over his face, and he stood from his seat. "It's time." He gave Trent a firm nod. "I got her."

Marie was waiting for Stan and asked now, "Cars are here?"

He glanced down to her. "Yes. Reese is almost ready to leave." He turned his robot-like face toward me. "We can go now, and we should if you want to get ahead of any press. I believe there's a sports reality show filming in the arena. You might want to avoid them now."

That was enough for me.

Dwayne looked confused again, tipping his head up to the side. His eyes skirting from me to Stan, or trying. They kept getting distracted by Marie in the middle. He paused, squinted, and he leaned forward now. "You're a player's girlfriend, aren't you?"

Marie snorted, standing up with me. "You're just now piecing it together about me?"

He was totally lost now. "Huh?"

She laughed shortly, holding her hand out. "I'm Juan Cartion's girlfriend."

His eyes bulged out. "You don't say?" He almost stumbled as he jerked forward to shake her hand, pumping it up and down. "It's a pleasure to meet you. I figured you belonged to someone, but I wasn't sure." His grin diminished to a shy one. "Took me all game to get my courage up to ask. I was hoping you weren't."

Marie barked out another laugh, pulling her hand free. "Yeah." She sidled up next to me. "Okay. We'll leave it at that."

He chuckled to himself.

Trent shook his head. "Okay. That's really our cue to go." His eyes found me. "Call me. Text me. Let me know if you need anything. Are you..." His gaze went to Stan, then back to me. "Are you going to remain here—"

"I've chartered a plane. We're going straight to the airport after this." He turned to me. "Do you have everything you need?"

"It's that bag I gave you in the SUV."

He nodded. "Then we're good to go."

My phone buzzed in that moment.

Reese: You're with Stan? Are you in the SUV?

Me: We're going now.

Reese: I got questions about you, just to warn you.

My throat swelled up. There he was, thinking about me when a part of his world crumbled today.

Me: Don't worry about me. How bad are you?

Reese: Getting through it. See you soon.

Reese: Love you.

Fuck the throat. A tear escaped my eyelid. I flicked it away.

Me: Love you back.

Reese: Feels good to type that.

Me: Yes, it does.

He didn't text again. Putting my phone away, all eyes were on me.

A sad smile stretched over Marie's face. "How's he doing?"

I lifted a shoulder up. "Said he got questions about me."

Stan swore under his breath. "I was hoping they'd hold off considering he lost his brother. Okay. That's it then. We need to go."

Hugs were done at the door. I hugged Trent, even Dwayne.

Trent murmured in my ear before letting me go, "Please reach out if you need anything. I travel a lot for my job. It's very easy for me to book a gig in Washington, just saying."

I stepped back, flicking him on the shoulder. "Go back and be with your woman. I like Lauren."

"She likes you too. And maybe I will."

He took Dwayne then, a hand on his arm as the guy was weaving all around people. With another wave over his shoulder, Trent and Dwayne went around the corner. We went the other way, and like before, I just followed Stan where he was going. It was a myriad of cement steps and back doors. Marie went with us, all the way to the parking area.

I wasn't ready for the attention, but we were getting it. As soon as we stepped out the last door, a woman with a camera was there. "Stan! How's Reese doing? Is that his girlfriend?"

Marie came to my other side, draping a sweatshirt over me and I tugged down the hood. This felt weird, adopting Reese's method of camouflage. A few months ago, I only had a cheating ex and a pervy grandpa in my life. That'd been it.

I paused in my thoughts as we walked down toward a row of SUVs waiting.

Breaking at one, Marie gave me a tight squeeze. "Stan has my number, but I got yours from him. Hope that's okay? I'm going to text you, see if you need anything. And I'll reach out once we get to Seattle in the morning."

Another squeeze, then she was off and getting into one of the other vehicles.

Stan had opened the door to the one we stood by, and I climbed in. He leaned in. The reporters had remained at the exit, but there were other people standing around, and a couple had their phones pointed at us. He blocked their view, his hands on both sides of the door. "I'm going to get in the front with the driver. Reese is heading out now. Do you need anything while I'm here? I can grab a water or anything else?"

My stomach growled. I hadn't eaten all day, but I shook my head. "I'm good."

I just wanted Reese.

He dipped his head down and stood back, shutting the door. He climbed into the front a second later, then we waited. The vehicle was silent, even the driver. Then a whole surge of activity happened toward the front. Lights were flashing, and out strolled a few of the players.

Garth Carzoni.

Lestroy.

Beau Michems.

Then Juan, and following him: Reese.

Everything raised a whole octave at Reese's appearance, but he walked through, ignoring everyone. Juan waited, and Reese bumped the side of his fist against his. Both separated. Juan went to where Marie was waiting, and Reese came to us.

He got in, tossing his bag in the back before sliding next to me. The door was shut, and he reached for my hand, entwining our hands. The SUV started, and within a minute, we were pulling away from the arena.

• • •

Life was a whirlwind after that.

We flew back to Washington that night. Both his parents were already checked into their respective facilities by the time we landed, and as Reese had said, they attended Roman's funeral. It was an emotional day for all of them. I sat beside Reese, holding his hand, and that night, I held him in my arms.

He was peppering kisses up my spine, his hand shifting over my hip as he rolled me to look at me. He was looming above me, resting on an arm to hold himself up.

The stark need in his eyes had me biting back tears. He'd had that look quite frequently this weekend, and I slid my hands up his arms, then moved one around his neck, going up into his hair and I fisted it there, pulling him down to me.

His mouth met mine. A soft graze. Loving.

It made me ache, but this time it wasn't a body ache. It was a soul ache. He brought me to life, and I just wanted to do the same for him now. I wanted to push all his haunts away.

He lifted his head. "What's wrong?"

My top lip curved up at that. "You're asking me what's wrong?"

He rested on his side, his hand tracing circles over my stomach. The sheet fell to the side. He was seeing all of me and he bent forward, his lips finding my breast, tasting me.

I closed my eyes, that soul ache shifting to peace. He filled me up in every way now.

Then I started talking, "You have not once pushed me away during this time. You've not once tried to avoid dealing with your parents or your brother. You've not once shied away from all the responsibilities on your shoulder."

That meant something.

He carried it all, and he did it without a thought, without breaking stride, and I knew he'd continue to do so as long as his parents were seeking help.

He lifted his head up, gazing down at me. "Yeah. Why would I?"

A half-laugh slipped from me. "I would've. I did. You changed me." I trailed a hand down his shoulder, his arm, his chest. "I couldn't even feel my emotions before. I asked those questions to evade it all, and here I am, actually feeling tears and peace and not shitting my pants because of it." I looked him in the eyes, drawing him back in. "That's because of you."

He shook his head, his hand going to the side of my face, tracing down my jawline. "No, that was you. You were starting to face the world again. I just happened to be in the way." His lip curled up, and he leaned down, nuzzling my jawline and moving south.

I closed my eyes, reaching up, grabbing a fistful of his hair.

My breath was shortening. Panting.

He was growing closer to my mouth.

He paused before touching his lips to mine and murmured, "You know my tattoo?"

I nodded. Did I? I admitted, "I might've salivated over it a few times." He lifted his head farther and moved so we could both see it on his side. "What does it mean?"

"It's Hebrew for teardrop shot."

"What?"

He was holding back a grin. "I know. It's kind of embarrassing."

"Why Hebrew?"

He laughed, burying his head in his arm for a second. "Because I thought it looked cool. I got it in college, and one of my friends was obsessed with learning Hebrew. I have no idea why, but we got drunk one night and resolved to get something that stood for our future. I got teardrop shot because it's rare and it's under utilized, and I wanted one thing to excel at in ball. I knew I was fast. I knew I could handle the ball decent, but I wanted one more thing that would make me stand out. I wanted to further pack my resume, I guess. But it also means more than that to me now." He paused, a dark emotion starting to blaze from his eyes as he gazed at me.

I whispered out, "Reese." My hand cupped the side of his face.

He caught my hand, bringing it to his mouth and kissing it. Then he rested it against the side of his face. "You think you had all this baggage when we first started."

I quirked an eyebrow up.

He relented, "And yeah, you might've, but you're going to be fine. You're going to be amazing. You can do anything you want, and I really believe that. All that stuff you went through, it didn't break you. It made you stronger, and I think it made you perfect for me." He paused, swallowing before he spoke again, his voice dropping low to a rasp, "Life with me is going to be hard. I'm the one with the baggage now. There's going to be fan pressure, women, publicity. Life's different at this stage, and I think, I really think, you're my teardrop shot. You're the high arch in my life. You're beautiful inside and out, and you're rare. So very rare." He leaned down, his mouth capturing mine.

All the love, pleasure, peace in me swirled up, flooding my senses.

I was blinking back tears, my hand moving to his chest. "There was a time when I thought I would never be happy again." My eyes held his. "I gave it up. I was just trying to find the will to keep going, then you happened."

Trent.

Owen.

Hadley.

Grant.

"I got back a part of my old life. I got a piece of a new life." Reese. "And suddenly, I could deal with losing a huge chunk of myself in the in-between. You think I was made for you. Well, I think you were made for me too." Then I grinned. "I mean, who else still responds to me when I randomly text for thoughts on beluga procreation?"

He laughed, his mouth closing in over mine. "That's true. I mean, if there's one thing that keeps me up at night, it's beluga fucking each other, especially at three in the morning when I'm lying right next to you."

I laughed, but then his mouth grew more commanding, and I knew the talking was done for the night. I was okay with that.

I was happy.

• • •

Reese was right. Life happened after that. A lot of life.

His father emerged from rehab six months later sober and he remained that way. Reese got his dad back. It wasn't quite the same with his mother. She was treated for chronic depression, survivor's guilt, and post-traumatic stress disorder.

Through the years, she had ups and downs, but she continued to struggle the rest of her life. She was in and out of mental hospitals, but she tried. She really tried.

As for Damian, the first day he met Reese, he beamed from ear to ear. He ate all of his meals. The nurses marveled at how happy he'd been. By that time, he'd already forgotten about me. I was his friend who watched sporting games with him, and then I became Reese Forster's woman.

I always got a little sad when he called me that. He never understood why, and I never shared. It was easier to go with the new name. It was the happiest for him. He was proud to know me.

He forgot AJ, but not Mickey or his mother. He remembered both to the end.

He passed in his sleep, five years from Roman's death. The nurses never heard his bed alarm. When they checked on him for their three am rounds, he was gone.

My family came around, but it wasn't a happily-ever-after ending with them. They were excited to meet Reese, but I was never able to get past what had happened with Damian. A piece of my heart had died, and though I tried to put it back, it never filled again. I was on polite terms with my family. Polite, but distant, and it stayed that way even while I worked close by in marketing for Echo Island Camp.

I remained with the camp for two years, going back and forth from Seattle.

I only needed to be there half the time, when I was in charge of photo ops and had to document all the busy camp schedules. Reese came with me if he wasn't training in his off-season, and during *my* off-season at work, I went where Reese was.

I put in my resignation when I was ready for a career change—and remember that book I said I was going to do for therapy? I finished it.

I published it.

And I'm pretty sure two people bought it: one was Reese, and the other was Stan.

Reese offered to post it on his social media, but I didn't want that. I wrote that book about Damian and me. It was our relationship, and I enjoyed knowing it was out there in the netherworld of sales. Over the next six months, three more people bought it.

Thank you, whoever you are.

As for Reese and I...

EPILOGUE

"I'm going to murder you!"

I was holding on to his hand in a death grip, my thighs spread wide, and it wasn't his head between my legs. A fucking basketball was coming out of me.

I know, I know.

I would love the little basketball. I would adore it. This twenty-two hours of pain would be worth it, or so I'd been promised. The outlook wasn't pointing that way, but then the doctor looked up. His face serious, his mouth in a perpetual firm line, he said the three most heavenly words that made me want to profess my undying adoration of him.

"One. Last. Push."

Well, I pushed.

I heaved.

I tried to punish Reese by breaking his hand, and he was cringing, but I knew it wasn't because of me. His gaze was fixed firmly on that doctor too, and then, with a last shove—I was trying here, so bad, but the epidural was working wonderfully—thank goodness—then the basketball was out of me.

I paused, holding my breath, tears streaming down my face.

The doctor lifted up our little basketball, curled up in a fetal position, all wrinkly and purple, and he was the most beautiful thing I'd ever seen.

"She's a girl!" the doctor announced.

She was the most beautiful thing I'd ever seen.

Reese was crying. I was crying, and a heartbeat later, she was crying. See. We were the most perfect family there was.

We named her Echo, call me a sentimental mess, but that's where Reese and I met. Echo Roman Forster, and yes, her last name matched mine because Reese and I tied the knot a year ago.

Holding Echo, holding Reese's hand, feeling a swell of feelings, I couldn't help myself. With the doctor still there, and a roomful of nurses, I asked no one in particular, "Thoughts on why we don't set toilet paper vertical instead of horizontal?"

THE END

For bonus scenes or more stories to read,
head to www.tijansbooks.com.

Other sport romances by Tijan:

Hate To Love You
Broken and Screwed
Fallen Crest Series
Ryan's Bed
And more are coming!

ACKNOWLEDGEMENTS

This book gutted me, and I hope, in a good way, that it gutted you too.

I hope it made you laugh. I hope it made you cry. And really, I just hope it made you feel.

Thank you to everyone who has helped me with this one!

To Amy, Eileen, Crystal, Mari, Kara, Paige, Chris and so many more.

Thank you to my readers in the Tijan Crew group! To those in my Audiomen group! To all the bookstagrammers and bloggers! If I miss a post, message me. I appreciate every single one of them.

I worked with dementia residents for almost twenty years, so I wanted to acknowledge them and their loved ones.

I'd like to acknowledge someone I know in my personal life who's going through something similar. This book is for you. This book is mostly for you.

Last, and I'm keeping these short for this book, just a thank you from me to *you*.

CPSIA information can be obtained
at www.ICGtesting.com
Printed in the USA
LVHW040847170619
621442LV00005B/571